A novel by Dorothy Gallagher

Copyright © 2023 by – Dorothy Gallagher – All Rights Reserved.

It is not legal to reproduce, duplicate, or transmit any part of this document in either electronic means or printed format. Recording of this publication is strictly prohibited.

Dedication

To Nicola, for her kind and constant encouragement, without which this novel would never have been completed.

Acknowledgement

With thanks to my editor Erica Mack, whose guidance and humour were invaluable.

Chapter 1

Eleanor tapped her foot and let her bag drop to the floor.

'Dear God,' she muttered. She had been at the head of the queue for at least five minutes.

Carl appeared at her side.

You've lost no time settling in then.' She nodded to his half-empty wine glass.

'What's the hold-up?' he asked.

'Seems like ticking off names and giving out badges is a more challenging task than you'd think.' Eleanor rolled her eyes in the direction of the receptionist.

'And that is why she is a mere administrator, and you are a... what was it again? A *top-shelf* academic.'

Eleanor gritted her teeth. She hated it when Carl adopted her sayings and voiced them as his own.

The man ahead of them finally lifted a key card from the desk and wandered off.

'Hi. May I take your names, please?' The receptionist smiled at them.

'Eleanor Bartlett, from the Institute for the Study of Human Development, Glasgow University, Scotland.'

'And Professor Thornton, same,' added Carl.

The receptionist consulted her screen.

'Professor Thornton.' She clicked on the tick box beside his name. 'And Bartlett?' She scanned the list again. 'Gee, I don't seem to have anything here. Is that Bartlett with a B?'

'Yep,' replied Eleanor, sighing. *What else could it be?*

The receptionist shifted her gaze from the main screen to her laptop.

'Okay, so I can see your name on the list of delegates…' She hesitated. 'But nothing is showing up for accommodation. You did place a reservation, didn't you?'

Eleanor looked sharply at Carl. As head of the department, he had insisted on dealing with all of the conference arrangements.

'Of course.' Carl smiled. 'The room will have been reserved in my name.'

'*Room?*' Eleanor glared at him.

'Ah, sure. I see it now. Sorry about that,' said the receptionist. 'You're down for a double.'

'No.' Eleanor shook her head. 'That's a mistake. We need two singles.'

'I don't think we have anything else, I'm afraid. The conference has already been oversubscribed. And no.' She looked up from her laptop. 'All the rooms are allocated.'

Eleanor rounded on Carl. 'We discussed this! I said I wanted a clear head for my presentation and no distractions!'

'*Distraction*, am I?' Carl drank down the last of his wine.

Eleanor turned back to the receptionist. 'Are there any other options? Local hotels, perhaps?'

Eleanor pursed her lips, seething. It was bad enough Carl had managed to wangle a place alongside her without having anything accepted for presentation. True, he had secured the funding for the research which she was to present, but that was it.

'We always share, Eleanor.' Carl pulled a small stack of business cards from his wallet and flicked through them.

'Always?' Eleanor scoffed. 'You mean Sweden?'

'Quite. What's changed since then? Ah, here it is.' He drew a card from the pile. 'Allen Swift.' He announced the name slowly, and at a volume Eleanor thought unnecessary. 'I promised Jack I'd pass on his regards. I'll leave 'check-in' to you.'

Carl drifted back into the crowd.

Eleanor turned back to the receptionist. 'I suppose it will have to do.'

She snatched the card from the desk and marched off, cursing under her breath, realising crossly she was partly to blame for the mix- up. She had wanted to finish things with Carl months before; their relationship had served its purpose for her. But when she learnt he would also be coming to Vancouver; she knew it would be better to wait. He could really mess things up for her here if he wanted to.

Eleanor joined the queue for the elevator and tried to block out the noise around her. From where she stood, she could see Carl working his way through the crowd, a fresh glass of white wine in his left hand, his right seeking the alpha male within each cluster.

'Eleanor?'

She felt a tap on her shoulder and turned round.

A tall man wearing stone-coloured chinos and a pale blue polo shirt greeted her. He looked, to Eleanor, as if he was heading for the golf course rather than an academic gathering.

'Allen Swift.' He held out his hand. 'Great to meet you. I've been looking out for you. Promised your director I would. Jack and I met at Oxford many moons ago.'

Eleanor stepped away from the stream of people entering the elevator and shook Allen's hand. He was handsome, around the same age as Carl but with the advantage of a tanned complexion and a good haircut.

'Come and meet the team. You won't have heard of them, but ever since that last paper of yours hit the press, they sure know who you are!'

Allen didn't wait for a response but turned back towards the foyer and pushed through the crowd, trailing an outstretched arm for Eleanor to follow. She slid her bag beneath a table displaying conference information and, thrilled by the realisation her work had been read internationally, caught up with him.

Eventually, he stopped beside an older man and a young woman.

'Here we are.' Allen didn't wait for their conversation to come to a halt. 'Simon? Sophie? I'd like you to meet Doctor Eleanor Bartlett.'

'Welcome to Vancouver, Eleanor. Simon Bouchard.' Simon's voice was softer and more hesitant than Allen's.

He did not offer his hand but instead leant closer to her and kissed each of her cheeks in turn. Eleanor felt her jaw stiffen.

'Simon spends a lot of his time at our research centre,' said Allen.

'It is true.' Simon laughed. 'In fact, I think my wife would say I practically live there.'

Eleanor liked the hint of French in his accent.

'And this is Sophie Ransom, my research assistant. She's a big fan of yours.'

'Hi.' Sophie smiled, giving a little wave.

Eleanor noted the sparkly earrings and matching necklace and found it difficult to imagine this young woman reading an academic paper. Suddenly, Carl was at her side.

'I was wondering where you'd disappeared to.' He smiled at Sophie then nodded to the men. 'Aren't you going to introduce me?'

Allen stepped forwards. 'Allen Swift.' He held out his hand. 'It's a pleasure to meet you, Mr...?'

'*Professor* Carl Thornton. I was about to track you down, but I see my protégée here has beaten me to it.'

He placed his hand on the small of Eleanor's back. She stepped away.

'Sure has. And we're all very much looking forward to her presentation.' Allen turned back to Eleanor. 'The Mitochondrial Matriarch — such a powerful idea! We're so glad you could make it over to tell us all about it.'

'Thank you. I was flattered to be invited,' she replied, pressing her lips together to suppress the smile that would give away her delight at finally breaking through into the world of serious academia. She wished Carl had stayed away a bit longer. She wanted to find her own place in this arena, distinct from him and his empire.

'No need for flattery, Eleanor. Your paper is one of the most keenly anticipated at the conference this year. There are a lot of big names out there just dying to ask you some very big questions. Me included.'

'It is true,' Simon added. 'We are intrigued.'

'And to think I was reluctant to get involved with this conference! So glad you twisted my arm, Simon. I think we may have a lot of research interests in common.' Allen held Eleanor's gaze.

Simon took up the theme. 'And your research has implications for… so many disciplines…'

Eleanor warmed to Simon, noting how his hands moved in synchrony with his words as if speaking a language of their own.

'Well, naturally,' Carl interrupted, 'Under my direction, the institute has been working on a number of topics around this field for some time. The issue of whether or not *both* parents have an equal genetic influence on their offspring. Now that's the question…'

A phone rang out, silencing Carl. Allen pulled his mobile from his pocket and read the display.

'Actually,' Carl continued, 'Eleanor's work forms part of a cohort of—'

'Sorry, guys. I'm going to have to take this.' Allen turned from the group.

Eleanor tuned out of Carl's pitch; she had heard it all before. She looked around. On one side of the foyer was a vast wall of glass, a window onto the snow-capped mountains that dominated the far horizon. She tracked their contours, the sharp rise and fall of each peak, the gentler slopes at their base. She began to feel them drawing her in. A chill of iced air seemed to catch in her throat. She gasped and rocked backwards as a strange energy gathered force within her, a quickening, new and yet familiar, like a haunting tune, half-remembered.

'You okay?' Sophie asked.

'No, I mean, yes,' said Eleanor, but she could feel her hands had started to tremble. 'A little cold…'

'I'm afraid the air-con can be a bit harsh in this place.'

Eleanor's eyes were still fixed on the frozen distance; she felt unable to look away. She had never been to Canada before, but there was something about these Rockies that made her feel detached from everything else around her. She felt herself pull away from reality as if she was floating alone in a balloon, towards the frosted peaks.

Sophie was talking to her now, and Eleanor forced herself to look away from the panorama and turn back to face the younger woman. She could see her lips were moving, but Sophie's words had blurred into a hiss of white noise that seemed to be growing louder and louder. Eleanor realised with horror she might faint.

'*Are* you okay?' Sophie asked again. 'You don't look so good.' She hurried to a nearby drinks table and fetched a glass of water.

Eleanor felt light-headed, but after a few sips of the cool drink, the room began to come back into focus, and she felt herself growing stronger.

'I think I'm just tired.'

'Would you like to sit down for a while?'

'No, please. I'm fine, really.'

Eleanor took a deep breath and checked the scene. She was relieved to see Carl was busy regaling Simon with some anecdote. No one, apart from Sophie, seemed to have noticed her moment of weakness.

Allen finished his phone call and swung back around to face the group.

'I'm afraid I'm gonna have to take my leave from this delightful company. I need to settle in our latest *delivery* at the research centre.'

'What is it?' asked Eleanor.

'I have absolutely no idea!' He raised his hands to the heavens. 'Another gift from Mother Nature, a frozen offering from the treacherous slopes.' He nodded to the icy peaks beyond the window. 'Most finds arrive in polystyrene boxes, covered with some dry ice, but this one, apparently, has required a large freezer unit, so I'll need to set it up, check the thermostatic settings, and so on.'

'What sort of things are sent your way?' Eleanor asked.

'Most of the larger finds turn out to be knots of vegetation whipped up by the fiendish winds of the high Rockies into *corpse-like* cocoons.' Allen's words were delivered with a flourish of drama. 'But animal finds are also common. In the twelve years I've been involved with the department, I've examined the remains of many unfortunate creatures that succumbed to the unforgiving climate.'

'And that's it?' Carl half-laughed his question.

'Not at all! Occasionally, we strike gold, uncovering prehistoric remains that provide new genetic data, and it's exactly the possibility of such a discovery that keeps my interest alive. It's exciting work and always a challenge. Certainly not for the impatient or the intellectually faint-hearted.'

Carl snorted.

'I'll catch up with you again tomorrow,' Allen said to Eleanor. 'Maybe we'll get a chance to chat after your presentation.'

And, without another word, he left. Eleanor watched as he marched through the sliding glass doors, out of sight. There was something about him. A force that both drew her to him and yet faintly repelled her.

Chapter 2

Eleanor woke the next morning to the sound of Carl sighing. He was flicking through the complimentary publication of the university's science faculty paper, *Gene-e-us*.

'The Proof, The Whole Proof and Nothing but the Proof: Evidence in Support of the Honesty Gene.' He snorted. 'Nothing like a big build-up, is there? Allen Swift certainly has the gene for self-belief, if such exists.'

'You know, you might just learn something interesting, Carl, if you can suspend your brutal cynicism for the duration of the conference.' Eleanor leapt out of bed and pulled on a light dressing gown. 'I'm actually quite looking forward to hearing more of what Allen has to say, so if you are going to find it difficult to suppress your disapproval, please do me a favour and keep your superior distance.'

'Cynicism? I don't think so. It's called scientific rigour. How on earth can anyone harp on about "proof" in the study of something as vague as honesty? It's nonsense.' He tossed the paper onto the bed.

***

Later, Eleanor watched from the wings of the auditorium as Carl marched to the front row of the central block of seating. There was only one chair still vacant, and that was beside Sophie. A pale pink cardigan and a handbag had been placed on it as if it was reserved.

Carl pushed his way past the first few occupants of the row.

'Do you mind if I join you?' Eleanor overheard him ask.

Sophie quickly cleared the chair, lifting the cardigan onto her lap and placing the bag on the floor.

'That's very kind of you. I had no idea this would be so well attended.'

Sophie smiled up at him. 'It's usually pretty busy.'

Eleanor watched as the young woman glanced behind her towards the door.

'I was actually saving this for Allen, but I can't see him anywhere.'

'Wouldn't worry about that, Sophie. I'm sure he can take care of himself. Anyway, possession is nine-tenths of the law, as they say.' Carl worked his back into the chair as he spoke.

Eleanor watched, puzzled, as Sophie cradled the cardigan in her arms, as if it were a baby. There was something oddly maternal about her that reminded Eleanor of her older sister. Olivia had always been the one who wanted to play with dolls when they were little, moving on to real babies throughout her teenage years, offering to babysit for their parents' friends, before eventually having three children of her own.

It had been an attraction Eleanor struggled to understand. It wasn't that she disliked children, but she'd certainly never wanted to be a parent herself. She had been shocked when her sister had announced her pregnancy so soon after graduating. She couldn't imagine that whatever Olivia got out of being a mother could possibly compensate for the cost to her career, her looks, and her quality of life. Thank God, she thought, she had never been cursed by the call of maternal longing.

Eleanor listened attentively to the first two speakers and then, at the coffee break, made her way to the restrooms. She needed to be by herself to call up that sense of calm focus that would carry her through her own presentation. When she returned, delegates were making their way back to their seats.

When her name was announced, she strode confidently onto the stage but was irritated to feel her fingers tremble as she plugged in her laptop. She had always been praised for her public speaking and usually relished the opportunity to impress, having outsmarted most of her debating opponents at school and university. But an ever- present fear of humiliation haunted her, and she had to fight hard against the quiet, insistent voice in her head that predicted such events, drowning it out with her own private, inspirational mantra.

She raised her head and smiled at the large gathering. As soon as she was a few slides, and witticisms, into her talk, she could tell she had them on her side and used their nodding heads and laughter to stifle her fears.

As she sailed through her well-honed delivery, she knew many in the audience would have read her paper and be familiar with much of what she was saying. She was excited, however, to finish with a research proposal she hoped would be well received.

With a dramatic flourish, she closed her laptop and gave the audience her full attention.

'In conclusion,' she declared, 'While it is now beyond doubt that Neanderthal, Denisovan, and modern man all coexisted and that an analysis of both nuclear and mitochondrial DNA confirms their interbreeding, I put it to you that this is not the whole story. More recent studies have unearthed the presence of another contributor to our gene pool, an ancient human lineage, as yet unidentified.

'The cause of its demise and extinction is unknown, but building upon the techniques outlined in this paper, I suggest it might be possible to derive from those mysterious strands of genetic code enough information to generate a hypothetical genome for such a subspecies and to discover what made them vulnerable and unable to compete with their superior peers. Thank you.'

There was a moment of silence before the applause began. She spotted Allen at the back of the room, writing something on a piece of paper that he shoved into his pocket before clapping along with the crowd.

'Any questions?' Eleanor cued the audience to quiet.

One hand went up. 'Doctor Bartlett, are you saying it might be possible to infer an entire genome from one or two strands of coding?'

'I think it might be possible to create an impression, at least. And remember, of course, it's not the same piece of information on every strand of DNA we come across. The summation of all the genetic data, once combined with information deduced from comparative studies, might just be enough.'

Eleanor caught sight of Allen again, pulling himself to attention and retrieving the paper from his pocket to write some more.

She nodded to another member of the audience waiting to speak.

'Are we talking nuclear or mitochondrial DNA here?' the woman asked.

'Both, although mitochondrial investigation is my main interest given its relatively smaller size and more durable structure.'

'Isn't that potentially limiting?' Carl called out.

'In that…?' Eleanor shot back.

'I would have thought it was obvious, Eleanor. Given that mitochondrial DNA only comes from the mother, you could be missing half the story.'

'Well, we now know that's not actually the case and that some paternal DNA does get through. That is exactly what interests me, as you know very well, Professor. We know there is a process of selective elimination of paternal DNA, so what is selected and why?' Eleanor smiled and looked away from Carl, determined to avoid the tedious dialogue and grandstanding which she knew Carl would feast upon.

But he wasn't done. 'The amount of paternal DNA that does remain is so small it's highly unlikely to have any significant consequences for the greater scheme of things.' Carl half-laughed at his own words.

'With respect, I don't agree. The evidence to date suggests quite the reverse. It now seems likely that all of our timeline calculations for human evolution may be incorrect, based as they are on the assumptions you have just so eloquently voiced. There can surely be few things of *more* relevance to the *greater scheme of things* than this.'

'Doctor Bartlett is absolutely right on that,' called a voice from the back. It was Allen. 'And I'd love to hear more about it but, sadly, we've over-run and lunch is served. I'm sure Doctor Bartlett will be happy to answer any further questions over the next few days.'

As Eleanor turned off her laptop and eased it back into its case, she saw Allen approach.

'Well done, Eleanor, just fascinating. Any chance of a quick chat before lunch?'

'Couldn't we do both?' Eleanor replied.

'I'm going to give the food a miss, I'm afraid. I need to head straight back to the research centre. But I could snatch a coffee?'

***

Allen chose the quietest corner of the bar and set two cups on the table. He pulled the paper from his pocket.

'Don't usually take notes.' He laughed. 'But sometimes my thoughts are so vague I need to catch them before they melt away.'

'Intriguing.' Eleanor took several sips of her coffee, the first of the day.

He looked at her intently. 'How does this link to your interest in the demise of subhuman species? It seems like a long way round, if you ask me, to try to work out what traits a "failed" species had rather than focus on what makes survivors superior, isn't it?'

Eleanor put down her cup. 'True, but that's what *I* would call missing half the story. The way evolution is portrayed tends to make us think everything is binary. You know, tail or no tail, opposable thumb or no opposable thumb. And the starting point is always what we have, and *inferior* beings have not. And this is all very important, but I'm also interested in those characteristics that might hold species back, like…'

'Bad breath or a tendency to gluttony?' Allen took a large handful of salted nuts from the bowl on the table and wolfed them down.

'Exactly.' Eleanor laughed. 'But seriously, we often focus on traits that favour physical survival, but that's not all it takes for your genes to survive. Our ancestors probably chose mates they were attracted to, physically and intellectually. Their cognitive and emotional dispositions would have been much the same as ours are today. Perhaps there were many other subspecies who were, for whatever reason, not attractive or successful mates, and I intend to investigate what made this so.'

'Very interesting.' Allen scribbled a new note on the bottom of his crumpled sheet. 'So much food for thought there, Eleanor. I sure wish I didn't have to rush off.'

Allen stood up, and Eleanor followed him to the door of the dining room.

'Don't let me take you from lunch and the queue of colleagues who'll be competing for a moment of your time.'

Eleanor spotted Carl, who was sitting with Sophie to his right, a vacant chair to the left. When he saw Eleanor and Allen in conversation, he got up and made his way towards them.

Allen turned to Eleanor. 'Why not come to the research centre and see what we do there? I think you'll find it fascinating. And as for our latest delivery, I have no doubt, given your research interests, that you will be just as intrigued as I am.'

Eleanor hesitated.

'If you come this evening, you'll not miss much here, apart from the after-dinner speeches, of course.'

'Splendid idea, Allen.' Carl had positioned himself between Allen and Eleanor. 'We'd love to come, wouldn't we, Eleanor?'

Eleanor pursed her lips. 'Of course.'

Superb,' said Allen, walking away from them as he talked. 'I'll have Sophie drive you over.'

Chapter 3

That evening after dinner, Eleanor slipped away while Carl and Sophie talked at the bar. As she passed behind them, she could hear Carl describing her current research as if it was his own, a habit of his which caused him no shame whatsoever. Sophie seemed engrossed, but when she noticed Eleanor, she looked up as if wanting to catch her attention. Eleanor smiled but didn't stop.

She told Sophie she preferred to make her own way to the research centre and privately thought if Carl shifted his attention towards Sophie, she would consider that a bonus.

She sat in the Uber in silence and closed her eyes. She was tired of talking and gave only monosyllabic responses to the driver's questions. Eventually, she felt her shoulders relax, and her breathing became deeper and slower.

She had never felt comfortable in groups. Even if she liked the individuals themselves, they always seemed to Eleanor somehow altered when part of a gathering. With very few exceptions, she felt the company of others was something to be avoided. But she knew such anxieties were a weakness, and the mere glimpse of this Achilles heel would be a gift to those who would revel in her vulnerability. And so, over the years, she had fashioned a second self, an outer self; a perfect image of the one that lived within and one which fitted exactly over her true self. Like Russian dolls, they shared their place in the world. The outer, with its rhino-tough skin, keeping safe the fragile Eleanor within.

They came to a halt in front of a low building; the evening sun giving its red brick a copper glow. Beyond, distant mountains faded in the dimming light so only a dark blue ridge could be seen. Eleanor stepped away from the cab without returning the driver's farewell and marched towards the double glass doors. A chorus of insects hummed from the untamed scrub around the car park, and for the first time since her arrival, Eleanor found the temperature bearable.

As she climbed the shallow steps to the entrance, she wondered what the evening might hold. A research sabbatical in Vancouver would be a career coup, she had no doubt about that, and Allen's invitation to visit the centre was a promising start.

'Shit!' She pulled and then pushed at the locked door. *Sophie must know the code*, she realised. How the hell was she supposed to get in?

Mosquitoes hovered beneath the pale yellow of the entrance light; their on-off buzz like doodlebugs threatening attack. Eleanor pulled a scarf from her bag and draped it over her shoulders. She didn't have Allen's number, so there was nothing else for it. She'd have to wait.

It wasn't long before she heard the crunch of wheels on the gravel and spotted Sophie's Nissan Micra approaching.

'Well, well, who's the early bird then? Can't get in?' Carl looked smug as he strolled towards Eleanor. 'Never fear; the cavalry's here.'

'Sorry, Eleanor.' Sophie caught up with them. 'I should have told you how to get in.'

'No apology required, Sophie,' said Carl. 'You can hardly be held responsible for the foibles of others. She should have waited for us.'

'I assume you know the code?' Eleanor looked only at Sophie.

'No, but there's another way in.'

Sophie took the narrow path that led to the back of the centre and pulled at the fire door. Carl and Eleanor followed her into a place of near darkness.

'Sorry about this,' Sophie said, 'It's a bit of a warren.'

They waited as Sophie ran her fingers along the wall until she found an array of switches then heard her sigh when nothing happened as she flicked each one in turn.

'Allow me.' Carl stepped forwards, rapidly working them up and down, to no avail.

'Never fear,' clipped Eleanor, 'The cavalry's here.' She smiled to herself as she fished her phone out of her bag and turned on the torch app. 'Is it far?'

'I don't think so,' said Sophie. 'Although I don't usually come in this way.'

She led them a short distance to a swing door that took them out into a corridor, dimly lit by low voltage strip lights.

'It's certainly a much larger operation than I'd imagined,' said Carl. 'Genetic archaeology must be big business over here.'

'I suppose it is,' Sophie replied, 'But these facilities aren't just for Allen's team. They're shared by several departments: veterinarian research, genetic and biomedical sciences, that sort of thing. And various clinics are run from here too.'

Eleanor walked ahead with Sophie while Carl trailed behind. Eventually, in the distance, she noticed a faint glow cast upon the floor, and as they got closer, she could hear the scuff of footsteps on a stone floor.

Sophie knocked quietly, but there was no response, so she pushed against the door.

Allen had his back to them. He clearly hadn't heard them come in. Eleanor watched him circle a large, rectangular-shaped unit. They waited for him to realise they were there, but he seemed utterly preoccupied. He stopped and peered into the container; its lid lifted like a casket in a funeral parlour.

Carl coughed.

Allen turned immediately; his cheeks indented by the pressure of his protective goggles. 'Aha! I have company. Welcome.' He pulled the goggles off and wiped their tinted lenses. 'So glad you guys could make it. Hope I didn't tear you away from all the fun?'

'What could be more fun than this?' Carl looked around the sparse room and gave what Eleanor knew to be a forced laugh.

Allen beckoned them forwards. 'Come and have a look and tell me what you think. Oh, and you'll need these.' He untangled a knot of rubber straps tying protective goggles to a hook on the wall.

Eleanor had seen pictures of frozen remains in various journals and often struggled to make any sense of them, so after putting the goggles on and approaching the container, she was not surprised by what she saw. Deep within the ice, she could just about make out a bundle, wrapped in what looked like a mud-coloured blanket. It was long, stretching nearly the entire length of the six-foot unit; its form undulating but slender.

'Is that it?' Carl asked. 'What is it?'

'Impossible to tell at this stage,' Allen replied. 'We just investigate every find we're sent.'

'Where was it found?' Eleanor was transfixed by the frozen puzzle.

'On Mount Meager, about ninety miles north of here, just above the west flank of the Lillooet River.'

'How long do you think it's been there for?' Sophie shrank back from the mysterious bundle.

'I really couldn't say, Sophie. It might only have been there for weeks or months, but it could be much older than that and only recently become visible.'

'Not much passing traffic up there, I imagine,' said Carl.

Allen nodded. 'True. But apart from that, even if it's been there for years, it might not have been lying on the surface. Mount Meager is a dormant volcano, so sometimes things that have been buried get moved around a bit and gradually work their way to the top.' He walked to a nearby table and picked up a bundle of documents. 'There's quite a bit of literature out there about this phenomenon.'

'Yes, yes, of course.' Carl took the papers from Allen. 'This stuff's been around for years,' he muttered, sitting on the only seat available and leafing through the sheets.

'What do you think, Eleanor?' Allen moved to her side.

'I really don't know what to think.' She studied the blurred fragments.

'So, what's the procedure?' Carl slapped the pile of papers to a close and tossed them onto the desk beside his chair.

'Well, that all depends.' Allen tapped his pen on the freezer rim. 'Generally, once we've identified the contents and taken samples for our own research, we pass the find on to whatever specialist group might be interested: plant biology, palaeontology, archaeology…'

'The police?' asked Sophie. 'Could be a crime scene.'

'We've never actually had to do that so far. Not one darned sinister find in all these years!' Allen laughed.

'What are you hoping for?' asked Eleanor.

'We use whatever we find to map out the genetic profile of life forms in the region. The conditions here are just perfect for this work; tissues are preserved so well it's possible to uncover ancient finds that throw up all sorts of data.

'Only last year, the tusk of a woolly mammoth was brought in — an amazing find! Eight feet long and around eleven thousand years old, and it's still throwing up all sorts of fascinating information. But even with all that, *this* one, for some reason, feels special.' He drew his open hand along the top of the freezer.

Carl rolled his eyes; a gesture Eleanor knew he wanted her to see.

Allen smiled. 'I thought it might tie in well with your mitochondrial research, Eleanor. Particularly what you were saying about the difficulties of using this material to estimate evolutionary timelines and the demise of substandard species. And that's what we're all about. It's exactly what we're looking for: information that will help us identify and understand significant evolutionary developments.'

'In all life forms? That's a bit ambitious, is it not?' Carl scoffed.

'Well, we have quite a varied team here, so we can cover a few bases. But as you can imagine, given my research interests, I'm always hoping for finds in the human line, although they've not been too plentiful. But you never know.' He pulled the lid down and checked the thermostat.

'Well, enough is as good as a feast,' Carl said, sighing emphatically. 'It's probably an old tree trunk. We have thousands of those back home. Got sick of the sight of them in first year archaeology! Anywhere I can find a drink around here? This dry air is getting to my throat.'

'Not here, I'm afraid. But if you think you've seen enough, then perhaps Sophie wouldn't mind driving you back to the conference centre? Eleanor and I can catch up with you shortly.'

'Excellent idea!' Carl looped his arm through Sophie's. 'Can't think of a more delightful companion for a cosy nightcap.'

Eleanor thought she spotted Sophie hesitate as Carl led her to the door, but she was not inclined to intervene.

Allen waited until the door had closed behind them before speaking again.

'Actually, I'm planning to stay here a while and start preparations for scanning. You'd be most welcome to stay if you want; see how it all works?'

'Sure.' Eleanor nodded, hoping her voice did not betray the satisfaction she felt.

Allen walked to the back of the room and slid open two large doors. Eleanor crossed to his side and peered into the newly exposed darkness; the dim glow cast from the workroom shed little light on what was in there. She could just about make out a bold outline reaching nearly to the ceiling.

Then the lights came, revealing the starkness of the chamber. To her left, Eleanor could see a window that stretched the full length of the wall; the blackness beyond pressing hard against it.

Allen strode in, and Eleanor followed. Without warning, he came to a halt and turned.

'Stop!' He pointed to a thick, red line she was about to step over. 'Do you have anything metal on? Jewellery, a belt?'

'Watch and earrings,' said Eleanor.

'They'll need to come off. Can't have them near this.' Allen nodded to the scanner. 'Magnetic.'

'Of course.' Eleanor removed them and placed them beside her bag.

The floor felt hard; its clinical covering coved to a seamless edge where it met the plain white walls. The only object in the room was the MRI; its long, narrow bed feeding into a doughnut-shaped portal.

'This looks impressive.' Eleanor drew her fingers over the touch screen of the control panel. 'Someone must like what you do here.'

'Sure hope so. But all the departments here have access to this equipment, although it's put to use by Simon more than anyone else. He runs his clinics from here. You met him yesterday.'

'I did, yes,' said Eleanor. 'What's his line of work?'

He's a consultant in obstetrics and gynaecology. Specialises in fertility treatment and all things related to it. You know, freezing embryos, cloning, surrogacy, and so on. It's big business over here. Same in the UK, I guess?' He crossed the room and turned the light down.

Eleanor followed him back to the storage unit and helped him heave open the lid. Once again, they gazed down.

'Looks pretty massive.' Eleanor squinted into it. 'Do you think it'll fit into the scanner?'

'That's the billion-dollar question,' Allen replied, 'But we do have the advantage of a machine that is veterinarian sized.'

'Of course.'

'Believe it or not, it's used more and more for non-vet cases. Bariatric medicine is becoming big business here too. Still, this block is probably too much for it to handle. It'll be safer if we shave a few centimetres off the top before trying to manoeuvre it.'

Allen selected some tools from an array arranged on the wall.

'It's not unusual for us to have to sculpt the ice a bit. You'll soon get the hang of it.'

'Now?' Eleanor gasped.

'Why not?' He handed Eleanor a small hammer and chisel, then dimmed the light to its lowest setting. She stood in silence and watched as he dropped to the floor and ran his fingers along the lower edge of the unit, flicking the switch that would lift its base. There was a slight pause, then a deep reverberation as the block slowly began to rise.

Eleanor recalled the snow-capped peaks of the mountain range beyond the conference centre and felt again the tremble in her hands. But this time, she knew what she was feeling was not apprehension, but excitement. A rush of energy swept through her that was unlike anything she had experienced before. A thrilling chill that seemed to burn open new pathways that had always been there but had lain dormant, as though waiting for this moment.

Allen sat back on his heels, and they watched the ice rise and begin to emerge. Its progress was slow but relentless, as if being unwillingly crushed out of the earth. Once it had risen a little above the edge, he brought the machine to a halt. Then he stood up and touched the newly exposed ice, pulling his fingers back sharply.

'We'll need these.' He handed Eleanor some insulated gloves and pulled his own from his pocket.

Allen adjusted the unit hinges, so the lid lay flat against its side. Eleanor watched as he tapped the ice, then, grasping the rubber grip of the slim, sharp hammer, she began to follow his lead.

The stillness echoed to the clang of hammer upon chisel. Soon, cracks appeared, and spearheads splintered to the floor. The glacial landscape changed; a smooth weathered surface becoming pitted and gouged. Then suddenly, they hit upon a seam; a fault line raced across its length, and the low hissing voice of liberated air broke a silence of centuries.

Allen wedged the fine blade of a long-handled spade into the newly formed fracture and forced it apart. A gasp of air raced beneath it, chasing itself from one end to the other.

'That should do it,' he said, fetching a trolley from the scanning suite. 'If you could just help me lift this.' He nodded to the far end of the storage unit, where Eleanor took up her position.

Forcing her fingers into the newly formed crevice, she helped him ease the upper layer onto the trolley. She could feel her gloved hands stick to the underside as they guided the freezing slab towards a chilled metal trough where it would remain until they were ready to replace it.

When they returned and looked at the block, they saw what appeared to be a dark blanket embedded in the ice, not the thin shroud Eleanor had imagined. It was quite separate from whatever lay beneath it.

'You know, if we manage to remove that section, we'll get a good view of what's down there. But we'll need to be careful. Whatever this is will be rich pickings for someone, I'm sure of it.'

Allen slipped again to the floor, and soon, more of the block rose into view. He scraped at the newly exposed surface and peered into it, swaying to and fro, trying to see around and beyond the opaque patches. Eleanor joined him.

'What in the name...?' She held her face as close to the surface as she could bear, before catching her breath.

Just inches below, a rippled sea of silk-like weave stretched across the expanse of ice. From a distance, it had looked dark — dirty, even — but now Eleanor could see it was intricately worked fabric.

Symbols in rich reds and deep greens were laced across its earth- brown length. When she examined it from each side, she had not seen any undulations, but from above, the pattern of the symbols somehow made it seem as if the fabric lay not flat, but rather formed rugged hills and sweeping valleys, a landscape that seemed to shift as she observed it.

'Wow...' Allen paced around the spectacle.

'Are you sure we should be doing this?' Eleanor asked.

'So long as we don't do any damage, it'll be fine. I think we can lift the fabric off in one piece; then we can have a look at whatever the hell is lying underneath.'

They worked on in silence. Finally, when the ice gave way, another great rift shot across it. This newly released section proved heavier and far more awkward to lift, but they eventually succeeded in removing it and, exhausted, wheeled their cargo to the metal trough. Eleanor sat down. She was shaking and realised she'd been holding her breath again.

'You okay?' Allen asked.

'Of course,' she replied. 'I'm intrigued.'

He strode back across the room but halted abruptly a few paces short of the unit. He stood with his back to Eleanor, but she heard him gasp.

'What?' she asked.

Slowly, he raised his right hand to shoulder level and beckoned her forwards.

It was not until she reached his side that she allowed herself to look down. A rush of iced air stole her breath. For there, not far below the surface, lay the perfectly preserved body of a young woman; her cornflower blue eyes wide open and staring up at them.

Chapter 4

The following day's programme no longer held any interest for Eleanor. She wanted to return to the research centre straight away, but Allen was busy all day and couldn't meet up until after dinner. The discovery had shaken them both. Eleanor recalled how Allen, too, had gazed in awe at the serene, ice-bound figure, how he'd recoiled, how they'd looked at each other, struck dumb by the vastness of the questions in each of their heads, and how they had both agreed there was nothing for it but to abandon all hope of research for the night and try to get some sleep.

The day dragged on, with one presentation blurring into the next. Eleanor was glad she hadn't sat beside Carl. Tiptoeing into their shared room the previous night and spending sleepless hours beside his snoring form had already been too much. But she was relieved he had been asleep; he would have sensed something and quizzed her, and she would have had to deflect him as she'd promised Allen she'd keep things quiet until they had a plan. Meanwhile, she knew she had a lot to prove at the conference, and so she utilised every fibre of her being to concentrate on what the speakers were saying and make time pass more quickly.

When at last, the sessions ended, Eleanor joined the slow-moving herd as they pushed out of the gloomy auditorium into the chilly dazzle of the atrium. She saw Carl in the distance, walking towards the bar with someone she didn't recognise. *Good*, she thought. She could slip back to their room, alone.

Locking the door behind her, she headed for the shower. Despite the chill of the air conditioning, her shirt clung to her. Peeling off her clothes, she let them drop to a limp pile on the floor, then turned the water to full power and cool.

She stepped into the torrent and closed her eyes, only to be faced with the vision once again. The body, in all its detail, a slim frame swathed in a robe of muted tones, limbs suspended in an elegant limbo. But it was the face, always the face, that stayed with her the most. Those eyes that seemed to stare into her own; her peaceful expression showing no trace of fear. Surely this was a death, either unexpected or fully accepted? Would she ever know?

Eleanor wrapped herself tightly in a towel. She must go back; she could think of nothing else. Nothing had ever made her feel like this before. She was entranced, for sure, but there was something else going on that was making her stomach clench to a frozen fist.

She waited until the last minute before dressing and going downstairs to join the others for dinner. As soon as she entered the foyer, she heard Carl's voice and spotted him, glass in hand, in the midst of a large gathering, orchestrating the discussion around him. She selected a mineral water from the tray of refreshments and turned to examine the batik prints on the wall.

'Eleanor!' Carl's voice hailed her like a passing cab. 'Do come and join us.'

Feeling snared, Eleanor walked over to them.

'There is no evidence for that whatsoever,' one delegate was saying. 'All the proof, as you call it, was never duplicated.'

'But does that mean the topic is not even a legitimate subject for discussion?' asked another, looking around for support.

'You're right, of course.' Carl had assumed the role of arbitrator. 'Today's theories are tomorrow's facts. What say you, Eleanor? We're just warming up for the debate tonight.' He waved the programme he was holding in front of her. 'The Nature of Nurture: Do We Inherit the Capacity to Care?' He held his hand out, inviting her to speak.

Eleanor sipped her water, buying time.

'Prefer to sit on the fence?' Carl goaded, giving her a look with which she was wearily familiar.

'I think it merits more than an impulsive reaction,' she replied as, to her relief, a bell sounded to summon the delegates towards the dining area.

'I have reserved the perfect table.' Carl steered Eleanor through the crowd to the quietest corner of the softly lit room. She saw his jacket already draped on the back of one of the chairs.

'Let's wait for the queue to die down a bit.' He nodded towards the line of people already snaking back from the serving area, beyond the glass doors into the foyer.

'Nothing like the smell of meat to bring them to the trough, eh?' He pulled out a chair for Eleanor then sat across from her and placed his hand over hers.

'I'm getting worried about you.' He looked into her eyes. 'There's something… different about you.'

Eleanor could smell the blast of stale wine from his breath and waited for him to articulate his complaint.

Carl filled his glass from a full carafe on the table, then leant across to pour some into Eleanor's. She shook her head and reached for her water. He rolled his eyes.

'Jesus, Eleanor, what's got into you? Forgotten how to relax?'

'Nothing's got into me, Carl. I just want to keep a clear head. I've got a lot on my mind.'

'Evidently.' He drank down half the contents of his glass. 'So, are you staying for the evening, or do you have a more pressing engagement?'

'I haven't decided yet,' she replied.

'Really? You know most *novice* speakers put a bit more effort into embracing the conference experience. Wouldn't like Jack to learn you were swanning off doing your own thing. Doesn't look good, Eleanor, and it certainly wouldn't help with any future funding requests.' Carl rose to his feet, returning his glass to the table with such force it shattered.

Eleanor pulled her chair back to avoid the red stream rushing towards her.

'Childish bastard,' she muttered, just loud enough for him to hear as he marched off to join the queue.

***

As soon as dinner was over, Eleanor caught Allen's eye and, holding up his car keys, he nodded towards the door. As she pressed through the crowd to catch up with him, she spotted Carl ahead of her, deep in conversation as usual. She hoped she could slip past unnoticed. But it wasn't until she got closer that she realised his companion was Sophie. She looked different in a tight-fitting dress and heels that raised her nearly to Carl's height. She smiled at Eleanor as she passed, then looked back to Carl, who was reeling off some anecdote as he refilled her glass from a bottle of Moët. Eleanor could hear his voice; its pitch and volume raised to deliver some punchline, followed by Sophie's laughter.

Sophie seemed calmer and less flustered by Carl's attentions than before. *Surely not, Carl*, Eleanor thought before muttering, 'I suppose there's nothing like the smell of fresh meat…' as she passed behind him and headed for the exit.

***

Eleanor and Allen sat in silence until they hit the highway.

'I've been struggling to get my head around what we saw last night,' Eleanor said eventually, staring straight ahead at the semi-circle of light cast onto the tarmac by the car's headlamps.

'Crazy, isn't it?' Allen replied. 'I've had to pinch myself a few times today too. My head's been… I couldn't tell you where.'

'Same.'

When they pulled into the centre, it was evident the place was deserted. Allen parked on the luminous chevrons of the disabled bay, right in front of the main entrance. Eleanor's heart fluttered as they crossed the threshold into the chill of the reception area.

'We'll set up the scanner before we raise her up,' he said as they marched down the dimly lit corridor.

He unlocked the door to his workshop and switched on the overhead light before sliding back the double doors that led into the scanning suite.

'Night shift,' Eleanor breathed.

'I often keep late hours; work better at night. I seem to have more stamina, if you know what I mean.'

Eleanor thought she saw him smirk.

'So, what will this scan tell us?' she said, ignoring the innuendo.

'Who knows?' Allen rubbed his palms together. 'In theory, it should give us a detailed, three-dimensional image of the internal organs and, if they have survived as well as her external ones, we should get a fair idea of her general health, maybe even cause of death.'

'She certainly doesn't give the appearance of having suffered any trauma. She looks calm… tranquil, even. I'd love to know what happened to her.'

Allen opened the doors to the scanning suite. 'Just going to turn the MRI on,' he called back to Eleanor. 'It takes a while for the magnets to stabilise.'

Allen strode back and opened the lid of the freezer unit, then raised the base, pulling on his thermal gloves while waiting for the ice to rise fully. The upper layers they'd eased off the day before had reattached, but it took little effort to prise them off again. They wheeled them, one at a time, to the trough.

Once again, the mass was raised, and they stood in silence as the body emerged. Eleanor felt a quickening in her heart as she watched it surface. Then, at last, she lay before them, suspended in her cloak of cloudy ice, her piercing eyes staring up towards a sky she could not see.

'Holy shit,' said Allen.

'She looks so peaceful. It feels intrusive to disturb her, like an act of desecration,' Eleanor murmured. She looked at Allen. 'Do you know what I mean?'

'Yeah, I guess so. But surely it would be more disrespectful to do *nothing* after all of this?' he said in a low voice.

Eleanor nodded.

'Come on; we've got no time to waste.' Allen checked the wheels of the trolley to make sure they were locked. 'The whole body can be scanned in about one hour.'

'Dear God! I'd no idea it would take that long!'

'I'm afraid so,' Allen said, sighing. 'Most people think it will just be a quick in and out, like a CT scan, but this is more thorough, more powerful, and, I'm afraid, a hell of a lot louder.'

'And that's okay? To keep her out for an hour? Won't the ice begin to melt?'

'It's not ideal, I know. We would normally space it out a bit, but we don't have time for that. She could be gone tomorrow for all I know.'

'Risky though.' Eleanor bit her lip.

'Needs must… It'll be fine, don't worry. I'll blast up the freezer when I put her back. And, in the meantime, I'll set an alarm on the scanner to alert us to any dangerous rises in temperature or humidity.' Allen worked as he spoke, raising the rails on the far side of the trolley, three horizontal bars which offered a low wall of support. 'If you could stand here?'

He crossed the room and selected a hammer and broad pallet knife from an array of instruments on the desk. Eleanor craned to watch as he eased the blade between the ice and the metal of the risen base. He tapped gently, working his way along its length like a sculptor, forming a groove. At last, she heard a snap and a sharp gasp like the release of a dying breath as the ice came away from its bed.

'That should do it.' He pushed again, and Eleanor saw the block slide towards her.

'Thank God,' she said, pressing hard against the rails to halt its progress.

Allen secured the open side, and together they wheeled their cargo to the scanning suite. Eleanor helped guide the trolley to the MRI then together; they eased the block onto the bed of the machine.

'Perfect fit,' said Eleanor.

'Sure is. Let's get on with it.'

A small room next to the scanning suite housed the controls, and the window that spanned the length of one wall offered a clear view of the MRI. They sat in front of a large screen as Allen tapped his instructions onto the keypad, then watched as the bed of the scanner slid into place, and the process began.

It wasn't long until images began to flash in front of them. They watched in silence as the patchwork of pictures appeared, each a different angle on a human skull and brain, with symbols and numerical data filling the spaces between.

'So, what does this tell us?' Eleanor whispered.

'I wouldn't pretend to understand it all,' said Allen, 'But from what I can see, she looks remarkably well preserved. She has indeed been flash-frozen.'

'Mummified,' said Eleanor.

'Looks like it.' Allen didn't lift his eyes from the screen. 'This is incredible! We can see the white and grey matter of the brain quite clearly, and the skull is intact. No sign of head injury.'

They fell back into silence as perfect image followed perfect image, from the brain down the spinal cord to the heart and lungs.

Eleanor could not lift her eyes from the screen, gasping at the sight of the bony skull encasing a brain etched with deep ridges and grooves. A face within a face, concentric worlds, like her own Russian doll selves. She shivered.

Soon, images of the head and shoulders gave way to those of the heart down through the stomach to the abdomen.

'As far as I can see, all the internal organs have been very well preserved,' said Allen.

'And look, she is definitely a *she*.' Eleanor pointed to the uterus and fallopian tubes.

'Yes.' Allen squinted at the screen.

Suddenly, an alarm sounded. Eleanor startled and turned to Allen.

He recoiled from the screen. 'Fuck… that's the thermo-alert!'

'Let's get her out of there!' Eleanor shot to her feet.

'No!' Allen insisted. 'We're nearly there. There's usually a generous margin of error in these things.' He slammed off the alarm.

'Surely we've got enough?' Eleanor argued, her throat tightening with fear.

'How can we know what we're missing? Just calm down; it'll be fine.'

Eleanor stared at Allen as he leant closer to the screen, his eyes bulging and his jaw clenched as if fixed by wires.

To Allen's right, reams of paper spilled from the printer and cascaded down to the floor: bones, heart, eye sockets, feet. Like pieces of a macabre jigsaw they had fashioned from a life once lived.

Allen gathered the printed sheets into a bundle and placed them in a folder that he stuffed into his bag. Pulling out others already in there, he handed those to Eleanor.

'A bit of background reading for you.'

She glanced at the titles. 'What? This study claims the age of the body *they* examined was estimated to be 3,500 years old! Is that possible? And the organs were so well preserved they were able to carry out biological and genetic testing?'

'Exactly!' There was a note of excitement in Allen's voice.

'Do you think ours could be as old as that?' Eleanor stared at the closed unit.

'Why not?' Allen shrugged. 'Once we've collected some tissue samples, we'll be able to find out for sure.'

'So, what will you do with all this data?'

'In the first instance, I need Simon to have a look. He has much more experience interpreting these scans than I have, so I want to hear what he makes of them. I won't tell him who the subject is, of course,' he added. 'Let's keep things simple and have him assume it's a normal modern woman.'

'Shouldn't a pathologist be looking at this?' Eleanor asked.

'Actually, a radiologist would be more useful, but all in good time. Better to keep this quiet for the moment.'

'But doesn't that mean you'll have to keep all of your findings secret? What would be the point in that?'

'For a while, yes, but ultimately no. There are ways of aligning oneself with on-going research. Anyway, often, these situations are more valuable in terms of the ideas they throw up more than anything else, and we would be giving ourselves a head start on those.' Allen's eyes flashed as he spoke, his hands held before him as if grasping for something. 'This is precisely the sort of unique opportunity that allows intellectual excellence to flourish, that imprints a name on the timeline of scientific history. You might imagine the world of academia to be awash with altruistic truth seekers, but the reality is it's an unforgiving sea full of ruthless sharks and charlatans.'

Eleanor noticed a tense twist in Allen's mouth as he spoke.

'You're telling me!' she snorted.

'People who play by the rules tend to lose by them too.'

Eleanor brought her hands to her face and tapped the hollows of her cheeks.

'But don't worry,' Allen said with a smile, 'We'll be done with her in no time, and no one will be any the wiser.'

Eleanor said nothing.

'Eleanor,' Allen went on after a pause, 'If you want to bail out now, that's fine by me. We'll just have to hope Carl doesn't blow the whistle on us.'

'But he knows nothing.' Eleanor felt her throat tighten.

'He knows something is going on. He's not stupid. He just doesn't know yet what that thing is.'

Eleanor nodded. 'I guess we can cross that bridge when we come to it.'

Suddenly, the timer sounded.

'Time's up.' Allen jumped to his feet.

Eleanor followed him to the scanner, where they waited for the body to emerge, ready for transfer back to the freezer.

As they prepared to lower the body in, Eleanor stared one last time into the young woman's eyes, finding it impossible to pull her gaze away.

'Ready?' She could hear Allen's voice, distorted, as if drifting away from her.

Suddenly, she could see herself from a distance, beneath a turquoise sea, swimming towards this beautiful woman who was smiling at her and beckoning her to follow.

'Eleanor!' She felt Allen's hand upon her shoulder and shot back to the moment. 'We need to get on with this. Push!'

Eleanor pressed her gloved hands against the ice, but then jolted to a halt.

'Wait.' She looked towards the door.

'What is it?'

'Can't you hear that?'

Allen listened. 'I can't hear anything. Come on; we need to get a move on.' He took a deep breath and lifted his hands. He looked to Eleanor, waiting for her to follow his lead.

'No, there it is again! Someone's coming.'

The handle on the workroom door rattled.

'Who in the name…?' Allen snatched up the hammer he'd thrown to the floor. He crept round in front of the trolley, hoping to shield it from view.

In an instant, the door flew open, and a well-groomed figure strode in.

Eleanor gasped. 'Carl!'

'You have the key card to *our* room, Eleanor. I thought I might find you here. The front door was unlocked, by the way. You might want to be careful about that, Allen.'

'Well, that's what I call an entrance.' Allen dropped his would-be weapon. 'But I hope you know that was not a clever approach. You could have caused a lot of damage.'

'To what, your reputation?' Carl's tone was clipped.

'For goodness sake, Carl, what were you thinking?' Eleanor glared at him.

'You know, under normal circumstances, I would be flattered by such an assumption,' said Allen. 'But your timing is dire. We are working against the clock here, and we don't have time for this nonsense.'

Eleanor snatched her bag from the table and pulled out her hotel key card.

'Here.' She held it out towards him. 'Strange that reception couldn't have found some way to help.' She sighed. 'Sorry if I've messed up your plans, Carl. These young girls do need their beauty sleep, don't they? But don't worry; I won't be back for about an hour, so that should give *you* more than enough time, I should think.'

Carl snatched the card out of Eleanor's hand, looking past her, over her shoulder, as he did so.

'What in the name of God…' He pushed Eleanor to one side and moved towards the icy specimen.

Allen stepped in front of him and folded his arms. 'This has nothing to do with you, Carl.'

Eleanor noticed Allen's fists clench.

'Oh, but it has now, Allen. It most *certainly* has.'

He peered through the gloom as he made his way closer to the block of ice, radiant in the near darkness. At the same moment, Allen stepped in front of the trolley and placed his hands against Carl's chest.

'I'm warning you, Carl. This is none of your business.'

Carl laughed. 'What do you plan to do, call security?' He looked from Allen to Eleanor.

Allen was still for a moment, then, after a glance at Eleanor, let his hands drop to his sides. Sighing wearily, he stepped aside.

Eleanor held her breath as Carl approached the trolley. The taut grip of his jaw eased, and his lips parted, moving to form words that did not come, until, at last, she heard him murmur, 'My God, I had no idea…'

Eleanor watched as his eyes roamed up and down the ice-bound woman.

'This can't be… surely?' He turned to Allen.

'Incredible, isn't it?' Allen stood beside him for a moment. 'But we need to put her back. She's been out too long already. You can make yourself useful and give us a hand.'

Eleanor stepped forwards, and they resumed their task of lifting her onto the raised base. Carl helped without question or comment.

It wasn't until they were driving back to the conference centre that Carl found his voice again. 'Right, Allen, I have numerous questions…'

'I don't have any answers for you,' Allen replied curtly. 'Anyway, none of this will matter in a day or two when she moves on.'

'What? Where to?' Carl sounded shocked.

'No idea. They never tell you with the big ones.'

***

Back in their hotel room, as Eleanor had silently predicted, Carl turned on her.

'Were you *ever* going to tell me?' He walked round to fill the space in front of her. 'I can't believe you! Surely this is the most… significant, astonishing find… and you were just not going to mention it?'

'It wasn't like that, Carl. Allen wanted—'

'What? To keep it for himself?'

'Well, you know as much as I do now, so what's the big deal? Anyway, you've been so preoccupied the past few days, and you were the one who wasn't interested in the first place, so there's no need to be so self-righteous.'

'Don't be ridiculous, Eleanor! Of course I wasn't interested in a daft lump of muddied ice! But I think you might have guessed… I mean, how long have you known?'

'Only since last night.'

'Well, at least that accounts for your air of mystery.'

'Look, Carl, just drop it, will you? I didn't know what to say. And it doesn't matter now.'

The conversation was over. Carl poured himself a whisky from the minibar and later, they lay in bed in a brittle silence that had them turn from one another to the sanctuary of their own thoughts.

Chapter 5

When Eleanor awoke the next morning, she was relieved to find Carl was not there. Her phone rang and she answered wearily, fully expecting it to be him, ready to spout a tirade of plotted revenge.

'You just got to hear this!' It was Allen. 'I've just spoken to Simon. He managed to have a look at the data.'

'And?' Eleanor leapt out of bed.

'Meet me at the centre as soon as possible. And for God's sake, *don't tell Carl.*

***

When her cab pulled up at the research centre, Eleanor was surprised at how busy the place seemed, as her previous visits had taken place out of working hours. She made her way through its corridors, hoping no one would question her.

As soon as she knocked on Allen's door, he unlocked it and let her in. The tail of his shirt hung loose from the back of his trousers, and he hadn't shaved. Papers were strewn across the desk.

He dragged another chair close to his own and waited for Eleanor to settle herself beside him.

'So, what did Simon make of her?' Eleanor held her breath as she searched his expression for clues to whatever he was about to reveal.

Allen leafed through several scrawled pages of a notepad, then rubbed his eyes before starting to speak.

'He confirmed the body was that of an adult female of above average height, in an apparently healthy condition. He noted no anatomical abnormalities and no signs of disease or trauma.' He paused.

'So?' prompted Eleanor, 'What am I missing? You did let him think he was looking at a scan of a live woman, didn't you?'

Allen nodded. 'I did. And… well… he commented on the presence of a slight swelling in one of her fallopian tubes.'

Eleanor shifted forwards in her seat.

'So, not only was our beautiful young lady a well-cared for and healthy woman, it would appear she was also, possibly, in the earliest stages of an ectopic pregnancy.'

'Oh… dear God!' Eleanor gasped and clutched her hands to her chest. 'I wonder if she knew?'

'Highly unlikely. I mean, we don't even know for certain that she is pregnant. It's only a hint of a possibility. And we would be talking of a very young embryo.' He re-examined his notes.

'How long had she been buried up there?' Eleanor shivered. 'Still and staring, like a film on pause…'

'That's exactly what we need to find out. We can arrange for a sample to be carbon-dated. I've already been in touch with a friend who does a lot of that stuff for the university's archaeology department. He'll be able to fast-track it for us.'

'How fast is a fast-track?'

'Well, that can depend on the quality of the sample, but he could have something back to us in a couple of days. And getting a sample shouldn't be too difficult; any part of the body will contain carbon. The most important thing will be to make sure that, once removed, the sample isn't contaminated. If it's okay with you, I'd like some technical help.'

Eleanor nodded, and Allen reached for his phone. She listened as he asked Simon if he could spare a few minutes, then hung up and smiled at Eleanor.

'He's on his way.'

Almost immediately, the door handle rattled, and Allen moved quickly to unlock it again.

'I know I said you should take care of this equipment, but to keep it under lock and key?' Simon laughed as he strolled into the room. '*Salut*, Eleanor.'

Simon's large, comfortable frame and friendly manner endeared him to Eleanor. He looked about twenty years older than Allen and gave off exactly the aura of trust she would hope for in someone in the gynaecological profession.

'So, how can I be of assistance to you? You have a problem?'

'Not a problem as such,' replied Allen, 'Although something has turned up.'

'Curiouser and curiouser!'

'You gave me your opinion on some data this morning.'

Simon nodded.

'And you asked no questions regarding its source.'

Simon sighed. 'Ah, I understand.' He turned towards Eleanor and proceeded in a measured, bedside manner. 'Eleanor, my dear, as I am sure Allen will have told you, it does look to me like an ectopic pregnancy, I'm afraid. But I would need some more details…'

Allen's confusion rapidly gave way to a quiet laugh.

'Sorry, Simon,' he interrupted, 'I'm leading you in the entirely wrong direction.'

Eleanor smiled.

'Okay,' said the older man, 'So now I have absolutely no idea what you are talking about.'

'Eleanor has been helping me with a little bit of detective work with a local find. I wonder if you could give me an opinion on it, before I move things along?'

'And this is to do with the data you showed me earlier?'

Allen rose from his chair and walked to the storage unit. Eleanor followed. Before lifting the lid, he checked all the doors were locked then dimmed the overhead light. He bent down to the base of the unit and flicked the switch. Soon, it began to rise.

From his chair, Simon watched in silence as the pair eased off the upper layers of ice and wheeled them to the trough. Once invited forwards, he approached the unit slowly.

As soon as he reached its edge, he halted and peered down into its depths. Eleanor watched as he raised both hands to his chest. For several minutes, he remained there, perfectly still, until, at last, he leant in closer, narrowed his eyes, and stared down. Still, he said nothing. It was some minutes before he stood up.

'The source?' he breathed.

Allen nodded.

'*C'est pas possible*! The MRI… it looked just like a living woman! I have never seen anything like it!'

'It is rare, but it's not the first find of its kind.' Allen handed Simon some of the papers he'd gathered. 'A number of bodies have been found that have been mummified in this way, perfectly preserved.'

'And, of course, it is not exactly unheard of in modern medicine either, I suppose,' said Simon. 'We borrow this very freezing technique with embryos, for deferred implantation.'

Eleanor helped Allen replace the upper crusts of ice then watched solemnly as the woman was returned to her resting place.

'So, what now? Have you any idea what you will do next?' asked Simon.

'We want to know the age of this find,' said Allen. 'To do that, we need a skillful bit of surgery to obtain a sample for carbon-dating, and that's where we hope you might come in.'

Simon nodded, but his thoughts seemed focussed elsewhere.

'Does anyone else know about this?' he asked eventually.

'One other person,' said Allen.

'Carl,' said Eleanor.

'Ah yes, we met at the conference.'

'Oh, and Sophie,' said Allen, 'You know, my research assistant. But she has only a vague sense of what is going on, and she's expressed no curiosity about it.'

'So, you would like some help to remove a small sample in such a way that it might never be detected?' asked Simon.

Allen nodded.

'It will be tricky, I think, but… I could try.' Simon looked at his watch. 'I must go to my clinic now. But this is not something to rush. I will think about it, work out a plan…'

'Of course,' Allen agreed, 'Let's talk it through, all brains on deck as it were. But we don't have that much time — how about we brainstorm it tonight over dinner at my house?'

'Of course,' said Simon, 'Bring a good bottle of wine, and your brightest ideas will not be far behind.'

Eleanor sighed heavily.

'Problem?' Simon asked.

'What about Carl?'

'What about him?' Allen rubbed his hand across his stubbled chin. 'Interfering bastard.'

Simon's eyes narrowed. 'Seems I have a lot to catch up with.'

'Quite,' Eleanor clipped, 'But I don't think we have any choice. Heaven knows the chaos he could whip up with just one phone call, and this find would be lost to us for good.'

'We have to keep him on side; more's the pity,' murmured Allen. 'Damn him!'

'Don't worry,' Eleanor spoke in a tone as chilled as the dead, 'I'll ask him along. And if ever he does decide to go public on this; I'll find a way to guarantee that he'll stand to lose much more than we do.'

Chapter 6

When Eleanor got back to her hotel room, Carl was already there, stretched on the bed, fanning his face with a newspaper. The window was open, but little air seemed to be circulating. Fresh from the shower, he wore only his towel. His eyes were half-closed, and he looked as if he was about to sleep but pulled himself up as soon as Eleanor appeared.

'Didn't expect to see you here,' Eleanor said.

'Yes, how strange I should be in my own room.'

'I thought you'd be busy.'

'I was.' Carl got up and pulled on a dressing gown. 'Spent the afternoon giving feedback on a bunch of presentations by juniors. Mostly tedious.'

'Anyone worth looking out for?'

'Well, Sophie was very good, of course, if a little nervous. She could do with a bit of help on presentation skills. I've offered to give her a few tips over dinner tonight.'

Eleanor's hear leapt. She smiled wryly. 'Ever the *mentor*, Carl.'

Carl ignored the dig. 'What about you? I haven't been able to get that... frozen woman out of my mind. Any developments?'

Eleanor hesitated, but before she had a chance to reply, Carl's phone rang out.

'Well, hi there, Sophie.'

Eleanor rolled her eyes as he adopted his sexy phone voice.

Carl knew nothing of the ectopic pregnancy, considered Eleanor as she pretended to read her emails. They'd both be flying home in a few days, and, as far as he was concerned, it could all end there, the trail just running cold. But not for her; Eleanor would make sure that she remained a part of it, at the centre of it, the very heart of it.

'Okay, maybe tomorrow then.' Carl's telephone tone had cooled from smoking hot to lukewarm. 'Looks like I have to postpone my plans,' he growled, tossing his phone on the bed and walking to the window.

Eleanor sighed. Now she had no choice but to deliver the invitation.

'Well, why don't you join us for a brainstorming session at Allen's tonight? He's making dinner.'

He sniffed and checked his watch. 'I'll see if I can squeeze that in.'

***

They took a cab to Allen's house, which was a ranch-like home in a suburb halfway between the university and the research centre. Allen answered the door, holding a bottle of red wine in one hand and a wad of papers in the other.

'Come in, come in!' He smiled, beckoning them into a spacious hallway that led into a bright living room, with open doors to a decked area beyond.

Simon was already there and stood to greet them as Allen reached for two more glasses.

'So good you could join us, Carl,' Simon said, smiling.

'I had a cancellation,' Carl replied, 'So, you're in luck.'

'I hope red wine agrees with you both?' Allen polished each glass with the cloth that was draped over his shoulder.

'Absolutely,' said Carl.

Allen poured the wine, then slipped behind the island that separated the dining area from the kitchen and continued preparing dinner. He seemed to work effortlessly and had no difficulty sustaining the flow of conversation as he chopped and seasoned.

Immediately, Carl launched into a tale of his own culinary efforts, and Eleanor noticed Allen's teeth clench. The methodical slicing of onions became a frantic chop as the *ratatatatat* of the knife on the board sent silver half-moons flying. But before long, the meal was ready, and Allen was ushering them to the table as he held aloft a large platter of paella.

'Not a bad effort,' said Carl, helping himself to a generous portion.

As soon as they'd finished eating, Allen gathered the dirty dishes and piled them in the sink. He ran a cloth along the table's wooden surface, gouging grains of saffron-coloured rice from its grooves. He then brought over four fresh glasses and another bottle of wine. There was a moment of quiet as he eased the cork away and filled each glass in turn.

'Okay,' he began, 'Where do we go from here? I take it Eleanor has kept you abreast of developments?'

Carl nodded. 'Of course.'

'Actually, I haven't told Carl about today yet,' she said.

Carl glared at her. '*More* secrets?'

'No time,' Eleanor shot back, 'Especially as you were running off somewhere for dinner.'

'Well, we are here now,' Simon mediated.

'Precisely,' said Allen. He took a sip from his glass and turned to Carl. 'As you know, we have in our possession an astonishing corpse, frozen in ice. We don't know when she lived, or how or why she died.' He paused. 'And yesterday's scans seem to indicate that the remains have been perfectly preserved.'

'And?' Carl asked coolly.

'And I asked Simon to have a look at the data from the scan. When he reported back to me this morning, he said it hadn't crossed his mind that the subject was anything other than a young female, alive today, such was the quality of preservation.'

Simon nodded.

'Okay, that is remarkable,' Carl admitted.

'And even more,' Simon picked up the tale, 'When I said the scan was typical of the many I routinely see, I meant exactly that.' He held Carl's steady gaze.

'Meaning?'

'Meaning, she just might be in the early, the very early, stages of an ectopic pregnancy.'

Carl sat in his chair, staring at everyone in turn. 'Now that is something,' he said, 'That really is…'

'So, now we need to decide what to do,' said Eleanor, 'How do we make the most of this?'

'It's such an opportunity,' said Allen, 'I say we brainstorm it tonight. Any ideas you can dream up, just spit them out, no matter how *out there* they might seem. Get them on the table, and we can think through the practicalities later.' He produced a notepad and pen from the drawer of the sideboard behind him. 'Fire away.'

'I think we've got to start with the carbon-dating, find out for sure exactly how old this cadaver is,' said Eleanor.

'Agreed,' said Carl, 'But before that, can we give the poor girl a name? An evening of euphemisms for *corpse* could become rather tiring, don't you think?'

'So long as it's not Eve,' said Allen. 'I can't bear clichés.'

'No, something symbolic,' Carl mused. 'Who's the goddess of love?' He turned to Eleanor.

'Aphrodite or Venus, depending on whether you prefer Greek or Roman,' she replied.

'Why go halfway round the world?' Simon cried. 'She is Canadian!'

'Okay, so who's *your* goddess?' Carl topped up his glass.

Allen tapped the question into his phone and frowned. 'Don't see a goddess of love, but what about A'akuluujjusi … the great Creator Mother?'

'Very catchy,' snorted Carl.

'Where was she found again?' asked Eleanor.

'Just south of the Lillooet Icecap, on the west flank of the Lillooet River,' said Allen.

'Lillooet then?' she suggested.

They looked at each other and nodded.

'Lillooet she is,' said Simon.

Allen took up his pen again. 'I agree with Eleanor. Some indication of the age of… of *Lillooet* will provide the critical context for all the other information we currently have and will gather in the future. But in addition to that, I would like some DNA samples to map out her genetic profile.'

'I see no problem in that,' said Simon, 'Obtaining the sample, that is. Even the smallest piece of tissue would give you all you need for both those investigations.'

'And I'd be looking for some mitochondrial DNA,' added Eleanor, 'To identify Lillooet's maternal inheritance. See which genetic line she belongs to. But we could get that from the same sample.'

Simon had left his chair and was pacing the floor behind the table.

'That just leaves you, Simon,' said Allen.

Simon returned to his chair and cleared his throat before speaking.

'I am thinking…' He waved his arms as he spoke. 'Excuse my presumption, but this is so… so very new and interesting… that perhaps I would be just a little more ambitious? Although…' He came to a stop and drew his hand across the rough of his chin. 'I realise this might not be possible… but if I could have any part of Lillooet for investigation, I would, for sure, have the embryo.'

A giddy silence electrified the room.

'I mean, what have we here?' he went on after a few moments, 'A woman of unknown origin, possibly from thousands of years ago, who carries within her the blueprint of her people, whoever they might be. It is astonishing. And as it looks like she has just conceived, that tiny bundle of cells could tell us so much! I'd like to see precisely how it has grown so far and to compare it with contemporary foetal development.'

Eleanor gasped. 'Dear God, of course!'

'I mean, would it act like any other frozen embryo?' Simon continued, barely looking at the others. 'That's what I would *really* like to know.'

'And could it be defrosted?' Eleanor joined in, her voice trembling, 'Maybe we could watch it, observe it, as it reawakens?'

Simon nodded. 'Perhaps, and I cannot believe I'm saying this, but… even try to multiply itself into life?'

Eleanor cringed as Carl burst into a volley of over-loud laughter.

'Impossible!' he cried, 'You imagine you could revive something so inert? You're out of your mind!' He gulped more wine, shaking his head.

'But why?' Simon replied. 'What is the difference between being freeze dried beneath an ice cap for however long or within a flask in my lab? Does the embryo know its environment? It is true that, as an ectopic pregnancy, this embryo will be a little more developed than those we usually manage, but the principle's the same.'

'But in your lab, you control temperature, humidity, and so on,' Carl pointed out.

'Precisely!' replied Simon, 'But in doing that, we're only trying to mimic nature, to trick the embryo into believing it's within a normal set of circumstances. And there's the irony! This event has been driven by nature. It's way more natural than anything I could ever hope to contrive.'

Simon's words were met with a solemn silence.

Carl left the table, returning with another bottle of red.

Allen leant forwards. 'Imagine for a moment that you *did* manage to coax this embryo back to life again, Simon. Is it at all possible that it could ever achieve its original goal?'

'Of life?' asked Simon, 'Grow into a living being?'

'No, not spontaneously. At least, what I mean is, not *independently*. But if it were capable of coming back to life in a Petri dish, could we not try to do the same with Lillooet's child as you have done with other embryos?'

Eleanor turned the idea over in her mind and felt her reaction shift between hope and horror.

'Would that be possible?' Allen was staring at Simon.

'No, no… definitely not.' Simon shook his head emphatically. 'This embryo is weeks more developed than the bundles of cells we work with in IVF. That sort of thing has never been achieved, as far as I am aware. With very few exceptions, ectopic pregnancies are doomed. If Lillooet had lived a while longer, both she and the foetus would almost certainly have died.'

'It might never have *been* achieved,' said Carl, 'But has it been *attempted*?'

'To my knowledge? *Non*,' replied Simon.

'Why not?' Carl challenged.

'Generally, we do not know a pregnancy is ectopic until the mother is in pain, and then it is too much of a risk to her to delay things. And I do not think that an embryo that big could be transferred without compromising it.'

'Okay, I get all that, but as regards to your worries about causing the mother harm, that surely is irrelevant in this case?' Allen had stood up and was pacing the floor.

'Well… yes… it's true.' Simon nodded.

'And is there anything to lose in trying to transfer the embryo? It's not got any chance of life as it is,' Eleanor surprised herself by joining in.

They all stared at each other in silence. Eleanor felt her heart thud in her chest, and she could see by the looks on their faces that the other three were just as excited.

Simon broke the silence. 'Ah no, even if we did manage to retrieve the embryo and defrost it, it would be inert, for sure. But if there was any spark of life in it, I should think it would not last for long.'

'But wouldn't that be fascinating in itself?' Allen's eyes gleamed as he spoke. 'How far would it go? Why no further? What's the same as now? What's different? Has development evolved?' He seemed to be racing to catch up with his own thoughts.

'And then supposing you find it does revive fully and does look viable,' added Eleanor, 'Would we do nothing to try to sustain it?'

'To go any further, we would need a surrogate, and I do not think that would be possible. Who in their right mind is going to agree to that? The women who come to see me do not want to be anthropologists; they want to be parents. Anyway, you would never get approval.'

'But what if we don't seek approval? What if we keep this strictly amongst ourselves?' said Allen.

'You mean implant this… *thing*… without telling the surrogate, it is not hers? That is outrageous, Allen. You surprise me!' Simon spluttered.

'No, that's not what I mean. Of course, we wouldn't trick one of your patients!'

'So, who *is* going to host this embryo?' Simon looked around the table.

They sat in silence for some minutes before Carl turned to Allen. 'Do you think, perhaps Sophie might…? She's young, not too inquisitive, you said…'

'Certainly not!' Simon interrupted, 'She is young, yes, and has her life ahead of her…'

'And I'm pretty damn sure she's still a virgin,' Allen added, 'So, I doubt she'd agree to something like this!'

Eleanor saw Carl shift in his chair and recognised the signs of an appetite whetted. He emptied his glass and reached for the bottle.

Quiet resumed until Eleanor caught sight of a loaded glance that shot between Carl and Allen, then, unmistakably, in her direction.

She glared at Carl. 'Absolutely no fucking way!'

'*Bon sang*!' Simon snapped, 'I hope I misunderstand you. Eleanor as host? Unthinkable!'

'Why?' Carl asked, 'Which part exactly would you find it hard to think about?'

'We do not know who this person is or why she died. For all we know, we could be putting the host at biological risk,' replied Simon.

'Highly unlikely, as you well know, Simon.' Allen shook his head. 'When it comes to a competition between mother and non-viable life, the established life normally wins.'

'*Normally*, yes,' repeated Simon, 'But this? Normal?' He shook his head. 'We have no idea what demands might be made upon the host body.'

Eleanor leapt to her feet. 'Pardon me for interrupting, gentlemen, but this is now *my* body you're talking about, and I have absolutely no interest in lending it out as some sort of laboratory wet nurse!'

She sat down and took a large gulp of wine, her cheeks burning. No one spoke for a while, and it was Carl who finally broke the silence.

'You're absolutely right.' He stretched in front of Eleanor to reach the bottle, spilling it as he overfilled his glass. 'Now I think of it, I can understand why you're not keen on the idea. As much as it would be an incredible experiment, the ultimate in living science, let's be honest, it *would* be a risk. I mean supposing, just supposing, this thing did take, and you became pregnant?' Carl looked around the table, laughing. 'No one in their right mind would expect someone like *you* to go ahead with a pregnancy. Some people are destined for motherhood, and others are, well, you know…'

'Carl, what on earth are you saying?' Simon jumped to Eleanor's defence, but she cut him off.

'Yes, what exactly do you mean, *someone like me*?'

Carl tilted his head back, a knowing smile playing around his mouth.

'Eleanor. Some women just aren't maternal material; horses for courses and all that. Don't feel bad. It's a pity we can't recruit a more likely candidate. Someone bright enough to understand the importance of it all, but able to deal with the fallout and settle into motherhood if need be.'

'Whoa, whoa, whoa!' Allen held his hands up towards the pair.

Eleanor ignored the intervention, overcome with fury. 'Someone bright, but not too bright, you mean? She's beginning to sound more like the ideal wife than the perfect mother!'

'Oh, don't go all feminist on me, Eleanor!' Carl laughed. 'You know exactly what I mean. It was daft of me to consider you; I should have known better. But I thought that, well, given your age and stage in life, you wouldn't be sacrificing as much as a younger, more maternally inclined woman would, that's all!'

'You are *way* out of line, Carl,' Allen cautioned.

'But it's true, isn't it?' Carl insisted, 'You're hardly likely, at your age, to change your mind and do all the mummy bit for yourself now, are you?'

'And your point is?' Eleanor clenched her fists beneath the table.

'Just that, Eleanor, if you don't want to use what remains of your procreative potential for yourself, then you might have thought about donating it to science. But hey, I'm not trying to talk you into it.'

'Just as well, because you're doing a shit job,' Eleanor shot back.

'As I said,' Allen continued, with an air of self-satisfaction, 'Now I've thought it through a bit more, I realise it's not such a good idea. Apart from the microscopically small chance of success in the first place and the associated risks, not everyone's cut out for parenthood. It's potentially a lifelong commitment, demanding mountains of patience and endless self-sacrifice.'

'Clearly not qualities necessary for fatherhood then,' Eleanor snorted.

'No, I see your point, Eleanor,' Carl persisted, 'It was a stupid idea. You as a parent?' He forced another laugh. 'It could never work.'

As Carl sank back in his chair, he smirked. Eleanor noticed the red stains etched from the corners of his mouth, making a clown of his face. She rose to her feet.

'I've had enough of this circus for tonight.'

She gazed down at Carl, wondering what had ever drawn her to him. This drunken buffoon, with whom she had so often shared her bed over the past two years. She thought of her younger self, impressed by the bluster and the promises, and knew that once this conference was over, she would never allow it to happen again.

'I'm going,' she announced, gesturing towards Carl. 'I'll leave it to you guys to pour this ideal exemplar of paternity into a cab at some point. Good luck with that.'

Chapter 7

When Eleanor arrived at the research centre the next day, the car park was still empty.

'This the right place?' the cab driver asked.

'Yep.'

Eleanor paid him and walked towards the main entrance. She turned as he was leaving and could see he was staring at her in his rear-view mirror. As soon as he was out of sight, she changed direction and followed the narrow strip of paving stones to the rear of the building, the path she had taken with Sophie on that first night.

The area behind the centre was stacked with wooden crates, and an open bag of cement spilled its weathered contents down the slope of the scrubland. She could hear the chirrup of insects from the wild grasses that grew on the undeveloped land, but she could see no signs of other life. A carpet of rough grass stretched out before her to the towering ridges that dominated the skyline.

Beyond a fringe of pine, she marvelled at the giant Mount Meager, a dark blanket of night shadow drawn up to shoulder height. A Peach Melba sky lay crushed between its icy ridges and the blue-black clouds above. She had gasped at the sight, overawed by the colours of the twilight palette, only then to curse herself for falling prey to sentiment. But she wanted to see the mountains again, and now, she found herself struggling not to cry.

Was that where she was found? Eleanor tried to imagine Lillooet's last moments and the final thoughts that had left her with such a peaceful expression. She sat on one of the upturned crates and closed her eyes. How long had Lillooet lain there? And how many lives marked the distance between them?

But it was not just time that separated them. Eleanor folded her arms and ran her hands up along smooth, warm skin to the dome of her shoulders. Lillooet had at one time been a soft, vital, thinking creature, with full use of her limbs and cognitive skills. But now she lay brittle and chilled, her mortal remains at the mercy of fortune, while Eleanor's body was vital, warmed by the rich blood that coursed through her veins. And *she* could still make choices.

Cradling herself, Eleanor closed her eyes and lowered her head to her chest. Tired from the night before, she drifted to that place between sleep and waking, where her thoughts seemed cast in the soft weave of a silky web. She saw Lillooet stroll along a woodland path, a newborn nestled in her arms. The dappled sunlight made a mosaic of her features, but it was evident who she was. Eleanor walked close behind her, straining to hear the lullaby Lillooet sang, captivated by its cadence. But when they reached a stream and Lillooet picked her way across its stepping-stones, Eleanor sensed she shouldn't follow, at which point Lillooet turned and smiled, as if telling her to trust her instincts.

She opened her eyes and rose unsteadily to her feet. She was not sure how long she'd been there, but by the time she pulled herself away and walked to Allen's room, she found him already engrossed in conversation with Simon.

'Good morning.' Eleanor took a seat beside the two men.

'*Salut*, Eleanor, how are you this morning?'

Eleanor could hear genuine concern in Simon's voice.

'I'm fine, thanks.' She hoped they wouldn't dwell on Carl's drunken rant the night before; she wanted to move forwards.

'Is he coming?' Allen looked to the door.

'I hope not,' Eleanor replied.

At that moment, the door swung open, and Carl strode in.

'Morning, all.' He sat down. 'Not late, am I?'

'We weren't sure if you would be joining us today.' Allen stared at him.

'Whatever gave you that idea?' Carl smiled. 'Last night? Come on!' He laughed lightly. 'A bit of academic rough and tumble never did anyone any harm. So, what's on the agenda?'

Eleanor held her lips tightly shut. She would not be provoked into more verbal combat.

Allen looked to Simon, who had brought a sheet of notes with him.

'I have been thinking over what we discussed last night, and I, for one, am still fully committed to extracting the embryo for examination and observation.' He looked around at the others.

'Absolutely!' Carl rubbed his hands together.

Allen and Eleanor nodded their agreement.

'Now we have all accepted that the whole implantation idea was a… pipe dream, as you would say—' Simon began.

'Albeit a tempting one,' Carl interrupted.

'We have rightly agreed to let that pass,' Simon continued. 'We now need to focus on strategy.'

'What are you thinking?' Eleanor asked.

'Actually, I think the procedure will be quite straightforward. The fact that our subject is so deeply frozen is, of course, vital as the embryo and all Lillooet's internal fluids and organs are held in a motionless state. So, with the existing data, we can derive the coordinates of the exact location of the embryo and then use stereotactic instruments to guide its removal.'

'How can that be done without leaving a trace?' asked Eleanor.

'That's what we were discussing when you arrived,' said Allen. 'This embryo is only about the size of a sesame seed. We will use a core biopsy needle to bore through the ice and retrieve it without leaving a mark.'

'But won't that introduce air into the body and damage it?' said Eleanor.

'*Non*, I think not. If we refill the channel immediately with some of the defrosted ice, it should refreeze instantly and become indistinguishable from the rest.'

'Ingenious.' Carl slapped his hand on the table. 'Sounds like we could get away with that.'

'Surely the plan has to be faultless, not just one with a reasonable chance of *getting away with it*?' snapped Eleanor.

'I believe it will be.' Simon replied.

'Timeline?' Allen looked at him.

'We should do it right now, I think, before she is no longer with us.'

Allen checked his watch. 'I can't hang around, I'm afraid. I'm on the inter-university panel all day. Can you manage without me? I won't be much help with this part of the process anyhow. Not my field.'

'And I have commitments too,' said Carl, 'But as you'll have gathered, I'm more of a thinker than a doer, always been top-heavy on the skills front. But Eleanor is free.' He waved his hand in her direction.

'Well, thank you, Alexa!' Eleanor hissed, turning sharply to face Simon. 'I would love to assist.'

Eleanor felt relieved after Carl and Allen had gone. Just being near Carl made her bristle, and she wanted to clear her thoughts of emotional junk.

'There are one or two things I should fetch from the clinic, Eleanor, then I will talk you through the procedure.' Simon walked to the door.

'Sure,' said Eleanor, pleased her voice sounded strong and steady, 'I'll make myself useful if I can.'

As soon as she was alone, Eleanor walked to the storage unit and heaved up the lid. She knew she would see nothing beyond the grey silver screen but gazed into it anyway. She held her hand above the spot where she thought Lillooet's heart might lie, just inches below her palm, and imagined how it might look if it were to return to life. A weak pulse splitting the ice around it, blood warming and oozing into thawing tissues until they, too, softened and gave way to the life- giving flow. Eleanor's own heart rate quickened to a double beat, each pulse an echo of itself. She took deep, slow breaths, trying to still its racing rhythm.

She wasn't sure what she was feeling. Compassion? perhaps, but there was something else, a far more powerful undercurrent.

Longing.

She realised she envied Lillooet, her freedom from the web of modern life, and the incessant call of people and events demanding her attention. She envied her blissful state, unconscious as she was of the decisions now being taken on her behalf; a destiny determined by others. What, she wondered, would Lillooet choose for herself?

As she heard Simon approach, Eleanor closed the lid just in time before he bustled in, carrying several cases.

'Much of what we need is already next door in the scanning room,' he said. 'And, of course, we will have to scrub up for this, just like any invasive procedure, yes?'

'Yes.'

Eleanor watched as Simon opened the cases, each containing an array of sealed packets, and placed them on a trolley.

'I want to make sure everything is ready to go so there will be no lag between discussion and action; that is where the problems sneak in.'

Eleanor longed to see Lillooet again. She needed to stare into her face and try to understand the pull she felt, as if they were joined by a cord, an umbilicus, woven together by strands of pain and ecstasy.

As Simon outlined the procedure, describing what each step would require of her, Eleanor took notes, her hand trembling at the thought of what they were attempting to do. Terrified, she realised, not at the possibility of being caught doing something that was surely illegal, but at the idea of robbing Lillooet of her treasure, only to destroy it.

'So, we are ready?'

Eleanor nodded and followed Simon to the freezer. She said nothing as they brought the body to the surface and removed the upper layers of ice.

Simon ran a gloved hand down the length of the ice tomb.

Eleanor wished she could have some final time alone with her. She turned to Simon. 'Hang on; we must take photos. Do you have a decent camera?'

'But of course!' Simon clicked his fingers and walked back to the door. 'One minute.'

As soon as he was gone, Eleanor moved back to Lillooet's side, like a grieving relative paying a final visit to a loved one.

'Lillooet,' she heard herself whisper as she stared into her eyes.

She remembered the woman singing in the woods, babe in arms. She removed one of her gloves and placed a warm finger on the spot above her cheek. She leant in as close as she could, trying to align her own eyes with Lillooet's, and when their eyes did lock, she gasped. Her finger shot from the ice, as if struck by lightning. It burnt, and she was forced to replace its protective clothing. Then, cautiously, she drew close to her again.

'Lillooet,' she spoke as if trying to rouse her. 'What would you have me do?' Her finger traced the contour of the translucent face, her mouth, her eyes. She was not ready to lose her.

Eleanor closed her eyes and saw herself standing face-to-face with Lillooet, a wall of barbed wire between them. Like a mother and child facing an imminent separation, she wanted only to hold on to that moment, to promise she would find a way for them to be together again. She would not be abandoned. She sensed Lillooet, too, was reaching out to her, urging her to breach the divide and take a leap of faith.

She felt a welling in her chest, a rugged rock of grief, the kind that lodges in the heart in times of loss.

You are not mine to mourn, she thought, kissing her finger and pressing it above the frozen lips. *And yet, you are. Somehow you now share the space of everything and everyone I have ever cared about, and fear losing.*

The door handle rattled, and Eleanor swung round to face Simon. She had made her decision.

'Are you alright?' Simon asked, peering at her. 'You know, if you are feeling uncomfortable with this, you can step out at any time.'

'No,' she said, 'It's not that. Simon, I have changed my mind, but not in the way you're thinking.'

Simon walked slowly towards her, stopping so close she could see the dark rim that circled the clear blue of his eyes.

'How different would things be today if we wanted to keep open the option of implantation?'

Simon's jaw dropped. 'You mean…?'

Eleanor nodded.

'*Really?*'

Eleanor could hear the shock in his voice. 'Yes.'

'I see you are someone who knows her own mind, Eleanor, but… are you sure?'

Again, she nodded.

'But just last night, you were so very much against the idea?'

'I needed time to think about it. In fact, it's all I've thought about all night. I want to do this, Simon.' She clenched her fists.

'What do *you* think? I thought you were holding back last night too.'

'It's true. I felt anxious on your behalf, Eleanor. It is a huge thing to ask of anyone, even if the chance of success is minuscule. I did not want there to be any pressure on you.'

'What do you feel now?'

'For myself, I… I am blown away by the idea. It would be the highlight of my career, no doubt about it. But are you certain?'

'Yes.'

'Fantastic!' Simon punched the air and hurried to fetch his notes from the table. 'A whole new frontier!' His face glowed as he spoke. 'What might we uncover? Having said that…' He took a deep breath as he sat down. 'It is unlikely, *highly* unlikely, that the procedure will be successful. Theoretically alone, the chances are remote, but in terms of the practicalities, we are talking millions… no, *billions* to one.'

'I know that. But, as Allen said last night, we could learn a lot even if it doesn't go to plan.'

Simon nodded.

'So, do we need to alter anything we're doing right now, or do we proceed as planned?' asked Eleanor.

'We proceed as planned,' said Simon, scribbling on his sheet. 'The embryo was going to be placed in a storage flask at any rate, so that is no different. It is the next phase that alters now. As soon as this procedure is complete, we should meet in my clinic to discuss and assess your fertility profile and talk through the process itself, just as I would do with any patient. Is that okay with you?'

'That won't be hard. I know exactly where I am.'

Simon shot to attention. 'And?'

'Day fifteen of twenty-eight.'

He frowned. 'Sure about this?'

'One hundred percent. Ovulate day fourteen, always do.'

Simon raised his eyebrows.

'I'm thinking of researching sibling issues in cycle variation. A purely professional interest,' Eleanor continued. 'Carl was quite right. I have no maternal inclinations whatsoever.' As she heard her own words, Eleanor thought about Lillooet and felt a wave of disloyalty wash over her. 'I want to do it, Simon. Tonight.'

Simon leapt to his feet and paced the floor in front of her. '*J'en reviens pas!* I wouldn't have thought ten minutes ago it could be possible to feel any more focussed, but now…' He looked into Eleanor's eyes and shook his head. 'We will, of course, need to discuss this with Allen and Carl, but, for the moment, we just have to get on with this.'

He handed her a sealed plastic bag. 'You need to wash your hands thoroughly, up to the elbow, and put these on. The locker room is just along the corridor.'

When she returned, Simon was ready to start. Like Eleanor, he had changed into sterile scrubs; a paper mask covered the lower half of his face, and a theatre cap was pulled over his hair. Eleanor felt reassured by his appearance, as if the garments themselves endorsed the procedure.

She watched as Simon set to work. He ripped open one of the double wrapped packages and eased out a slender needle. Then, holding the clear plastic syringe with both hands, he pushed the plunger fully in.

'Right.' He checked his laptop and attached a fine cable from it to the base of the syringe. He tapped on the keyboard, and instantly Lillooet's image was transformed from two to three dimensions, encased in a cage of intersecting lines.

'The red X you can see on the screen is the marker, our target, and the yellow one tracks the path of the needle.'

Eleanor looked from the screen to Lillooet and back.

'Now, according to these coordinates, the optimal insertion point is here.' He lowered the gleaming shaft to the ice and pressed firmly. They waited for it to slide in.

'*Quel bordel!*' He stopped after a few moments. 'It is not breaking through.'

'I suppose they're designed to pierce soft flesh, not solid ice.' Eleanor could see no impact whatsoever had been made.

'True, but I had hoped the heat produced by the friction of the metal on the ice would be sufficient.' He paused. 'But no… we'd need a drill to get through this, and we don't have time to set that up.' Simon tried again, scraping at the face of the ice with the needle's point. 'It is no good, Eleanor. We cannot risk exposing her to this temperature for the length of time we'd need to do the procedure.' He looked utterly defeated.

'Heat,' Eleanor persisted, 'That's what we need.'

'You think? But the harm…'

'Just a bit, surely? A hot needle to make an indentation and get the process started…'

'Or, better still,' Simon put in, 'What if we create a fine channel by cauterising?' He thrust the syringe into Eleanor's hand and ran to the scanning room. She heard drawers open then slam shut, the rustling of paper and the clang of metal falling to the floor. Eventually, he reappeared.

'We have nothing to lose,' he panted, unravelling the long blue cable from what looked to Eleanor like an electric toothbrush. He tore open another packet and attached a needle. Within seconds, he was pressing into the entry point.

Eleanor watched as the hot-tipped, silver steel slid effortlessly beyond the tiny scrape the previous needle had managed to make. Water began to trickle from the channel.

'We will need that,' Simon told her. 'Unwrap one of the larger kidney dishes and catch as much as you can.'

Eleanor fumbled with the slippery cellophane and ripped the metal bowl from its bag. She dropped to the floor and held it in both hands.

'Let us see if that's done the trick. Hopefully, the biopsy needle can do the rest.' Simon withdrew the cauterising needle and slipped the original into the groove. He leant hard against the ice.

'*La vache!*' He shuffled closer.

Eleanor felt the limp green cotton of his scrubs press against her face. She heard him mumble more profanities.

She stood up, still holding the bowl in place. 'Why not just power on with the cauteriser?'

'Are you crazy?'

'What's the alternative?'

'We put her back in her box and walk away.' Simon sighed heavily.

'No!' Eleanor shook her head. 'I'm not doing that. I can't.'

'Thought you wanted to play it safe?'

'I did. But now I don't. I'll do it if you don't want to.'

Simon glanced at the screen; time was moving on. 'No, I will be faster for sure.' He slid the cauterising stick back into place. 'I will keep an eye on this if you can monitor the screen. We need to stop just short of the embryo and push through the final stretch with the other needle.'

Eleanor was desperate to see what Simon was doing, but she knew she must keep watch on the screen, and so she forced her gaze to remain there. She didn't have to wait long.

'Stop!' she barked.

Simon turned to check how close he was. He threw the heated needle to the floor and pushed the original into the clear channel. This time there was less resistance, the thawed flesh parted without much of a struggle, and soon he reached the target.

Eleanor held her breath as the long blade reached out to the tiny bundle of cells. Simon withdrew the needle.

'Did you get it?'

'I hope so, but it is barely visible to the naked eye.' Simon's voice was still muffled by his mask. He pulled back the syringe plunger, and a hair-like column of cloudy white filled its chamber. They squinted into it as if trying to read a crystal ball.

Eleanor felt different, even from an hour before; somehow responsible, yet no longer in control. But she felt certain this was what Lillooet wanted her to do.

'We need to work quickly, Eleanor. I have a feeling that whatever is in here is beginning to thaw.'

Eleanor pulled on her thermal gloves and moved quickly to remove the flask from its chilled casing. She unscrewed the lid, releasing a swirling mist of iced air, and by the time she returned, Simon had eased the contents of the syringe into a clear tube. He fastened the lid and handed it to Eleanor, who slipped it into the flask, securing it immediately.

Then he drew up a small quantity of melted ice water from the dish and injected it into the channel he'd created.

'*Dac!*' He pulled off his mask and gown, and, taking the flask from Eleanor, left the room.

Eleanor approached Lillooet and looked into her eyes. Immediately, she felt a fresh surge of energy gather force within her. Her hand trembled, but not in fear, as she reached out to her.

'I will do my best, I promise,' she whispered, 'And now we are connected, forever.'

She raised the camera and began to take pictures, snapping continuously, anxious no detail be left to the mercy of memory alone.

When Simon returned, they quickly replaced the upper layers of ice and lowered the base of the unit. They watched in silence as they finally laid her to rest, disappearing from view, as she travelled backwards in time to her icy grave.

***

Simon's office was comfortable and reassuring. Three soft chairs were arranged in front of an uncluttered desk. Well cared for parlour palms swayed in the wash of the gentle breeze from a freestanding fan. Simon sat in the single chair in front of his desk and gestured to Eleanor to make herself at home.

'I hope you will not find this too intrusive, Eleanor, but this will involve gathering information of a personal nature.' He took up his notepad and pen.

'Fire away.'

'Is there any chance you could be pregnant at the moment?'

'Dear God, no!' Eleanor felt her stomach twist.

'Ever been pregnant?'

She shook her head.

'And have you ever tried to get pregnant?'

'Absolutely not.'

'And you are certain about where you are in your cycle?'

Eleanor nodded.

'Well, it seems we are in luck. Things could hardly be better, Eleanor. Your hormones are already primed, ready to kick in. They are preparing the nest. It is perfect! But we need to act quickly; this window of opportunity will soon pass.'

'And I'm scheduled to leave tomorrow.'

Simon sighed, drawing his fingers through his already tousled hair. 'Now, that is not so perfect. Normally, I would want to keep an eye on things, on *you*. Make sure you are well…'

'I'll be fine,' Eleanor insisted. 'Anyway, as you said yourself at dinner, there is nothing *normal* about this at all. Please, Simon, believe me, I am fit and healthy.'

He nodded slowly. 'Okay then, today it is. But we will do a bit of hormonal massage first, just to help things along. It is not as much as I would like, but it will be better than nothing.'

'How much does this differ from your usual approach?' Eleanor asked.

'The main difference is the developmental stage of the embryo. We normally transfer between day two and day six, but this one is more mature, so it is unlikely to take root. I have certainly never heard of it being done before.'

'And it's been frozen for longer than normal,' said Eleanor.

'I assume so,' Simon said, smiling, 'And that could be a problem too. We normally use a cryoprotectant to preserve the embryo's state, so it is highly likely this one will have degenerated beyond usefulness. But there is no manual for this; all we can do is our best and see what happens.'

'So, where do we go from here?' asked Eleanor. Now that she'd committed to the project, she was determined to make it work.

'Hormone shot, straight away.'

'And then?'

'Then the embryo will be thawed and brought up to body temperature.'

How long does that take?'

'Once we remove it from the flask, it will be ready in about forty- five minutes.' Simon was scribbling notes as he spoke. 'So we have plenty of time to prepare for implantation. We can do it this evening.'

Simon pulled his phone from his pocket.

But, of course, we cannot do anything until we've discussed this with Allen and Carl.'

'Do we have time for that?' asked Eleanor.

'I think we must. They are just as invested in this as we are, and this is Allen's find.'

Simon lifted his phone and called Allen. It rang out for some time before Eleanor heard him leave his message. 'Simon here, Allen. Call ASAP; this is urgent.' He turned to her. 'Can you call Carl?'

Eleanor had no doubt Carl should be informed and that his knowledge and experience would be valuable. But she was also well aware of the toxic tip to his dented ego and knew her actions so far would already be viewed by him as sufficient provocation. She thought of her career in Glasgow.

Perhaps she should wait and see if there was any point in telling him at all. Successful implantation was so unlikely, whereas serious consequences of his vengeful rage were not.

'Think I'd rather tell him in person,' she said.

Simon nodded.

'Well, I say we do the hormone shot now, then meet up at nine o'clock this evening for the next stage. This will give you time to talk to Carl, yes?'

Eleanor nodded.

Simon stood up and strode through to an ante room. He returned moments later, a small tray in one hand and a box of surgical gloves in the other.

He pressed a fine needle syringe into a small bottle of liquid and drew up its contents. 'This shot might just help things along. As I said, it is nothing like the usual prep I would give, but it is better than nothing.'

He threw the empty vial in a bin and held the needle upright, pushing the plunger gently until a trickle of liquid escaped.

'If you could just make yourself comfortable?' He nodded to the high bed behind her. 'These drugs are most effective when delivered as close to the uterus as possible, so if you could roll up your top.' He turned his back to her.

Eleanor felt self-conscious as she loosened her shirt.

'This will feel cold; it's alcohol to make sure the skin is clean.' He pressed a moist wipe on her abdomen and moved it outwards in a steady circular motion. She felt her skin tingle and chill.

'Good.' He turned to pick up the syringe. 'One quick jab and phase one will be done.' He pinched her skin with his left hand and then quickly pushed the needle in with the other.

Eleanor felt the sharp point pierce her and burrow deep inside. Stunned by the pain, she struggled to remain still.

'Well done,' he said, turning away and peeling off his gloves. 'That is the easy part, Eleanor. The real work is yet to come. You should try to rest this afternoon. Sleep if you can. These things work best when the recipient is relaxed.'

'Think I'd better pack, actually. Knowing I'm organised and ready to leave in the morning will do more to help my blood pressure than a nap,' she said, laughing.

'Then we will rendezvous at nine? I will have everything ready by then.'

Eleanor pulled her shirt down then lay still for a moment, her hand resting on the injection site. Her skin felt burnt and bruised. *Dear God*, she thought as she climbed off the bed and prepared to leave Simon's office. *What on earth have I let myself in for?*

Chapter 8

Eleanor managed to pack, but not to sleep; her fitful attempts bringing only restless frustration. She was grateful Carl was nowhere to be seen, absolving her of any guilt she might have felt about withholding information, and so it was with a light, if racing, heart she made her way back to meet Simon, arriving at nine on the dot.

He showed her into a consulting room, handed her a sterile package, which contained a paper-thin gown with ties at the back, and left her to change.

'Are you ready?' He knocked gently on the door of the consulting room he had led her to.

'Yes, thanks,' said Eleanor, her efforts to sound calm, making her voice louder than she intended.

Simon entered, barely recognisable in his green theatre gown, gloves, and mask. His eyes, though still kind, did not linger on Eleanor; his focus was on the items and implements he had brought with him. His manner was contained; he maintained a comforting distance without seeming cold. Nervously, she clutched at the straps that tied at the back of the thin paper gown.

'I'll get my things,' Simon said. 'Please, make yourself comfortable.'

She lay on the hospital-style bed and tried to relax. There was a blanket folded at her feet. She reached down and pulled it up, although it only stretched as far as her waist.

She looked around at the white walls, decorated with framed certificates, and at the drawers whose printed labels she could not read.

She closed her eyes so she could focus on what was happening. She didn't want to fritter away her attention. She wanted to be aware of each step, believing that if she could, she would *will* this being into life. But as she lay there, she saw herself, as if watching from above. A pale, naked figure, beneath a flimsy gown, waiting for a man she barely knew to take hold of the hem of her paper weave garment and fold it up to her chest, exposing her, looking at her, touching her, impregnating her.

She swallowed hard against the lump that had formed in her throat and wondered if she had time for one more visit to the washroom. But there was nothing to be gained in delaying things, she told herself. She would just have to try to block out all those images and get on with it. She would soon be home, in her flat in Glasgow, and this awkward moment would seem like a dream.

In the distance, beyond the dark shape of the door, she heard the scuff of steps. They seemed to start and stop, start and stop. She heard the squeak and click of cupboards opening and closing and pictured Simon gathering together the tools of his trade.

She felt her hands tremble and drew them down to where a baby might grow, to that part of her that might soon swell with new life. She caressed her abdomen, her moist palms warming in their friction with the paper robe. Closing her eyes, she thought of Lillooet, lying only a few corridors away. She mimicked her position and tried to style her own features into the expression that graced Lillooet's face, vowing to take over from where she had left off.

Simon returned carrying a metal tray covered by a muslin cloth and positioned himself at the foot of the bed.

'Simon?' she whispered, 'What exactly is going to happen?'

He moved a little closer to her and looked into her eyes. 'Well, before I explain the procedure, I need to tell you that I estimate the embryo to be about four- or five-weeks' gestation, so my guess is, Eleanor, your body will reject it outright.'

Eleanor shivered. 'I understand.'

'But for now, the embryo has reached room temperature. I have added a culture medium for ease of transportation. The fluid will be drawn up into a syringe…' He mimed the action with both hands. 'And passed through your cervix into the womb. The procedure itself is actually quite straightforward and only takes a few minutes, but I have to warn you, there is usually a degree of discomfort.'

Eleanor exhaled audibly, only realising then she had been holding her breath as he spoke.

'I will say to you once more, it is not too late to back out, Eleanor.' Simon reached over as if to place his hand on hers, but seemed to change his mind and withdrew it.

'Absolutely not, Simon. I want to do this, and the process doesn't worry me. I have every confidence in you. I know you've been doing this work for years.'

'Indeed so. Much of my working life has been in this field, and, as it happens, we ended up having to go down this route ourselves, Anna and I, to have our daughter Sarah. I'm sure Anna would not mind me sharing that with you. She was quite relaxed about the whole thing, but then, it was different for us.' He hesitated, eyeing Eleanor with some uncertainty.

'In that?'

'Well, Anna was desperate for a child. I think she would have put herself through anything to get pregnant. And that drive is what made it all tolerable for her. I think that is the same for most of the women I work with. I cannot imagine what it would be like to subject yourself to this procedure and the high possibility of an unsuccessful outcome, without the call from Mother Nature that generally underpins it.'

'Simon.' Eleanor leant towards him. 'Don't worry on my account. I know what I am doing, and I am perfectly at ease with it. Who is to say that the drive of my enquiring mind is any less powerful than someone else's need for womb fulfilment?' She stared into his eyes. 'I'm just marvelling at the apparent straightforwardness of it all. It sounds almost too simple to work.'

'Shall we?'

Eleanor nodded slowly and closed her eyes. She hadn't allowed herself to think through the mechanics of the procedure and what it would feel like. She watched as Simon adjusted the position of the stirrups at the foot of the examination couch and swung a low stool between them.

'Right,' he said, 'This procedure requires you to be in a more… accessible position, which means your legs need to be supported by these stirrups. You will have to organise yourself, Eleanor, as there's no nurse to assist you, and I am scrubbed up.'

He turned his back, and Eleanor realised this was the cue for her to get on with it. She tugged at the blanket and let it slip to the floor beside her, then raised each leg into the stirrups, their cold rubber and metal hands gripping her behind each knee. She lay back down before telling Simon she was ready. He swung back round to face her, holding a neat bundle of folded paper coverings.

'We need to place these over your legs and abdomen to maintain a sterile environment and isolate the target area.' He had adopted an instructive and authoritative tone as he unfolded the first package. 'So, if you could lift your gown a little,' he directed, averting his eyes.

A flush of embarrassment washed over Eleanor as she grasped the edge of the faintly patterned gown and lifted it to her waist. Simon briskly draped one and then another paper covering over her abdomen and down each leg before opening the third package, which contained a single sheet with a circular window. She felt his gloved hands manoeuvre this last covering, so it exposed only that part of her critical to the intervention.

Wheeling his stool closer, he took up his position between her legs. She could see only the top of his head; his white, thinning hair barely covering his scalp. She felt his gloved hands against her skin but allowed herself to dwell no further on that. He was a machine; she told herself, a drone performing an essential task, nothing more.

She scrambled to adopt a mind-set that might make the experience tolerable, trying to imagine she was a patient undergoing routine treatment, but the pace of her heart told her otherwise, and images from the past began to intrude. Her first boyfriend, how desperate he had been to have sex with her, and how terrified she was at the thought of pregnancy. But urged on by a rush of hormones and the scent of his excitement, she had allowed him to wrestle her to the floor of his student room. Then, as he fumbled in the tightening pocket of his jeans for a condom, his roommate had burst in, bringing the frenzied scene to a sudden halt.

Eleanor tried to shake off the old memories, but they would not leave her. She sought her usual unfailing escape route — detachment — only to uncover a new truth. With sudden amazement, she realised her tendency to use sex as a currency, a means to an end of *her* own choosing, was more a consequence of past experiences than a clever strategy of her own devising.

'The next thing you will be aware of will be the insertion of the speculum into the vagina.'

Eleanor was pulled abruptly back to the present.

'The noise you hear now is the speculum opening. This allows access to the cervix which will be gently swabbed with a saline solution.'

Eleanor realised she would rather he spared her the voice-over and just did what he had to do.

'*C'est partie gagnee*. You might feel a little discomfort now as the solution is injected through the cervix into the womb, a sort of cramping sensation. This sometimes recurs over the next ten days or so — if, indeed, the implantation lasts that long — but it is natural, and it will pass.'

This was the moment; this was what it was all about. Banishing all trivial thoughts, she called upon her deepest power, her will, her hopes, and her intent. She felt the gentle surge of the fluid, the sensation of it washing through her, inside her, its temperature indistinguishable from her own. She tried to picture what was happening but saw only colours, swirls of rich greens and reds and blues that twisted between and around one another. She began to feel a swell of pleasure as the colours merged to form a hue she did not know and embraced it as her own. Then, when the wave subsided, her fears, mixed with excitement, gave way to a deep contentment. She brought her hands to rest upon her abdomen and forgot about the loss of dignity she had felt only moments before.

'Okay,' Simon eventually said, sighing, 'That's as much as anyone can do.'

He gently lifted her legs down from the stirrups and, picking the blanket from the floor, placed it over her, before peeling off his gloves.

'Ideally, you should lie still for about thirty minutes; give it every chance.' He looked around the room. 'This might help.' He flicked a few switches that simultaneously summoned the soothing tones of spa music and dimmed the lights to a womb-like glow.

'I will leave you to relax for a while, Eleanor. Are you warm enough?'

'Yes, I'm absolutely fine,' murmured Eleanor. 'I'll just lie back and think of England.'

'Well done, Eleanor,' he whispered, as he closed the door behind him.

Eleanor pulled her gown back into a respectable position and heaved a heavy sigh. She felt suddenly tired and weak, her legs aching from the grip of the stirrups and the effort of holding them still. All she had to do now was wait, Simon had said, but the sudden cramping in her abdomen made her want to curl into a foetal fold.

Was the mission accomplished? She closed her eyes and drifted into the anonymity of darkness. Then, turning onto her side, she allowed the weight of her limbs to sink into the firmness of the day bed. The procedure had been more traumatic than she'd expected. And becoming aware of the gentle trickle of tears upon her cheek, she considered that perhaps she did not know herself quite as well as she had assumed.

Chapter 9

Eleanor stood in a daze at the front door of her flat, scrambling through her bag for the key. It was unusually warm for Glasgow, but she felt chilled to the bone, jetlagged and exhausted. She was relieved the journey was over and that Carl had slept for most of it, leaving her free to wince at the rise and fall of each cramping sensation that coursed through her lower abdomen. She longed for her own bed but knew she would be unable to relax until she'd soaked away all traces of the night before and with it, she hoped, the squirming embarrassment she felt when she allowed herself to dwell on the details of the event.

Bolting the door behind her, she abandoned her luggage in the windowless hallway and headed for the bathroom. She poured scented oil into the tub, set the taps to full, then undressed slowly, delighting in the peace and certainty of her own space. She could enjoy this time, knowing she would not be interrupted or called upon to listen to yet more of Carl's endless, self-indulgent tales as she had endured on the long flight home. She slipped easily into the water and spoke aloud, although there was no one there to hear her.

'That was too long to be away.'

She allowed herself to sink further into the steaming bath.

'But am I… am I still alone?'

She looked down at her smooth, taut skin. Could she be pregnant? She felt suddenly too hot, the cramping sensations had returned, so she ran the cold tap until the temperature lost its bite. When the cramping stopped, she slipped back down into the cooler water. She would have to be more careful.

Reminding herself of the unlikelihood of pregnancy, nonetheless, she ran her hand over and around her abdomen. She tried to imagine what lay inside, beneath her palm. She saw her fingers quiver as they swept across the smooth, pale landscape of her belly.

Suddenly, she sat up and buried her face in her hands.

Dear God, what have I done? What if I give birth to a monster?

Her stomach churned, and she felt a sickening chill rise up and through her. She leapt out of the water and grabbed a towel from the rail, pulling it tightly around her, wrapping it like a shroud as she perched on the edge of the bath.

But then, how could it be a monster? *This is Lillooet's child.*

She summoned up her favourite vision of Lillooet, that first time she saw her, lying majestically within her icy tomb.

Gradually, she felt her breathing calm. She gripped the soft, deep pile of the bath towel and rubbed its warmth into her. Then, fixing upon her vision of Lillooet, she walked to the bedroom and slipped between the cool, crisp sheets of her own bed.

She sank instantly into a heavy, unmoving sleep only to become trapped in a seamless loop of bizarre images.

She was running up a steepening track, desperate to reach the platform of a deserted station. It was cold and dark, but she could just discern the outlines of figures seated in a locked waiting room. They sat in motionless silence, but she knew they were alive, watching to see what she would do.

A train approached, a loud, dark gathering presence. She would escape on the train, free herself from the cold scrutiny. But as it approached, she saw it was destined for the platform opposite, and the dilapidated railway bridge was too far away to reach in time. Her only chance was to cross the track.

She stumbled through a carpet of tangled, withering flowers, dry and matted, ensnaring her feet. Her legs felt impossibly heavy, but there was time if she persisted. She knew she was still being watched and thought she heard the watchers whisper: *she must decide*.

Reaching the platform's edge, she picked her way across high, razor-sharp railings and began to haul her cut and bleeding body up onto the other side. But they were there, the silent ones, prising off each successful grasp. The train drew to a halt. She struggled, only to find herself back on the steepening path to the station.

***

She woke, hours later, to the shrill call of her alarm, groggy with disbelief that morning had arrived so quickly. Still half-asleep, she showered, dressed, and made her way to the car. She didn't feel like breakfast, and even though it was not unusual for her to eat nothing until lunch, she felt queasy. *Could it be a sign?*

She usually enjoyed the brief journey from her West End flat to the university, where the Institute for the Study of Human Development was based, especially during term time. She would watch as streams of students trickled in from all directions, merging to become a swell of backpacked youths, pressing towards the main buildings. But it was quiet today; the new semester was still some weeks away.

The institute was housed in a beautiful old Victorian terrace once occupied by Glasgow's middle class before being bought over by the expanding university. It comprised three soot-darkened, sandstone mansions, pressed hard against each other like soldiers standing to attention, shoulders high and tight. A short flight of weathered steps led to the main entrance in the middle of the three buildings; the doors to the other two being permanently locked.

As she entered the dimly lit hallway, Eleanor felt the haze of jetlag begin to lift. Gradually, she remembered the tasks she had been working on before Vancouver, and by the time she had climbed the stairs to her departmental base on the second floor, she'd already drawn up much of the day's to-do list in her mind.

It was normal after conferences away for Carl to regale the team with a personal account of the main events of his trip. He relished these occasions, assuming centre stage as he fed his favourite anecdotes to his captive audience of junior academics and aspiring postgrads. Eleanor listened, anticipating the sound of his commanding voice and the customary swell of laughter and exclamations, but all was quiet, and she was surprised when she opened the coffee room door to a subdued scene of business as usual.

'Welcome back,' said Jane, the admin assistant, as she entered the airless coffee room. 'Carl won't be in today, food poisoning. He thinks it must have been something he ate on the plane.'

'Really?' Eleanor suppressed a smile as she recalled losing count of the number of times he had summoned the flight attendant for more wine. 'That's too bad.'

She decided to have her coffee in her room. She walked through to the spacious office she shared with Tom, the research assistant, and Kyle, a PhD student. Reaching her desk, she opened the top drawer and took an anti-bacterial wipe from the packet she kept there. She swept it across the light oak surface before organising the stationery she stored in a lower drawer.

Sipping her coffee, she began to type up a synopsis of the conference and her personal reflections on its benefits to her work at the centre; she would be asked for this at her annual appraisal. She then turned her attention to the backlog of emails. Organised by date, they awaited their turn for her attention. She worked her way through them, responding to each as required and allocating further tasks to her list.

As she approached the end of her unread messages, her eye was drawn to the bold print that headed the email at the very foot of the page.

PREGNANCY.

Like a child guarding schoolwork, her hand involuntarily reached to cover the screen. She glanced towards the two other members of the team, now seated at their desks, and drew her chair closer to her laptop. She clicked on Simon's message.

Salut, Eleanor

Hope you had a good flight home. How are you feeling? I assume no news is good news, but as I am sure you are aware, everything can change in an instant. Countless miscarriages happen without anyone being any the wiser, as whatever was there is just washed out as part of the normal cycle. This is by far the most likely scenario in your case. However, if you do manage to hold onto things for a couple of weeks and then begin to experience new cramping or vaginal bleeding, the best you can do is rest.

I have been thinking about monitoring events. You should start now. I know this might seem premature, especially given what I have just said, but I would rather we gathered data we will never need, than miss the chance to capture it.

You should start taking blood pressure readings and keeping a diary of signs or symptoms like breast discomfort, fatigue, food fads, metallic taste, frequency of micturition and so on. And you should do regular pregnancy tests, of course. Let me know how things are going. Despite the ridiculous odds of success, every thought, at the moment, seems to take me there.

Meanwhile, things have not gone so well with Allen. He was (and remains) furious that we did what we did. Never seen him so angry. He seems to think Carl somehow had a hand in this, wants the project for himself etc. etc. Thinks he is taking his find back to Scotland and will not keep us informed. I know he is upset, and he will calm down, but perhaps a few lines from you could reassure him. Or even from Carl, but that might make things worse. Must confess I, too, have my worries about Carl.

He certainly loves the spotlight, and I wonder what he might risk to hold on to it?

Let me know what you think and get a recording!

Kind regards, Simon

Eleanor read over the email once more before shutting her laptop down and scanning the room to see if anyone was watching her. She headed back to the coffee room, where she dispensed some cool water into a paper cup that trembled in her hand. She dropped into the nearest chair.

Everything felt so different now she was back in her usual environment. The possibility of pregnancy seemed unimaginable. How would she deal with it? How would she explain it? Not that she would have to explain anything, she quickly reassured herself. This was a personal matter. But she no longer felt that rush of delight at being part of clandestine research. She felt entirely alone. And it was not the comforting solitude she generally craved; it was a clammy aloneness she knew associated itself uniquely with regret.

She needed air. Hurrying back to her desk, she picked up her cardigan and grabbed her bag from beneath the chair. She walked briskly through the coffee room, and reception area, then ran down the stairs, back out into the August sunshine. She made her way out of the campus and headed down the hill to the noise and bustle of the crowded midday street. The school holidays were nearing their end. She watched a mother, clutching bags of uniforms and school supplies, restraining her children as they pressed pedestrian lights at the crossing. Turning right, she headed towards the Botanic Gardens at the far end of the road, where she often ate her lunch on summer days.

Is this really what you want? Eleanor asked herself as she paced towards the only vacant bench. She sat down, closed her eyes, and commanded herself to take control. *Dear God, if this is how I react to one email about the possibility of pregnancy, how would I cope with the reality of an actual child?*

She shook her head and rubbed the furrows on her brow. What in heaven's name had made her think she wanted this child?

Two more mothers strolled by, pushing prams. They were chatting and laughing. One of them reminded her of her sister, Olivia, or at least a younger version of her, when she still smiled. A plush caterpillar toy fell from the pram and landed at Eleanor's feet. She scooped it up, gazed at its crinkly legs and mirrored face, before handing it to the young mum.

'How old is she?' Eleanor surprised herself by asking the question.

'She's eight months, nearly nine,' the mum replied proudly, sweeping away the wisps of hair that had fallen in front of the infant's eyes.

Eleanor stared at the baby and was rewarded with an instant grin. She smiled back and felt her throat tighten, as if she was going to cry. But that was wrong — she knew she felt suddenly happy, as if the smile was a sign of approval. Olivia's children had never seemed very fond of her, and they only ever spoke to her when pushed into it by their parents or their gran.

'She likes you,' the mum said, more to the baby than to Eleanor.

Maybe, *maybe,* she could do it after all?

Just then, the other mum turned and, looking behind her, yelled at full volume. 'Christopher! What on earth are you doing? Stop that this instant; you're hurting her!'

Eleanor followed her glare to a small boy who scowled, clutching a scooter, as another child lay screaming on the path. Both women turned and ran back to the scene.

Eleanor walked away, seeking the quiet of the humid greenhouse, where the hush of water being finely sprayed over the tropical plants and the smell of the rich, moist earth instantly calmed her. She followed the cobbled path through the exhibits.

It was ridiculous to imagine anything could ever come of this anyway. She had to regain control; whatever happened from here on, she couldn't allow herself to crack. She barely recognised herself in her emotional display.

'Pathetic,' she muttered. One way or another, things would play themselves out, and everything would be fine.

She strode out of the glasshouse and through the park gates, making her way back to the institute, grounding herself in the familiarity of all that passed around her. At last, she felt her breathing settle. From now on, she would plan her strategies and, in the highly unlikely event she was actually pregnant, she would organise some form of monitoring programme. And after work, she would buy some pregnancy tests.

***

Back at the office, no one remarked upon her uncharacteristic absence, but by the end of the day, she was exhausted and deeply regretted having promised her mother she would pop in on the way home. But she felt uncomfortable about disappointing her, so she headed for the quiet suburb, a fifteen-minute drive from the university, that contained her childhood home. Her heart sank when she rang the doorbell and heard the noisy stampede of children's feet in the hallway. Eventually, the door swung open.

'Aww, it's only Aunt Eleanor,' called twelve-year-old Bertie, Olivia's eldest. He turned and ran into the living room, where the television was blaring.

Miriam Bartlett's hallway always looked dark, even on the brightest of days like today. But the shady front of the property was well compensated by the glorious sunshine that always seemed to fall on the neat and spacious garden to its rear.

'Charming,' said Eleanor's mum, smiling broadly as she emerged from the gloom and approached the door to greet her daughter. 'Nothing like a hearty welcome, is there, my darling?' She pressed a kiss on the side of her cheek, holding her flour-covered hands aloft. 'Olivia shouldn't be too long. Some sort of meeting at school.'

Eleanor followed her mother back into the light-filled kitchen. The back door was open, and the sweet scent of newly cut grass seemed to bring the garden into the house. She stood for a while, staring beyond the fruit trees to the old shed at the foot of the lawn where she and Olivia had played as children.

She turned to watch her mum as she rubbed the flour from her hands before flicking on the kettle and taking two china cups from the shelf.

'Heavens, I can't believe that's you back already. It seems like no time at all since we were waving you off.' Miriam finished drying the dishes before popping the newly formed bread into the oven.

'Yes, back on home turf at last,' Eleanor said, sighing.

'Did it not go well then, dear? You look exhausted.'

'Oh, it was fine, Mum. I'm just tired. Anything happening here?'

'Everything's just fine here. The children go back to school next week, and they're ready for it. Enough is as good as a feast when it comes to school holidays.'

Eleanor's mum tilted two scoops of tea leaves into the warmed pot. Miriam Bartlett was the only person Eleanor knew who had not yet made the transition to tea bags.

'Actually,' she continued, in slightly lowered tones, 'I think Olivia was quite relieved to be back at work today.' She brought the tea to the table and sat opposite her daughter.

'I don't know what Olivia would do without you,' said Eleanor.

'That's what families are for,' Miriam replied.

Eleanor watched as her mum absent-mindedly stacked and rearranged the Lego bricks scattered on the wooden table. When she concentrated on her hands alone, with their timeless duo of wedding and engagement rings, Eleanor could almost imagine the woman they belonged to was still the younger mother she could remember. The reassuring mum who never embarrassed her in front of friends, the proud Miriam Bartlett who sat smartly dressed and glowing with pride on prize-giving day. The mother who didn't seem to have any needs of her own but was constantly there to support and encourage her family. Even now, Eleanor sometimes found it difficult to believe her mother existed independently of her offspring.

'Mummy's here!' They heard the cry go up as the front door opened.

Eleanor sighed; she had begun to hope she might get away before her sister arrived.

'Hello, my darlings!' Olivia always sounded at her warmest with the children. Eleanor heard her kiss and embrace each one. 'We'll discuss that later,' she heard her promise as she made her way through to the kitchen.

'Oh.' She fixed briefly on Eleanor. 'You're popular tonight, Mum.'

'Hi, Olivia,' Eleanor replied. She glanced up at her sister and thought how she had aged since she last saw her. Or maybe she was just noticing for the first time the dark bands beneath her eyes and the marionette lines appearing on each side of her mouth.

'Any tea left in that pot?' she asked.

'Of course.' Miriam rose and made her way to the sink, where she gave the tea strainer a quick rinse before balancing it on Olivia's cup and pouring what was left of the tea into it. 'I was just saying to Eleanor that it seems like no time at all since she left.'

'Mmm,' murmured Olivia. 'Mind you, these last few days have felt endless from where I'm sitting.' Olivia stirred a spoonful of sugar into her tea.

'More tea, dear?' Miriam looked at Eleanor as she refilled the kettle.

'Not for me, thanks, Mum. I'll be off in a minute.'

'So soon? You've only just got here.'

'This was just a quickie, Mum. I'll come for a proper chat on Sunday.'

'That would be lovely,' her mum replied.

'You didn't happen to bring back any Canadian dosh, did you?' Olivia brightened and looked back towards her mother before adding, 'Bertie has started a collection of foreign coins.'

'Probably. Have a look.' Eleanor drew her purse from her handbag and slid it across the table. She held onto it briefly, waiting to see if Olivia could be drawn into eye contact. But it was pointless. For years now, Olivia had done little to hide her dislike of her sister, but things had definitely got worse over the past year. She had no idea why she felt so resentful, but she did wish her sister would at least try to hide her feelings from their mother.

'Bertie!' Olivia called through to the lounge, 'Come and have a look.'

Olivia unzipped the bulging leather pouch and rummaged inside, fishing out a handful of cents and quarters as well as a ten-dollar note.

'Bertie!' She called louder this time.

The boy came running and picked up the coins his mum was lining up on the table.

'Sweet,' he said, picking one up and studying it.

'And look at this too.' She handed him the crumpled note.

'Aww, nice.' He unfolded it and smoothed it out.

'What do you say?' Miriam prompted.

'Thanks, Aunty Eleanor.' He smiled briefly in her direction.

'My pleasure.' Eleanor rose from the table and rinsed her cup.

'Don't forget this,' Olivia half-chastised, dangling Eleanor's worn-looking purse by its zip. 'Although God knows, it would hardly break the bank to buy a new one.'

'Thanks,' replied Eleanor coolly before heading down the narrow hallway, her mother at her heels.

'She's had a bad week, Eleanor.' Miriam placed a hand on her daughter's arm as they paused at the living room door.

Eleanor turned to face her mum. 'Isn't every week a bad week for Olivia?'

Miriam sighed and shook her head.

'Sorry, Mum, it's not your fault.' Eleanor gave her a hug and then called into the lounge where Olivia's daughters were watching television.

'Bye, girls.'

There was no reply.

'Aren't you going to say goodbye to Aunty Eleanor?' Miriam called.

'Bye,' they chorused dully.

'See you on Sunday, Mum.' Eleanor closed the door behind her and headed for home.

**

As she made her way back through the quiet streets, Eleanor tried to concentrate on the practicalities of the task ahead and the advice outlined by Simon, but waves of emotion kept drowning her thoughts: her mother, her sister, and the father she had lost to cancer five years before.

She thought about the embarrassment she'd felt when shopping for pregnancy tests earlier that day. She'd been reading the small print, trying to work out what made them different from each other, when she'd sensed someone was staring at her. She tried to ignore it, then panicked, wondering if it was someone she knew, someone who would let the cat out of the bag before she'd had time to befriend it.

She had looked challengingly in the observer's direction but saw only an uncomfortable-looking young man in shop overalls.

'Can I help you?' He had a slight stammer and drew his tongue across dry lips after speaking.

'No, I'm fine, thanks. Just doing a bit of research.' Eleanor cringed at her sheepish explanation. That was when she felt herself blushing. She then marched to the cash desk and bought two different kits even though, for the sake of consistency, she would only use one of them and then, if she needed to, stick to that brand.

This self-pity has gone far enough, she thought. She couldn't let her feelings get the upper hand, not after all these years and not after what she'd just been through. There was no going back. She had made her decision in Vancouver, and she was going to stick to it.

***

She rarely saw her neighbours and certainly never talked to them. The communal areas were maintained by a factor, and there was no other reason to approach, or be approached by, fellow residents. And that was exactly how she liked it.

The apartment itself was small and neat, its furnishings simple. Eleanor disliked clutter, a term she applied to any item that was devoid of clear purpose. In fact, she realised the home she had created for herself was about as far removed from her mother's as it could be.

When Eleanor woke the next morning, she was grateful for her foresight of the night before. Her morning routine was so automatic she'd worried she might forget to use the pregnancy test, so she had placed it on the floor at the entrance to her ensuite. Despite knowing it would still be too early for a positive result, Eleanor felt a flush of excitement as she opened the box. She had used test kits before, but always with dread. This time was different. She had chosen the most expensive test available, one that claimed it could detect pregnancy eight days after conception.

She ripped open the packaging. *Even if I am pregnant, I'm still some days short of the mark,* she thought. But she did it anyway, for the sake of completion. This was research, and there were few things she hated more than empty grids on a results table.

She read the instructions again: hold the stick in stream of urine or collect in a clean cup and dip for five seconds. Result will appear in the window within one minute.

She fetched a paper cup from the kitchen. It had been years since she'd had to collect a sample.

A short time later, standing by the sink, she dipped the white-tipped stick into the cup and slowly counted to five, then emptied the rest and flushed, before placing the stick on the edge of the bath. She saw her hand tremble as she tried to find its point of balance.

Dear God. She turned away and walked back to her bedroom, where she sat on the bed and chewed on the loose skin of her knuckles. *What an overreaction.*

She stared into the face of her watch, counting the march of each tick, letting three minutes pass until she pulled herself up and made her way back to the bath side. Still, several paces away, she could already read the result. *Negative.*

She was not surprised, but she was unsettled by the feeling of emptiness that accompanied it. Flicking open her laptop, she recorded the result then headed off to work, reassuring herself that so far, all was going to plan.

***

Entering her office, Eleanor saw Carl had made a remarkable recovery. He was regaling the staff with his account of events from Vancouver, as she had predicted the day before. She was relieved to catch his speech as she would be able to monitor any references he might make to her activities and anticipate the questions she could be expected to field as a result.

But Carl was winding up. 'And if all goes well,' he concluded, 'We might be graced with the services of one of their brightest starlets for a sabbatical period, to help with some joint work we are negotiating. *Funding* provided,' he added ambiguously, before turning towards Eleanor and smiling. 'Have you got a minute? My office?'

Eleanor followed him through the workroom to the large bright office which lay beyond it.

'Great to be back, eh?' Carl threw himself into his favoured chair, eyeing her with obvious suspicion. 'What's up? You seem tense.'

'Not in the slightest. A little tired, certainly. Are you over your *tummy bug*?'

'Yes. Any word from Vancouver?'

'Just an email from Simon, hoping we'd had a good journey,' she offered vaguely. 'You?'

'Well, Sophie, of course, has been in touch. She is so keen to join us for a while. I'm rather touched.' Carl swept a hand along and down his neck, like a preening cat, post-lunch.

'I don't doubt it,' Eleanor said, sighing.

Carl echoed her sigh, making his longer and tinged with unambiguous contentment. 'I'm going to talk it over with Jack later this morning. He seems keen too. I was thinking she could slip well into your latest project, Eleanor. I was telling her all about it, and she was quite fascinated by your ideas on the role of mitochondria in speeding up the evolutionary process. Might even make Jack warm to it a bit more too, you know, be a bit more generous when parcelling up the funding.'

'Carl! You had no business telling *anyone* about the details of my research proposal. Least of all, Sophie!'

'What's that supposed to mean? She's brighter than she appears, you know. You don't have to be frigid to be smart.'

'Fuck off, Carl. You know exactly what I mean. My proposal is strictly confidential. Until the ink has dried on my name beside it, anyone could claim it as their own work!'

'Calm down; it's hardly a Nobel contender. And who do you imagine is going to steal it? *Allen?*' Carl scoffed. 'He's not exactly one to watch. Hasn't had anything of significance published in the last decade.'

Eleanor felt tired and queasy. She pursed her lips furiously. *Untrustworthy shit!* Thank God, she hadn't told him anything about the implantation.

'Well, I'm going to tap out some ideas and see what Jack has to say to it anyway,' Carl announced, 'I know he's keen to accommodate Allen, although God knows why. Don't see those two as buddies.'

Eleanor knew Carl's motives towards Sophie were more personal than professional. Even before she'd become involved with him, she'd heard rumours in the office of his affairs. But she hadn't been looking for a life partner, so none of that had put her off. He was sharp-witted and entertaining, and offered her the sexual outlet she had wanted at that time. But things were so very different now.

She smoothed the fabric of her skirt and stood up.

'You look magnificent, as ever.' Carl stepped between her and the door. 'I'll pop round tonight after the gym.'

'I don't know, Carl. I'm really tired.'

'Just for a few minutes. I'd like you to look over the proposal. That shouldn't take too long.'

'Well, give me a call first and make sure I'm not in bed then.' Eleanor walked around him to reach the door.

'And why should that stop me?' He smiled.

'I'm still jet lagged, Carl. I need some time to synchronise body and clock. Not tonight.'

Carl's face was close to hers. She could see the flecks of green, like splinters, in his sharp, blue eyes and smell the mix of musky aftershave and sweat that used to draw her to him. She could so easily just kiss him, like she had that first time two years before, on this very spot, and know that this alone would keep things going, uncomplicated, for a while.

She stared at Carl, through him, beyond him.

'I don't want you to come round tonight.' She pushed him to the side and pulled at the door. 'Or any other night, for that matter.'

Heading straight for the washrooms, she locked herself into one of the cubicles and leant against its cool Formica door.

Things had changed, and she knew it was only partly to do with Carl. Ever since the implantation, she had peered further into the dark corners of her sexual past, drawn repeatedly to scenes and sensations that, she now realised, she had tried to forget. Binding and gagging their ghostly echoes, she had suppressed them, only to discover she was not free of them at all; she had buried them alive.

Chapter 10

It was Sunday at last. Eleanor rolled onto her back and threw the bed cover aside. It had been only three days and a few hours since implantation. She pictured the neat pile of boxes of extra pregnancy test kits she'd purchased the previous evening stacked on the shelf above her sink. She'd bought far too many. She felt bloated, tired and unaccountably angry, that tiresome trinity that usually preceded the onset of her period. *Definitely pointless*, she told herself and, pulling the covers around her again, she drifted back to sleep.

When she next opened her eyes, she glanced at her phone and realised she'd have to hurry to reach her mother's house in time for lunch. She forced herself to sit up, but despite having enjoyed around ten hours' sleep, her eyes still felt heavy. She felt queasy and drained of energy and thought she might cancel. She was wondering how to excuse herself when her mobile rang.

'Carl?' Eleanor was surprised. He didn't usually risk Sunday calls.

'Good news,' he announced, 'We've got the green light for Sophie.'

'Really? After all the cuts they've rained on us this semester? I don't get that. Management must have more money stashed away than they ever admit to. When is she coming?'

'December. Not ideal. Could be tricky getting accommodation at that time. I mentioned you'd be able to put her up, though.'

Eleanor sat up. 'Absolutely out of the question, Carl! Not even for one night. Why don't *you* put her up? She's going to be your research assistant after all.'

'*Our* research assistant, Eleanor. And she can't possibly stay with us. I'd have to ask the girls to share a room, and there's no way we can do that and have peace on Earth this Christmas.'

'Well, I'm sorry to spoil your festive plans, but you should have consulted me before you made the gallant offer. I don't do guests. It's not my problem, but if it was, I'd get onto University Accommodation and sort something out with them.' Eleanor ended the call and tossed the phone aside.

'The nerve!' She stomped into the kitchen and slammed the kettle onto the hob. If ever she needed proof that Carl knew nothing about her, then this was surely it.

***

By the time Eleanor arrived at her mother's house, Olivia was already there. She was sitting on her own in the living room; her legs curled beneath her on her favourite spot on the settee. In that moment, Eleanor remembered the young Olivia, sitting in that very position. She had been so pretty, far more popular with boys than her younger sister, a situation that had pleased Olivia immensely. There had been a constant stream of them at the door, phone calls and, of course, a flurry of cards on Valentine's Day. Olivia, it seemed, had the world, or at least the world of boys, at her feet. So, it was quite a shock to everyone when she had become engaged to Charles.

He seemed to be everything Olivia was not. Conservative in dress and political outlook, rule-bound, a corporate kind of man. He was proud of Olivia and wore her like a badge of honour, but to Eleanor, he lacked warmth and didn't seem to really know the woman he was planning to marry.

Flamboyantly dressed and socially vivacious, Olivia was the girl most of her friends aspired to be. Her style seemed effortlessly creative as her gift for transforming vintage clothes into contemporary items gave her the unique, non-high street look she coveted. Young Olivia could usually be found in smoky basement coffee shops and gallery cafes frequented by the arty types. How she came to meet Charles at all was something Eleanor had often wondered about, and it wasn't until the bump started to show some months later that Eleanor understood their engagement.

'We'll just have to make the best of it,' she heard her dad say to their mum from beyond the half-closed bedroom door, his voice flat and disappointed, but Eleanor imagined she could hear his acceptance of the situation and his determination to support his daughter.

Eleanor glanced at her sister. A band of dark roots gave lie to the flounce of blonde floating above it, and the slightly over-applied blusher offered only a sad reminder of the girl she had once been. Eleanor felt an unexpected surge of compassion and would maybe have reached out to clasp her sister's hand had her mum not entered.

'Nearly ready!' Miriam bustled into the sitting room. 'Is Charles not coming today?'

'God knows.' Olivia idly stirred her gin and tonic.

'What a pity,' she soothed, plumping the already perfect cushion. 'I haven't seen him for such a long time. Is he very busy?'

'Apparently.'

'Maybe next week, darling.' Miriam smiled, tidying her way out of the room.

'So, how was it then?' Olivia asked, throwing back the rest of her drink. 'Vancouver?'

Eleanor sat in the opposite corner of the settee. 'Oh, it was fine, quite interesting in parts,' she replied as she half-heartedly took a tiny sip of her drink.

They had got into the habit of an aperitif before Sunday lunch several years before, when they'd accidentally allowed the Christmas ritual to extend beyond its normal season and decided just to incorporate it into their Sunday routine.

'It must cost the institute, or whoever funds these things, a fortune. I can't see the Education Department coughing up the cash to send me on a jolly like that,' Olivia sniffed.

'They almost certainly do. You just don't know about it. They'll be sending their high-ranking management to all sorts of events, most likely.'

Eleanor suddenly felt sick and set her gin down onto the coffee table.

'Waste of taxpayers' money, if you ask me.' Olivia slammed her empty glass down beside Eleanor's nearly full one. 'You not wanting that?'

Eleanor shook her head.

'Too much of a good time across the pond? You're looking a bit more pasty than usual.'

As Olivia reached for the full glass, Eleanor thought she saw her hand tremble.

'Everything all right?' she asked, avoiding her eyes.

'As if you care!' Olivia clipped.

Eleanor softened her tone. 'Olivia, why do you make everything so hard? Is there a problem?'

'Just the usual stuff that you've been wise enough to steer clear of. Charles just wants time to *chill*, he says. Never seems to cross his mind that I wouldn't mind a few hours off now and again too.'

'Is there anything I can do?' Eleanor regretted the words almost as soon as she'd uttered them. Olivia hated offers of help, especially from her younger sister.

'What, like lend me one of your married men to see me through for a while?'

'God, Olivia, give it a rest, please. I don't feel well. I'm so tired…'

'Tired?' Olivia rolled her eyes. 'So go to bed! You don't have screaming kids to stop you, and you don't know what tired is until you have, believe me!'

Eleanor bit her lip. She would not be pulled into an argument, not today.

Olivia drained Eleanor's glass swiftly and lifted the gin bottle from the table.

'You're not driving home, are you?'

'What do you care?'

'A lot, actually.' Eleanor placed her hand on her sister's arm.

'Well, I don't need your pity, thanks, or a sanctimonious sermon on the evil of the demon drink. You'll be buddying Mum to church next.'

'Well, hopefully, I won't be buddying you to AA meetings.'

'Fuck off, Eleanor. You haven't a clue about me and my life.'

'At least I take responsibility for mine,' Eleanor quipped.

'What's that supposed to mean?'

'I don't constantly blame other people for everything that goes wrong in my life.'

'And I do?'

'Yes, you do. You've always played the victim, Olivia. *Poor me* is the subtext to everything you say! But you're the loser. If you blame the world for your problems, you give away control of your life.'

Before Olivia could fire back, their mother appeared at the door.

'Lunch is served!' she trilled.

The sisters rose in silence and followed their mum through to the dining room. Eleanor was annoyed she had allowed herself to be baited by her sister, especially at their mother's house. But it was so difficult to rise above their conflict. Somehow, they were stuck in the tension of their teens, those distant days when all that was good between them died, and a barbed fence erected itself in its place, for reasons she had never understood. Eleanor often scanned backwards in time, trying to pinpoint the moment or event that changed it all, but she could never find it. Good times just seemed to have blurred into bad, like water seeping its way up through a colourful painting, the lines and tones becoming distorted, contaminated, with no clear point of transition.

Eleanor took her place at the table and tried to put their argument behind her. Olivia was unhappy. She had been for a long time now and seemed to delight in punishing everyone else for her misery. But she knew these family times were important to her mum, so she vowed to do her best to continue tolerating them.

As she glanced around the table, Eleanor realised her own adherence to routine was probably not a habit that had spontaneously evolved. For years, their mother faithfully followed well-worn templates for each household event. As children, they had privately mimicked her stock phrases, laughing hysterically at any change in emphasis or tone they could muster. They enjoyed each other in those days, trusted each other.

'Have you washed your hands?' Olivia adopted her mummy voice to each child in turn as they ran in from the family room where they had been watching cartoons.

At five, Beth was the youngest and sat between Olivia and her gran so they could help cut up her food. Bertie sat to his gran's other side, then Eleanor, then Charles' empty chair and finally, eight-year- old Hannah. As each child had been brought to the table as infants, they had been designated a slot which had, like everything else, become set in stone.

It wasn't a big room, and its appearance was made all the smaller by the large, dark oak furniture that had filled it since Eleanor's parents moved into the house not long after their marriage. Despite the moderate temperature and the sunshine that did its best to brighten the room, a fire crackled in the hearth, as it always did on Sundays.

Eleanor watched her mother as she spooned the measured quantities onto each plate. It seemed to Eleanor she lived in a time bubble. Change for her was something to be avoided, a deterioration in standards rather than progress. The children sat patiently, waiting for everyone to be served. Olivia had trained them well, Eleanor conceded, in some respects.

Miriam placed her hands together and offered her customary, simple grace: 'Blessings on our meal.'

Silence fell as they started to eat, but Eleanor hesitated. She sat with cutlery poised, regarding the meal upon her plate: roast beef, Yorkshire pudding and vegetables steamed to perfection. Her stomach twisted. She hoped she might manage a few mouthfuls, for her mother's sake.

'Gravy?' Miriam offered her the gravy boat.

The sight of the thick, heavy sauce, its surface slightly congealed, made Eleanor's stomach heave harder. She swallowed.

'I'm so sorry, Mum, but I don't think I'm going to be able to eat this.' She quietly replaced her knife and fork.

'Can I have it?' Bertie intercepted keenly before being silenced by a sharp look from his mum.

'Whatever is the matter, dear? Are you not feeling well?' Miriam stopped eating in sympathy.

'I'm fine, still working on transatlantic time perhaps. I think my stomach thinks it's breakfast time.' Eleanor tried to smile.

'Let me put it away. You might feel like it later.' She rose instantly. 'Would you maybe like a cup of tea for the moment?'

'Really, Mum, I'm fine with water. You sit down and enjoy your lunch. It looks lovely, don't let it go cold,' urged Eleanor. 'And don't look so worried. It's nothing, believe me.'

'Once a mother, always a mother,' Olivia managed between mouthfuls. 'Hostages to fortune, we are.'

'Apparently,' sniped Eleanor, 'But only if we choose to be.'

Eleanor could see she had hit a chord. Olivia shot to her feet and stormed out of the room into the kitchen.

From beyond the door, they could hear Olivia sobbing.

Miriam glared at Eleanor. 'Shall we go to the living room for a word, dear?'

It was not a question for which 'no' would be an acceptable answer. Eleanor followed her mother to the door.

'There's ice cream to follow for children with clean plates.' She paused at the door to remind the children. 'And I'll be back in a few minutes to check.'

They passed by the kitchen door, now closed, and could hear Olivia wailing on the other side.

'Poor Olivia,' said Miriam as soon as they were out of earshot of the children. Eleanor knew her mum's words were an appeal for sympathy, but she felt too drained to rise to the challenge of understanding her volatile sister.

'Poor Olivia, nothing, Mum!'

'Don't be so harsh, dear. She's in a bad place right now…'

'And no wonder. Mum, all this "*poor Olivia*" nonsense hasn't done her any favours. Ever.'

Olivia suddenly marched into the room. 'And what's that supposed to mean?'

Eleanor took a deep breath and made sure her voice remained calm and level. 'You're always being treated like you're some sort of emotional invalid, Olivia, and it stops you taking responsibility and making a go of things. You're so quick to complain about your life instead of trying to make something of it. And I believe an indulgence of sympathy has only served to encourage your sense of vulnerability.' Eleanor glanced apologetically at her mother.

'Oh?' Olivia drew back. 'And Eleanor Bartlett is a self-made success?'

'I've taken charge of things, yes.'

'Well, I suppose you have to, now Daddy's not around!'

'Girls, enough!' Miriam closed the door to the hallway. 'You might be comfortable having it out like this, but I'm not. Especially when there are children about.'

Eleanor could see anger in her mother's eyes, an emotion she rarely gave way to.

'I'll just go.' She stood up and marched towards the door.

'Please don't.' Miriam's tone softened. She caught Eleanor's hand.

'Actually, Mum, I'm not feeling too good. I shouldn't have come.'

Miriam followed her daughter to the door.

'I'll call later,' Eleanor promised as she left.

Through the dining room window, she could see Olivia's children, seemingly unperturbed by the raised voices. *Probably something they are well used to,* thought Eleanor as she pulled away and headed for home.

All the way back to her apartment, a hideous nausea gripped her stomach. She willed herself to hold on, desperate for the sanctuary of her own home.

Once there, she felt barely able to stand still long enough to unlock the door, searching frantically for her keys and snatching at them desperately as they slipped from her grasp onto the polished tiled surface of the communal landing. Covering her mouth with one hand, she wriggled the key in the lock with the other, before throwing open the door and letting it slam behind her as she raced to the bathroom.

It was some time before she staggered into her bedroom and flopped lifelessly onto her smooth, silk bed throw. Her legs felt weak, and her hands trembled as she recovered from the retching of a few moments before.

Thank God, I made it home, she thought, wincing at the idea of embarrassing herself by throwing up at her mother's or, worse still, in the street outside her flat. She made her way into the kitchen and prepared a cup of camomile tea, settling down to drink it in the calm of her living room.

Eleanor massaged her stomach, her hands working slow circles over its tight muscles. She wanted to feel normal again, for her body to function in its usual way.

She was rarely sick and knew this was a sign something different was happening. She wished it away, all of it. Then suddenly, a shock of pain had her clutch her abdomen. She gasped as its force gathered and, dropping to the floor, rocked back and forth, praying for it to pass. Surely this was the end, the final push to rid her body of the intruder. She was tired of all thoughts of pregnancy and the physical trauma that seemed to accompany it. But as the crisis resolved, a vision of Lillooet, looking bold and beautiful, began to flash before her eyes, and her resentment slowly began to fade, replaced with a renewed resolve to hold on to the embryo for as long as fate decreed.

Some minutes passed before the pain faded enough for her to crawl back onto the settee. Tender, but no longer cramping, she reached for her laptop. She would read more on pregnancy and on possible indications of miscarriage.

As soon as she opened her laptop, a notification flashed on the screen. She had two new messages.

Hi Eleanor

Hope you had a good journey home and are settled back into life in Glasgow. We don't have Lillooet anymore. As soon as we passed on an outline of the situation to the authorities, she was collected and transferred. They wouldn't say where but did say they would keep me informed and asked me to keep things quiet in the meantime. Still waiting for feedback from carbon-dating. There was an error in the first set of results, so having to repeat tests. Hope we get something. No chance of a redo now, is there? Will let you know as soon as I hear anything. Hope all's good with you. I hear Sophie has agreed to visit for a while. Glad you're there to keep an eye on things.

Hope you're well. Keep me posted on how things develop with you.

Talk soon, Allen

Eleanor read the email a second time, scanning for hints of the anger Simon talked of, but she could sense none. Should she bring it up, or was he unaware of what she knew? She returned to her inbox and clicked on the second email.

Hi Eleanor

Carl has probably told you that I have decided to take up his offer of a sabbatical in your department. He mentioned you'd very kindly offered to put me up for a while. That is so very thoughtful of you, but I wouldn't like to impose. Anyway, it's probably better if I organise something permanent from the start. Think that will help me settle in. Just wanted to say thanks anyway.

Looking forward to working with you, Sophie

Eleanor closed her laptop and stretched out on the settee, falling asleep instantly.

She slept so soundly she did not hear the alarm and had it not been for the incessant ringing of her mobile, she would probably, for the first time ever, have been late for work. Reaching the phone just as the ringing stopped, she noted the missed call from Carl. She headed for the shower. Her body moved heavily and reluctantly from bed to kitchen to bathroom. She could not remember ever feeling so exhausted. Perhaps she was ill. The pink of the box on the bathroom shelf caught her eye. She tore open the cellophane and, after using the stick, placed it on the shelf.

She swayed beneath the spray of the shower, waiting for the warmth to work its usual magic, but could feel only weakness in her limbs.

The phone rang out again. She turned off the water and, pulling a bath towel round her, reached out to answer it.

'Hello,' she said, her voice sounding sharper than she intended.

'Is that you?' Carl asked.

'Of course, it's me, Carl.' Eleanor sighed heavily. 'Who else would it be? Sophie hasn't moved in yet.'

'Hilarious,' he replied, 'Have you checked your email today?' He spoke rapidly.

'No, not yet.'

'Well, have a look as soon as you can. There's something interesting from Allen.' His voice sounded excited but subdued. *Must be calling from home*, Eleanor thought.

'What does he say?' She hastily pulled some clothes from the wardrobe and threw them onto the knot of bed sheets.

'Just read it. I'll catch up with you in the office,' said Carl, 'Need to go.' He ended the call.

'What a drama queen!' she muttered, wrapping her wet hair in a towel and perching on the side of her bed as she searched for Allen's email. Locating it almost immediately, she began to read.

The carbon-dating results have just come through. At first, it looked like the findings were erroneous, but apparently not. Just incredibly unusual. The specimen is, apparently, too old to age by this method. As you probably know, the half-life of carbon is around 5,700 years, so this method can only calibrate ages up to a finite limit. This seems to suggest that our sample, Lillooet, is at least 50,000 to 60,000 years old! Is this possible? Clearly, I couldn't reveal the true source of the material to the lab, so I couldn't ask them what this means for us. I still can't take it in. Need to read up a bit on ancient man. Let me know what you think. Simon, of course, is beside himself with excitement.

'Fuck!' Eleanor cast her phone to the floor as if it had become suddenly hot. 'More than sixty thousand fucking years?' What the hell kind of a creature did that make Lillooet, then? Was she even *human*? And her child? Thank God it felt like her body was rejecting it. Eleanor clutched her abdomen and started to heave. She rushed to the bathroom, where retch after retch produced nothing other than water and a yellow-green fluid. Her mouth burnt from the acidic bile, and as soon as she managed to pull herself to her feet, she leant down and drank eagerly from the cold tap.

In the mirror, she caught sight of the white plastic stick awaiting her attention. A strange heaviness welled up; her legs felt fragile, and her fingers trembled as she reached for the stick. She covered it with her hand; did she want to know?

She took it through to the bedroom and sat on the edge of her bed, then steeled herself and whipped it into full view. She stared at the small grey window, and there it was, confirming what she somehow already knew. She was pregnant.

Chapter 11

Eleanor paced between her bed and the bathroom sink before whipping her laptop open and reading over Allen's email again. At least fifty or even sixty thousand years old; where would that place Lillooet on the evolutionary timeline? A knot twisted in her stomach, her moist palms struggled to steady trembling fingers that fumbled out urgent enquiries to an uninterested web; carbon-dating, ancient finds, palaeontologists, oldest human remains. Each word generated its own cascade of information pathways that fled from her like liquid mercury.

She slammed it shut and examined the white plastic stick again, willing it to flash up an error sign, praying for a reprieve.

'No fucking way am I spawning this!'

A new image of Lillooet flashed before her, that delicate and fresh-looking face. But it now seemed sinister, her 'almost smile' twisting to a sneer, the clarity of her eyes speaking ruthlessness, not truth.

She felt another warning heave and rushed to her spot on the floor beside the toilet bowl.

I'll just need to get rid of it, she reassured herself between gripping belches of empty air. *I'll call Simon. What an irresponsible, thoughtless… stupid, fucking idea!* She picked up her laptop and stomped into the living room. There was a message from Carl.

Where the hell are you?

'Fuck off!' she yelled, checking her phone. 'Ten past nine, you can wait!' She turned her phone off and threw it onto the settee opposite.

Eleanor tapped out her question and chewed on the nail of her thumb as she scrolled down the replies.

The morning after pill works for up to 120 hours after unprotected sex. However, the sooner it is taken, the more effective it is likely to be.

She ignored the offer of a discreet online delivery and turned instead to a map highlighting the location of nearby outlets.

She threw on her clothes and raced downstairs to her car. The closest pharmacist with the drug in stock lay only ten minutes away, where she had so recently bought the pregnancy kits.

'A hundred and twenty hours,' she mumbled, not noticing the red light as she sped through the crossing. A fury of horns erupted. She did not care.

'That's five days. Shit, shit, *shit*.' She tried to calculate how many hours she'd been pregnant, taking account of time zones, but the numbers slipped and slid away from her. So, instead, she tried to convince herself she was just within the time limit as she marched towards the pharmacy door.

Moments later, she returned to the car, ripping open the cardboard box and peeling the single tablet from its foil wrapper. She washed it down with a mouthful of cold tea, left from the day before. At least she had taken decisive action. She congratulated herself, beginning to feel in control once more. Never again would she place herself in such a vulnerable position; she did not want to live by committee. She would follow her own rules.

She raced back to her flat. She needed to talk to someone, and it would have to be Simon. His phone rang out for quite a while before he picked up.

'Eleanor?' His voice sounded tired and old.

'Sorry about this, Simon. I know it's the middle of the night there, but you're the only person I feel I can…'

Just one minute, Eleanor,' he whispered back.

She heard rustling, then the creak of a door.

'I was hoping you would call.' His voice sounded stronger now. 'That is a spectacular result, is it not?'

'I'm finding it a bit hard to believe, Simon. More than fifty to sixty thousand years old? That can't be right, can it? The sample must have been compromised in some way.'

'*Non*, I think not,' he replied, 'The result was replicated a number of times. We are in uncharted territory here. Let us just pray to the high heavens that we weren't successful in our… manoeuvres. We could easily be prising open a genetic Pandora's box.'

Eleanor remained silent.

'You think not?' he pressed.

Eleanor found herself sobbing inside.

'Eleanor? Are you all… please God, no! You cannot be!'

'I am, or rather, I was.'

'*Horreur!*' he gasped.

'I've taken care of it.'

'I mean, what were the chances? Whatever it is must have been determined to survive.'

Eleanor remained silent.

'So, how did you take care of it?' Simon asked.

'Morning after pill. Think I was still within the five-day limit.'

'Of what?'

'Since implantation…'

Simon groaned. 'But no, Eleanor! That is not how it works. That kind of medication can only prevent implantation. If you have already had a positive result before taking it, then nothing will have changed. It has no effect on an established pregnancy.'

Eleanor sank to the floor as she felt her knees buckle beneath her.

'Eleanor, listen to me. You are going to be fine. But I suggest you organise a D&C. There will be agencies around that can do that for you. Believe me; all will be well.'

Eleanor felt her breathing slow to a calmer pace. A D&C. That was the answer, of course!

'In the meantime,' Simon continued, 'I suggest we say nothing about these developments to Allen and Carl. I get the impression you're not looking to be talked out of this, so we will keep it simple, if that is possible.'

Eleanor agreed although his warning was hardly necessary. She had no intention whatsoever of enlightening Carl, not only because she didn't want him to know anything about what they'd done but also because she couldn't risk him seeing her as untrustworthy. There were other important issues to consider, other aspects of her work that could be in jeopardy if he knew she was capable of such treachery. He knew nothing at present about her hypothesis proposing the existence of a third genetic axis, the sort of work that would not only strengthen her voice in the world of academia but could also gain her a place in scientific history. If Carl got wind of it, she had no doubt he would become the headliner.

Simon had said he would call later. In the meantime, she would have to simply play a role. Act normal. Go to work. Be herself.

***

As soon as Eleanor walked into the reception area, Jane pounced.

'Carl's waiting for you.' She rolled her eyes in the direction of the coffee room.

'Well, good morning to you,' Carl announced her arrival in a booming voice, interrupting his discussion with his PhD student. 'At least you've managed to arrive in time for morning coffee.' He stood up. 'Your room or mine?'

Eleanor followed him through the general workroom to his den. He checked the door was tightly shut before sitting opposite her.

'Don't even ask.' She raised her hand to put a stop to the inquisition before it started. 'I'm just feeling a bit under the weather.' 'Ah, women's troubles?' He poured her a coffee and placed it on the table in front of her. 'We men get off so lightly.' He sighed. 'Anyway, what do you make of the carbon-dating?'

'I'm not so sure.' She shrugged. 'On the one hand, I understand Allen's excitement, but I can't deny that my gut feeling is that someone's got their maths wrong. She looks far too modern, too *homo-contemporary*. And her clothes, they just didn't look…'

'Prehistoric enough?' Carl looked surprised. 'A very mature and considered response, especially from one so enthralled with all things Lillooet.'

Eleanor loathed his patronising tone. 'So, what's your view?' She hoped he would, as usual, be happy to speak at tedious length. The embers of her nausea had quite suddenly been reignited by the very mention of Lillooet's name, and she needed time to compose herself.

'Eleanor, I don't think you're getting this. If this information is correct, we're looking at something quite different from the early man we all assumed. In fact, I doubt we're looking at early man as we know him at all.'

'You think this is an authentic result?' Eleanor struggled to sound calm.

'These procedures are usually pretty accurate. But what does it mean?' Carl shrugged. 'Ancient civilization? Travellers from a different universe? The genius manifestation of a chameleon-type virus? God knows.' He shuddered. 'At least we didn't try to bring the damn thing back to life. Now that could have been the stuff of nightmares. Jurassic Park with bells on…'

Eleanor gripped the sticky plastic seat of her chair.

There was a knock at the door, and Jane appeared.

'Your visitor is at reception, Professor,' she said, smiling.

Carl rose to his feet. As he walked to the door, she saw him glance in the mirror. Eleanor caught his reflection, smirking back at her and shuddered. *How much did he know?*

Back at her desk, Eleanor was determined to research abortion clinics, but no sooner had she begun her search when the fist that had clenched her stomach all morning suddenly released its hold, sending waves of warning. She leapt from her chair and hurried to the washroom where she slammed into a cubicle. Just in time, she managed to kneel on the floor. With one hand, she piled her hair above her head. With the other, she gripped the cool porcelain of the bowl, trying to steady herself as wave after wave of retching left her weak and utterly drained. It was some time before she felt she had the energy to push herself up and sit for a while on the lid.

Her legs were shaking, and her eyes watered so much she could hardly focus through the blur. She took a few deep breaths and leant back on the cistern. *This will pass*, she thought, but deep in her stomach, she felt a fresh assault gather. She knew she would have to go home. And that meant she'd have to stand up and get back out there. It hardly seemed possible, but after a few minutes, she forced herself to her feet and moved out of the cubicle. She placed her bag on the table in front of the mirror and began to fumble through it until she found what she was looking for. She returned to the cubicle and sprayed it with perfume; a cloying veneer settled over the pungent pall. She wasn't sure it was an improvement.

In all the years of her employment, Eleanor had prided herself in never having missed a day's work. Today, however, was different.

She would pass it off as a migraine. She hurried back to her desk, where she pushed her laptop into its case then swept all the remaining items into the top drawer. She scribbled a note to Jane and placed it on the receptionist's desk before heading for freedom.

Once safely in her flat, Eleanor locked and double-bolted her front door, relieved she would not have to open it again that day. With the drawbridge raised and portcullis secured, she cast off her office- armour and slipped into a pair of brushed cotton pyjamas that had been abandoned immediately after being unwrapped several Christmases before. She pulled the curtains to a close and arranged her duvet around her on the settee. Then, with a steaming mug of blackcurrant tea placed on the table to one side, she opened up the emails on her laptop and felt a stab of panic as she saw the most recent one was from Allen. Steeling herself, she opened it.

Hi, Eleanor

What do you make of the carbon-dating bombshell? If accurate, then this find is unprecedented. As far as I'm aware, it is estimated that modern man first populated North America 30 to 40 thousand years ago, probably crossing the land bridge that then connected Siberia to Alaska, although this was possibly not the only colonising group. In short, little is known about this. There's a lot of hypothesising but scant solid information. Fewer than 35 skeletal remains uncovered in the New World have been dated as older than 8,000 years.

Fascinating stuff I'm sure you'll have uncovered much more than I have. Please keep me informed.

Best wishes, Allen

Eleanor slid the laptop to the far end of the table. Allen seemed to be playing dumb. Perhaps he was trying to push her to open up? She rocked gently, trying to stave off the waves of sickly pain gripping her stomach yet again. How could she so quickly fall apart, not just physically, but emotionally?

Shivering now, she pulled the quilt around her, hoping its warmth would hasten sleep and that sleep would help her heal. But despite her exhaustion, sleep did not come readily. A collage of faces, Carl, Simon and Allen amongst them, twisted in and out of focus, their images multiplied and distorted as in a hall of mirrors. She could hear Olivia somewhere in the background, crying and laughing in alternate bursts. She saw her mother sobbing as the infant she clutched was wrenched from her arms and dropped into the crevice beside which she crouched, wailing.

'Please stop!' Eleanor called out, wiping her moist cheeks. As the tears released her sorrow, so, gradually, a blanket of calm settled around her.

The collage melted away, and in its place, a field of waving green emerged. There was sunshine and warmth, and Eleanor felt herself drawn into its beauty. A solitary bird circled above before settling on the branch of a nearby tree. She heard water and turned to see a clear stream gambol over and between a shallow bed of earth and rocks. Then from the other bank, she thought she heard music, the soft, lilting tones of a lullaby. And there she was, standing by the water's edge, a sleeping child held close. Lillooet. She smiled at Eleanor and nodded.

'*Everything is as it should be,*' she seemed to say, although no words were spoken.

Eleanor looked into her eyes and no longer felt any fear. She saw only beauty and truth. She tried to hold the image fast, but soon it faded, casting in its wake the gift of sleep.

***

A buzzer sounded, very faintly, from somewhere beyond her concern, but failed in its repeated attempts to rouse her. It came, and it went, each shrill demand for attention seemingly hours apart. A familiar sound, but no more than that. She dismissed it, burying deeper into her den. Surfacing briefly, she noted the lack of light beyond the curtains and considered making her way to bed but was soon sucked back into an overwhelming vortex of sleep, unable to muster the strength to overcome it.

When she awoke, it was to that energy of stillness that commits itself to no time of day or night and offers no immediate clues to help guide the newly awakened.

Suddenly, the front door shuddered violently; someone was outside, pounding upon its surface. Eleanor leapt out of her makeshift bed and rushed into the hallway. Hand poised on the panic button, which was located by its side, she pressed her eye to the spy hole, afraid of what she might see. A man stood outside, his back towards her.

'Who is it?' she asked.

'Eleanor?' Carl swung round. 'For God's sake, open up. What's going on in there?'

The panic that had seized her rapidly gave way to relief that just as quickly became fury. She threw back the bolts and pulled open the door.

'What on earth are you causing such a racket for? The neighbours will be up in arms. Come in, for God's sake.'

Carl kicked off each shoe and followed Eleanor into her living room.

'You've been missing in action for three days.'

Eleanor froze.

'Everyone's worried sick. You're lucky that it wasn't the police at the door!' Carl pushed the duvet aside and flopped onto the settee. 'Where in God's name have you been? You haven't answered your phone, your email…'

'Three… days?' faltered Eleanor. 'Three days, are you sure?' She dropped down beside him. 'I haven't been anywhere.' She held her head, trying to order her thoughts. 'What day is it today?' She eyed Carl in disbelief.

'Thursday.' Carl moderated his tone a little.

'Thursday…' Eleanor rubbed her brow as if trying to remember what the word meant. 'Thursday?' She repeated.

Carl surveyed her from head to toe. 'I better call a doctor.'

'No, no need for that. I was just so very tired. I remember coming home and falling asleep, but that was on Monday, wasn't it? I just can't believe I've slept that long. Maybe bad jet lag, maybe some kind of virus, maybe both…' She fell quiet.

'Let me get you something.' Carl rose to his feet and walked beyond the breakfast bar to the open plan kitchen. 'Coffee, tea?'

'Tea would be good, and anything you can see in there for eating. I'm suddenly horribly hungry.' Eleanor half-laughed. 'So, I can't be that ill, can I?'

'So, you just felt *tired*?' he asked a few minutes later, handing Eleanor a mug of milky tea and placing a packet of cereal bars on the table in front of her.

'And a bit sick,' she added, tearing off a wrapper and biting desperately into the snack. 'Maybe I've got whatever it was you had,' she suggested, raising her brows.

'Well, you had us all worried. We thought you had either died or eloped.'

'Neither likely,' she replied.

'So, what is going on then?'

'Who says anything is going on? I'm ill. End of.'

Eleanor shivered as Carl narrowed his eyes. He knew something. Had he been in touch with Allen? She thought of her research and her need for his trust.

'Look, Carl. I think I've done something… risky.'

She watched as he shifted forwards in his chair, his mouth twitching as if ready to declare his response. He cocked his head a little as if keen to miss nothing.

Eleanor walked to the large picture window and drew back the curtains, admitting a welcome torrent of sunshine. 'I think I know what's going on.' She swung round to catch his immediate reaction. 'I think I might be pregnant.'

Carl shot to his feet.

'Well, not to me, you're not!' he shouted.

Eleanor's jaw dropped. Of all the reactions she had anticipated, this was not one of them.

'Really?' She felt suddenly enraged. 'And what makes you so sure of that?'

'Had the snip, years ago. Two's quite enough for me, thanks. There's no way I'm picking up the tab for this.' He was red in the face. 'Do you really take me for such a fool? Think I don't know about Allen?'

Eleanor hesitated.

'That shark's gone quiet, and I can only guess why. But I'm surprised at you, Eleanor. You hardly know the guy. Wouldn't have put you down as the easy type, but there you are.'

'What a fucking hypocrite you are, Carl. Get out!'

Eleanor marched to the front door and yanked it open, kicking Carl's shoes out into the hall on her way. She slammed the door before he was barely across the threshold, clipping his heel as he left. She listened to him curse as he put his shoes back on and made his way downstairs.

She pulled the door wide open again and rushed to the railing above the stairwell.

'And don't ever come back!' she yelled.

'Don't worry, psycho. No chance of that!' He slammed the main door behind him.

Fired up with a new energy, Eleanor remained in the hallway until the thunderous echo of Carl's departure had dissipated. She was glad she had spoken her mind and relieved she had told him nothing he wouldn't soon learn anyway.

'Everything is as it should be,' she found herself saying. She would own this pregnancy, she would nurture this child, and she would start anew, by telling her mother.

***

The following Sunday, Eleanor arrived early for lunch, keen to make sure there would be plenty of time before Olivia and her gang arrived.

'You're early.' Her mum was delighted to see her daughter at the door a good hour ahead of schedule. 'I'm still peeling the potatoes.'

Eleanor followed her into the kitchen and leant against the radiator, as she had done so often as a schoolgirl. She would stand on that very spot, telling all the tales of the day while her mum prepared dinner.

Eleanor watched as Miriam drew the peeler over the rough surface of a large potato, forcing a long tongue of mottled skin out between its blades. She remembered how, as children, she and Olivia had made a game of measuring the longest lengths of potato skin and scoring their mother's efforts out of ten. *Everything was so straightforward then*, she thought. Her stomach felt tight. She would say something now, she decided.

'Mum,' she started. She could hear the quiver in her own voice.

Instantly, her mum stopped peeling and turned to face her.

'Yes?' She looked worried. 'Is everything all right?'

'Yes, everything's fine, Mum.' She couldn't stop now. 'But I do have something to tell you. Something important.'

'Yes?' her mum repeated, wiping her hands on her apron as if freeing them for some greater purpose.

'Well, I'm pregnant.' Eleanor looked briefly into her mum's eyes then down to the floor. Standing there, at the radiator, her back warmed, her finger tracing the groove along the ridged top of the metal, she felt she had slipped back in time some twenty years. She waited for a response.

'Good heavens, dear.' Miriam rushed towards her. 'That's... that's marvellous news. Isn't it?'

'Yes.' Eleanor smiled back. 'I'm thrilled.'

'So, when's the baby due? And who knows about this? Can I tell people?'

'Oh, it's still early days, Mum, but I wanted you to be the first to know. And I didn't want you to guess.' Eleanor patted her still flat abdomen.

Miriam sat down on the nearest chair. 'When do I get to meet the father?' Her eyes sparkled as she spoke.

'Mmm...' Eleanor tried to remember what she'd decided to say.

'Sorry, dear. Shouldn't I ask?'

'Not at all, Mum. It's a very sensible question. It's just that I don't actually know him...'

Miriam clutched at her chest. 'Oh no, darling, you weren't...?' She started to rise from her chair.

'No, no, nothing like that.' Eleanor waved her mum back down. 'What I mean is, I wanted to do this on my own, so there is no father as such, or rather there is, but he won't be acting as one. I've had IVF, Mum. I didn't really think it would work, so I thought I'd keep it to myself.'

Eleanor watched as shapes formed on her mother's lips that would have been words, but none were spoken. They were the questions her mother would like to ask. But Miriam knew her daughter well and had learnt over the years that the more she asked of Eleanor, the less information she received.

'Well, darling, you're going to be a mummy!' Miriam embraced her daughter. 'I'll need to set my knitting needles to work. That's so exciting! When did you say the baby's due?'

Before Eleanor could answer, she heard the front door burst open.

'Olivia's early too!' Miriam looked at the kitchen clock. 'Can I tell her?'

'Of course.' Eleanor struggled to smile; she wasn't sure she was ready for this.

Suddenly, Beth ran into the kitchen. 'Granny, Mummy's crying!' The little girl was wide-eyed and anxious.

'Again!' grumbled Bertie's voice from the hallway.

'Oh, dear.' Miriam looked apologetically to Eleanor. 'From one extreme…' She paused when Olivia slammed into the room and flopped onto a chair. She said nothing, but dropped her head to the table and sobbed, her slender fingers furrowing her hair.

Miriam dropped to her knees beside her daughter. 'What is it, Olivia? What has happened?'

Olivia shuddered a few more times before pulling herself up. 'He's left. Charles. He's walked out. Cheating bastard!'

'Shh.' Miriam signalled to Eleanor to close the kitchen door.

'I knew there was someone, but oh no! How could I even suggest such a thing…?'

Eleanor watched Olivia's tears drip onto the table. Her heart ached for her sister. She often didn't like her, but she did still love her.

Miriam wrapped her arm around her firstborn and rocked gently as she held her. 'I'm so sorry,' she whispered.

It was some minutes before she stood up again. 'I'll make us all a cup of tea, shall I?'

'All?' Olivia revived a little and, sitting up, looked around the room. She sighed when she spotted Eleanor. 'I didn't see you. You're early.'

Eleanor just nodded her reply, aware that any words at this point might not be well received.

'Yes.' Miriam spoke for her. 'We were just having a chat.'

'About me, I suppose. The tragic and hilarious source of family entertainment.' Olivia swept a tissue beneath each eye, spreading the smear of mascara as she did so.

Eleanor sighed.

'And what does that mean?' Olivia tossed her hair from her face. 'That I'm right?' She stared at Eleanor as if daring her to reply.

'Why would I come here early to gossip about you?'

Miriam placed three mugs on the table. 'No one was talking about you, darling. Now, tell me about Charles. When did all this happen?' Miriam gently nudged the conversation forwards.

'It kicked off last night. He'd left his phone in the bathroom, and I saw it, a text. From "L" and ending with xxx. Of course, I challenged him about it, and he didn't even try to deny it! *These things happen*, he said!'

'Bastard!' Eleanor remembered her fury with Carl.

'But that doesn't mean he's leaving you,' Miriam reasoned.

'Oh, you'd better believe it. As far as I'm concerned, he's already left!'

'Don't be too hasty, darling. Sit on it for a few days. You've got the children to think of too…'

'Don't you think I fucking know that?' Olivia gestured wildly, knocking over the chair between her and Eleanor, the chair on which Eleanor had placed her bag. Its contents scattered across the lino.

Eleanor began to gather up her possessions.

Olivia watched as her sister put the spilt coins back into a purse and checked to see if her pocket mirror was broken. Suddenly, she froze.

'What is that?' Her voice sounded less hysterical.

'What?' Eleanor searched around her but could see nothing unusual.

'That.' Olivia pointed to a pink cardboard box, a pregnancy kit, that tumbled out with all the other rubbish that cluttered her bag.

Eleanor cringed.

'No way… uh… you're having a laugh, aren't you?' Olivia looked at her mother.

Eleanor closed her bag and glared at her sister. 'I see, so now I'm the pitiful entertainment, am I? What's so hilarious about me owning a pregnancy kit?' Her sympathy for her sister was rapidly freezing back into a brittle rage.

'At your age, Eleanor? And with your OCD attitude to life?' Olivia snorted.

'Well, you'd better start laughing now, Olivia, because I'm pregnant. And I'll tell you this; I'll not be messing this child up by stomping around like a self-obsessed drama queen all the time.'

Eleanor snatched up her bag, abandoning the items not yet gathered, and marched to the front door. Slamming it behind her, she caught sight of three pale faces at the living room window. A stab of guilt stopped her in her steps. She turned and waved, but only Beth, the youngest, waved back.

Chapter 12

Eleanor seethed all the way home. What on earth had happened to her relationship with her only sister? Her mind raced back to their childhoods, their hopes and dreams.

'I'm going to be an artist when I grow up,' Olivia had often announced.

'Colouring in won't pay the rent!' their dad had grumbled, each time he overheard her.

He could be like that, Eleanor mused, full of opinions he was always ready to proclaim. He had done nothing but encourage Eleanor in her academic aspirations, but Olivia... not so much. Eleanor vaguely remembered her dad steering Olivia away from her dreams of art school, towards an art degree at the university.

Eleanor replayed her sister's words in her mind. Perhaps she had a point; their father had never been even-handed in his approval of them, even before Olivia's shock pregnancy.

What would he say of Eleanor now?

***

Back in her apartment, Eleanor's thoughts turned to Carl.

'Fuck you!' she cried aloud. She paced the floor, running over what she might say to him — if anything. 'You have no idea what's going on. You are in the dark, and that's where you'll stay until *I* decide otherwise.'

She smiled, feeling suddenly powerful, but then she remembered Allen. She needed him on side and he deserved to know; Lillooet was his find, after all. He would be furious if he thought she was deceiving him, and that had never been her intention. She whipped open her laptop.

Hi, Allen

Hope all is going well with you.

Can we talk?

Eleanor.

She stared at the screen. It wasn't long until he replied.

Good idea. When?

Now? She tapped out.

Sure. I'll call you.

No, let's FaceTime. I'll call you.

Eleanor went to the bathroom and examined herself in the mirror. She brushed her hair and practised her smile; this had to go well.

Back on the settee, she took a few moments to calm herself and rehearse her opening words. She pressed the key that would summon Allen, and within seconds, his face filled the screen.

He stared at Eleanor; his left hand cupped beneath his chin as if poised to proclaim judgement.

'Hi.' She smiled, momentarily forgetting what she had planned to say. 'How are you?'

There was no smile in return. Eleanor felt sick.

'Plodding on,' he replied. 'You?' His voice sounded flat and impassive.

'Look, Allen. I think we have some serious catching up to do…'

'I know what you're going to say, Eleanor. Simon had the good grace to fill me in about the implantation. Thanks. And here was I thinking that at least we had *something* left of Lillooet to study, a piece of ancient history that would be ours to decode, instead of being flushed to nothing around a U-bend. *Good work!*'

'We had no intention of hiding anything from you. Please believe me. We had to be decisive. It was a now or never thing.'

Allen's expression didn't alter.

'And Simon tried to call you, repeatedly,' Eleanor continued.

'So he said,' Allen snapped back, 'But he could at least have tried to call my secretary, or one of my colleagues. I'm sure they'd have found a way to get a message to me. I was hardly on the moon.'

'Allen, none of it was planned. Our heads were spinning. Simon had no idea I was going to revisit the whole implantation possibility. He was shocked, excited… and didn't want to let the opportunity pass. Neither of us did. The timing was perfect…'

'But you somehow managed to reach Carl?'

'I didn't even try.'

'Really?' Eleanor watched as Allen's eyes widened and jaw slackened. 'You didn't run the implantation by him first? Whoa! How did that go down when he found out?'

'He didn't. Still doesn't know.'

'What?'

'Why should he? He wasn't a main player in this, so I decided to proceed on a need-to-know basis.' Eleanor was beginning to feel more confident now, seeing that Allen was eager to hear more.

'Will you ever tell him?' Allen's brow furrowed. 'I suppose, as you say, if he doesn't need to know, then why would you?' Now he was nodding his approval.

'Well...' Eleanor swallowed hard. 'That's just it, Allen. In fact, that's why I called you.'

'Meaning?'

'Meaning...' She paused, studying his expression. 'Looks like he will need to know. It worked. I'm pregnant.'

Allen said nothing, his expression frozen, but his eyes widened.

'Oh. My. God.' He leant closer to the screen. 'That's...' He shook his head. 'No, no, no, no... that is... incredible... crazy, fucking *amazing*!'

Eleanor smiled, strengthened by his enthusiasm.

He leant back in his chair, clutching his head. 'I can't believe this.' He stood up and walked out of her view, reappearing sporadically as he paced the length of his office.

'Okay.' He eventually faced her again. 'A plan. We need a plan.' He snatched a pen and sheet of paper. 'Does Simon know?'

Eleanor nodded. 'But only because he was going on about the carbon-dating bombshell and praying for the failure of the pregnancy.'

'I get that, of course. We do need to talk about all of that.' He scribbled something on the paper. 'And what about you? Are you comfortable with… all of… this?'

'Absolutely,' Eleanor replied. 'It's the scientific journey of a lifetime.'

'You'll have to tell Carl, Eleanor,' Allen murmured, 'This is a really big deal.'

'Not yet, Allen, trust me. I think I'll stick to my need-to-know tactic. I don't want him taking over.'

Allen nodded. 'Fair enough, nor do I. Good. I'm glad we're on the same page.'

'He does know…' Eleanor tailed off.

'What?'

She had been on the point of telling Allen that Carl did know she was pregnant, just not that it was Lillooet's child, but she knew Allen would quiz her on his reaction, and she would have to go into details of the row, how Carl had decided it must be Allen's baby and stormed out. She couldn't face that conversation right now.

'I think he knows something's up, that's all,' she finished lamely. 'Sorry, but I have to go, Allen. I'm feeling a bit queasy.'

'Sure, great, fine. I need to get my head around all of this too. Make some plans. Thanks for calling, Eleanor. We'll talk soon. Oh, and look after yourself.'

***

When Eleanor arrived at work the next morning, still queasy, Carl was locked in an animated huddle with several research assistants and PhD students from his department, including Kyle and Tom.

'Exactly my point!' she heard him announce, 'Development versus manifestation! So many hypotheses on the presentation of these disorders have sought to understand and explain them — predominantly with reference to the influence of either inherited or environmental factors. But even a casual consideration of ethological observations indicates quite clearly their dual roles.'

Eleanor watched as Kyle attempted to offer a contribution, but Carl bulldozed on.

'Yes, yes, there's a lot of interest in "spectrum disorders" at present, and drug companies are keenly awaiting any developments that could inform a treatment regime.'

'But do you—' Kyle tried again.

'—and that is exactly why I am on the brink of being given the green light — and a very generous grant — to pursue this line of research.'

'So, what exactly will I be looking at?' Tom asked.

For a brief moment, Carl looked baffled. Then he laid his hand on Tom's arm. 'Oh no, no, no! This piece of work will require a top-notch researcher! That's why we're being given the services of Sophie Ransom from Vancouver. She has already touched on the subject of critical periods of development in the first year of life, which is why I made sure I managed to secure her involvement.'

Eleanor could see Tom trying to hide his mortification.

'Oh, okay,' he mumbled. 'So, when will this start?'

'Well, my proposal has been very well received by management, and it's really just a formality from here on in, a question of dotting the I's, etcetera.'

Eleanor walked through to the workroom and closed the door behind her. She had heard enough. Carl had done his usual. He'd made a fizzing cocktail of an idea out of Sophie's PhD thesis and was already claiming it as his own.

***

Eleanor spent as little time with Carl as possible over the next few weeks, although his focus on planning for Sophie's arrival meant he barely seemed to notice. This suited her well as she was constantly tired, and her frequent episodes of morning sickness left her little energy for Carl management.

It wasn't until about three weeks after learning she was pregnant that Eleanor began to feel more normal. She found it easier to get up in the morning and no longer felt she was under constant threat of needing to rush to the bathroom.

But then, one Monday morning, as she stood waiting for a document to spill out of the printer, she could sense Jane staring at her. Turning to face her, Jane blushed and looked down at her desk, but said nothing. Later, that same afternoon, she walked into the coffee room, creating silence as she entered. Kyle and Tom immediately started talking about a film they were planning to see, but Jane merely turned and left the room, looking flustered.

What the hell is going on? Eleanor wondered, trying to quieten the rising feelings of paranoia that whispered rumours in her head. She had never joined in the office gossip, so it wasn't that she felt excluded, but she did feel unsettled by the sense she was its focus.

It wasn't until the next morning, when she caught sight of herself in the full-length mirror in her hallway, that she realised what the murmurings were almost certainly about. To her astonishment, there, beneath her tight skirt, was a discernible bump.

'No!' She turned and twisted, waiting for her reflection to resume its slender form. 'Impossible! Surely? I can't be more than five weeks!'

Before setting off for the office, she called her local surgery and booked an emergency appointment for that afternoon.

The young doctor listened attentively. 'Don't worry,' she soothed, 'It is not at all unusual for people to get their dates mixed up, or even for some transient bloating to make a pregnancy appear more advanced than it is. But you've done the right thing checking it out. I'm going to arrange a scan for you as soon as possible so we can get an idea of exactly where you are.'

Relieved, Eleanor decided against returning to the office for the last hour of the working day. Instead, she made her way to the town centre to buy some loose clothing which would hopefully stem the chatter for a while.

A few days later, she received a text from the ante-natal clinic; they could fit her in that afternoon. Feeling something of an imposter, she made her way to the south side of the city where the maternity services were based. She was grateful for the distance from her home neighbourhood and the anonymity it offered. There was little chance she would meet anyone she knew.

She took a seat in the corner of the crowded room and waited for her name to be called. Despite the fact her small, swollen abdomen seemed like an outsized appendage, she found herself surrounded by women who made her feel inappropriately slim. Trying not to stare at the tight balls bursting out from their bellies, she found it impossible to imagine she might ever be that huge. She watched as one woman, much younger than Eleanor, hobbled into the waiting room, clutching her back. She groaned as she eased herself into the only vacant seat.

'Eleanor Bartlett?' An older lady clutching a thin, buff file had appeared in the doorway.

Her pregnant peers watched as she sprang to her feet and followed the nurse along the corridor and into one of the many side rooms.

'If you could just pop up onto the bed, the sonographer will be with you shortly.'

Eleanor nodded. She could feel her legs tremble as she lay, waiting for the door to open, longing for the procedure to be over with.

Eventually, a woman dressed in crisp blue scrubs appeared. 'Hello,' she said. 'I'm Catherine, and I'll be conducting your ultrasound today. Have you had one of these before?'

'No,' Eleanor replied, with some emphasis.

'That's fine. It's a painless and straightforward procedure. If you could just pull up your top and push down your jeans, please.' She selected a tube of gel from a nearby trolley.

Eleanor had fully expected to be questioned at this point, but nothing was asked of her. Instead, the sonographer read over the notes in her file then set to work, squeezing the thick gel over her skin.

'Sorry about this. It's a bit cold, I'm afraid.' She set the dials on the machine and turned down the lights.

'So, it's a confirmation of dates we're looking for?' The sonographer didn't look at Eleanor as she spoke, concentrating instead on moving the metal wand back and forth over her abdomen and peering at a screen that only she could see.

'Well... yes,' Eleanor stammered, 'Exactly.'

She scanned the technician's face, waiting for some sort of response and praying it wouldn't be a gasp of horror at the vision of whatever monster was growing within her.

'Ah, here we are.' She pressed harder on the spot she'd found and touched the pad of the console beside her. 'Just measuring now. This gives us a fairly reliable estimation of the length of gestation.' Her voice sounded calm, which Eleanor found reassuring. 'Would you like to see?' She smiled at Eleanor.

'Of course.' Eleanor craned her neck as the screen was turned towards her. 'Dear God!' she exclaimed, pulling her hands to her face.

Immediately, she forgot about all her misgivings. There, before her, was an image of a perfectly formed foetus, and she watched in wonder as the tiny promise of life, powered by a visible heartbeat, kicked and stretched within her.

'First baby, isn't it?' The sonographer looked back at her notes.

Eleanor opened her mouth to reply but found she could say nothing.

'It feels like a miracle every time, don't worry.' She made a note in the file then placed it back on the trolley.

Eleanor continued to stare at the screen. She scrutinised the tiny creature but could see nothing unusual. It was a baby.

'Would you like a photo? One for the scrapbook?'

Eleanor nodded. She felt she would cry if she tried to speak, so chose silence instead.

'Here we are.'

A short length of thin paper rolled out, like a receipt, from the machine. A column of stills framed with numbers and dates. The words 'Baby Bartlett' were emblazoned across the top.

'How pregnant am I?' Eleanor suddenly remembered the purpose of the visit.

'Around twenty weeks, I'd say.'

Eleanor gasped. 'No!' She shot up and held the pictures closer to her. 'That's not possible. Are you absolutely sure?'

'As sure as current technology allows us to be,' she replied.

'Twenty weeks? That's five months.' Eleanor tried to count backwards. How on earth could that be? Perhaps it wasn't Lillooet's child after all. Perhaps it was Carl's... Dear God, that was even more unthinkable!

'Not really.' The sonographer was tidying things away. 'Closer to four, I'd say. Gestation is calculated from the first day of your last period, and conception is usually around two weeks after that.'

'All the same... I... I'm certain that can't be right.' Eleanor shook her head and racked her brains for an explanation. 'Is there any syndrome or condition that could make a baby grow more rapidly than it should?' She stared up at the sonographer, unsure what kind of answer would calm her fears.

'Not really.' The sonographer turned to face her. 'I mean, there are obviously conditions, like macrocephaly, where babies do have an enlarged head, but... your baby is perfectly in proportion. I could see if there's a consultant around to talk over any concerns you have, if you want?'

'No.' Eleanor instinctively shied away from the possibility of a detailed discussion about the conception. The less attention she drew to herself, the better. 'You're right, it's fine. Just the shock of it, I imagine.' She lay back on the bed and closed her eyes for a moment. She would have to go home and think this through.

'Of course.' The sonographer walked to the door. 'But if you do change your mind, we can arrange for a consultation at your booking- in appointment.'

***

When she was back in her car, Eleanor took the roll of black and white pictures from her bag and unfurled them. She sat for a while, motionless, just staring at them before tracing her finger around each tiny image. Suddenly, she felt a welling of something inside her, a longing to reach out and touch the tiny being, to cup it in her hands and brush its cheek against her own, to whisper soothing words and feel the tiny heartbeat upon her chest.

The images, taken in rapid succession, seemed to capture the motion of the child, turning to face her, a hand reaching up towards her. Eleanor placed a trembling finger on the outstretched limb and instantly felt a shock of energy run through her, a tingling warmth that seemed to wash away all fear and doubt, coursing through her and filling her with hope.

'Everything is as it should be,' she heard herself say.

Eleanor's mind-set had shifted almost instantly; the toxic smog of fear seemed to dissolve before her eyes, bringing clarity in its place. Of *course,* this wasn't Carl's baby! This was Lillooet's child, she was certain. Nothing about the progress of the pregnancy itself had been conventional, so why on earth would she expect anything different of the foetus itself? This was no ordinary pregnancy and, in all likelihood, no ordinary baby. And although she had no way of knowing this for sure, she felt the force of the bond already formed between them was in no way ordinary either.

Eleanor folded the paper carefully and tucked it into her bag, then headed for home. She no longer felt scared or alone but was instead gripped by a new determination to protect this pregnancy and do everything in her power to help the child draw its first earthly breath. But as she took her place in the rush hour traffic queues, she became aware of another change, a shift in her emotional gears that made this pregnancy no longer feel like a struggle. She was curious, engaged and excited, but not as she had been in Vancouver. Her attachment to this project, she realised, was no longer purely scientific. She now longed for the child itself.

Chapter 13

Four months after Eleanor's return from Vancouver, the long summer days had given way to the near constant darkness of Glasgow's winter and relentless rain spilled from cluttered gutters onto puddled pavements.

It was a dark Friday morning in December, and Eleanor could hear hailstones battering against her bedroom window. All night the wind had wailed like a grieving mother, her cries keeping Eleanor from much-needed sleep. She did not want to leave her bed and pulled the quilt more tightly around her. *Christmas holidays soon*, she thought and tried to settle back down. But she was awake now and became aware of someone walking around in the flat above. Footsteps that started and stopped, then started and stopped again.

She heard little of her upstairs neighbour and had no idea which of the strangers she occasionally passed on the stairs lived above her. This was the only person she could hear in the building, and for years now, she had listened to their solitary steps, early in the morning or sometimes late at night. Whoever it was, thought Eleanor, also lived alone.

She wondered if the person below listened out for her too. Did they know who she was, and had they noticed she was pregnant? She began to imagine herself pacing the floor with a baby, the person beneath hearing her weary steps.

She had often watched Olivia try to hush a crying infant, walking the length of her mum's living room only to turn and repeat the action endlessly.

'Shhhh,' she would say, pressing her lips against the hot, moist cheek of her fractious child.

Will I have to do that? Eleanor wondered.

She felt a soft turn within her and drew her hand down from the collar she had made of the quilt, to massage her now significant bump. With each passing day, the movements had become stronger, firmer, feeling less a part of her own body. Of course, the child still might not survive, she knew that, but it was her job to keep things going for as long as possible.

She swept her hand across the taut skin of her belly and felt a ripple of response from within. Sometimes she could identify a beaded string of knuckles or the soft bend of what could be either an elbow or a knee. She no longer feared this baby; she had overcome her early self-consciousness about being pregnant, and the nightmares of delivering a barely human, hirsute form had faded from the day of her scan. She had agreed to her role in this experiment and was determined to make the most of it; accepting these unspeakable anxieties was a price worth paying for scientific gain. Although she couldn't deny, with each day that passed, the bond she felt with this child grew stronger. Books on pregnancy and child development replaced those on genetics and research techniques that previously cluttered Eleanor's bedside table. At least once a day, she consulted the one that outlined exactly what should be happening throughout each week of pregnancy, but she found it impossible to place her progress on the typical timeline.

It was clear the pregnancy was advancing at an accelerated pace, with each stage outlined in the textbooks occurring in Eleanor's body well before its allotted time. Her own work on mitochondrial DNA had made her familiar with the mounting evidence suggesting that different species of man had coexisted hundreds of thousands of years ago, but it wasn't until after the scan, when her fears of being colonised by some parasitic intruder had subsided, that she properly read up on the subject. And the more she learnt, the more intrigued she became. Species of humans had come and gone, interbreeding, some surviving, some dying out, leaving only traces of their existence upon the earth in the DNA of modern man, a genetic calling card. Was Lillooet one of these extinct people? Human, but not the kind we know today? Some *other* kind, perhaps?

Eleanor grew comfortable with the uncertainty. She, after all, had been the one who decided of her own free will to resurrect this genetic memory, delivering it into a time and place unknown to any of its kind.

She was careful, however, to hide any signs of emotional attachment from Simon and Allen, ensuring instead that each word she wrote and each gesture she made in their video conferences projected a purely professional attachment to the project. As for Carl, they had barely spoken since the argument, communicating only by email and staying out of each other's way.

Eleanor congratulated herself that her pregnancy was no longer the subject of much interest to her colleagues. Few even made the usual enquiries, well aware of her preference for privacy and only Jane asked about the due date for the baby in response, to which Eleanor replied as vaguely as she felt was reasonable: *sometime in February.*

In truth, it was impossible to tell. Even the obstetrician had revised the due date forwards, telling Eleanor she must have got her dates wrong. Meanwhile, Carl's continued avoidance of her was raising eyebrows. She knew her colleagues assumed the baby was his and she did nothing to disabuse them of their assumption.

Despite it being the last working day of the university term, it was the day of Sophie's arrival at the institute. Eleanor was the last to arrive in the office and was just taking her seat around the table for the Friday meeting as Carl started to address the small group. He explained this arrangement would give Sophie time to settle in and meet people before the real work began and had organised a full diary of social events that would keep her by his side for most of the holiday period.

'Attention, everyone.' Carl chinked his teaspoon onto the side of his mug.

The chatter thinned to quiet.

'I would like to introduce you all to Sophie Ransom, from Vancouver, who will be working with us for the foreseeable future.'

He raced through a round of cursory introductions, pointing to and naming each member of staff in turn, leaving Eleanor until last.

'And, of course, Sophie, you'll remember Eleanor Bartlett…'

'Lovely to see you again.' Eleanor smiled. 'Welcome to Glasgow.'

'Thank you,' Sophie replied, 'I'm excited to get started.'

There were few items on the agenda that day, but Eleanor knew the first would probably expand to fill the entire morning.

Carl rubbed his hands together as if anticipating a feast. Eleanor rolled her eyes.

'I can think of no better way to end one year...' He beamed, pausing to survey his audience, 'Than to plan an exciting project for the next. As you know, I will be embarking on a major piece of research that will draw to us, once again, the attention of the scientific community. My research proposal has been very well received and funding approved. In fact, on the mere basis of a brief summary of my hypothesis, I have already been asked to present at next year's Paris Conference!'

Kyle and Tom exchanged glances and Sophie brought her hands together as if to clap.

'Sophie will be carrying out the basic research and data compilation and will report solely to me.'

Sophie nodded eagerly.

'So, I hear you ask, what will be the meat of this?' Carl clicked the small black switch he clasped in one hand and the first page of his PowerPoint flashed onto the screen before them.

In Search of the Fulcrum: Critical Periods of Development on the Autistic Spectrum

Eleanor held her phone beneath the table and quickly checked her latest email from their director, Jack. She glanced around the table and saw a furrow form on Sophie's brow.

Carl was pulling a bundle of papers from his bag.

'Clearly the detail of methodology etcetera is of particular importance to Sophie and me.' He smiled towards her. 'The Dream Team!'

Sophie blushed.

'But it is of critical importance that you are all well versed in what we are doing and to that end, I urge you all to read this document. I anticipate a great deal of media interest in this, so the last thing we want is one of you being asked questions and having no idea about what's going on! Communication is all.' He brought his fist down forcefully onto the table.

'Carl, I was wondering—' Eleanor began.

But Carl raised his hand, palm towards her. 'There will be a time for questions after the presentation.'

He pushed on, dragging the small gathering through a seemingly endless series of pages that could, Eleanor believed, easily have been heavily abbreviated.

'And so you have it,' he eventually announced, glancing at his watch. 'And perfect timing too. Tea-time.'

'Carl?' Eleanor raised her hand to speak. He turned to face her.

'How does this tie in with Jack's email?'

'That's what I was thinking,' Tom chimed in. 'Look, here.' He turned his laptop towards Carl.

Eleanor watched as he scanned the document. His face grew red and his lips tightened.

'This is preposterous!' he eventually declared. 'I am one hundred percent certain this has been sent in error.' He whipped out his phone and punched in a number. 'Jack? Carl here.'

They all listened in silence as Carl attempted to right the wrong of the email. 'No… I've received no such thing… Well, I haven't had a chance to read it then. Too busy preparing the presentation for our next project…'

Eleanor couldn't hear Jack's words, but his voice carried to her. He sounded calm and matter of fact.

'Absolutely no way!' Carl bellowed. He turned his back to the group and walked to the window. 'Well, I can't accept that, Jack. I've put a lot into this…'

Eleanor looked at the others. Sophie was biting her lip but Tom and Kyle looked like they were trying not to laugh.

'Yes, I will do that, Jack. In fact, I'm on my way now.' Carl ended the call and marched back to the table. He glared at Tom. 'Did you know about this?'

Tom nodded. 'Got an email from Jack last night, detailing everything.'

'Oh, very good, so you just thought you'd let me carry on…'

'I did try—' Eleanor started.

'Well, sod this.' Carl marched to the door. 'I don't give a damn about Allen's contribution, bloody cheek of him. This is my research and I'll do it my way.' He slammed out of the door just as a young man entered.

'Ready?' he asked.

Eleanor got up and walked over to him. 'Paul, hello! Just about, if you could give us ten, we'll get the place organised. Meeting ran over a bit, I'm afraid.'

'No problem, I'll tell the others.' Paul smiled and left.

'Kyle, Tom? Would you mind moving the table to the side?' Eleanor asked. 'Jane, could you bring in the drinks and snacks, please?'

Sophie appeared at Eleanor's shoulder. 'What is going on?' she asked.

'Right now, or generally?'

'Both, I suppose.' Sophie stepped aside as Tom and Kyle shuffled past, heaving the conference table over to the window.

'It's the last working day of the year and it's our turn to host the end of term do, so all the other teams will be joining us. It's going to get busy here, I'm afraid.'

'And Carl?' Sophie asked.

'Looks like he was outbid on the research front and he's not too happy about it.'

Eleanor had known for some time that Allen had persuaded Jack to accept his proposal; a longitudinal study of newborns, tracking early development. They had spent weeks discussing how they could properly assess this child, should it live, without raising suspicions and she had thought Jack would break the news to Carl earlier, but as soon as he had begun speaking, she realised he was still out of the loop. She hoped she had succeeded in disguising her delight at his ignorance.

'I see.' Sophie looked worried.

'But nothing changes as far as you're concerned, Sophie. If anything, in fact, your role here is even more important. Allen's department is part funding this project and you will be reporting to him.'

The door opened behind Eleanor and a cluster of people pushed in, making a bee line for the refreshments.

'How was the flight?'

'Long.' Sophie rolled her eyes. 'At least now I'll appreciate what everyone else goes through when they come over to visit us.'

'How's Allen?' Eleanor sipped iced water from a plastic cup. 'He'll miss you, I'm sure. He manages to keep you very busy.'

'I imagine he'll survive.' Sophie laughed. 'Although I think he plans to keep me busy here too. He seems to be very interested in this project. *Obsessed,* even.' Sophie laughed again. 'He's an all or nothing kind of person and his attention to this research definitely falls into the former category! He's already sent me a stack of papers to read on child development.'

'Maybe I should read them too,' said Eleanor, patting her bump lightly as she upgraded her opinion of Sophie. She was more articulate and observant than she had realised.

Eleanor wasn't sure what had been said to Sophie about her pregnancy. She would know about it, of course, from Allen, but she would have been told nothing about its true origins. As far as Sophie was concerned, it was a happy coincidence that Eleanor's baby was due in time to be part of this research project, and that was all she would ever know.

'Of course, congratulations!' said Sophie. 'You must be getting excited. I imagine the baby's due pretty soon?'

'Believe it or not, that's a matter of some debate, but I'll be ready whenever the stork chooses to fly by.'

Carl marched back into the room and drank down most of a glass of red wine before approaching a group of older men standing in the far corner. It was only a few moments before Eleanor saw him look in their direction.

'Sophie!' he called over

'Well, you look amazing, Eleanor,' Sophie said, smiling and turning towards Carl. 'See you later!' She headed across the room to join him.

Eleanor felt hot; the room was not really big enough for the twenty or thirty now gathered there. The path between her and the drinks table was full of people she might have to talk to if she tried to push through, so she decided to make her escape and return to the peace of the workroom.

She pushed her way through the tight group in front of the door, slipped away from the gathering and returned to her desk. No one else had come back to work, choosing instead to linger in the party atmosphere. In the past, Eleanor would have stayed on too, but today she preferred to clear all outstanding tasks before the office closed over Christmas. But despite the quiet, she found it difficult to concentrate. She shifted in her chair, trying to find a comfortable position. Nothing seemed to work. Her back ached, her neck felt tight and she longed for a soothing bath. At four o'clock, she decided to give up; she would finish the last few jobs in the comfort of her own home.

***

Breathing a sigh of relief as she reached the sanctuary of her car, she switched the radio station over from news to Christmas carols. She didn't feel like listening to stressful stories of doom and gloom. She wanted to feel calm and soothed. She longed to be home, to retreat from the world for a while and she would be there soon — ten minutes if the traffic stayed quiet all the way, thank God. But just as she approached the junction that led to her mother's house, she remembered she'd promised to pop in to see her that evening. It was only a fifteen-minute detour, but it would probably mean she wouldn't be home for another hour or two.

'Shit,' she mumbled, trying to make up her mind before the lights turned green. She decided she ought to go, thinking of her mother looking out of the window for her.

She found a parking space right outside her mum's gate, which was a blessing as the rain had become more forceful, pounding off the pavements. She held her collar tight around her neck as she struggled against the wind to wrench open the wrought iron gate. A cruel December chill spilled through each gap in her clothing, frozen fingers of ice slipping beneath her scarf as she fought her way to the front door.

Through a glass panel framed by a holly wreath, she could see the reassuring glow of the mock Tiffany lamp on the hall table, a Mother's Day present she and Olivia had saved up for some twenty-five years before. In the window of the front room stood the little Christmas tree they'd had since she was a child, a kindly sentinel, guarding the Christmas spirit and all those wishing to embrace it. All was as it should be.

As soon as she pressed the brass button of the bell, she saw Miriam stand up and place her knitting on the low table that pressed against the side of her chair. Eleanor heard the quiet tread of her slippers on the wooden boards and watched the image of her face blur back and forth through the ripple of the small glass pane as she unlocked the door.

'Come in, my dear, come in.' Eleanor's mum helped remove her wet coat and scarf. 'Let's put these near the fire and see if we can dry them off a bit before you have to go back out into that dreadful weather. Or you could always just stay here for the night?' Miriam locked the door behind her daughter.

'No, Mum, but thanks. I'm not far away, I'll be fine.' Eleanor walked ahead into the living room and sat in the seat opposite her mum's, the one closest to the flickering fire. The room was bathed in a reddish glow from the tree lights and the flames of the coal fire.

'Here we are.' Miriam returned with a tray holding two cups of tea. 'I didn't bring any mince pies, dear, because I've made a good, proper dinner for you. It will be ready in ten minutes.'

She placed the tray on the coffee table and handed Eleanor a cup before settling herself back into her own chair on the other side of the fire.

'Look.' She held up her knitting; a white, fine-needled, baby cardigan. 'What do you think?'

'It's just beautiful, Mum. Makes me almost wish I'd let you teach me how to knit, although I would never have had the patience for it,' Eleanor said, laughing.

'Well, you were always so busy with your studies. And then there was your music and ballet. You didn't sit still long enough to learn to knit.' She weaved a gentle defence for her daughter's lack of interest in traditional domesticity. 'What a pity you've just missed Olivia. I had little Beth to keep me company today. She had a bit of a cold, poor lamb.'

'Mmm.' Eleanor was listening, even if only superficially. *Beth*, she considered. *Yes, that was a pretty name*. She had noticed Olivia's children more than ever before in recent weeks, and, perhaps, slightly less critically.

'Have you come up with any names yet?' Miriam seemed to read her daughter's mind.

'I've not really given it much serious thought.' Eleanor warmed her hands around the mug. 'But I think I'd better get on with it.'

Her mum nodded, glancing over at Eleanor's bump. 'It all seems to have happened very quickly. Are you quite sure of your dates?'

'No, actually.' Eleanor had been expecting this question for some time. 'In fact, the obstetrician has now suggested that the previous IVF did work after all, but, rather unusually, went unnoticed.'

'Really? How fascinating. So, where would that place you, time- wise?'

'More pregnant than I thought.' Eleanor patted her baby bump and laughed as casually as she could manage. 'Maybe by about two or three months?'

'Well, that sounds more like it, darling. I didn't want to say. The only other idea I had was that maybe it was twins…'

'Dear God, no!' Eleanor grimaced

'So, have you got things in place, dear? Have you thought about childcare? You do know I'll help you all I can, Eleanor. That is, all you would like me to.'

'I know that, Mum. You've already been more supportive than I could ever have wished for. But as it happens, I'm having this baby at a rather convenient time. The institute is starting up a crèche in January, so I've signed up for that.'

'Really? That is handy. But will they take new babies? Aren't those places usually meant for older children?' Miriam looked worried.

'I couldn't say what they usually are, but this one is only for new babies, actually. It's part of a research project that my department is running, a longitudinal study of child development.'

'So, what will they be observing?' The needles stilled temporarily.

'A whole range of things: physical development, socialisation, language skills, intellectual skills.' Eleanor gave a casual summary of some of the observational fields that had preoccupied much of her thinking in the previous weeks.

'I see.' Miriam's brow furrowed. 'So, they'll be part of some sort of experiment?'

'Well, that makes it all sound a bit sinister, Mum, but really the babies won't notice a thing. They will be looked after in a beautiful and very well-equipped nursery, with a generous ratio of staff to children. They will be very well cared for.'

'What's the purpose of this *study*?' Miriam had resumed her knitting.

'We're trying to look at the development of some aspects of personality, trying to separate out genetic and environmental influences. To do that you need to keep as many other variables as constant as possible. Things like diet, exercise, the sorts of toys you're given and things like that. And this is about as close to environmental control as we can ethically get,' Eleanor explained.

Miriam frowned. 'And are all these parents quite happy to place their children under that kind of scrutiny?'

'Well, there will be only six babies involved, just two from mothers working in the institute, and another four babies from other university departments and local businesses that happen to be due within a three-month period. And yes, they're all delighted in fact, because the nursery fees are being heavily subsidised and all parents will receive dietary supplements and a whole range of other supports.'

'Ah. Very good.' Her mother nodded, perhaps a little disappointed her babysitting services would not be much called upon. 'Well, you know I'm here anyway, if you should need me. And Olivia too. I'm sure she'd like to be of use to you, despite her recent troubles.'

'Of course. I knew things had been a bit tense between the two of them recently, but I really was quite shocked when Charles actually left. Has she heard much from him?' Eleanor asked.

'I don't know. Olivia has gone a bit quiet recently. I think she's more upset than she's letting on. Probably trying to be strong for the children.'

'That's too bad,' said Eleanor.

'I know you girls have…' Miriam hesitated. 'Well, gone your separate ways, I suppose, but you can still be helpful to each other, *be there* for one another as people say nowadays.'

'I'm sure we can, don't worry, Mum. We're both going to be just fine.'

Eleanor swallowed against the tightness in her throat. She knew it must have been hard for her mum to be so frank and to ask for her support. She wanted to reach over to her, to embrace her and have all these warm reassurances reciprocated, but her limbs felt heavy, immobilised by familiar embarrassment.

'Let me see if your dinner's ready.' Her mother brightened, placing her work to the side then bending to kiss her daughter's forehead as she left the room.

Eleanor waited until she knew her mother could not hear her.

'I love you too,' she whispered.

Chapter 14

Christmas used to follow a well-established routine in the Bartlett household. The family would gather at home on Christmas Eve and make their way on foot to the local church to take part in the carol service. Then, once home, they would sit in the living room and raise their glasses to the season of goodwill before sliding into the cold sheets of their childhood beds.

Since her wedding, Olivia would not join them until Christmas Day. Eleanor disliked the noise of the over-excited children and the mess as gifts, carefully chosen, would be unwrapped and only fleetingly acknowledged.

Fortunately, this year, Olivia decided she would prefer a quiet Christmas at home so their mother accepted the invitation to spend the day with her own recently widowed sister, leaving Eleanor free from any obligation whatsoever.

It was a wintry December, very cold but dry, so when the snow did fall, it lay thick, like a perfect blanket. Eleanor had spent Christmas alone only once before and this Christmas morning, as she looked down upon the white and silent scene from her first-floor window, she recalled that day, some twenty years before.

Frozen railway points had forced the cancellation of trains and, like many other students that Christmas Eve, Eleanor had been turned away from the station, her rucksack heavy with hastily wrapped gifts. She felt upset hearing the saddened voices of her parents as she broke the news to them over the coin-operated telephone outside the station but as she journeyed back with the crowd, she had been surprised to find herself suffused with a strange elation at the prospect of being by herself.

Slow to form friendships and uncomfortable with casual conversation, she felt strangely at ease in this company of near-strangers that day as they forged their way, pilgrim-like, back to their student residencies. Resisting kind offers of company, she had returned to her room filled with a greater sense of joy than she could ever recall. When a fresh snowfall started, she sat by her window, in dim candlelight, looking down onto the parkland surrounding the student village, watching as the trailing footprints of fellow students were slowly erased and marvelling at the grand postures of the ossified trees.

From the room above her, another student placed a record on repeat play.

'*In paradisum,*' it sang out, again and again, until Eleanor could see in her mind the arm of the record player lift and return between each rendition. Entranced by the angelic chorus, her mind slipped effortlessly into reverie.

She missed Olivia and the closeness they had enjoyed as children, and from her ringside seat in her simple student room, replayed in the otherworldly arena below her the highlights of their innocent pleasures.

Two small, spinning children, heads held back to the heavens, tongues stretched out to catch the falling flakes. Stumbling and giddy, they engineered collisions that brought forth squeals of joy and their agreed mutual exchange: 'Sorry! Sorry! Sorry!'

The Sorry Game, they called it. It was a game best played in inclement weather, such as rain, high winds or snow. Round and around they would spin, enjoying the contact as hands clipped hands and arms flailed before they crumbled together into a common heap, unself-consciously intermingled.

The following morning, Eleanor had tracked down her neighbour to ask for details of the record so she could buy it for herself. It was Gabriel Fauré's 'In Paradisum' and ever since, it had remained her favourite piece.

She rose from her recollections of two decades before and, lifting her phone out of her bag, scrolled through the menu; surely, she had it in here somewhere.

There it was. She smiled to herself and selected continuous play. As the first notes sounded, she inhaled sharply, holding the breath within her as if it was the source of the bliss she now felt.

'*In paradisum.*'

The voices consoled her, their soothing strains flooding the apartment.

'*Deducant te angeli.*'

The music followed her into the bedroom where she tumbled into the satin arms of her bed.

'*In tuo adventu, suscipiant te martyres.*'

She closed her eyes and, in her mind, cast a line, fishing for visions, for reassurance that all would be well.

'*Et perducant te.*'

She felt a gathering within her, a swelling of emotion.

'*In civitatem sanctam.*'

It was only music, and this piece in particular gave her access to this part of herself.

'*Jerusalem, Jerusalem, Jerusalem.*'

She let herself fall into the music, accepting its energy as her own. She felt her limbs tingle as if something new, some hope-giving drug, was coursing through her veins. She felt happy and sad, excited and terrified, exhilarated and exhausted by it all. And when she felt the tears melt down her warm cheeks, they brought a calm relief that led her to a motionless sleep.

In paradisum.

She floated, in a sea of blue, buoyant vapour, a delirious ecstasy carrying her into her otherworld. The vapour mist around her cleared to reveal a brilliant sky which scrolled above a deep meadow, wildflowers swaying to a warm breeze, casting their intoxicating scents.

In paradisum.

She drifted to the side of a clear, gurgling stream that tumbled over sparkling nuggets of rose quartz. Beyond the clear water, a shady wood of broadleaf trees beckoned and, picking her way across stepping-stones, she began to discern, from the rustle of lush vegetation, sounds of a different sort.

Neither song nor cry, they called to her; wordless voices uttering their silent command. Approaching a shaded clearing, she became conscious of a groundswell of longing that pulled her closer to the sound. And there, beneath an ancient oak, within a moss-lined hollow, lay an infant, a tiny child.

Asleep and still, it made no sound, but the song rang on around both it and her. She knew she had a choice: to turn away and resume her journey, independently, free from this responsibility, or to go forwards and accept the child.

In paradisum.

She stooped and gathered it in her arms.

A gush of warm water drenched the sheets, bringing Eleanor to sudden alertness. Bolting upright, she swept her phone to silence and struggled to realign her thoughts with the present. Again, the warm wetness came, accompanied this time by a dense pressure that seemed to grind into her pelvis.

'Surely, it can't be? Not yet!' She threw back the covers.

The colourless moisture clung to her thighs, rapidly cooling upon contact with her cotton pyjamas and rippling the sheets below her. Jumping up, she ran to the bathroom where another outpouring followed, flooding the tiled floor.

'Okay, okay!' She peeled off the sodden garments and threw them into the shower. 'This must be it. Oh God…'

Given the accelerated progress of the pregnancy, she had, of course, expected the baby to arrive earlier than normal, but not this early; she was barely five months. Surely this baby could not survive? She reached for her phone but wondered who to call. Her mother was hours away and Olivia was at home alone with the children.

The hospital? She started to tap out the number but then stopped and tossed the phone onto the laundry pile and paced the damp floor.

This is a child stolen from history, a birth uninvited by nature. Perhaps she had been arrogant, or foolish, in trying to bring it back to life. Perhaps it would be for the best just to let nature take its course, sixty thousand years later than planned. But then, she thought, if it has survived so far, surely it deserved the help any other new life would receive? She clutched her head in her hands, pressing her fingers as far into her flesh as she could bear.

A massive cramp gripped her abdomen and she sank to the floor gasping as she clutched the rigid bulge. Eventually, she felt the tension begin to ease beneath her fingers. Perhaps it was already too late to call for help, but she decided she would have to try. She snatched hold of the abandoned phone and dialled 999.

'I'm in labour,' she panted to the voice that asked her which service she required. 'Yes, I'm certain… no, that won't be possible, I'm on my own… and don't think I could drive… six or seven months,' she exaggerated. 'I'm not sure.' She fell silent as a new wave of pain gripped her brick-hard abdomen, its iron force crushing down upon her. It was some while before she could talk again and was barely able to stammer out her address.

'Yes, all right, I'll do that.' She clutched the side of the sink and pulled herself to her feet. 'I'll make sure the door is unlocked.' She shuffled to the front door, turned back the key and released the chain.

Gingerly returning to her bedroom, Eleanor attempted to pull off the damp sheets, but wave upon wave of pressure left her trembling and unable to sustain the effort required to reorganise the bed. Eventually, she managed to drag her quilt onto the bedroom floor and fell upon it.

Again and again, the agonising waves battered against her. Eleanor was glad she was on her own and felt free to give full voice to her agony. Staggered by the severity of the pain, yet amazed at her body's ability to survive it, she tried to ride it out rather than resist it.

Between contractions came moments of no pain, when she tried to regain control by focussing on all that remained normal around her: the snowflakes outside that drifted slowly to their destination and the phone that had been cast to the floor.

Leaning against the side of her bed, she rocked to and fro, sometimes dropping to all fours, swaying, until the next sickening wave started to gather once again.

As the agonies expanded, so the rests between them grew shorter. She lost interest in everything around her and gave up hoping for the arrival of help. She turned inwards, bringing all her will to bear down upon this task, this immediacy, this urgency of now, until finally the crisis dawned, the infant crowned and a spark that had been ignited eons before came blazing into life.

The pain ceased.

Eleanor reached between her legs and felt the warm wetness of the baby slip into her grasp. It did not announce its arrival with the squeal she had expected, but it did inhale sharply when she picked it up and brought it to rest upon her chest. He was certainly breathing and looked in good shape as far as she could tell, but still, he was not crying. Wiping the vernix from his face, she saw him root towards her nipple and gasped as the infant's tiny lips latched on, sending a shock of agony through her. She watched in awe as he worked his jaws, first urgently, then steadily as the life-giving milk began to flow. Was this normal? She stroked his delicate face.

'Beautiful boy,' she whispered, at which moment he opened his dazzling, cornflower blue eyes and instantly, she knew she loved him.

Chapter 15

'Do you really need to get back to work so soon, dear? Six weeks is rather early, don't you think?' Eleanor's mother barely raised her eyes from the contented bundle she cradled.

'I feel great, Mum, don't you worry. Really. I feel well rested and very happy.' She stroked her son's cheek.

'Isn't he a delight?' purred Miriam. 'They don't all arrive quite so settled.'

'I know, I've been lucky on that score. He seems to have a very calm temperament. Serene, almost.'

Olivia appeared with a tea tray.

'*Angelic,* by any chance?' She raised her eyebrows and set the tray down heavily on the coffee table beside Eleanor's chair. 'That will all change for sure when you abandon him to a work crèche.'

'Can I hold the baby?' Beth came running into the room after her mother.

'Maybe later, when he's awake,' said Olivia.

'Okay,' the little girl accepted. 'So, who's going to be that baby's daddy?' she asked as she turned on her heels at the doorway.

'No one,' said Bertie from his seat by the window, 'Just like us now,' he added, turning away from his mother's glare to stare out at the front garden.

'We do still have a daddy though, don't we, Mummy?' asked Beth.

'Of course you do.' Olivia crouched down beside the little girl and cupped her hands around her daughter's face. 'He's just very busy at the moment.'

Bertie stomped out of the room.

'What's the matter?' Beth ran after him. 'Are you crying, Bertie?'

'Poor darling,' said his gran, 'He's confused and upset.'

'I know that!' Olivia said, her voice tight and controlled.

'Have you explained to the children what's going on, dear? It would probably help them. I'm sure some of their friends will have parents living apart. They might understand more than you expect.' She reached over to stroke her daughter's arm. 'Children are often more scared of the ordinary things they don't know, than the frightening things they do.'

Olivia stiffened to her mother's touch. 'I've explained all they need to know. Bertie will just have to get used to it, like the rest of us.' She pulled away from her mum to organise the cups and saucers.

Miriam quietly passed Gabriel to Eleanor and slipped out of the room.

Eleanor waited until Olivia's breathing had eased and she had taken her first sip of tea

'So, how's work?' she asked.

'A hell of a lot better than home,' replied Olivia, each word formed tightly and delivered on the shortest of leashes. 'Not surprisingly,' she added, in a voice sounding weary of its own fight.

'Well, if there's anything I can do to help…' Eleanor faltered.

'Like what?' Olivia glared at her. 'Spread some of your magic, happy dust around? What on earth makes you think you can be of any help to me? Or even begin to understand how I feel? You have no idea!' She clenched her fist and turned sharply away.

'Look, Olivia, obviously I feel for you right now and, of course, I can't imagine what you're going through, but there's nothing to be gained from shutting people out, especially not Mum, she's doing her best for everyone. And if you must be angry, at least direct your rage appropriately and tell Charles what you think of him instead of making everyone else suffer for your misery.'

'And what makes you think I'm not angry with you? Maybe I am. You are so fucking smug, Eleanor, waltzing into motherhood, assuming you know it all. The six-week expert! Maybe that is something that really makes me angry.' She glanced down at the sleeping Gabriel. 'And maybe it's people like you, who've never committed to anyone, who haven't invested years of their lives in one relationship, but who feel free to steal other people's husbands, just taking what they want from them and wrecking their marriages!' Olivia's nostrils flared, fury blazing from her bloodshot eyes.

'Stealing other people's husbands?' Eleanor laughed in disbelief. 'Honestly, Olivia, you have no idea what you're talking about.' 'Don't act all innocent, Eleanor. Do you really think we're all stupid? How many conferences have you gone to with… what's his name?'

'Carl, you mean? I don't think I'll be fighting Mrs Thornton over that buffoon, even if he was Gabriel's father, which, by the way, he is not.'

'Oh, I see, so little mister perfect here is what, a gift from God? An immaculate conception?' Olivia sneered. 'Or is he the product of yet another husband theft?'

'You know what, Olivia, you really need to take a good look at yourself and listen to your own toxic narrative. Maybe husbands aren't just stolen. Maybe they sometimes walk out of their own accord, to get away from bitter, jealous wives.'

'Eleanor!' their mother snapped. They had not heard her enter the room.

Gabriel woke suddenly and started to wail.

'I'd better be off.' Olivia turned abruptly. 'Kids? We're off, hurry up and get your shoes on.'

'No, stay a while, dear. Please.' Miriam followed Olivia to the table at the window, where she pulled a tissue from the box.

'Don't leave like this, pet. Everyone's a bit on edge just now, with so many changes to deal with.'

Eleanor saw her mother glance towards her. She knew what she wanted, for Eleanor to apologise, to ease the stress of the moment.

Instead, Eleanor turned her back on the pair and pulled Gabriel closer to her. He had stopped crying now but was staring up at her, his pupils wide and dark.

Olivia was pulling on her coat. 'No, Mum, really. I'm fine. And I do need to get going.' She glanced at her watch. 'The uniforms still need to be washed and Bertie has a project to finish for tomorrow. That's going to be fun and games.' She sniffed and stuffed the tissue into the pocket of her cardigan.

'Well, if you must, dear,' her mother said, her voice sounded strained. 'Maybe I'll call you later tonight?'

'Okay.' Olivia softened a little. 'I'll call when the kids are in bed. Might even get a chance to talk properly then.'

***

The next morning was Eleanor's first appearance at work since Gabriel's birth. She had been dreading this day since the moment she had looked into his eyes. The thought of handing him over to someone else he would smile at, reach out for, possibly even come to love, gouged a hollow in her heart.

She found it difficult to maintain her usual professional distance as her colleagues gathered around for a glimpse of the new arrival. Jane swayed to and fro as she cradled the baby in her arms. Carl kept his distance and seemed either unaware of, or not concerned by, the searching looks and whispers of colleagues as they gazed between him and Gabriel.

She would have to tell him the truth, she knew that, but wasn't sure how best to tackle it. Allen had been thrilled when she had announced Gabriel's birth and wanted to catch the next flight so he could see the child in the flesh. But, worried this would force her hand with Carl, Eleanor had put him off, saying she'd thought it safer to wait until he was more settled and had acquired some immunity.

Every Saturday though, she'd Zoomed Vancouver and talked through the weekly observations she had sent to them. But while she enjoyed seeing the thrill of Allen's excitement, she shivered each time Simon spoke, often focussing on possible dangers.

Carl would be furious and the longer she left it, the more difficult it would be. Would he ever trust her again? Would he support the research or do his best to sabotage it?

She noticed the time and realised she was already running late. Thanking the small throng for their compliments and good wishes, she made her way to the crèche.

She stood for a while in the elevator before pressing the button that would take them up to the top floor. They were alone again. She kissed the soft skin of Gabriel's forehead and held him tightly, folding herself around him.

'All will be well, darling,' she whispered, 'Please know that.'

She pressed the button and, breathing slowly and deeply, prepared herself for what was to follow.

***

'Hi there,' Sophie greeted her warmly, holding the door open as Eleanor entered the freshly painted nursery.

'What a beautiful room!' Eleanor gazed around her at the colourful wall displays. 'And so peaceful.' She looked over at the infant sleeping in a basket by the window. 'Is it always this calm?' Light melodic music filled the airy space.

'Not always,' Sophie said, laughing, 'But we only had three babies here last week. Gabriel is the first to join us this week.'

Sophie opened the folder she was carrying and handed Eleanor a booklet with Gabriel's name already printed on the front page.

'Would you mind completing this sometime today? It forms part of our baseline assessment.'

'Of course.' Eleanor flicked through the pages, scanning the headings of each section. She looked forward to the task.

'So, this is Gabriel.' A woman in her fifties approached. Her broad smile and outstretched arms immediately set Eleanor at ease. 'I'm Kara. May I?' she cooed, sweeping Gabriel into her arms.

'How do you do?' Eleanor held out her hand, keen to connect positively with the person who would probably form the next closest bond with her child in his early years.

'So pleased to meet you, Eleanor.' Her voice was deep and rich and she held Gabriel to her, pressed against her soft, round chest with an ease that spoke of many years' experience handling babies.

'Aren't you a cutie?' Kara lifted the infant to her face, holding him so close their noses nearly touched. 'I will be Gabriel's main carer here in the nursery,' she said to Eleanor, before turning her face back towards Gabriel, 'And we're going to get to know each other very well, aren't we?'

Gabriel opened his eyes.

'He's waking up... oh my, what beautiful eyes you have, little one!' Kara gasped. 'Looks like you've just stepped out of a Vermeer!'

Eleanor instantly liked Kara and, she knew, Gabriel did too.

Despite knowing a care regime had been agreed that would be uniformly implemented for all the babies, Eleanor could not resist pointing out a few aspects of Gabriel's personality and routine for particular attention. She was relieved and grateful to find Kara listened carefully and made notes. Then, feeling more wretched at the separation than she imagined possible, she kissed Gabriel's cheek and turned to go. Wiping the tears that slipped down her face, she was appalled to hear what she had rarely heard before — a wail of sorrow from her son.

***

Eleanor was relieved to find the workroom empty when she sat back at her desk. Kyle and Tom were chatting in the staff room and Sophie had returned from the nursery and was now with Carl in his office. Eleanor's head was throbbing. She massaged her temples, hoping to knead away the tension and tried to tune out of the chatter from the nearby rooms, until she heard something that pulled her back to attention.

'*Gabriel*, for God's sake?' exclaimed Carl, 'What sort of a name is that? The woman's become unhinged. I mean, Sophie, I know you're not the bitching type, but really, it's got to be a joke.'

'I think it's kind of cute,' she heard Sophie reply, 'And a baby's name surely has to be one the mother really likes.' There was a pause, before Sophie spoke again. 'After all, it might be her only chance to name a child.'

'And thank heaven for that, or there would be a whole host of angels floating around the office crèche,' Carl guffawed.

'Poor Eleanor,' Sophie said, 'She'll be exhausted coming back so soon and I imagine she'll be pretty upset at having to be separated from her baby all day when he's just six weeks old.'

'Pfff.' Carl barely stifled his amusement. 'I don't think you know our Eleanor terribly well. Just you wait and see, not a tear will be shed. That woman is made of steel.' Eleanor heard his derisory laugh. 'And the final two are starting today?'

'Yes.' Sophie's voice was quieter and more difficult for Eleanor to hear. 'I've printed off the observation and assessment schedules for the first week, with the changes you suggested. I hope they're okay, I haven't had much experience with tiny babies.'

'Oh, don't you worry, plenty of time for that. Anyway, we've managed to employ some highly experienced staff. I'm sure they'll be running a tight ship. Your job will be to keep an eye on the bigger picture, reset assessment parameters, if need be, analyse data etcetera. There's no need to get your hands dirty.'

Eleanor heard the rustle of papers, usually a sign Carl was winding up a conversation. As quietly as she could, she slipped out of the workroom and into the washroom.

'What a shit!' she exclaimed as loud as she dared, but still, she knew she would have to put thoughts like these to one side and win him over.

When she returned to her desk, she saw Carl deep in discussion with Tom.

'Do you have a minute?' Eleanor approached him.

Carl feigned dramatic surprise. 'She talks! Mother Eleanor has a voice!' He studied his watch. 'I'm a bit busy right now. Maybe in ten.'

'Fine.'

Eleanor returned to her desk and opened the booklet Sophie had given her. She scanned the first few pages before flicking through the rest of the document. There were a few open-ended questions, but most required the parent to select just one of a given range of options. This would be more challenging than she thought. Apart from those relating to weight, height and sleeping pattern, Eleanor could immediately see she would struggle to select answers that properly described Gabriel.

'Eleanor.' Carl had appeared at his doorway. 'I have a few minutes now.' He turned sharply and walked out of sight.

Eleanor sighed heavily then rose to follow him.

'So?' Carl had chosen to sit behind his desk, giving Eleanor no option but to take the hard, low chair opposite.

'Look, Carl, I know things haven't been easy between us recently, but surely we need to put our differences aside, even if just for the sake of our research.'

'Oh, *our* research, is it? So, is my name still on the paper, or is there no space for it now that Allen and Simon are topping the bill?

After you, of course.'

'Actually Carl, that's what I want to talk about. I was intrigued by your research proposal. You're absolutely right, spectrum disorders would attract a lot of interest and funding.'

Carl sniffed.

'Why not combine that research with what's about to start upstairs? I can't imagine it would require much modification to procedures, and the setting is perfect.'

Carl said nothing but he drew his hand across his chin and Eleanor thought she could see the glaze on his eyes shift from loathing to reluctant interest.

'I imagine the assessments you had planned could merge seamlessly,' Eleanor continued.

'It would mean a complete redraft of the assessment booklet,' Carl replied.

'Which might not be a bad idea anyway.' Eleanor picked up the copy lying on Carl's desk. 'I'm not sure about some of the parameters being set by the answer options.'

'Really?' Carl shifted in his seat. 'I thought we'd accommodated the slower developer comprehensively.'

'I'm sure you have. But I'm struggling to find answers that properly reflect Gabriel's progress to date. I think we might be running the risk of creating a ceiling effect.'

'A ceiling effect?' Carl echoed.

Eleanor thought, with a pang of panic, that she ought to tell Carl about Lillooet now. She could see his curiosity about the child had been piqued. But just at that moment, his phone rang and he answered immediately.

'Hi, Jack? Just about to call you, as matter of fact. I've had an idea about how to maximise research opportunities at the crèche.' Carl waved towards Eleanor; her signal to depart.

She did not return to her desk but decided instead to find Sophie. As she walked through the workroom and straight to the lift, she felt delighted to have a legitimate reason to return to the crèche. As soon as she crossed the nursery threshold, she felt that now familiar wave of contentment that being close to Gabriel brought her.

'Hi!' Kara appeared. 'Everything okay?'

'Yes. Sorry to come up unannounced, but I really need to ask Sophie about this.' She waved the booklet in her hand. 'She asked me to complete it today, but I have a few questions…'

'No problem, she's in my office.' Kara pointed to the first door in the corridor. 'I'm afraid I'll have to leave you to it; I'm scheduled for an interactive session with one of the babies.'

Eleanor knocked gently on the door before entering. 'Sophie?' She smiled at the young woman behind the desk. 'Do you have a few minutes?'

'Of course.' Sophie stood up and moved to the comfortable chairs in front of the desk. 'Please, sit down.'

On the wall to Eleanor's left was a large window looking onto the main playroom.

'I didn't notice this when I was dropping Gabriel off!' Eleanor exclaimed.

'Isn't it perfect?' Sophie smiled. 'It allows us to observe the infants without their awareness of being watched.'

'Ahh, good idea.' Eleanor wandered over and peered through. She could see Gabriel, asleep in a basket close to the window where she stood. She struggled to pull herself away.

'So,' Eleanor said, placing the assessment booklet on the table between them, 'I'm afraid I'm struggling a bit with—'

Suddenly, a loud thud resounded as the main door of the crèche slammed to a close. Eleanor and Sophie turned sharply to face the office door that Eleanor had left ajar.

Eleanor listened to the heavy tread of the visitor pace up and down, before stopping at the door across from the office.

'Aha! Just who I'm looking for!' Eleanor recognised Carl's voice immediately. She knew he'd want to have a look at Gabriel, especially after their conversation.

'With you in a minute,' Kara almost sang the words. 'Just completing this section of the interactive programme.'

'Ah, of course.' Eleanor recognised Carl's default charm offensive. 'Excellent, Kathy. I'm glad to see you're implementing the protocols as directed.'

They listened as Kara completed the nursery rhyme she had been singing.

'Thought I should see how things are progressing,' Carl said.

'I see,' replied Kara, a hint of lullaby buoying up her intonation. 'When would you like to come? As you know, the observable assessments are conducted daily at 10.00 and 14.00 hours. Shall I put you in for one of these?'

'No need for that, Kathy. I'll just have a quick look while I'm here.'

'I'm not sure that—' Kara started.

'No, no, don't worry. I'm not expecting a fanfare. Just seeing it as it is will be good enough.'

They heard him march towards the playroom door. Eleanor shot up and rushed to the one-way window. She watched as he scanned the room before asking, 'So, where is the latest arrival then, young *Gabriel*?'

One of the nursery nurses pointed towards the sleeping child. Eleanor's heart raced as she watched Carl approach. He came to a halt in front of the sleeping infant, so close to the window Eleanor could see the stain of coffee on the corner of his mouth. She watched, immobilised, as Carl scanned the child from top to bottom, then had to stop herself from calling out as he reached into the cot and started to unfold the blanket that swaddled him. Every instinct compelled her to rush in and snatch up her baby but she forced herself to stay where she was.

Kara was now by his side. 'Please don't handle the children. Especially when they're asleep.' She placed her hand gently on Gabriel's chest and eased Carl's away from the baby.

'For God's sake, Kathy.' Carl's voice was raised. 'You do know I'm in charge of this project, don't you?'

'Of course.' Kara remained calm. 'But there are protocols…'

'That I drafted!' Carl exploded. 'And they weren't intended to be used as trip wire for me!'

Gabriel stirred.

'See, he's waking up anyway.' Carl turned from Kara and stared into the crib. Eleanor clasped a hand to her mouth as the infant's eyes shot open.

Immediately, she saw the colour drain from Carl's face as he found himself caught in the child's gaze. She looked at her son. His eyes, those cornflower blue eyes, stared up at Carl, fully alert, yet in no way distressed.

Carl's jaw dropped.

'*Bloody hell…*' She read his lips as they twitched out their disbelief. He stared down into the crib and slowly nodded his head. 'Those eyes… I know those eyes… This surely can't be true…'

Pulling his gaze from the child, he stared straight ahead. Eleanor watched as his unseeing eyes fixed on her own, invisible to him behind the glass. His lips quivered, but still she could make out the whispered utterance.

'*Lillooet.*'

Chapter 16

When Eleanor arrived home that evening, Carl was already at her door.

'We need to talk.' His eyes darted between Eleanor and Gabriel, snug in his car seat.

'We do.' Eleanor placed the carrier on the floor and unlocked her front door.

Carl looked dazed and walked, trance-like, to the settee.

'I don't want to have this conversation in front of Gabriel,' Eleanor said firmly. 'Give me an hour, and he'll be settled in bed.'

'He's six weeks old, for Christ's sake…'

'One hour.' Eleanor held up a warning finger.

***

'So, when did you plan on telling me? Next week? Next year? Never?' Carl launched into his attack as soon as Eleanor had settled Gabriel and returned to sit opposite him.

'I did try, this afternoon.'

'You hardly made much of an effort,' Carl challenged.

'Whereas you?' Eleanor was determined to remain strong.

Carl eventually broke the silence. 'So, why the change of heart?' he demanded, 'About implantation?'

'Curiosity, science, new frontiers…' Eleanor shrugged. 'I just couldn't let the opportunity pass.'

'Shit… I can't believe you kept this from me.' Carl pursed his lips tightly. 'What else don't I know? Or did you plan to drip-feed the truth to me, as you saw fit?'

'Carl, give me a break. I was overwhelmed, stunned, scared, and I really didn't think it would come to anything…'

Again, he shook his head. 'How do I know this is the truth?'

'What brought you here tonight, then?' Eleanor felt more comfortable arguing about logic than emotion.

'Those eyes… they certainly look like Lillooet's, but…' Carl shook his head.

'Because they are!' Eleanor exclaimed.

'Do Simon and Allen know?'

She nodded. 'But not Sophie.'

'And do they think I know?'

'Sort of…'

'*Bastards*. Thanks, Eleanor. So, I take it this is why Allen plans to fly over for the six-month assessment meeting? Not just to *keep an eye on the project*.'

Eleanor sighed.

'Wait… does that mean Jack knows?' Carl looked hunted. 'Is that why the funding was approved?'

'Not at all. He just owes Allen, apparently. That's why he okayed the project.'

Carl sat with his arms folded tightly to his chest.

Eleanor remained silent.

'Well, we need a plan,' he said eventually, 'The fact he has survived at all is remarkable.' Carl pulled out his phone, tapping rapidly. 'I already have a few ideas. We've no idea how long he'll live. Not long, I'd guess, so we must make the most of it,' he continued as if talking only to himself.

Eleanor felt her stomach tighten. Carl's words filled her with terror, not because the idea of Gabriel's early death was new to her; it had already cost her many hours' sleep. But to hear this prospect given voice in the more reasoned light of day transformed what she had chosen to believe as a phantom fear into the flesh and blood of vital horror.

'We'll discuss all this tomorrow.' Carl rose to his feet. 'I'll get in touch with Allen tonight. Make sure I'm fully in the loop this time.' He articulated each word with an exaggerated precision.

***

'Shit, shit, shit!' Eleanor leant against her front door as soon as he'd gone. She had known he would work it out as soon as he saw the child, and now she wished she'd found a way to tell him first. But in some ways, it was a relief that he knew; he would be more interested and supportive of the project. But he would have his own agenda, and it would be more important than ever that she concealed her attachment to Gabriel. As far as Carl was concerned, Gabriel was a curiosity, a unique object for examination, not a baby she loved — *her* baby.

When she slipped into bed that night, she looked over at Gabriel. He was lying on his back, swaddled in a soft cotton wrap with a woollen blanket tightly tucking him into place. The room was bathed in the warm, red glow of a nightlight, and she could see from where she lay the gentle, reassuring rise and fall of the tiny body.

Her eyes settled on the framed picture that sat on the dresser beyond the Moses basket. It was her graduation photograph, showing a young Eleanor, smiling triumphantly between her proud parents. Would she ever see such an image of Gabriel? She shuddered and closed her eyes.

Sleep came quickly, too rapidly even to announce its approach. But all too soon, its comfort twisted from lifeline to noose. She was on a train, a dark and dirty train. There were other people there. She could see them in the periphery of her vision, but each disappeared as soon as she turned to grasp them in her sight. She held a bundle, a tiny infant, tightly to her chest. He cried with hunger, but she could not feed him. She had to get off the train, but they would not let her. They would stop her. They would take her child. The train was slowing. Surely, they would escape? The door flew open, and a lush landscape raced past them, light and bright and promising, it beckoned to them, but as she sidled towards it, the others forced her back, wrestling the infant from her arms and, hovering by the doorway, preparing to cast him out.

Eleanor shot up in bed to the panic of piercing screams. It took some seconds for her to realise the desperate cries were Gabriel's.

Racing to his crib, she found him wet with tears, his eyes wide with a terror he could not share.

'There, there, little one.' She rescued him and brought him into her own bed, knowing she would find as much comfort in his company as he would in hers.

'There, there,' she consoled again as she propped herself up on a cascade of pillows and placed him on her chest, before lifting the quilt to cover them both.

'Don't be afraid,' she soothed, feeling his rapid breathing settle to a calmer pace. 'Nothing will harm you. No one will harm you, my treasure. Everything is just as it should be.'

But as he settled back to sleep, Eleanor was reluctant to close her eyes once more. She wanted to rest, to slip away from everything and everyone, except Gabriel. But to sleep was to cast off the cords of reason and give full rein to the torment of her fears.

Dear God, she thought, *when will this all end?*

But as she lay, snapshots of the day flashed before her, and she knew this was only the beginning.

Chapter 17

It was Thursday morning, and although it was only eight thirty, Eleanor was already at work. She wanted to catch Sophie before the others arrived. It had been just over four months since Gabriel had started at the crèche, and the first formal review meeting was due to take place the next day. It had been impossible to get any information from the nursery staff about Gabriel's progress to date, but that was a condition she had agreed to. It was part of the protocol, a way of reducing parental inclinations to address any issues relating to a child's development and so skew outcomes. But Gabriel already looked bigger than all of the other infants, and there was no doubt that developmentally, he was also well ahead.

Eleanor knew Sophie had been working for some weeks now on the paper she would present and was keen to learn what would be said about Gabriel. She was terrified her reactions would alert the others to her true attachment to the child. Carl and Allen were to attend in person, while Simon would join them on FaceTime.

Eleanor tapped on Carl and Sophie's door, Sophie's desk having been moved there by Carl for 'ease of communication' not long after she arrived. When Eleanor entered, Sophie was studying sheets of numbers, tables and graphs.

'How's it going?' Eleanor asked.

Sophie sighed. 'I've read over everything countless times, and I think it's okay, but I still feel nervous.'

'Of course.'

'Sophie!' Carl suddenly breezed into the office. 'Aren't you the early bird?' He marched towards her. 'Will you give us a moment, Eleanor?'

Eleanor nodded tightly and returned to her desk, frustrated she hadn't managed to steal a preview of the report's highlights.

Once back at her desk, Eleanor felt restless and exhausted. She hadn't slept well. When she'd collected Gabriel from the crèche the night before, Kara had approached, asking her to meet for a chat at ten the next day. Her apprehension made her stomach churn, and she frequently consulted the office clock. There were so many things she did not want to hear and so many questions she would rather not be asked.

Back in Vancouver, when all this had begun, she would never have imagined feeling what she now felt for this child. She knew she would have a sense of responsibility, but more for the research itself than for any life form that might come of it. But from the moment Gabriel's beautiful eyes opened and found hers, she knew nothing in her life would ever be the same again. She no longer thought of life before Gabriel, unless it came with a shudder of pity for its relative emptiness, and she didn't want to hear of anything that might disrupt this idyllic calm.

***

'Is everything all right?' Eleanor asked as soon as she sat down in the nursery at ten on the dot.

'Absolutely,' said Kara. 'I'm so sorry if I've alarmed you. I just want to talk a few things over with you, compare notes.'

Eleanor scanned the nursery for her son and almost immediately heard the warm laughing gurgle he generally reserved for his mother. She allowed herself to relax a little.

'He knows you're here,' Kara said. They stopped briefly to listen to him before rounding the corner to the observation station. Gabriel was sitting there, unsupported, on a Caribbean-themed play mat.

'This little guy has pretty good hearing,' Kara said as she led Eleanor to the chairs which had been placed beside her son.

Eleanor beamed and leant towards him, kissing him gently on his forehead then smoothing down his now thick, sandy-coloured hair.

'How are you, my darling?' she said, prompting a broad smile.

'He's a very responsive little boy,' Kara began, 'And so aware of the world around him?' Her voice got higher towards the end of her sentence, giving it more the air of a question than an observation.

'Yes,' said Eleanor, 'He seems to be interested in everything. I suppose there's just so much to learn at this stage.' She glossed over what she knew had been intended as an opportunity for her to offer more.

Kara nodded and opened the file on her lap, flicking through various observation sheets and charts, each with Gabriel's name in bold print along the top.

'As you know, Eleanor, we have only six babies on this programme, all more or less the same age and living in similar circumstances.'

Eleanor nodded.

'I know this is your first child, but have you had much experience with babies before? I mean, have you had many opportunities to watch them develop over the years? See how things normally unfold?'

Eleanor swallowed back the word '*normally*' with a shiver.

'No, not really. My sister has three children but, to be honest, I was so busy when they were little I didn't take a lot of notice of how they grew or changed,' she said, with an unexpected pang of guilt.

'Well, as I said, we only have six babies here, not exactly a big sample for comparisons, but I have spent the last thirty years working with this age group, and I feel it is my duty to draw your attention to the highly unusual pace of development that Gabriel exhibits.' She looked towards the infant, who was carefully sorting and constructing the coloured blocks around him.

'Fine.' Eleanor held her gaze steadily.

'I'm just telling you, because the management team will be receiving its first detailed report from us tomorrow, and I know they will be asking questions about Gabriel, so I wanted to make sure you were aware of the situation.'

'Of course,' said Eleanor, 'But what does this mean, do you think, for Gabriel, for his future?'

'I'm no expert on these things, Eleanor, but I would have thought that if he continues to develop as he is at the moment, he could have a brilliant future. I mean, it's not just that he is cognitively miles ahead of his peer group; he is physically mature too. Look how well he sits, and he's already making attempts to walk. This is remarkable for an infant of six months. His coordination is very well defined, and his fine motor control is astounding.' Kara nodded towards the perfect column of wooden blocks. 'Socially and emotionally, he seems so calm and confident too. I have never met a child so at ease with himself and the world.'

Kara closed the folder and, sighing thoughtfully, turned back to Eleanor.

'My main concern is whether or not we will be able to stimulate him appropriately, so he doesn't become bored or frustrated. The programme we are required to follow here is pretty exceptional, but it is also very specific and quite, well… rigid. I'm wondering if we should perhaps be organising some more rigorous assessments and seeking advice on how best to meet Gabriel's needs. How would you feel about that?'

'I appreciate your concern, Kara, and I see your point. Perhaps you could write up exactly what you think the current assessments are lacking, and we can look at that more closely in the forthcoming review? But I wouldn't worry too much about Gabriel. He gets plenty of stimulation at home. I think we should just take this one step at a time. He seems happy enough to me at the moment.'

Eleanor reached out to the infant, who had ceased playing and sat regarding them intently.

'Oh, sure, he seems happy, very happy, and I really don't want to cause unnecessary alarm. It's just, there's something… *special* about Gabriel, and I want us to do the very best for him.'

'Thank you.' Eleanor smiled and rested her hand briefly on Kara's arm. 'I do appreciate that. But don't worry; I have every confidence that all will be well.'

***

That evening, Eleanor found it difficult to settle, moving between the kitchen and the living room, starting jobs only to walk away, leaving them unfinished. She couldn't stop thinking about her meeting with Kara and ran over the lines each had spoken. While she felt she had managed to strike the balance between parental concern and professional distance, a deep unease had gripped her. Suddenly, she froze. *That was it!* The nub of the problem.

She'd always known this was an experiment and the child might not present as normal, that she must remain professional in her management of the situation. None of this was, in itself, difficult for her to handle, either as a parent or as a professional.

But had she truly believed she could be both? That she could allow a child to become a mere object of interest? How irresponsible it had been of them to place a child in this position! And Carl had talked so cavalierly about the likelihood of Gabriel's imminent death… Eleanor shuddered as she continued to pace the floor.

A scream from the nursery alerted her to Gabriel's distress, finely attuned, she now realised, to her own. Running to his side, she gathered the sobbing bundle in her arms and kissed away his salty tears, promising to protect him forever, from the suspicions and intentions of others and from the folly of her own ignorance of the power of love.

Chapter 18

When Eleanor arrived at the office the next day, Carl and Allen were already there. Allen rose to his feet as soon as she entered the room and, walking to her with arms outstretched, brushed each side of his cheeks against hers. Over Allen's shoulder, Eleanor could see Carl scrutinise their contact.

'You're looking remarkably fresh for someone who's just weathered a transatlantic flight!' Eleanor stepped back from him.

'You're looking great too, Eleanor,' Allen said, beaming.

'Quite,' Carl joined in. 'Some women never get their figure back after a baby. I suppose that's one of the advantages of a premature delivery.' He allowed his gaze to roam freely over Eleanor's body.

'Lucky old me then,' said Eleanor, guessing things weren't going too well for Carl regarding his attentions to Sophie. 'So, what's new here?'

'Just doing a bit of catching up,' Allen said in a lowered voice. 'I can't wait to hear how things are going. I've had regular updates from Sophie; absolutely fascinating, but not the details of the statistical analysis. I'm preparing my brain for information overload!'

Eleanor forced a mild laugh. 'But remember, Allen, all reactions must be restrained until Sophie leaves the meeting.'

'Of course.' Allen nodded. 'And thanks for your copious notes. This has got to be the most closely observed pregnancy ever.'

'Have you and Simon managed to make anything of it all yet?' asked Carl.

'Quite a bit, but we're nowhere near finished. There's a mountain of data to get through.'

'But what's the story so far?' Carl pressed.

'Well, as far as we can tell, much of what happened throughout your pregnancy was very similar to any normal pregnancy, Eleanor. Your body appears to have undergone the same changes, in more or less the same order, as any other woman. The big difference was the *pace* of everything. So, even though it was much shorter than normal, every physical, hormonal and biochemical change did occur as expected, just at an accelerated rate.'

'Any ideas why?' asked Eleanor.

'I don't know for sure,' said Allen, 'But my guess is that something within the foetus determined the rate of progress, somehow stimulating your reproductive system to respond directly to its developing needs.'

'You mean, hormonal catalysts or something like that, triggered by the baby?'

'Something like that,' Allen replied, 'Although we could say that's more or less what happens in any pregnancy. But in this case, it was almost as if the growing baby took the lead, determining the physiological mood of its own creation.'

'Very poetic, Allen,' Carl sneered, 'But a touch too romantic for my liking. From what you're saying, it sounds as if this developing child could just as easily be seen as a little dictator, taking control of resources for its own ends.'

'Let's stick to what we know,' said Eleanor. She felt panic at this new idea of her son. 'This fast-track pregnancy was designed to produce a fully developed baby more rapidly than happens now. Do you think all pregnancies would have been that quick back then?'

'Possibly,' said Allen, 'Maybe they needed it to be speedy. In a primitive society, they would have lived such precarious lives. It might have been essential to reproduce quickly. And perhaps the question we should be asking now is not why pregnancies were so fast then, but why they've become so much slower now?'

'And the catalysts you mentioned, have you identified them? Are they familiar to us?' asked Carl.

'No idea,' said Allen, 'We have a freezer full of Eleanor's blood samples, but it could take forever to get through them on our own. And we can't risk passing any of this on to the centre's labs, although that would speed things up. We could sure do with Sophie back in Vancouver now!'

'Speaking of Sophie, she's probably already in the meeting room,' said Eleanor.

'Yeah, and Simon too, bleary eyed, waiting for our FaceTime.' Allen rose eagerly and marched to the door as Eleanor and Carl followed.

***

Eleanor sat motionless as Sophie gave her presentation of Gabriel's development. It was not just that she was determined to hide any trace of the pride she was feeling at her son's accomplishments, but she was also stunned by Sophie's delivery. Her handling of the data was thorough and intelligent, demonstrating an excellent grasp not just of the concepts and behaviours under scrutiny, but also of the power and limitations of statistical analysis in its interpretation.

So, in conclusion…' Sophie closed the folder. 'Gabriel is currently functioning beyond the third unit of standard deviation on all measures considered by the research to date.'

Eleanor scrutinised Sophie's face as she sat impassively, waiting for questions. Sophie was no authority on child development, Eleanor knew that, but she was clearly an excellent statistician, and these results, regardless of what was being studied, would surely prompt some sort of reaction. She felt the twist in her stomach tighten.

'Excellent work, Sophie.' Carl took it upon himself to round things up. 'A promising start. You've given us plenty to think about.'

'Yeah, good job, Sophie,' Allen agreed. 'We're a bit short of time today, so no questions at the moment, but I'll catch up with you later.'

Eleanor watched as Sophie packed her papers into a neat bundle and rose to leave. *I've underestimated you, Sophie Ransom,* she thought as the young woman closed the door gently behind her.

'I've never heard of anything like it,' said Allen as soon as Sophie was safely out of earshot, 'He's in the top 0.015 percent of the population for every intellectual, physical, social and emotional measure available to us at present. The child is a prodigy, a true prodigy!' Allen stared at the graphs before him.

'If accurate,' added Carl.

'What on earth does it mean for him?' Eleanor wondered aloud.

'In our society, or in what would have been his own?' asked Allen.

'Maybe he would have been exceptional even in his own time, or perhaps the process of freezing caused something unusual to happen?' Simon suggested, his face filling the screen of Allen's laptop.

'Or maybe they were all like that back then,' said Eleanor, 'He could be just a normal kid.'

'Highly unlikely.' Carl pursed his lips and shook his head. 'I mean, how old did you say this life form was, more than fifty or sixty thousand years? That would just fly in the face of reason and of everything we know about evolution. We need to redo the dating, using Gabriel's DNA.'

'Definitely,' added Simon, 'Find out exactly what kind of a human we've got here… if, indeed, he's human at all.'

'Dear God,' Eleanor murmured, in sharp contrast to the chilling scream that was beginning to consume her inner world.

'We could certainly do with more solid information,' Allen agreed. 'If what we've just heard is accurate, we urgently need to think about where we're going with whoever—'

'Or *whatever*,' Simon cut in.

'—this is.'

'What do you have in mind?' Eleanor tried to sound matter of fact.

'Some sort of… I don't know… risk assessment?' Allen shrugged. 'We suddenly have even less of an idea of what we're dealing with here. Just imagine how unmanageable the situation could become if Gabriel continues to develop at this rate! Before we know it, we could have numerous… *Gabriels* to contend with, not to mention their genetic legacy…'

'Absolutely,' announced Carl, 'Contamination of the gene pool would be impossible to prevent. Unless we can get more specific genetic information, as a matter of urgency, we might not want to hold on to these *stolen goods* for too long.'

Eleanor swallowed against the sudden dryness in her mouth. She wanted to reach for her water but decided against it, fearing the tremor in her hands would give too much away.

'What about your mitochondrial investigations, Eleanor?' asked Simon, 'Couldn't that tell us something?'

'Very much so. These are exactly the sorts of issues my research can address. I feel confident we can get some unequivocal answers to the questions you've raised regarding Gabriel's essential nature.'

'How long will that take?' asked Carl.

Eleanor shrugged. 'As with most research, the correlation between the specificity of information required and time needed to unearth it is usually pretty strong. If we want to do this properly, it will take some time.' Eleanor was relieved she sounded cool and in control.

'In the meantime, any chance of a glimpse of the subject himself?' Allen tidied his papers neatly into his briefcase. 'I can't wait to see him in the flesh. This experiment will seem so much more real then.' *Experiment.* Eleanor shuddered but took care to maintain her composure. 'Certainly,' she said. 'I told Kara to expect a visit.'

'I'm afraid I'll have to leave you to it,' said Carl, 'I've got a conference call from Paris coming through. They're trying to pull me into some grand project they're organising; they need a *figurehead,* apparently,' he preened. 'But we certainly must talk this through some more. What about dinner at my house tomorrow evening? Would that suit you both? Around eight?' He turned to the screen. 'You're done for now, aren't you, Simon?'

Despite her anxiety, Eleanor couldn't suppress a smile as she watched Simon slowly shake his head before logging out of the call.

'Sure,' said Allen.

Eleanor nodded. 'Of course,' she said levelly, 'Thank you.'

***

Kara welcomed Eleanor and Allen warmly and led them into her office, though Eleanor could tell by the way Allen was looking all around him he was paying little attention to what she was saying.

'So, given we restrict access to non-essential visitors,' Kara continued, 'We've made sure to place Gabriel close to the observation window for the duration of your visit.'

Before Kara had managed to fully draw aside the curtain, Allen was at her side, eagerly scanning the room. Eleanor joined him, keen to catch another glimpse of her child. She felt a deep sigh of contentment as she anticipated catching sight of his sparkling eyes and just the thought of his broad smile filled her with pride and joy. She looked forward to seeing the impact that first sight of him would have on Allen.

'So, where is he?' Allen searched the room.

'There.' Eleanor pointed to the child seated only feet away from them, his back turned towards them. She looked from Gabriel to Allen and back again. 'Engrossed in something.' She smiled to herself.

'So, that's Gabriel,' Allen murmured.

Instantly, the infant stopped what he was doing and turned to face them.

'Whoa.' Allen pulled back a step from the window. 'Do you think he heard that?'

'Maybe.' Eleanor smiled and waved at her son.

Gabriel pulled himself to standing and turned to face them. He smiled at Eleanor and waved back.

Allen moved again to the window's edge and peered down at the child. Immediately, Gabriel fixed him in his gaze.

'Good God,' he stammered, 'He's…'

Eleanor turned to face him, to share in his excitement. But instead of the admiration she expected to see, Allen's face had paled.

'Well?' she probed.

Gabriel made his way to the window.

'He's… wow, he's… incredible…'

Gabriel walked cautiously to the spot directly opposite his observers. Behind him, a wooden puzzle had been completed.

'He did that? Amazing…' uttered Allen.

Gabriel seemed to be studying Allen's face, scrutinising each feature in turn. Allen coughed and looked at his watch.

'Gee, I'd better get a move on.' He took a step backwards.

'Bye.' Eleanor waved then blew a kiss as she drew the curtain back across the window, quite sure Allen's back was now turned.

'Who would have thought?' Allen turned to Eleanor as they stood waiting for the lift doors to open.

Eleanor sensed Allen was looking for some sort of emotional response.

'I know,' she replied, without a trace of emotion as the doors closed behind them.

'God, Eleanor, you're doing some job.'

'I just do what any mother would do; it's more demanding than...'

'No, I mean...' Allen interrupted, 'God, what *do* I mean?' He shook his head.

Eleanor didn't move from the lift when its doors opened onto her floor. Instead, she pressed the button that would close them again.

'Well?' She searched his face for a hint of what lay in his heart.

'I mean... don't you find it all a little... disconcerting?'

'Of course!' she exclaimed, 'In fact, there were times during the pregnancy when all I could feel was sheer terror wondering what I was going to give birth to. But since his arrival, I've come to terms with things. He looks so normal, I'm just not as scared, I suppose.'

'He might *look* normal, Eleanor, but clearly, he's anything but. I don't know what I expected to feel, but it wasn't this.'

'Give it time,' Eleanor reassured, 'I'm sure Carl felt the same at first. We can talk it through tomorrow night. I've got loads of data to get through today, so you'll have to excuse me.'

Eleanor opened the lift doors. She had had enough of the conversation and doubted whether she could contain her true feelings much longer. Rushing to the washroom, she shut herself in a cubicle.

'Fuck!' she exclaimed before covering her mouth with her hands, feeling them tremble against her dry lips. 'They're scared, they're backing off… even Allen! Fuck him!'

She sank onto the toilet seat, rocking back and forth, considering her options.

Any hint of persuasion regarding Gabriel's normality from her could, she knew, be counterproductive, possibly pushing them closer to a panic reaction. She had to stay cool.

She rose to her feet and leant on the locked door, pressing her forehead against its cool panel, reaching a decision at last. She would have to try to feed their personal ambitions rather than their private fears; make them believe that research into Gabriel, even for a short time, could pave the way to professional gold and, at the same time, buy her some time to come up with a plan.

Chapter 19

Normally, on a Saturday, Eleanor would take Gabriel to the park. That was their routine. But today, she had resolved to work on the samples Allen and Simon had sent her.

Scientific research had always been her life, her passion, but since Gabriel's birth she found she had developed an aversion to clinical investigations. Just going into the lab now made her think of those early discussions in Vancouver and the emails she had exchanged with Simon and Allen once she told them she was pregnant.

Eleanor remembered nodding as Allen had cautioned her at the start that there would be *nothing normal* about this pregnancy. And she recalled the relief she had felt when he reassured her that whatever happened, she should not feel the full weight of responsibility for any child that emerged.

'Not your property,' he had said firmly. And while no one had specifically put it into words, it *had* been understood, from the beginning, that the continued survival of any experimental life form would be conditional upon its low impact on contemporary society.

She shuddered now at the memory of how they had planned, in abstract, the future of someone they did not know, a real human being they had objectified and assumed ownership of. It was madness. And it all seemed so heartless now; Eleanor no longer recognised her own, dispassionate voice in those past discussions. But had she ever *truly* believed a live being would emerge from all this?

Combing back through all that had happened, Eleanor realised in the beginning her determination to proceed had been mainly driven by her instant attachment to Lillooet; the idea that she might house her child, forge a link between them, womb to womb, the promise of an eternal link with this mesmerising woman.

In fact, she could see now that each of them had been propelled by their own undeclared motivations: Allen craved professional recognition, Simon was driven by intrigue, and Carl, as ever, pursued prestige and money. The three men had no real, emotional attachment to Lillooet, seeing her and the embryo as a means to fulfilling their own ends and while there was, as of yet, no evidence Gabriel could be viewed as any kind of threat to modern man, she knew not one of them would have qualms about acting promptly were that to change.

So, for now, she would have to appease them; she would have to appear, at least for the time being, to be on target with the… *experiment*.

***

'Oh, aren't you getting more handsome every day?' Miriam cooed at Gabriel as he snuggled close to his mother.

Eleanor was standing in the hallway of Miriam's home, with Gabriel in one arm and a bulging bag in the other.

'What are you feeding him, dear?' Miriam half-laughed. 'I don't remember you girls being nearly so well grown at this age.'

Eleanor laughed, hugging Gabriel closer to her. 'Probably a boy thing. Thanks for looking after him today, Mum. I'm a bit behind on a few things.'

'Not at all. It's hardly a sacrifice,' said Miriam.

'And you're sure you're okay about having him overnight?'

'Of course, dear. Please don't worry. We'll be fine. I think it'll be harder for you than for me.' Miriam smiled at her daughter.

'Everything's in the bag.' Eleanor lowered the large holdall onto the floor. 'And if you have any worries, anything at all, Mum, please call me. I'm only going to Carl's for dinner, so I'm not far. But it'll be a bit too late to waken Gabriel and take him home.'

'Honestly, Eleanor, we'll be fine, won't we?' Miriam smiled at Gabriel. 'I'm sure I had all of Olivia's children overnight many times by this age.' She kissed him on the nose

'So, what are your plans for the day then?' Eleanor placed Gabriel on his feet between them.

'Well, Olivia might pop in on her way home from the shops, then I thought we might go to the park and then maybe the library. You'd like that, wouldn't you, sweetheart?'

'Yes!' Gabriel stamped his feet in delight.

Eleanor scrutinised her mother's gaze of amazement.

'How very clever you are, darling.' Miriam crouched down to his height. 'Well, this is all very new.'

'It is,' agreed Eleanor. 'Gabriel has had a couple of things to say this past week. Just thought I'd keep it a surprise for you.'

'My, it's all happening so fast.' She drew herself up to full height. 'Mind you, I'm probably forgetting how you girls were. I couldn't quite believe it when Gabriel tottered between the chair and the settee last week, and look at him now, he's so steady on his feet.'

'Well, I'd better be off, Mum.' Eleanor checked her watch. 'Sorry to leave so quickly, but I'll call later.'

Eleanor lifted Gabriel into her arms for one last hug before leaving.

'I need to go now, Gabriel. Mummy is going to be very busy today. And tonight, you're going to stay with Granny and sleep in Mummy's old room. Then I'll come back for you tomorrow and I'll hear all about the fabulous time you've had. Does that sound good?'

'Yes!' Gabriel hugged Eleanor tightly.

'See you soon.'

Eleanor walked down the path to her mother's gate then turned to wave. She knew they would be at the living room window. Gabriel looked perfectly happy with his gran. She blew him a kiss then closed the gate behind her, determined not to give way to the tears she felt welling up.

As she approached her car, she saw Olivia park across the road. The back door opened and the children scrambled out. Bertie first, as usual.

'Don't push,' she heard Hannah complain.

'Careful,' Olivia called to them, 'And don't cross the road yet. Wait for me.'

Eleanor watched as Olivia gathered up a pile of coats and a carrier bag from the front seat. It was only since having Gabriel she had begun to realise how much time and effort Olivia put into her children.

'It's Aunty Eleanor,' Hannah said, pointing.

Olivia looked over to where Eleanor stood.

'Hi.' Eleanor waved.

'What brings you to this neck of the woods on a Saturday morning then?' Olivia took Beth's hand and crossed the road, ushering Hannah and Bertie in front of her.

'Need to get on with some work today. Mum's taking Gabriel,' said Eleanor.

'*Gabriel* is going to be here today?'

Eleanor thought she saw Olivia recoil.

'Isn't your all-singing, all-dancing nursery open twenty-four-seven then?' her sister continued.

'Oh, ha ha! At least I don't land my entire brood on Mum twenty- four-seven,' Eleanor snapped back.

'You know, I thought you'd give all that obsessive stuff up, now you're a *mother.*' Olivia stared at Eleanor with a blank expression.

'It's my job, Olivia. I can't just give it up. I need to earn something.' She felt her stomach tighten. It was so hard to talk to Olivia. Every comment felt like an accusation.

'But you don't need to work all the hours God sends. What's the point of having children if you don't have time for them?' Olivia looked away as if she was just thinking aloud.

'I don't have time for this.' Eleanor turned to go.

'That's right, do your usual, run away.' Olivia called after her.

'What are you talking about?' Eleanor wheeled around.

'Come off it, Eleanor. You've never had time for anything or anyone except yourself. I'm just surprised that even *Gabriel* hasn't managed to snap you out of it. And you know as well as I do that all that work, work, work is just a big cover. You've done it since you were a kid. You run away from the big, bad world and hide behind your books.'

'Christ, Olivia! What is your problem? Could you not just have said "hi" back to me and left it at that? Well, thanks for the advice on how to run my life, but I'm not sure you're in a position to show me the path to fulfilment. Anyway, Gabriel has just as much right to be here as his cousins.'

'Pfff, *cousins,*' Olivia sneered.

Eleanor felt her blood chill. 'What's that supposed to mean?'

Olivia turned from her sister. 'Give these to Granny, will you?' She handed Bertie the bag, overflowing with crisps, snacks and cartons of juice.

'Let me carry something,' Hannah called out to Bertie as the two girls chased after him, round the side of the house to the garden where there was a door into the kitchen.

'Well?' Eleanor pursued her sister.

'I think this family nest might have had a little visit from the cuckoo, that's all.'

'Olivia! What on earth are you saying?'

Eleanor could see a faint smile on her sister's face.

'I'm sure I'm not the only one to notice how… *different*… Gabriel is.'

'What?' Eleanor could feel her heart thump in her chest.

'I don't think Gabriel is genetically any more yours than mine!' Olivia shrugged as she stared Eleanor in the eye.

'I have no idea what you're talking about. And I don't think you have either.' Eleanor's throat felt so tight she found it difficult to form words.

'You may have had IVF, darling, and you may have been pregnant and pushed that… child… out. But you're kidding yourself if you think I believe you created him. You might be the scientist in the family, but we all know about egg donation!'

Eleanor felt her knees weaken beneath her. *Thank God*. She took a deep breath and composed herself.

'That's fine, Olivia. You believe what you want. I really don't give a damn.' She turned sharply and marched to her car, without waiting for Olivia's comeback.

***

When Eleanor reached the car park, she tried to turn her thoughts to the day ahead, but she still couldn't focus. Olivia's words had terrified her, and the thought others might come to see Gabriel in the same light as her sister, immobilised her with terror.

She unlocked the building's heavy front door and locked it again behind her, before making her way across the tiled hallway to the flight of stairs that hugged the back wall, leading down to the basement. She regretted having waited so long to get started on her part of the Lillooet research, but she hadn't anticipated Gabriel's rapid development, how quickly he would be viewed as *not normal* and how utterly desperate she would feel to protect him.

The basement was a place of permanent twilight. It had no windows so none of the sunlight from the streets ever found its way down there. It was a vast cave occupying the space beneath the three buildings above it and was lit only by pale, thin strips of opaque glass tubes that emitted a constant background hum.

In the past, the lab had felt like Eleanor's territory, a place where she was comfortable, fully herself. Ever since her schooldays, she'd been fascinated by the idea that all living things were made of tiny building blocks, cells, each a world in itself, with patterns of behaviour that determined the nature of its life.

After graduating from Edinburgh with her first class degree in cell biology, she had been one of the few students to be awarded funding to complete a PhD in archaeogenetics in London and she had relished every moment.

She saw herself as an explorer, a crusader for truth. And she had always seen truth as a worthy prize. Simply knowing she had helped to reveal something, to free others from an ignorance or misunderstanding, no matter how small, had often consumed her with a missionary zeal and pride.

But since Gabriel's birth, she realised, she had been shying from truth, anxious it might harbour distasteful consequences. Now, she looked suspiciously upon the ultimate goodness of objectivity and hoped she would uncover only those truths that would protect her son.

She took off her jacket and swapped it for the lab coat hanging on the wall beside her desk. Maybe today, she would discover something that would change the way they saw Gabriel, something that would help her solve the puzzle of his life and, ultimately, perhaps even save it.

Chapter 20

It had been some time since Eleanor last visited Carl's house. When she first started working at the institute, she had been invited to quite a few events there: a barbecue, a Christmas party and other social gatherings. But since she and Carl had begun sleeping together, she hadn't been back. She'd bumped into Carl's wife, Lydia, on a number of occasions but they didn't talk. She felt uneasy now as she made her way to the front door. She didn't know if Lydia knew anything about her husband's infidelity and Carl had regularly mentioned how difficult and unreasonable Lydia could be, so she hoped she wasn't about to become embroiled in anything uncomfortable. She would have preferred a different venue for dinner, but reluctantly understood the need for privacy.

Carl answered the door and led her into the living room where she found Allen already seated, sipping a glass of wine. She noticed how handsome the Canadian looked in his chinos and crisp pink shirt, his skin glowing from years of exposure to the comfortable Vancouver climate. Carl walked to a wine rack that stood against the back wall of the living room and picked out a number of bottles, examining the base of each in turn, selecting only those with the deepest dimple for the table. He may not have invested the time to acquire cooking skills to match Allen's, Eleanor thought, but he did know a thing or two about wine.

He handed Eleanor a large glass of red.

'Your favourite,' he said with a flourish.

Eleanor was glad of the distraction of something to hold.

The door opened and Lydia entered the room.

'Why hello, Eleanor, I didn't hear you come in.'

Eleanor stood up to greet her.

'I hear congratulations are in order.' She pecked Eleanor on the cheek. 'How are you coping, dear?' Her voice sounded warm and genuine.

'Really well, thanks. He's quite an easy baby though.' Eleanor sat back down, relieved the first hurdle, their greeting, had been overcome.

'Well, you enjoy every minute of it. It passes so quickly. And before you know it, they're off to university.' Lydia looked to Carl.

'Yes,' he said. 'How's dinner doing? Should we come through?'

'Exactly what I came to say. I'm serving now.' Lydia smiled and left the room.

***

Eleanor was pleased to find herself seated between Allen and Lydia. She felt more in control of the conversation when she sat opposite Carl and could read his expression, knowing his unpredictable skill for shifting the mood of a conversation in an instant, wrong-footing those less aware in his company.

'So, who's got baby tonight then? Daddy?' asked Lydia, passing round a bowl of roast potatoes.

'No, my mum,' said Eleanor. 'She loves being with her grandchildren.'

'So, does she have him during the day too then?' Lydia pressed.

'No, I managed to get a place for him in the institute's nursery.'

'That's handy. Didn't have any of those in our day, did they, Carl?' Lydia smiled at her husband.

'No, indeed not,' said Carl in a matter-of-fact voice. 'These young mums just don't know how lucky they are.'

'Although, it can't be easy working when your child is still a baby.' Lydia's tone sounded soft and concerned.

'How many children do you have?' Allen asked Lydia.

'Just the two girls, but they've kept us busy enough. Haven't they?' Lydia looked to Carl who seemed lost in his own thoughts.

'Indeed,' he replied. 'Have you read that article, Allen, on how much it costs to raise a child these days?'

The Canadian shook his head as Carl, predictably, began to relate, in minute detail, the story of the article.

Eleanor regarded Lydia out of the corner of her eye. She had never before allowed herself any feelings of guilt about her relations with Carl, convincing herself his wife was either unaware of, or not interested in, his flirtations with other women. Besides, it wasn't as if she had ever wanted Carl to leave his wife for her — the very idea gave her an involuntary shudder. But now as she sat next to Lydia, she noticed the slim frailty of her hands with their faint traces of age spots. Time was passing for them. They'd shared their youth, raised children together and now they should be growing old, peacefully, as a couple. But Carl barely seemed to notice his wife. In fact, he hardly looked at her, even when Lydia spoke to him. Eleanor felt sad and sickened. How, she now wondered, could she so easily have shut out any thoughts about her?

Everything felt so different now. Since having Gabriel, Eleanor was no longer able to block out the feelings of others so readily. And while this made life more complicated, robbing her of her old, useful, easy ruthlessness, it added an emotional depth to her relationships, a dimension and new responsibility of which she had been previously unaware. Thinking now of her younger self, Eleanor felt sure that, should she meet her, she would almost certainly despise her.

As Carl talked on and on, Eleanor looked around the room at the photographs on display. She had been in this room before, but now she noticed the faces smiling out at her. Carl and Lydia as youngsters in ski gear, hugging each other in a snowy landscape. Eleanor guessed from their plump and fresh-faced smiles they had been in their early twenties when the picture was taken. Next to that was a gilt-framed photo of a bashful young Lydia in a 1990s wedding dress, with a slim-looking Carl by her side, dressed in a morning suit. On the mantelpiece was arrayed a series of baby photos, then children in uniform and on the sideboard sat the most recent picture. It looked like a professional family shot, with Carl and Lydia seated together, their teenage daughters on either side.

This is a real family, thought Eleanor, *a family like my own.* She wondered how she would have felt if her own father had been unfaithful and how she would have coped. She felt sick at the thought of how the younger Eleanor would have viewed it all.

Maybe Olivia was right? Maybe she had been a heartless home-wrecker after all.

'Coffee anyone?' Lydia stood up and started to gather in the plates. 'Eleanor?'

'Oh, no, thanks, you're very kind.' Eleanor felt herself blush as she replied. She was grateful for the dimmed lighting, knowing it would hide the truth of what she was feeling. She had never felt so ashamed.

Allen touched her arm. 'So, explain to me again, Eleanor, just how this mitochondrial research of yours works? It's been a while since I read your paper, I'm afraid, and I need to get back up to speed.'

Carl topped up the glasses. 'Lydia?' He raised the bottle in her direction.

'Not for me, thanks.' She smiled. 'This all sounds very interesting, but I hope you won't be offended if I leave you to it. I have a rather good book I'm sure I can hear calling to me from the lounge.'

'Thank you, Lydia. That was delicious.' Allen rose to his feet.

'Can I carry these through?' He reached for his plate.

'Not at all,' she reassured him, 'But thank you for offering. I can easily clear things later.'

Eleanor watched as Lydia slipped quietly out of the room and was reminded for a moment of her own mother. They were so similar, she thought. Each provided the invisible scaffolding of family life upon which had been built the impressive edifice of their husbands' careers.

'So, Eleanor, what can your specific research tell us about Lillooet?' asked Allen, turning his chair towards her as soon as the door had closed behind their hostess.

For the first time that evening, Eleanor had the full attention of both men. She'd rehearsed her lines in the taxi on the way to Carl's, determined to engage their curiosity whilst taking some control of the situation, tempting them with the possibility of scientific treasure.

'Actually, it can tell us remarkable things.' Eleanor adopted her professional voice. 'Children inherit their mitochondrial DNA from their mothers and then pass it on, unchanged, to their children and so on, down through the generations. We can trace a maternal line back through centuries, millennia even, to its initial source.'

'But don't we all come from the same root ultimately?' asked Allen.

'Yes, in Africa,' said Eleanor.

'Mitochondrial Eve.' Carl yawned as if this was old news. 'About one hundred and fifty thousand years ago.'

'Possibly older, actually. More modern estimates put it closer to two hundred thousand.' Eleanor enjoyed being sure-footed in her facts.

'Okay.' Allen shifted in his chair and pulled it closer to Eleanor. 'So, what about Lillooet?'

'Hopefully, we'll be able to get some idea of whereabouts on this timeline she falls and which branch of the tree she comes from.'

'So, *when* will we have this data?' Carl eased another cork out of its bottle.

'I'm working on it now,' said Eleanor, 'With any luck, we should have another piece of the jigsaw to consider shortly.'

'And what a puzzle it's turning out to be.' Allen placed a hand over his glass. 'Any idea how long you'll need?'

'I'm not sure, but so far it's going *rather* well.' Eleanor offered her best Mona Lisa smile. 'And I'm confident that what I will ultimately be able to put before you will be well worth the wait.'

When Eleanor spotted the glint of intrigue in Allen's eyes, she congratulated herself that the bait seemed to be working. But she could see Carl needed more.

'I don't want to jump to conclusions,' she went on, 'But I think we could be on the brink of a significant discovery, the implications of which extend well beyond Gabriel and so could form the basis of quite discrete new research.'

'Nice.' Allen nodded to himself, seemingly savouring his own research hopes.

Carl said nothing.

'Gabriel is… so… *different* from our assumptions,' Allen continued, 'His existence could call into question so much of our established thinking about the evolution of man and—'

'Quite!' Carl interrupted. 'He's not exactly the deficient genetic throwback we anticipated, eh?' He sat back in his chair and stared intently at Eleanor. She noticed the slight curl of his lip as he spoke and wondered what was coming next.

'Indeed not,' said Allen. 'I've spent the last twenty-four hours trying to make some sense of it all, to get over… the shock of seeing him.'

Eleanor tensed further.

'But now,' continued Allen, 'I can't wait to get down to understanding what makes this little guy tick. Can you imagine what secrets his genes could unlock?'

'Exactly!' Eleanor joined in eagerly. 'What we learn from Gabriel's genome could shape the world of genetic modelling. I mean, for example, what parent wouldn't want to buy into a therapy that could comprehensively advance aspects of their child's development? The possibilities could be infinite!'

'So much for Gabriel shedding light on the nature of the intellectual and physical *limitations* of early man!' agreed Allen.

'Well, maybe he was never going to *illuminate* us in that regard for one very simple reason!' Carl placed his glass onto the table with such force that the cups and saucers rattled.

'And that is?' asked Eleanor.

'Maybe he's no more an example of early man than you or I. Maybe he presents no challenge whatsoever to our understanding of human evolution.'

Eleanor was stunned.

'Excuse me?' Allen sat upright.

'Where are you going with this?' Eleanor stammered.

'You read the report on carbon-dating, didn't you?' Allen challenged.

'Oh yes, the *carbon-dating*. What about it?' Carl shrugged. 'Come on, guys. A wild finding like that would normally be tested and retested a hundred times to assess the reliability of such a result. You know it as well as I do. This test was only run, what was it, *once*?'

'Twice, actually, but—' Eleanor started.

'And as for Sophie's stats,' Carl bulldozed on, 'I wouldn't mind running my eye over the details. The results were far too… *neat*… for my liking.'

'Where has all this come from, Carl?' Allen spoke in a low voice.

Eleanor could see his knuckles had turned white.

'Don't get me wrong, Allen, I'd love to believe it, like I'd love to believe in Santa,' Carl scoffed, 'But my gut is telling me otherwise, that either someone is mistaken, or… that you two, and Simon, are viewing the information a little *optimistically*, shall we say?'

'Or maybe,' Eleanor fired back at Carl, 'If we accept, for one moment, that the dating is accurate, that Gabriel is a true example of some ancient tribe, is it beyond our imagination to envisage that some of our ancestors were at least as developed as we are today?' Eleanor looked to Allen for support.

'Rubbish!' Carl shook his head. 'Come on, Eleanor. I think playing out this maternal role is beginning to taint your judgement.'

'On the contrary, Carl, *playing out this maternal role*, as you put it, is costing me a great deal, personally and professionally. And, believe me, I'd be the first to draw a line under it if I thought it was a waste of my time,' Eleanor snapped, smarting from the pain of her own feigned disloyalty towards her son.

'Whoa! Steady on, guys.' Allen put down his glass and stared from Carl to Eleanor and back. 'It's only natural we're going to be challenged by this.' He waved his hand up towards the ceiling and the sky beyond it. 'Surely at this stage, we should be keeping an open mind, considering all the possibilities?'

Eleanor could see Allen was confused by Carl's abrupt change of attitude, but she had seen Carl do this kind of wrecking move before. It was one of the reasons she would have preferred to keep him out of the Lillooet project altogether. Either he was jealous, or he had an ulterior motive which had nothing to do with Gabriel and everything to do with his own personal gain. Perhaps both.

'I think you'll eventually find this whole thing has been blown out of all proportion and is a colossal waste of brain power.' Carl took out his phone and scrolled down the screen as he spoke. 'My guess is that, in a few years' time, there will be a five-centimetre column in one of your local rags, Allen, stating that a body found in the ice on Mount Meagre or whatever it was, has been positively identified as Mavis Somebodyorother, who sadly disappeared after a fancy dress party a few years ago.'

'And everything else is just a coincidence?' Eleanor challenged. 'The accelerated pregnancy, Gabriel's abnormal physical development, his exceptional cognitive skills! And I saw you, Carl, when you…' Eleanor tailed off. She had been going to remind Carl of his reaction to Gabriel's eyes, how he saw instantly that they were unmistakably Lillooet's, but stopped herself, suddenly recognising the escape route this theory of Carl's could offer. 'Of course… okay… yes, it *is* possible.' Eleanor's voice softened. 'You're quite right to look at all possibilities.'

'Fair enough,' added Allen, 'We must make no assumptions. Coincidences happen, as does the unlikely. Our research has to satisfy the rigors of scientific objectivity.'

Carl emptied his glass. 'Anyway, I doubt very much that the nursery project will be funded beyond the one-year trial.'

Eleanor grew cold. 'What?'

Carl smiled, clearly pleased his words had hit their target. 'Management is making the kind of noises that usually precede those of a plug being pulled.'

'And you're just going to let them?' Allen's eyes narrowed.

'Nothing I can do to stop them,' Carl said. 'Anyway, as I said, I say we all take a reality check here. No one on the planet has ever managed the transfer of an ectopic pregnancy to the womb, despite what some of our transatlantic politicians might have tried to argue lately. It's the stuff of fantasy. And you mums have had a pretty good deal out of the free childcare, so everyone's benefited.'

'And Eleanor's pregnancy?' asked Allen.

Eleanor's heart was pounding.

'These things happen. Even after the most fleeting of relationships.' Carl smirked.

'I'm not going to dignify that with a response,' Eleanor said quietly. 'Have you even applied for next year's funding?' She held her hands flat on the table. Everything in her wanted to slap him.

Allen seemed to read her feelings and placed a hand on her arm. 'So, are you saying that will be it? No more nursery, no more research, no more data? Are you *mad*? What about Gabriel?' Allen stared at Carl. 'And the other children?'

'What about them?' Carl shrugged. 'The others are only there as a cover. I'm not interested in their bog-standard development in the slightest. Never was. And if Gabriel turns out to be the contemporary child I now suspect him to be, all this assessment and fuss has been a waste of time.'

'Weren't we just agreeing to keep our options open? Supposing you're the one who's got this wrong, Carl?' Allen pursued him.

'If something should miraculously turn up from Eleanor's research that does suggest he is as *special* as you seem to think, then clearly, at some point, we would have to deal with him. But I rather think we've been spared that… inconvenience because I don't buy into any of this. It's not science it's fiction, science fiction, and I've already wasted enough time on it. As far as I'm concerned, the game's up.'

Deal with him. Eleanor tried not to flinch at Carl's easy talk of the eradication of the life she most cherished. She sat motionless; her face drawn into a fixed mask of disbelief. Yet another Carl masterstroke, the bastard! If she accepted his opinion, told him he was probably right, then the nursery and the research would go. But if she unearthed evidence of Gabriel's uniqueness, then the threat to his life would be ever-present. She was trapped.

She could tell by Carl's casual dismissal of Gabriel's situation he would have no difficulty in taking on the task of *dealing* with him. She hesitated to speak, worried she'd give herself away, but she could not remain silent.

'You really have excelled yourself this time, Carl. I am utterly shocked at your callous lack of concern for everyone else who has invested in this.' She opened her mouth to say more, then pursed her lips and shook her head.

'These things happen, Eleanor, and life goes on.' Carl shrugged.

'I don't get it,' Allen put in, 'You have nothing to lose, or rather, *we* have nothing to lose, by at least putting in an application for continued financial support for the project. I know for certain my department will match it, dollar for dollar, as agreed.'

'Unless, of course, you need the money for some other project that's caught your eye? Paris, perhaps?' Eleanor was fighting to keep her tone level. This had to be it. It was Carl all over.

'Trust me,' said Carl, 'There's no point in chasing after more money for this one. No one *upstairs* is interested.'

'Trust *you*?' Eleanor slammed her fist on the table. 'I don't think so! You've just decided on behalf of us all that this research shudders to a sudden end and you want us to *trust* you? My God, Carl, do you really expect everything to go back to the way it was before, and that things will settle down?' Eleanor tried to secure some eye contact with Carl, but he wouldn't look at her, staring instead at the glass in his hand which he had refilled to the brim.

'There's a child involved in this, Carl,' interrupted Allen, 'And, according to the data which we currently have, a biological mystery to be unravelled. This is a unique opportunity. It could give us the most incredible vision of mankind's earliest history, and yet you seem resigned to denying it and turning away? Quite frankly, I'm lost for words.'

'Look…' Carl leant in towards the other two. 'You really shouldn't take this personally. You know how these funding decisions are made. You should all just be grateful I managed to rein in any resources at all for this project and I have secured a commitment to see the year out. And until then, nursery life, and "research" activities can continue as per—'

'Oh, brilliant,' Eleanor cut in, 'And what do you think will happen as soon as word gets out that the nursery's going to close? Staff will immediately start to look for jobs elsewhere and all the consistency and continuity of the care environment will just fall apart.' Her voice was raised but she didn't care.

'I'm not saying I *want* the project to run aground.' Carl spoke a little more gently. 'I'm just telling you how things stand. We're all too familiar with the shifting sands of research finances. God knows it's hard enough to stay ahead of the game even with the big projects. But when you're looking at a minority interest like this, with scant data and no immediately obvious benefit to any cause or company…' He paused. 'It's pushing it.'

'I'm not buying it, Carl. You've done a deal with finance, I know you have,' said Eleanor, trembling with rage.

Carl waved the notion away.

Allen exhaled sharply. 'Look, let's give ourselves a bit of time to think through the options. This project should be running for, what, another six months?' He was clearly struggling to maintain his customary, tightly controlled tone. 'Leave it with me. Don't say anything to anyone just yet and I'll see if there is anything we can do, funding-wise, to keep things going beyond that.'

Carl said nothing.

Eleanor rose abruptly. 'I'm going home.' She couldn't bear to be in Carl's company a moment longer. Snatching her coat from the back of her chair, she marched to the door and slammed it shut behind her.

All the way home, she stared out from the taxi window onto the leafy suburbs of Carl's life and loathed it all. She thought about Olivia's cruel words earlier that day, then Lydia's face and the sudden guilt she had felt. It all crashed down upon her at once, like snow from an avalanche. She felt drained and confused, tired of everything and everyone.

Apart from Gabriel.

The thought of him needing her, looking for her, crying for her, slowly brought her back to full strength as the taxi weaved through the late evening traffic.

An idea was seeding itself in her mind. A terrifying, hopeful idea. Perhaps she would leave them all, start again somewhere else. A life of glorious anonymity for them both, mother and son! *Safety*!

But then, she reasoned, could she really do that? On a practical level, of course, she was hardly the first to raise a child on her own. But would they have anonymity? If Gabriel continued his fast-track development, how long would it be until people pointed it out? Before teachers questioned his uniqueness? Doctors? What if he became unwell with something she couldn't handle? Without a team around her, their anonymity could soon turn into isolation and what would be the point of that? Why drag a life across millennia, away from its eternal resting place within his natural mother, to face the sterility and uncertainty of such an existence?

'No,' she announced emphatically to herself as she turned the key in her apartment door. She would not do that to Gabriel, to herself or to Lillooet.

And lying alone in bed that night, the room hollowed by the absence of her son, Eleanor visited again her vision of Lillooet and the gift of Gabriel she had entrusted to her. She felt held by Lillooet's silent presence and comforted, as if she herself was cocooned within Lillooet's womb. She felt her breathing settle and knew she would find a way to keep him safe. All would be well.

Chapter 21

Eleanor longed to be with her son again and, after a restless night, arrived on her mother's doorstep half an hour earlier than their prearranged time of eleven o'clock.

'Hello, my little darling!' she exclaimed, whisking Gabriel into her arms and kissing him on the cheek. 'Have you had a wonderful time with Granny?'

'Yes!' He nodded eagerly, his soft sandy hair falling across his clear, smooth brow.

'He was good as gold,' Miriam said, smiling.

'What did you do?' She sat him on her hip and followed her mum into the kitchen. It was only then that she spotted Beth, balanced on a stool by the sink.

'We've been to the park,' said Beth.

'Hello, Beth. Wow, that sounds like fun! And are you helping Granny with the dishes?'

'Yes, I am,' she replied, sweeping her hair off her face and leaving a cloud of bubbles on her forehead. 'And I watered the plants in the garden, and I helped Granny put the washing machine on, and I didn't argue and cry like Bertie and Hannah.' She reeled off her accomplishments, practical and moral.

'Well, aren't you a clever girl?' said Eleanor. 'Oh dear, Mum, sounds like you've had a busy time.'

'Oh, it's been fine, dear. Edited highlights always lend a sense of drama to the mundane.'

'Sorry anyway. I didn't realise Olivia was leaving the children with you this weekend as well. I would never have left Gabriel for so long if I'd known.'

'Oh, nonsense, Eleanor, you make it sound like a burden and you know that I like nothing better than a full nest.' She lifted Beth from her precarious perch at the kitchen sink.

'When will Olivia be back?' Eleanor hoped she could leave before her sister arrived. The last thing she wanted was for them to argue again, especially in front of their mum. But she couldn't imagine being civil to Olivia, not yet.

'I'm not sure.' Her mother glanced at the clock. 'I think she has rather a lot going on today.' Miriam sighed.

'Mummy was crying,' Beth said nonchalantly.

Eleanor's stomach lurched. 'What a shame,' she said. 'Maybe she's not feeling very well.'

The two women exchanged pained glances.

Eleanor turned Gabriel to face her. 'What did you do at the park?' She bent towards him, their noses touching.

'We went on the swings and the slide, didn't we?' Miriam said.

'Feed ducks,' Gabriel announced, beaming.

Miriam clapped her hands. 'Why, indeed we did! My, my, *two* words. You are such a fast, little boy. You know I think you are going to be even more clever than your mummy!' Granny laughed. 'And that's saying something!'

'Is my mummy clever too?' Beth tugged at her granny's skirt.

'Why yes, of course she is,' Miriam reassured the child. 'However else do you think she managed to have three such wonderful children?'

'Are three children more clever than one children?' asked Beth.

'Well…' Her granny hesitated. 'I suppose it means she has been very clever three times.'

'Our mummy's very clever, because she's got three children, not just one.' Beth ran to inform her siblings.

'Oh dear.' Miriam frowned. 'Not my best effort, I fear. That's not quite how I meant it.'

'That's a five-year-old's view of the world, Mum.' Eleanor laughed. 'And anyway, maybe she just heard what she needed to hear and surely that can't be so bad? Sounds like Olivia's not too happy.'

'Charles is seeing someone else,' Miriam whispered.

Eleanor did not know what to say.

'I thought things were getting better, that maybe there was a reconciliation of sorts on the horizon. I suspect Olivia thought that too. She was a little perkier last week. But… apparently not.'

'Oh dear. Poor Olivia. Even when you think a relationship is over, it's still hard to face that kind of rejection,' said Eleanor.

'We'll just have to help all we can,' her mother said. 'I'm so very glad you're around these days, Eleanor, even if the two of you…'

Miriam stopped talking as Hannah threw the door open and marched in.

'Granny, Bertie won't let anyone else choose what's on the television and we don't like car programmes!' she cried, her face flushed and shiny, not yet registering her aunt's presence.

'Hello, Hannah. Have you had your hair cut?' Eleanor asked.

Hannah nodded reluctantly.

'Let me see.' Eleanor placed Gabriel on the floor. 'My, you really suit it like that. Do you remember how I used to wear my hair at that age, Mum?' Eleanor approached the distressed child.

'How could I forget?' Granny laughed. 'I had to get you out to school in the morning and you would insist on your hair being just so.'

'Have you got a brush and some bands, Mum? How would you like me to give you the very special hairstyle I always wore at your age, Hannah?' she asked the little girl. 'I used to call it my lucky hairstyle.'

Hannah nodded a cautious assent, reluctant to abandon entirely her righteous complaint, but drawn towards her aunt's uncharacteristic attention to her.

Miriam rummaged around in a drawer and produced a hairbrush with several coloured hair ties wrapped around its handle.

Eleanor stood behind Hannah and gently swept the tangle of hair off her face, gathering it up into one thick bunch at her back. She eased the brush down through the auburn locks.

'I think your hair is going to be just like mine when you grow up,' said Eleanor.

'Yes.' Miriam looked over. 'It's certainly the same colour. Not Gabriel though.' Her eyes rested on the little boy.

'Too early to call that one I'd say. But you, Hannah.' Eleanor steered away from talk of Gabriel's appearance. 'You have inherited the beautiful Bartlett locks. You lucky thing!'

Hannah smiled and wiped a hand across her damp face, trailing with it the marks of her distress. Eleanor brushed, firmly now but still gently, with a soothing rhythm and felt, with a glow of pleasure, Hannah relaxing into the moment, succumbing to the seductive comfort of grooming. From the annals of her own childhood, Eleanor heard herself humming a playground tune as she drew the brush down through the newly gleaming hair.

'I know that one, Aunty Eleanor.' The little girl turned to her with joy in her eyes as she proceeded to sing along. And as she fixed her in her trusting gaze, Eleanor felt warm tears prick her eyes; tears of happiness for the moment, of sadness for missed opportunities and for the dawning of what she knew to be a new and very different bond with her sister's child.

Gabriel, on the floor at her feet, looked up from the colourful book he was holding and smiled. *He* was the source of this new love, he had opened the door to this powerful depth of feeling within her and, she suspected, he was conscious of it.

***

That night, after tucking Gabriel into bed and placing kisses all around his beautiful face, Eleanor searched through the cupboard in the hall where she stored those things that, in a house, would have found space in the attic. Things one did not want ready access to but would find it difficult to part from entirely. Eventually, she found what she was looking for: an old photograph album. She eased it out from its place in the pile of abandoned clutter. She curled up on the settee and folded back the impressive front cover.

It was an old-fashioned book, with sheets of faintly patterned tissue separating each display, like curtains waiting to rise upon a stage, each semi-opaque film prompting that same delighted anticipation. Her mum had given it to her shortly after her dad's death, and while Eleanor had appreciated the gesture, she hadn't looked at it since, believing her most treasured memories were stored in her heart, not on scraps of paper. But something about Hannah, her eyes, perhaps, as she turned to look up at Eleanor earlier that day, had triggered off a cascade of memories, faces from the past. And now, as she turned the pages, each faded image greeted her like an old friend; loved ones gazed at her, coaxing smiles and sighs, posing long forgotten questions with their unblinking eyes.

Like an archaeological dig, the photos emerged from the past in definable strata, the grandparent era, her parents as children, their wedding and early days, until eventually, the arrival of their children. Eleanor sank into this other world as pictures of two became pictures of three and then four, with a broad-smiling Olivia being helped to hold baby Eleanor on her knee. Then on through their childhoods, with baby faces becoming toddler faces, until toothy gaps appeared and unself-conscious grins became smiles, half-suppressed, as adolescence blossomed.

Eleanor traced the faces with her finger: her father, her mother, her sister, herself. She loitered awhile on the pictures of Olivia and noticed for the first time how like her at that age Hannah was now. Flicking back to the first photos, Eleanor sought out her own mitochondrial line, from maternal grandmother, through her mother, to Eleanor and Olivia. They were connected, all of them, like threaded pearls floating in a primordial sea, their connecting string hidden from view.

As Eleanor flicked to the back page of the album, a more recent photo lay loosely between the leaves of an otherwise blank page. Olivia and her three children standing in front of her mum's front door. It was a few years old now, Beth still a babe in arms.

And so, the string of pearls grows. Eleanor drew an imaginary line from Olivia through each child in turn. She thought of Gabriel and tried to imagine his image, pressed upon the same page, gazing through the thinning tissue, staring into her eyes. It was not only his appearance that would single him out. He would never be part of the cord that connected all the others. Her only physical tie to Gabriel, she knew, had been severed at birth.

Surprising herself by the depth of her sigh, she was called sharply back to the present by the ping of her phone, alerting her to a text message. It was from Allen.

Hope not disturbed you. Am away tonight but would like to talk before then. You free now?

Eleanor consulted her watch. It was eight o'clock.

No problem. She added her address, pressed send and put on the kettle.

She knew they had to talk and come up with some sort of a plan, but she wasn't ready for the conversation yet. She had no idea what she would do if the nursery closed.

It wasn't long until he arrived.

'So sorry to barge in on you like this. Hope I didn't waken the little guy, tried to knock as gently as I could.'

'Don't worry about Gabriel. He's as much an angel at night as he is during the day. He sleeps like a log. Drink?'

'Sure.' Allen handed her the wine he'd been clutching.

She poured two glasses and returned to the living room. She felt nervous, expecting questions about her plans. Questions she couldn't answer.

'I was wondering if we'd be able to meet up before you had to go.' She sat opposite him and sipped from her cautious measure.

'Yeah, it would have been too bad to leave things as they were after dinner at Carl's. But I'll get to the point. Frankly, I was shocked by Carl's behaviour last night. He's not an entirely predictable operator, if you don't mind me saying so.'

'Don't hesitate to speak your mind, Allen. Nothing you have to say about Carl could offend me,' she said.

'Well, I want to put something to you, something for you to think about over the next week or so, no pressure. But I've made a few preliminary enquiries and, if you were interested, it might be possible to arrange for you to spend some time at the research centre in Vancouver.

'I'm not sure yet what the terms would be, but I do know our people are very impressed with your work and would be honoured to have you on board, as would I, not to mention my interest in having closer contact with Gabriel. As I said, you don't need to say anything yet and nothing is guaranteed at present, but if you might be interested, then I'll make it my priority to progress things when I get back.'

Eleanor said nothing for a while. She sat quietly, letting the idea sink in.

'Thank you. I'd really have to think that over, Allen. Not that I'm dismissing the idea.' She rose to her feet and, walking to the window, gazed down at the familiar scene below She pictured her mother's stoic acceptance of such a decision, followed, she knew, by private tears, and flinched at the thought of living up to Olivia's taunts about running away from her difficulties.

'I just have to think what would be best for Gabriel.'

'Of course,' Allen replied, 'And for you, Eleanor. Back at the research centre, we would be able to continue monitoring his development and, hopefully, put into place provisions as appropriate: educational, health or whatever.'

Eleanor nodded.

'And it would ease Carl out of the frame. I don't trust that man. It might look like he's walking away now but I'm convinced he'd burst back onto the scene if there was even the faintest whiff of success.'

Eleanor knew he was right, and it was a sensible suggestion; in many ways it would offer solutions to issues that had been troubling her. In Canada, they would be anonymous, and no one would need to know Gabriel's true age. There would be fewer questions and he would be safer, away from those who felt entitled to question and pry, especially Carl, who had many an axe to grind and no conscience about collateral damage.

She knew that, to him, Gabriel was a mere commodity in which they each had an equal share, and he had no intention of giving his up unilaterally. He had already made casual references to the child's *dispensability* and Eleanor knew that despite his dramatic announcement of the previous night, so long as Gabriel was alive, so his interest would be also.

'I'm afraid I need to go.' Allen looked at his watch. 'Sorry this is so rushed, but I'm actually en route to the airport.'

'Of course.' Eleanor pulled away from the window and walked towards him. 'I'll definitely think about it, Allen. I'd have to be sure.'

'No problem.'

Eleanor walked with him to the door, closing it gently behind him.

She returned to the settee. Allen's suggestion had taken her by surprise. It was certainly a tempting offer, but was it the right thing and could she do it to her mum? She closed her eyes and instantly the faded images from the album filled that space in her mind she had sought to clear. She knew Gabriel could never be one of them, another gleaming pearl in her family line, but in Canada she could hold him close and spin for him a safety net that would bind him to her and hopefully, in time, to her family.

They would remain attached forever by an umbilicus forged from love; one no man could ever sever.

Chapter 22

There was an uncharacteristic buzz at the nursery on Monday morning. Parents, who normally settled their children before hastily departing, huddled in a group in the corridor, talking in rushed whispers. Eleanor nodded briefly to the familiar faces and instantly read their unease. Something was up. Eleanor wondered if rumours about closure had already circulated — she wouldn't have put it past Carl to make sure he was first to break the story.

But as she approached them, the most animated of the group stopped talking while another glanced towards Eleanor, her flat expression telling her all she needed to know.

Dear God, she thought, *this has something to do with me.*

Eleanor held Gabriel closer to her and braced herself for whatever was to follow.

Before she had a chance to settle Gabriel down to play, Kara appeared, beckoned her into the office and closed the door firmly behind them.

'I'm so sorry,' Kara began, 'I have absolutely no idea how this has happened, but I'm quite certain it has nothing to do with any member of my staff.'

'I don't know what you're talking about, Kara.' Eleanor placed Gabriel on the rug at her feet and handed him a colourful pop-up book from the shelf.

Kara took a copy of the local paper, the West End View, out of her drawer and slipped it across the table to Eleanor.

'Experimental Nursery Turns Infants into Einsteins!' screamed the headline. Aghast, Eleanor began to read.

The West End View can exclusively report that a local childcare facility located within one of the city's universities has been employing special techniques to promote a hot-housing effect in the intellectual development of tiny babies. Reports suggest that the programme includes feeding the babies superfoods and one unconfirmed report claims the department involved is in the process of developing a drug to make our babies bigger and brighter...

Eleanor read on, her eyes darting from line to line, terrified of what she might read next. Then, as she neared the end of the article, she froze.

One little star, reportedly angelic by name and by nature, has, our source reports, already been offered a generous contract to be the face of a range of soon-to-be-launched miracle products.

Reeling, Eleanor pushed the paper back across the table. 'But this is ridiculous! It's simply not true!'

'We know that, but people love a good story.' Kara folded the paper and returned it to the drawer. 'I've asked all the parents not to talk to the press, but I can't guarantee anything,' she continued.

'Of course,' Eleanor whispered.

'What I mean, Eleanor, is that I can't guarantee Gabriel's anonymity.' She fixed Eleanor in her gaze. 'Because, as I'm sure you will have realised, they mean him. There's a pretty big clue in the piece.'

Eleanor nodded slowly, picking Gabriel up and hugging him close.

From the street below, she heard a raised voice and followed Kara to the window. A young man, brandishing a camera, stood at the bottom of the stone steps that led to the main entrance, a university security guard at his side.

'Obviously, he is safe from prying eyes in here,' Kara went on, 'But I think you should be careful.'

***

Eleanor waited until the knot of parents had undone itself and returned to their desks, bursting, she imagined, with gossip that could cause this uncomfortable interest in Gabriel to spiral out of control. Once safely back in her own department, she headed for Carl's office, overruling her earlier determination to give him a wide berth today.

From beyond the closed door, Eleanor could hear Carl whistle a tune to himself. He sounded smug, self-satisfied and, in her rage, she decided against any formality, pushing the door wide open and marching in.

'Was it you?' She glared at him.

Carl was at his desk, the West End View splayed before him.

'Calm down, Eleanor. You knew this was on the cards. Maybe someone has done us all a favour by bringing it to a head so quickly.'

'Oh, I see, so maybe someone who knew that funding just might be withdrawn soon, decided that a sudden death might free up the cash a bit more quickly for another pet project?'

'That's what I call truly delusional, Eleanor.' Carl didn't take his eyes off the paper as he spoke.

'No, that's it, isn't it? I'm right! You made the call to some pathetic little journalist friend of yours, desperate for any shit story, didn't you? And why? Because you're tired of this whole thing and maybe you are more than just a little bit jealous.'

'Jealous?' Carl looked up at Eleanor and shook his head in apparent bemusement. 'You're not only very wrong, Eleanor, you're quite insane. What have I got to be jealous of?'

'Jealous perhaps of Allen's integrity, of my happy independence from you and of Sophie's attraction to men her own age!'

Carl's jaw tightened. Eleanor was glad to see she'd hit her mark.

'You really are pathetic, Carl,' she said levelly, 'You strut about this place as if you were a Nobel Prize winner. But you're nothing special at all, not in *any* department.'

Eleanor watched as Carl's face fired red with fury. He slammed his fist on the table and opened his mouth to speak. But before he had the chance to reply, she had stormed out through the wide-open door.

Tom, Kyle and Jane watched, open mouthed, as Eleanor pulled her jacket from the back of her chair, snatched up her bag and strode to the door.

Heart pounding, she made her way to the nursery. She had to get Gabriel away. As she hurried down the corridor, she could see everyone else looked quite normal, getting on with their work as if it was the most ordinary day in the world. But she had made up her mind. She would take Gabriel to her mother's.

***

When she entered Kara's office, she found Kara and Sophie in sombre conversation.

'I'm sorry to interrupt,' Eleanor began, 'But I think I should take Gabriel home, while the wolves are at bay.' She attempted a light- hearted tone.

'I think that would be for the best.' Kara nodded. 'At least for a day or two until all this fuss calms down. Anyway, Gabriel doesn't seem to be himself this morning. He's been fretting ever since you left — maybe he's brewing something.'

'Perhaps, although he seemed perfectly well this morning.' Eleanor knew exactly why he was distressed: he sensed what was going on.

'Is there anything I can do to help?' Sophie asked.

'Yes, thank you,' said Eleanor, 'Perhaps you could slip Gabriel out by the fire exit while I go for the car? I could pick him up just outside the library?'

'A wise precaution, Eleanor,' Kara said.

'I'm so sorry,' Eleanor said.

Kara smiled. 'Don't worry. It's only a local rag so I doubt there will be much interest beyond today. There are no facts to back up the story.'

'That might be true, but since when has the truth offered protection from media intrusion?' Eleanor replied as she hurried to the door.

Within minutes, she was in her car. The streets were busy with students and shoppers. With a surge of relief, she saw Sophie walking towards her, hugging the infant close. Eleanor jumped out and opened the back door, lifted Gabriel from Sophie's arms and strapped him into his car seat.

'I'm so sorry for all this,' Sophie said.

'What on earth do you have to feel sorry for, Sophie? Unless you're telling me you're the one who called the press?'

Sophie shook her head, her distraught expression telling Eleanor all she needed to know. She was telling the truth.

'I'm sorry you've been dragged into all of this,' Eleanor went on, 'Research wasn't meant to be like this, was it?'

***

When she pulled up at her mother's house, Miriam was in the front garden, filling terracotta pots with colourful plants. She looked delighted to see her daughter.

'What a lovely surprise!' Miriam said as Eleanor carried Gabriel up the garden path to his granny. She laid down the trowel beside a large bag of compost and pulled off her gardening gloves. 'To what do I owe this pleasure?' She lifted the child from his mother's arms and hugged him.

Eleanor had decided during the drive she would tell her mother there was a tummy bug going around the nursery, but at the last minute she decided against spinning that yarn, opting instead for an understated version of the truth.

'Just a bit of a kerfuffle at the nursery, Mum, nothing to worry about, but I thought it might be better to steer clear for a while.'

'Really?' Miriam sounded surprised. 'What kind of a kerfuffle?'

'Just nursery politics…' Eleanor faltered.

'Politics? In a nursery?' Miriam's brow furrowed.

'Just a stupid article in the local paper, making out the nursery's a breeding ground for child prodigies. A lot of nonsense. It's sure to blow over soon enough.'

'Really? So, did all the parents take their children home?'

'Those who could arrange an alternative did. No one wants their child caught up in that sort of nonsense. Where on earth they got the idea from God only knows, interfering—'

'Oh dear…' Miriam interrupted. She placed Gabriel on the grass and brought a trembling hand to her forehead.

'What is it?' Eleanor watched as her mother paled, suddenly looking much older than her sixty years.

'I do hope this has nothing to do with that rather inquisitive lady we met at the park on Saturday.'

Eleanor froze. 'What was this? Did you mention it to me?'

'No, I didn't think it was important at the time. I just put it down to natural curiosity…'

'So, who was this woman and what did she say?' asked Eleanor.

'I have no idea, and she didn't say much at all, but she did ask such a lot of questions. She wanted to know how old Gabriel was and then raved about how advanced he was for his age.'

'What else did she ask, Mum? Did she ask about Gabriel's nursery or anything?'

'Yes… she did… and I think I said that being at nursery always brought children on, especially one like Gabriel's where they're very careful about diet and routine…'

'Go on, please.' Eleanor could see her mum would rather end the conversation there.

'Then she asked where it was, because she might send her children there if it was so good,' her mother recalled in some distress. 'I'm so sorry if I spoke out of line, Eleanor, but a child like Gabriel is always going to attract attention…'

'A child like Gabriel? What is that supposed to mean, Mum?' Eleanor could hear an edge to her voice she had not intended.

Miriam flushed. 'I only mean that he is such a beautiful and clever little boy that he's bound to... stand out. Surely you've noticed?'

'Noticed *what*?' Eleanor challenged.

'Nothing bad, darling. He is the most delightful child ever... but he is, well, different from the others. Don't you think?' Miriam took a step closer to her daughter and placed a hand on her arm. 'Different in a good way,' she added.

'Of course, I've noticed.' Eleanor forced a smile. She looked into her mother's eyes and wanted more than anything to be wrapped in her arms, protected as she always had been as a child and reassured all would be well. But she was a mother herself now, and she had to be strong.

'That's just the way his genetic dice have landed; his lot in life,' said Eleanor, 'And it's my job to protect him and help him to be the happiest little person he can be.'

Miriam placed her arms around Eleanor and held her close.

'Of course, it is. And it's a job you do extremely well.' Miriam kissed Eleanor's cheek.

'I should be going.' Eleanor looked over to Gabriel, who was watching them closely.

'Of course, darling.' Miriam's voice sounded calmer again. 'Don't worry; this will pass.'

Eleanor gave Gabriel one last hug before walking to her car and waved to them as she drove off, Gabriel perched on his granny's hip, her mum smiling and blowing her a kiss, as if nothing had changed. But as she drove away, she knew a corner had been turned and from now on everything would be different. No matter how hard she tried, she would not be able to disguise Gabriel's uniqueness from those around him. Stemming the flow of questions and investigations was already moving beyond her control. She would have to make changes, big changes, to their lives. Whatever else, she must ensure this unfortunate trail went cold, and did so quickly.

Chapter 23

Eleanor was relieved when Gabriel fell asleep shortly before their arrival in Vancouver. By the time they were passing through airport controls, he was in his pushchair, still fast asleep and looked more like the infant depicted on his passport photo, rather than the toddler he had become.

As soon as she'd collected her bags, Eleanor looked for the cab Allen had organised and as they drove off, Gabriel woke up and began to take an interest in his new surroundings. Glasgow's dull October morning had become a warm, bright, cloudless Canadian afternoon and before long, they were speeding along a wide highway that carried them north across a high bridge.

Gabriel peered down at the water below them. 'Ocean?' he asked.

'Fraser River,' the taxi driver said. 'First time in BC?'

'Yes,' Eleanor fibbed.

'Sure is a lot to see here.' He began to list his recommendations, far too quickly for Eleanor to keep up.

Soon, they left the commercial district and quite suddenly a view of the mountain peaks opened up in the distance. Eleanor gasped.

'They're quite something, eh?' the driver called back.

Gabriel shot to attention and, wriggling free from his seatbelt, knelt on the chair and pressed his face as close as possible to the glass. Eleanor could see his reflection, his eyes wide, his mouth moving as if he was speaking. But his silence told her these were words he did not wish to share.

After a few minutes, Gabriel held out his hand towards Eleanor, his eyes still fixed on the rugged, white-iced mountains.

'Home,' he said.

Eleanor stopped stroking the small hand, now cupped by her own. 'What was that?' She leant closer towards him.

'Home.' He turned to look at Eleanor, his smiling eyes sparkling as if mesmerised.

'You wanna go home, kid?' The driver laughed. 'You just got here!'

Gabriel glanced at the driver then at his mother. She had noticed recently that his speech seemed to regress when they had company, unlike their times alone together, when he was now able to communicate with her quite fluently.

'Home,' he whispered to her.

Eleanor felt her heart lurch. *What did he mean?* She studied his face, and for a fleeting moment imagined he no longer looked familiar. He was staring into her eyes, the cornflower blue colour more dazzling than ever.

I'm being ridiculous, she told herself, *projecting my own feelings onto Gabriel. He doesn't know anything about this place…*

'Yes, home, darling.' She sat up and smiled at her son, aware the driver was listening. 'We'll soon be in our new home.'

***

After a while, they turned off the highway and travelled along a narrow road lined on either side by open fields. Sophie had provided her with a meticulously curated list of accommodation options, and Eleanor had chosen to live in an apartment on the edge of a new development. She guessed her neighbours would be commuters, mostly single or childless, as was the case in similar locations around Glasgow, so any fleeting contact she might have with them would, she hoped, benefit from their lack of experience with children.

'This is it.' The driver pulled into a paved area in front of an apartment block.

It was four stories high and sat on its own in a plot of rough grass. About two hundred yards behind it, Eleanor could see a similar development was being built, although no one seemed to be working on it. All she could see was a digger and piles of materials.

'Need a hand with this?' the driver asked as he lifted the case from his trunk.

'No, I'll be fine.' She counted out the unfamiliar Canadian dollars.

Pushing the buggy with one hand and wheeling her case with the other, Eleanor made her way along a paved walkway that cut through a stretch of grass towards their new home.

They took the lift to the third floor, where four identical doors were spaced evenly on either side of a narrow strip of dark red carpet. There seemed to be too many doors for the length of the corridor, and Eleanor began to worry her apartment was going to be tiny. But when she walked in, she found herself in a bright and airy space, filled with sunlight that flooded in from the lounge window, which lay straight ahead of her. It was a large room, the smell of fresh paint and new carpets still in the air, and almost the entire wall facing her was made of glass. The view beyond it seemed to stretch out forever across uninhabited grassland, to a densely wooded area that sat below a jagged backdrop of still more towering, snow-capped mountains.

Eleanor lifted Gabriel out of the buggy and followed as he ran to the picture window.

'Wow!' he exclaimed, clambering up onto the low sill.

'Wow indeed,' Eleanor agreed. 'I think I can live here!'

'Me too.' Gabriel pressed himself flat against the glass.

'So, you like this place?' Eleanor crouched down beside her son.

Gabriel just smiled and nodded. Suddenly, he turned to Eleanor. 'Is Granny coming too?'

Eleanor drew a hand to her chest as if to soften the blow to her heart. She forced back the tears that threatened to rise as she replied.

'No, darling.' She wrapped her arm around him. 'I'm afraid Granny needs to stay in her own home. She has so much to do there. But we can write to her and email her and...' Eleanor struggled to think of more ways of keeping in touch that wouldn't involve Granny seeing or hearing her rapidly developing grandson.

'I love Granny.' Gabriel turned back to face the view.

'So do I,' she just managed to say.

Eleanor was grateful when Gabriel wandered off to explore the apartment. Staring at her own reflection, she followed the trails of her tears, salty tramlines that seemed to etch a new pathway, perhaps the one she was now on, without knowing the destination.

Eventually, she dragged her gaze back to the interior of the apartment and to Gabriel who was now darting around opening cupboards and drawers, casting anxious looks in all directions.

'Are you looking for your toys, darling?'

'Yes!' he cried, tugging at her sleeve. 'Are they coming?'

'They should be here already. Let me have a look.' Eleanor searched around for the two large boxes she had sent over in advance, keen to help her son settle in as easily as possible.

She had only packed a few of their belongings, mostly Gabriel's. All things of value were stored at her mother's house, leaving only essential furnishings in place for the newly installed tenants of her Glasgow flat.

'Look! Here they are.' Eleanor walked through to the kitchen area and spotted the containers with *Bartlett* and their new address in bold print across them. 'Let's open these up and get this place organised.'

Gabriel rummaged through the box until he found his favourite blanket, a patchwork of colourful squares knitted for him by Granny. Eleanor bit her lip as she watched him haul it out, hold it to his face and smell it.

'Why don't you put that on your bed, make it cosy for your first sleep here?'

Gabriel nodded and, folding the woollen memory carefully in his arms, trotted off to his bedroom.

Eleanor sensed he needed time alone, so she did not follow him but instead threw herself into the task of creating order and comfort. She walked to and fro, placing the remnants of her old life upon their new stage. First, she unpacked Gabriel's clothes. She hadn't brought much for him, knowing nothing would fit for long enough to justify shipping them across the Atlantic. He was growing so rapidly he sometimes only wore things once or twice before Eleanor had to pass them on.

When Gabriel reappeared, he went straight to the box of toys. Eleanor tipped it onto its side and a landside of treasures tumbled out. Gabriel seemed happy to explore its contents, rejoicing at times at new discoveries, as if meeting up with old friends. Eleanor watched, enjoying his delight. Then she saw him stretch in and pull out a gift- wrapped box.

'What's this, Mummy?' Gabriel carried it to her. He sat on the floor at her feet and drew his finger along the paper caravan of reindeer, flying in a twinkly sky, hauling a sleigh laden with toy-filled sacks.

'Ah,' said Eleanor, sitting down beside him, 'That's for later.'

She waited until he had had his fill of the magical scene and wandered away before lifting the parcel and sliding it to the back of the high shelf in her wardrobe. She remembered there was a similar package in another box, papered with teddies holding birthday cakes. She would look for it now and hide that too. Eleanor had suggested to her mum that shipping Christmas and birthday gifts with the rest of Gabriel's toys would save her the expense of sending them later and reduce the chance of them going missing in transit.

Since deciding on the move, she had spent many a wakeful night devising strategies that would conceal the truth about Gabriel's precocious development. She knew her mum would want photos and regular updates, so had decided to chart his progress in virtual time, creating a chronology of events that might pass as believable. It would be complicated, she knew, and would require careful planning. Soon, she would stage Christmas and birthday celebrations, the photos of Gabriel opening these gifts to be posted in two months' time.

When the boxes were finally empty, Eleanor could see Gabriel was slowing down he was tired and hungry. They would go somewhere to eat then back home to bed. She called a cab. Tomorrow, she would hire a car and drive to the research centre for the first full day of their new lives.

***

The hire car was delivered right on time the next morning.

'Are we going out?' Gabriel asked, jingling the keys in his hands.

'Yes, we are!' Eleanor kept her tone as breezy and confident as possible, though when Gabriel slipped a small hand into hers as they made their way to the door, she had a feeling he was reassuring her, rather than the other way round.

Soon, they were speeding along the highway. The roads were quiet, a welcome change, Eleanor thought, from the start-stop of Glasgow city driving. Gabriel stared out at the trees that lined the roadside, showing the first hint of their autumn livery, bright greens mellowing to lime; reds to gold.

'Where are we going?' His voice brought Eleanor back from her daydream.

'Now that is a very good question, young man!' Eleanor looked back in time to catch Gabriel's proud smile. 'We are going to visit Mummy's new workplace.' She checked his expression in her rear- view mirror. 'Do you remember where Mummy used to work, in Glasgow?'

Gabriel nodded. 'And the nursery.'

'That's right! You went to the nursery at Mummy's work. Well, that was where I worked then and this is where I will work now!'

'Will I go to nursery?' Gabriel caught his mother's eye in the mirror.

'No, Gabriel, I'm afraid there is no nursery here.'

She watched as his arched brows fell and his smile returned to neutral.

'But once we've had a look around and met Simon, one of the people I will be working with, we are going to do something very exciting.'

'What?' Gabriel wriggled in his chair.

'We're going to meet someone *very* special who is going to look after you while Mummy is at work!'

'Kara?' Gabriel beamed, bolting upright in his chair.

'No, darling, not Kara. I know you liked her very much.'

Gabriel nodded.

'The person we are going to meet is called Christina and she is very excited about seeing you.'

Eleanor held her breath, waiting for Gabriel's reaction. He said nothing but turned to stare out of the window. She had taken Gabriel from everyone he knew and loved, from the only family he would ever have, and to what, she asked herself. To a lonely life in which people would have to remain strangers?

Gabriel fell silent and Eleanor's thoughts turned to Simon. She liked his gentle style of talking and the way he gesticulated as he spoke, as if spinning words with his hands. She appreciated his considered contributions to their many recent discussions, a helpful counterbalance to both Allen and Carl's more reactive styles.

She remembered with gratitude his calm professionalism during the cataclysmic moments of the embryo transfer and all the reassuring emails he had sent once she had decided to join them. He was kind and clever, she knew she would enjoy working with him. He reminded her, she realised, of her own father, a professor of history at Glasgow University, who'd encouraged both his daughters to work hard at school, then university. He had been so proud of their successes, yet her sister had grown more distant from him during her teenage years and beyond. Eleanor had no idea why.

As she neared her destination, she began to recognise her surroundings: the four-way stop, the pizza parlour and the sign bearing the university emblem that pointed the way to the research centre. She turned into the car park and sat for a moment before unstrapping Gabriel from his seat.

'Here we are,' she said, lifting him out, balancing him on her hip and making her way in the dry heat towards the low, brick building. 'Hi,' the receptionist said as Eleanor walked through the front door. She beamed at Gabriel. 'Aren't you a little darling! How old are you, sweetie?'

Eleanor opened her mouth to trot out another untruth when she heard footsteps approach from behind her.

'Eleanor! How wonderful to see you,' Simon exclaimed.

He hugged her lightly before standing back to study Gabriel. He seemed to freeze.

A phone rang out and the receptionist excused herself.

Eleanor watched as Simon pressed both hands to his temples before sliding them down to cover his mouth. He closed his eyes and took a deep breath before opening them again, as if to test the reality of what he was seeing.

'What a fine young man you are,' he stammered out, eventually, shaking his head as he spoke.

Eleanor hugged her son closer to her.

Simon opened his mouth to say more but stopped when the receptionist reappeared.

'And you are looking marvellous too, of course.' He smiled at Eleanor, although she could hear he was struggling to sound casual.

'Why, thank you!' She laughed.

'Eleanor, this is Florence, our office manager.' Simon introduced the woman Eleanor had assumed to be the receptionist as soon as she reached his side. 'And Florence, meet Eleanor. You may remember I mentioned a while ago that she would be joining the team here.'

'Hi.' Florence smiled. 'Welcome!'

As they shook hands, Gabriel started to wriggle free.

'Allow me.' Simon held out his arms. 'Looks like he is quite a weight.'

'No need.' Eleanor placed him on the floor. 'You prefer to walk by yourself, don't you, darling?'

Eleanor's heart swelled with pride as Gabriel tottered off along the corridor.

'*J'en reviens pas*!' Simon stared at him, then back at Eleanor, his mouth open. Eleanor was unsure if he was lost for words or holding back in front of Florence.

'Shall we… go to my room?' he stammered. His gaze remained fixed on the little boy.

'I can watch Master Gabriel. Might give you two a chance to talk.' Florence smiled, reaching for a crate of toys she kept for enquiring infants. But Gabriel had other ideas, running towards Eleanor and clamping his little hand in hers.

'Thanks, that's so thoughtful of you,' said Eleanor, 'But I think Gabriel is still reeling from all the changes. He'll be fine with me.'

As soon as they were in his room, Simon closed the door firmly then turned to face Eleanor.

'*Non*, Eleanor, is this really… him?' He stared at the child. 'I… I… not sure I can get my head around this.'

Eleanor nodded then placed a finger on her lips.

Simon nodded back.

She fished some paper and coloured pencils from her bag and arranged them on the coffee table. Her mind drifted back to the last time she'd been in Simon's room, the meeting when she told him of her intention to go ahead with the procedure. She turned to look at Gabriel. He had walked to the bookshelf and was drawing his finger along the spines of some neatly ordered texts.

'Would you like to do some drawing, darling?' she asked.

Gabriel trotted back to his mother's side.

'And would the young man like something to drink, I wonder?' Simon asked Eleanor.

'Water, please,' Gabriel replied.

Simon paled. 'Of course.'

He disappeared once again. Eleanor could hear the clank of cups being organised, the thud of something dropped on the floor and the rustle of paper as snacks were unwrapped.

'Do not worry, Eleanor, I am… adjusting,' he said when he returned, clutching a plastic cup of water and a plate of biscuits. 'I know you have kept me fully informed of developments and I have read Sophie's assessment summaries and, of course, had a full report from Allen when he visited you in Glasgow. But nothing prepares you for the reality of something as… unusual as this.'

He placed the drink on the small table where Gabriel had already made himself busy.

'I know,' said Eleanor, quietly delighted at Simon's appreciation of the child. A valuable protection, she hoped, from possible inconceivable horrors.

'I did not think you would make an appearance today. Thought you'd be sleeping off the… jetlag.' He didn't take his eyes off Gabriel as he spoke to Eleanor.

'Actually, I rarely suffer from jet lag when I travel westwards, but I pay for it when I go home,' said Eleanor as brightly as she could.

'Plenty of time before that debt is due then, eh? We are all ready for you here. In fact, I was just finalising your teaching schedule. Not too much for you, I hope. I have tried not to give you too many early starts or late nights — these things can play havoc with childcare arrangements as I recall.'

'Thanks for that, Simon, but I think I've got that side of things covered.'

'You have? I feel so bad we cannot provide on-site childcare. Not quite up to the Glasgow standard, are we?'

'Don't be daft,' replied Eleanor, 'It didn't even cross my mind that you'd consider it. Anyway, I'm not sure another placement like that would be a good idea. The Glasgow nursery was fabulous, but under the circumstances, it was time to reconsider arrangements.'

'Of course. Allen told me about your brush with the media.' He shook his head. 'So, what arrangements have you made?' He watched Gabriel as the little boy concentrated on his drawing

'I've organised a nanny. Not live-in though; I couldn't bear that. She's Slovakian. Her last placement was in Toronto but she's moving here to live with her boyfriend, so that suits me fine.'

'*C'est partie gangee*! You have not wasted any time!'

'Needs must.' Eleanor sighed heavily. 'I'm a complete novice when it comes to organising childcare but once I'd contacted a few agencies and learnt the lingo, as it were, it wasn't too hard to find what I wanted.'

'But you have not met her yet? Is that not a little… risky?'

'I know, but we've Facetimed several times and I called her previous employer, so I think that's about as much as I can do. And we're going to meet Tina today, aren't we?' Eleanor placed a hand on Gabriel's back. She knew he was listening to the conversation.

'Yes,' he replied, without looking up, 'I'm going to meet Tina.'

'That is a pretty name, is it not?' Simon leapt at the opportunity to engage with the child.

'Yes,' said Gabriel, glancing up.

For a moment, there was silence as his bright eyes fixed upon Simon's. Eleanor watched Simon's transfixed expression. He was staring back at the boy as if trying to peer into the depths of his being.

Eleanor thought she saw his eyes moisten.

Simon pulled his gaze back to Eleanor. 'Do you think, perhaps, she might soon be asking questions? Seeing him every day…'

'I'm sure she will.' Eleanor watched Gabriel as she answered. 'But I've worked my way around the major issues for the moment, I think, and I do have a longer-term plan…'

'Mummy?' Gabriel handed Eleanor his drawing, an oblong stretched across two unsteady circles, the blue smudge on top, a clue to its inspiration.

'What a lovely fire engine! I think we should take that home and find a good spot for it.' Eleanor placed the picture carefully on her lap and patted a clean sheet onto the table in front of Gabriel.

When she looked up, Simon was again shaking his head.

'What the…' he began.

Eleanor silenced him with a raise of her brow. He nodded.

'Well, I'm glad you are here now. There are so many more… detailed… examinations we can conduct, given our facilities.'

'What do you have in mind?'

'Physical tests, medical assessments, scans…' He paused. 'Things you couldn't easily organise in Glasgow.'

Eleanor nodded and forced a smile, a tight-lipped barrier to what her heart would have her say. She looked at her watch.

'I think it's time we went home.' She rose to her feet, tidied Gabriel's paper and pencils into her bag and lifted him into her arms.

Simon accompanied them to the car park.

'See you tomorrow,' he called as Eleanor strapped Gabriel into his car seat.

Eleanor nodded, but as she pulled out onto the highway and headed for home, she felt she would rather never return. The thought of her son, her baby, being subjected to invasive tests was unbearable. Visions from her university days resurfaced when she had relished the task of dissecting rats, examining the spoils beneath the harsh beam of her microscope. She thought of Gabriel, pinned to a board, screaming out to her…

'Shit!' She slammed her foot on the brakes just in time to stop the car from running a red light.

Gabriel cried out as he swung forwards and when Eleanor checked her mirror, she could see fear and alarm in his face.

'Sorry, darling. Are you okay?'

He nodded uncertainly.

Focus! Eleanor admonished herself as she crawled forwards when the lights changed. *For Gabriel's sake. I need to stay strong.*

***

'Hello, I'm Christina.' The young girl smiling at the door of Eleanor's apartment held a piece of paper tightly in her hand. Eleanor could see her own name and address printed on it. 'Tina?' She pointed to herself. 'This is right place, yes?'

'Hello, Tina, come in.' Eleanor held the door open. 'Yes, this is the right place. Come and meet Gabriel. He's very excited to see you.'

'Gabriel!' Eleanor called. 'Tina is here!'

The little boy came running from his bedroom and stood smiling up at them.

'Hello.' Tina crouched down beside him. 'I've been looking forward to meeting you.'

Eleanor warmed to Tina instantly. She liked the gentleness of her voice and the way she dropped down to her son's height. Gabriel rewarded her with a broad smile; it was clear he liked her too.

'Let's go and sit down, shall we?' said Eleanor.

'Yes.' Gabriel jumped up and down. He reached up for Tina's hand and led her to the living room. 'Here.' He patted a cushion at the back of the chair. 'Sit here, Tina.'

'Thank you very much, Gabriel.' Tina sat down.

'Would you like to see my pictures?' Gabriel asked.

'Yes please,' said Tina. 'You like drawing?'

'Oh yes!'

'That's wonderful, Gabriel! What else do you like?' Tina encouraged him.

'I like stories and walks and making things…'

'Why don't I make us a coffee while you get to know each other?' Eleanor could see Tina's eyes widen in surprise at Gabriel's language. She was relieved Gabriel had chosen to speak to Tina as he did at home, using his full vocabulary rather than the single-word expressions he adopted with strangers. Daily life would be frustrating for him now without verbal communication. *But how had he known that?*

'That's great, because I like all those things too!' Tina laughed. 'I think we get on very well.'

By the time Eleanor returned, Gabriel had surrounded Tina with all the treasures he wanted her to inspect.

'I have an idea.' Eleanor turned to Gabriel. 'Why don't you draw a *very* special picture for Tina while we have a chat?'

Gabriel ran off to get started on the task.

Eleanor and Tina looked at each other and laughed.

'What a wonderful little boy you have,' said Tina, 'So full of fun and so... smart?'

'Thank you,' said Eleanor. 'He's interested in everything.'

'Perhaps you run me through his routine?' Tina took a pen and notebook from her bag.

'Actually, I've typed it out for you.' Eleanor fetched the prepared document from the kitchen, impressed nonetheless by Tina's attempts to organise herself.

'I'm sorry I don't drive,' said Tina, 'If you need me to take Gabriel to park or kindergarten, this could be a problem, yes?'

Eleanor had quietly delighted in this aspect of Tina's CV. 'It shouldn't be a problem. As you will see from Gabriel's schedule, he doesn't often mix much with other children.'

Tina read down the sheet of paper. Eleanor saw her frown as she read.

'So, he doesn't play with other children. Ever?'

Eleanor took a deep breath and cast an eye to the door to make sure Gabriel was still in his room. She hoped she could follow through with the lie she had so carefully sculpted on the journey from Glasgow.

'I'm afraid Gabriel has…' She took another deep breath and bit her lip before progressing. 'He has a medical condition that makes him rather… vulnerable at the moment.' Eleanor found she couldn't meet Tina's gaze.

'So sorry.' Tina placed the full cup back on the table.

'Yes, I can't deny it's been a struggle to come to terms with it myself.'

'He is such lovely boy,' Tina sympathised.

'Thank you.' Eleanor looked up again. 'He is. And everything should work out fine.' Her voice brightened. 'But he has a tumour… a brain tumour…' Eleanor paused, as if the words themselves caused her pain.

Tina sighed and her bright smile vanished.

'But it is benign…'

'Benign?' Tina looked confused.

'It won't spread anywhere else,' Eleanor explained.

'I see.' Tina was silent for a moment. 'So, that is why he cannot play with others?' she asked.

'No, not because of the tumour itself.' Eleanor was surprised Tina was following the details. 'But the treatment, the radiation therapy, weakens his immune system.'

'Ahh.' Tina nodded.

'But it won't be forever,' Eleanor added. 'Once the treatment is over and he becomes stronger, he'll be able to live a normal life again.' Eleanor swallowed hard, struggling this time with the real pain of knowing the lie of such a future for Gabriel. 'But for the moment, he could catch anything and everything and not be able to fight it.'

'Of course, I understand.' Tina's words were quiet and gentle.

'But he's a very happy little boy,' Eleanor went on, sounding as reassuring as she could manage, worried she might be scaring Tina away. 'He loves to play at home and he's a bright little thing, so everything interests him.'

'What will you do when he goes to school?' Tina surprised Eleanor with her forward-looking concerns.

'That's still some time away. He is only three,' Eleanor continued the deceit she had started in her emails. She glanced at the door to see if Gabriel was close enough to hear this lie, but she couldn't see him.

'Of course.' Tina looked a little embarrassed at having asked the question. 'He is big... eh, tall?'

'Yes.' Eleanor took her chance to embellish the story. 'That is part of his condition. The tumour is causing that.'

'I see.' Tina looked like she was about to ask more questions, so Eleanor was relieved when Gabriel suddenly reappeared, clutching a drawing in his hand. He ran to Tina.

'For you.' He held it out to her, jumping up and down with excitement as he waited for her response.

Tina looked at it. Her eyes widened. 'You did this?' she asked.

Gabriel nodded proudly.

'This is very good, Gabriel.' Tina turned the picture to face Eleanor.

'Wow!' Eleanor exclaimed.

A jagged line had been scratched along the full width of the page, its many peaks scribbled over in white, its base scored with green.

'What is this?' Tina traced her finger along the graph-like outline.

Gabriel beamed and pointed to the window.

'Of course! The mountains. This so good, Gabriel. May I keep?'

'It's for you,' he said, grinning.

'Thank you. Maybe we draw together when I come to look after you?' Tina looked to Eleanor.

'That's a very good idea, isn't it?' said Eleanor. 'Can you start tomorrow? Eight thirty?'

'Yes, I would like that.'

'Perfect. We'll see you on Monday then.' Eleanor stood up.

Tina picked up her bag, clutching the drawing in her other hand and followed Eleanor and Gabriel to the door.

'Bye, Tina!' Gabriel called out as Tina walked along the corridor that led from their apartment to the lift.

As soon as she was out of sight, Gabriel ran to the living room where he stood on the windowsill and watched as Tina walked away from the apartment block, turning one last time to wave up to Gabriel.

'You like Tina then?' Eleanor asked.

'I do,' he answered thoughtfully. 'She is kind,' he said with an air of maturity that no longer surprised Eleanor.

***

'What makes me three?' Gabriel asked his mum as she tucked him into bed that night.

'That is the number of your age,' she replied, trying to sound convincing. She had learnt Gabriel was quick to pick up on any hesitation or ambiguity in her voice.

'I am three.' He smiled. 'I am Gabriel, and I am three.' He threw his arms around Eleanor's neck and held her close.

'Yes, you are,' she replied, kissing him on the forehead. But as she turned down the nightlight and left the room, she felt weighed down by a heaviness in her heart. She loved this little boy, more than she had loved anyone in her life, more than she imagined she ever could love. But to keep him safe, to keep him close, she knew she must spin a web of lies that would forever form a gulf between them.

Chapter 24

Within a few weeks, things settled into a routine and Tina's initial questions about Gabriel's unusual rate of growth and development gradually gave way to an acceptance of his *condition*.

Every work morning, Eleanor would watch the little boy climb onto the living room windowsill so he could spot Tina as she walked up the path to their apartment.

'Tina's here!' he would call out and run to the door to greet her.

It was a comfort to Eleanor that her son seemed so happy. She felt confident as she made her way to work each morning, knowing she would be able to focus without worrying about what might be happening at home.

Allen had been generous in the time he had allowed her for research. He had kept her teaching commitments to a minimum, allowing her to focus on the detailed scrutiny of Lillooet's mitochondrial DNA. Moreover, with Carl out of the way, she was free to pursue her emerging hypothesis on the key role played by mitochondrial DNA in the extent to which an inherited trait is expressed. Eleanor knew her idea was novel and bold, but she had a gut feeling she was onto something and was glad she was a long distance away from Carl. She had to make sure he didn't take ownership of it.

It was a Monday morning in December and Eleanor made her way, as usual, to Simon's office, where she met with him and Allen to discuss issues arising from the week before.

'Looking forward to hearing how you're getting on with the Lillooet samples, Eleanor,' Allen said from behind the newspaper he continued to read. 'And now Gabriel has had time to settle in, I'd like to add physical assessments to his developmental profile.' He folded his paper and looked over to her.

'Yes,' Eleanor agreed, 'That's been on my mind too.'

'It would be too bad if he slipped through our fingers before we got anything concrete from him.' Allen sighed heavily.

Slipped through our fingers? Eleanor shuddered. *What was he talking about?*

'You mean…?' she started.

'I mean removed from our bailiwick… like Lillooet. I still think we should have kept quiet about her.'

Eleanor's heart had begun pounding. 'Ahhh, I see. But don't you think keeping quiet about Lillooet would have been too risky? It would only have taken one accidental sighting, a curious student, a caretaker…'

'Sure, but is that really any different from Gabriel? In fact, he's worse. We can't exactly keep him in a freezer.'

Eleanor gasped at Allen's words, quickly disguising her unguarded utterance as a cough. Despite the fact he had met and marvelled at her son in the flesh, Allen seemed to have no difficulty in casting both Lillooet and Gabriel as mere objects for study.

'Heard any more about Lillooet?' she asked, feigning lightness in her tone.

'Nah.' Allen shook his head. 'As soon as we contacted the National Board, they took the matter out of our hands. We haven't heard a word since. But that could mean anything, from *nothing worth mentioning* to *top secret*. It might be years before we get anything back.

'In fact, if they do decide to give out information, we'll probably read about it in the press before they get round to telling us. As far as they're concerned, we just sent them an odd-shaped block of ice for random study. Who knows when — if ever — they get around to it.'

'Just as well,' said Eleanor, rubbing her arms. She suddenly felt cold. 'The less anyone knows about us, the better.' *For as long as possible*, she added inwardly.

'So, can we fix a time for Gabriel to come in? Out of hours, of course.' Allen whipped out his phone and scrolled through his diary.

'Sure.' Eleanor did the same.

'Monday?' Allen suggested without lifting his eyes from the screen.

'*Next* Monday?' Eleanor would have preferred more time to prepare Gabriel, and herself, for this event.

'Is that a problem?'

'No, not at all. What kind of assessments do you have in mind, to kick off?' She held her breath.

'First visit, let's keep it simple… weight, height… basic parameters, you know.'

'Sure.' Eleanor nodded. 'Who'll be dealing with this? I'm quite happy…'

'Actually, Simon and I thought that perhaps we should take over from here. We were going to ask Sophie to do the first assessment now she's been released from Carl's grasp, but Gabriel has altered so much…'

Eleanor nodded. 'But she will still ask questions.'

'Yes. We thought we could use the brain tumour story you fed Tina?'

'Good idea.' Eleanor relaxed a little. 'That will also cover why she can't visit him — risk of infection.'

'Sorry!' Simon burst into the room. 'Just wanted to double check this stuff before I brought it to you.' He eased a bundle of loose papers onto his desk and selected a few from the top of the pile.

'Sounds interesting already.' Allen rubbed his hands together.

'Cold?' asked Simon. 'I think you might find our winters a bit difficult, Eleanor. Especially on days like today, when the furnace is not up to speed.'

'It can't be any worse than Glasgow's constant rain.' Eleanor wrapped her cardigan snugly around her.

'Well, perhaps you can let us know which you prefer once you've had a few months of this.' Simon buttoned up the woollen cardigan he wore over his thick shirt. 'And how is Gabriel enjoying his first Canadian winter?'

'His first full winter, really, although that's rather difficult to grasp,' said Allen. 'It's almost impossible to believe he was born just one year ago this month.'

'He's fascinated by the idea of seasons and different types of weather,' Eleanor said, changing the focus. 'He spends a lot of time gazing out the window at the snow. He wants to know everything about it, so we've made a few visits to the library to do a bit of research.' Eleanor kept her tone measured and informative.

'Wouldn't the internet do the same job?' Allen suggested. 'It would be a lot simpler and would keep Gabriel out of the public eye.'

'True, but I can't keep him inside all the time, that wouldn't be healthy. I try to make sure we have a few expeditions a week and next to the museum, the library is a firm favourite. Not many young children there.'

She knew Allen and Simon would rather she kept Gabriel in isolation. Not that she blamed them, after all the fuss that had erupted in Glasgow. But it was difficult to argue Gabriel's case without betraying her compassion for him.

'It cannot be easy, Eleanor, keeping him in the shadows,' Simon sympathised, 'And he is such an alert child. Does he ever ask you why he does not go out more?'

'He hasn't actually, and he seems perfectly happy with things as they are. I see no need to rock that boat.' Eleanor knew Simon was giving her a chance to speak from the heart, but she couldn't risk it. She would rather be thought of as cold than attached but nonetheless, she could see he sensed something. She would have to be careful.

Simon nodded then turned his attention to the bundle of papers.

'I have read over your pregnancy data a number of times now and I still do not understand the full picture.' He flicked through the document. 'Look...' He paused at one of the graphs and, folding back the opposite sheet, placed it on the table before them. 'I have been trying to tease out the flow of hormones and neurotransmitters present in the samples you sent to me throughout your pregnancy, Eleanor. Most traces are typical, if accelerated, in their presentation. But this one here...' He tapped the paper heavily. 'This is the one that interests me.'

'What is it?' Allen craned his neck to read the labels on the graph.

'Endorphins; the brain's *feel-good* factor,' said Simon. 'You know, the ones we produce during exercise, sex, when we laugh and so on.'

'Production is normally increased in pregnancy though, isn't it?' Eleanor studied the page of data.

'Yes. In fact, it is possible that their sudden drop-off after pregnancy is what sometimes triggers postnatal depression. But what is important here are the astronomical levels circulating in your bloodstream throughout parts of your pregnancy.' Simon traced the dramatic contours on the chart before him.

'Looks like you were one happy lady,' said Allen.

'It does,' Simon agreed, 'But what particularly interests me is *when* these endorphins are produced. I think there might be a pattern. I have been trying to match it with markers of the development of the foetus, to see whether or not these surges are in any way related to important prenatal events.'

'And?' Eleanor frowned.

'I am still just hypothesising, of course, but it does seem to me that there is a strong correlation throughout the pregnancy between significant growth events and endorphin surges.'

'What do you think that means?' she asked.

'Well, this might sound a bit, eh… *imaginaire*, but do you remember we talked some time ago about the way the foetus throughout this pregnancy seemed to orchestrate things? Well, perhaps it was a bit more than that. It would appear that immediately following each transition period, a rush of endorphins was triggered, almost like a form of encouragement, perhaps?'

'You mean like some kind of conditioning of the host body?' asked Allen.

'I am not sure I'd put it in those terms. That makes it sound rather cold and clinical,' said Simon. Eleanor was aware at times of Simon's attempts to protect her from Allen's brutal objectivity. 'But there is no reason to assume that to be the case. In fact, the whole interaction seems to be a very positive one.

And, of course, we do not know why this was happening. A correlation does not necessarily mean there's a causal link. But perhaps it suggests this pregnancy was a more... cooperative interaction than normal.'

'I suppose this kind of relationship between a mother and her developing baby could be seen as highly adaptive,' said Eleanor. 'If pregnancy was a learning opportunity for the host body, if it had some sort of memory of a successful pregnancy, then a second pregnancy would learn from the first and be more efficient.'

'And what about the foetus?' asked Allen. 'What could this say of the unborn child? Is this an entirely instinctive system? How does it know its development is proceeding well and when to reward?'

'I have no idea,' said Simon. 'Does it too have some sort of idealised memory to work from?'

'Maybe the memory is at a genetic, rather than a conscious, level and is part of the reproductive process rather than the foetus itself,' said Eleanor, 'But is that any different from the norm?'

Simon shrugged. 'The important thing, I suppose, is that although there is much that is similar between this pregnancy and every other, there is also something very different about what was happening here. And, as far as we can see, whatever did happen yielded positive outcomes, for the mother's sense of wellbeing and for the progress of the pregnancy itself.

'So, why, then, are pregnancies not like that today? Why have we evolved away from that?' asked Eleanor.

'That, Eleanor, may well be the key question.'

***

'Letter, Mummy.' Gabriel selected one envelope from the bundle Eleanor had collected from her mailbox in the foyer and left on the table by the front door. He ran the length of the hall to his mum's bedroom to deliver it. 'From Granny,' he said, settling himself onto the bed.

Eleanor emerged from the en suite where she had been running Gabriel's bedtime bath.

'Why, so it is,' said Eleanor, sitting down beside him.

'Granny's writing.' Gabriel drew his index finger across the neat, cursive script.

'Would you like to open it?' asked Eleanor.

Gabriel carefully pulled at the fold of paper, eventually extracting a colourful card. On it was a picture of children, wrapped in warm winter clothes. They stood on a patch of snow that sparkled with the reflection of the lights decorating a huge fir tree. The children looked like they were singing.

'Always the first to send her Christmas cards.' Eleanor read aloud her mother's seasonal greeting. She studied the neat script with its familiar hoops and crosses. Holding it closer, she caught the faintest whiff of Miriam's perfume.

'You're sad, Mummy.' Gabriel moved closer.

'Oh, I'm just missing Granny a little. She's my mummy, you see,' Eleanor said.

He nodded. 'And Granny's sad too.'

'I imagine so,' said Eleanor.

'She is,' said Gabriel, picking up the card. 'Here.' He handed it to her. 'You can feel it.'

'What do you feel?' Eleanor took the card from her son.

'The sad,' he replied simply, 'In her words.'

'You think her words sound sad?' Eleanor asked.

'They *feel* sad. Feel them.' He took his mother's hand and drew her fingers across the black, inky text.

Eleanor took hold of the card and observed Gabriel intently. His brilliant eyes stared back into her own, his fresh, young face awash with compassion and concern.

'See?' he whispered. 'Granny is sad because Aunt Olivia is sad.'

Eleanor closed her eyes. She didn't know what to say.

She thought about her mother and Olivia all evening, hoping there was nothing wrong. She waited until Gabriel was asleep before checking her email for any messages from home but found nothing new.

She couldn't dismiss Gabriel's words though and wondered, not for the first time, about his incredible sensitivity to the feelings of others. How could he have *felt* the sadness?

***

'How did the *explanation* go with Sophie, Allen?' Eleanor asked when she next met with him and Simon.

'I said you had taken him to a paediatrician because you were worried about his rapid growth and that the ensuing investigations identified the cause as a brain tumour. I also told her it will ultimately kill him. Probably when he's quite young.'

Eleanor felt her stomach turn at Allen's casual reference to Gabriel's death.

'Did she question anything?' she asked.

'No, she swallowed it whole; hook, line and sinker.' Eleanor could hear the satisfaction in his voice. 'Most of the time she just shook her head, once she'd stopped crying.'

'What about the rapid growth bit? Did she accept that?' asked Simon.

'Completely, said she'd read about that sort of thing before, even knew the medical term for it: acromegaly. That took me by surprise, I must admit.'

'And his advanced skills, his speech, motor development and so on. How did you account for that?' asked Simon.

'I told her we weren't sure if Gabriel would have been like that anyway or if it was a consequence of his medical condition, and said that was why we wanted her to continue assessing him.'

'Genius!' Simon nodded eagerly.

'Yes, perfect,' added Eleanor. 'This can definitely work.'

'Yup.' Allen sounded pleased with himself. 'I've taken the liberty of drawing up a list of possible investigations.' He pulled out a bundle of booklets from the file he was holding and handed one to each of them.

Eleanor scanned the document, swallowing back her horror at some of the proposed assessments: MRI, blood tests, tissue samples, parameters of tolerance to sensory stimuli, pain threshold… Her heart began to race. *Dear God, my poor darling!*

'Look good to you two?'

'Of course.' Simon nodded. 'Very comprehensive, but we will need to discuss our methods…'

'Naturally.' Allen looked inquiringly towards Eleanor.

Eleanor was determined to stay in role but in her heart, she swore she would not ever allow Gabriel to be subjected to these tests, some of which seemed nothing short of barbaric. She would have to somehow ensure they didn't happen and if she failed, then they would have to leave, and as soon as possible. But that would mean outsmarting her colleagues and to do that, she would need to convince them of her loyalty to the experiment and of her heartlessness.

'Yes,' she said, nodding calmly, 'We need all of this. But I wonder if we should be extending our assessments to one other dimension of Gabriel's development?'

Allen looked up in surprise. 'Really? What have I missed?'

'His sensitivity,' said Eleanor, 'And I don't mean pain sensitivity. He seems to know exactly what I'm feeling, even when I think I am disguising my feelings well.'

'I'm not sure that's so unusual, Eleanor. Children can be very in tune with their parents, especially if they don't have much contact with other people. They become over-attached.'

'True, but this feels different, Allen. Gabriel isn't just picking up on my feelings. He seems to have a sensitivity for other people's feelings too.'

'Maybe he is sensing your mood?' suggested Simon.

'No, it's more than that,' Eleanor insisted. 'What I'm talking about goes way beyond astute observation of social cues. Gabriel picks up on things that have no local expression. He is sensitive to the feelings of people who are nowhere near at the time. He has a sort of remote sympathy for people he is in some way attached to.'

'In what way?' Simon leant towards Eleanor, crossing his arms.

'You mean like a mind reader?' Allen raised an eyebrow.

'No, more of a… heart reader, I suppose,' said Eleanor.

'Come on! What's triggered this?' Allen half-smiled.

'A few things, but the other day, for example, my mother phoned. She was updating me on my sister's personal circumstances, and Gabriel asked me later why his aunt was so angry…'

'Good hearing, perhaps?' Simon suggested.

'No, her anger, which *is* indeed significant, wasn't mentioned…' Eleanor tailed off. 'Besides, he was asleep at the time.' She wouldn't have mentioned this trait had she not needed some way of buying time.

'I think you're reading things into this that don't exist. He's almost certainly mirroring you…' Allen shook his head.

'Except I'm not the sensitive type, as you may have noticed,' replied Eleanor.

'True, but I think it's a red herring nonetheless.' Allen waved his hand as if flicking away an irritating insect.

'Perhaps the best you can do at present is to keep a journal of events, write down all the things he says you think are significant and then, perhaps, we look at it?' suggested Simon.

'That's exactly what I am doing,' said Eleanor, 'But I have the sneaking suspicion I'm just scraping the surface of… *something*, although I do realise I might be mislabelling it. But I would like to investigate it, so I've sketched out some preliminary assessments.'

'What is there to lose?' Simon shrugged.

'Nothing,' Eleanor jumped in before Allen had a chance to air his opinion. 'I will need some time to set things up though, and the assessments themselves will need a few weeks to run. Also, given the need to control all other emotional factors, it is critical this study precedes the physical tests, which could alter his attitude and disposition.'

Allen sighed heavily as Eleanor awaited his objection.

'Sounds good,' Simon spoke first. 'The more, what do you say… bang for our buck, the better. Right, Allen?'

'Just as long as it *is* a bang and not a whimper,' Allen muttered. 'Send me your proposal, Eleanor, and I'll think about it.'

Simon glanced at his watch. 'I must go.' He stood up. 'I promised to help organise this afternoon's Christmas party. All the IVF children and the staff kids come to it. It is crazy!' He laughed. 'Are you bringing Gabriel?'

'Just briefly,' said Eleanor, disguising the delight she felt, as she recalled Gabriel's excitement. 'Paradoxically, I don't want to draw attention to him by keeping him away from everything.'

'Be careful.' Allen frowned. 'This place is just as full of prying eyes as Glasgow was.'

***

The party was in full swing and few people noticed Eleanor and Gabriel's arrival. As soon as his jacket was off, Gabriel ran to join the other children, leaving his mother to wonder at his confidence, given the little contact he had with his peers.

She watched as one game followed another and cautious exchanges between children grew into relaxed grins and squeals of delight. Her eyes followed Gabriel as he ran and danced around the room. The children seemed to be immediately drawn to him and soon began looking to him to take the lead in their games.

'Great to see them having so much fun, isn't it?' One of the lab technicians had taken up the vacant chair across from Eleanor. She had noticed him before in the staff canteen, but they'd never spoken. 'The kids just love it. This is our third year here.'

He dipped his hand into a bowl of salty snacks and, gathering a handful, tilted his head back to pour them in. 'It's Brian, by the way.' He wiped his hand on his jeans then held it across the table to Eleanor. 'I'm from Melbourne originally. Sounds like you're not from these parts either. Scotland?'

'You're right. I'm Eleanor,' she said, smiling. She glanced at her watch, willing Santa to deliver his gifts so she could leave with an easy conscience.

'So, which one's yours?' Brian asked, looking around the room as he spoke. 'No, hang on. Let's see if I can guess. I'm good at this.'

He stared at Eleanor, then scanned the floor, repeating the actions several times.

'Okay, so I'm going with the girl in the red tartan dress?'

'Good guess,' said Eleanor, 'But that's my son over there.' She pointed to the circle of children passing round a parcel to the intermittent music. 'Blue shirt,' she added.

'Right beside my little fella.' Brian grinned. 'Bradley. He'll be four next month.'

Eleanor braced herself for the next enquiry and, noting Gabriel was a little taller than Bradley, decided to further enhance the lie of his age. But just then, Bradley's father became distracted by a commotion on the floor. The music had stopped just as his son had passed the parcel to Gabriel and a wail of disappointment filled the room.

'It's only a game, little fella,' Brian soothed, running to his son's side.

'Here.' Gabriel passed the parcel back to the crying child.

Bradley stopped crying and stared in disbelief at Gabriel.

'It's okay. I won the last game.' Gabriel smiled.

'Why, thanks, son.' Brian stared at Gabriel with bemusement. 'That's very kind of you, but you don't have to do that, you know. Rules are rules.'

'It's fine.' Gabriel smiled and skipped back to his mother.

'That was very kind of you,' said Eleanor.

'I felt sorry for him.' Gabriel shrugged. 'He was sad.'

'Time to go, darling?' Eleanor thought it wise to leave before much could be said about Gabriel's heroism. 'Would you mind awfully if we miss Santa's presents? I can collect yours tomorrow?'

'Okay!' He smiled. 'I've had loads of fun.'

***

It was dark by the time they got home. The grass in front of their apartment was deep with a fresh fall of snow that glistened in the moonlight. Gabriel ran through it, tossing armfuls of the freezing white powder into the air then spinning around, trying to catch it. He held out his tongue and giggled as the chilly snowflakes landed.

'That reminds me of a game Olivia and I used to play when we were little.' Eleanor stood close to him on the snow-covered grass. She stretched out her arms then started to spin slowly beside him, gently brushing into him as she did so.

Gabriel started to spin too.

'Sorry!' Eleanor said when their hands collided.

'Sorry!' Gabriel called back, giggling.

'Sorry!' called Eleanor, turning just a little faster.

'Sorry!' replied Gabriel, spinning faster too.

They continued the game, turning faster and faster, their eyes turned up to the starry sky.

'Sorry!' They took it in turns to call out, laughing heartily until eventually, exhausted, they collided and fell together onto the soft ground. As they tried to catch their breath, they cast clouds of moist air into the darkness around them, just visible in the light of the moon.

'It's very cold,' Eleanor said at last, rubbing her hands together. 'We'll need to go in.'

Gabriel stared up at Eleanor. 'That was the best fun ever, Mum.' His cheeks glowed and his eyes sparkled. He looked into her eyes. 'Did Aunt Olivia laugh when she played this game?'

'Yes, she did! We both laughed and laughed until we cried.'

'But now she only cries.' Gabriel sighed.

Eleanor gasped. She crouched down to his height and took hold of his snowy, gloved hands. 'She will laugh again, Gabriel. Everyone feels sad sometimes.'

Gabriel nodded, then called out, 'Race you!' and ran ahead to the apartment door.

Eleanor followed, laughing.

That night, as she tucked Gabriel into bed, he called her back into the room just as she was closing the door.

'I've had a wonderful day, Mummy.' He held her tightly around the neck as she bent over to give him one last kiss. 'When can I play with the children again?' he asked.

'I don't know, Gabriel. Those boys and girls probably only meet up once a year, at the Christmas party,' said Eleanor.

'So, are they alone for the rest of the year too?' He pulled himself up onto his elbows.

'Is that how you feel, darling? Alone?' Eleanor sat down on the edge of the bed.

'Don't worry, Mummy. I'm not lonely. I have you,' he said, 'And Tina.'

Eleanor ran a finger down the contour of his cheek.

'And I have you.' She kissed him on the forehead, pulled the quilt around him and left the room, furtively wiping tears from her eyes.

Back in the living room, she sat on the settee and looked around her. In a few days, it would be Christmas Eve and beneath their modest tree lay a small stack of gifts.

Only one year had passed since Gabriel had come into this world, yet already he was a caring, articulate child, with a love of life and so much to offer the world he had come into. She could not hold him back much longer, she thought, as a virtual prisoner in this little apartment.

She would have to think of another way of making it all work, of helping Gabriel to be everything he could be and of doing all the things he might like to do. But could she do that and keep him out of the limelight? Because that, she knew, would be the only way to keep him safe.

Chapter 25

When Eleanor arrived at work, the car park was a plane of snow, as smooth as icing on a cake. As she drove across it, she could hear the soft crunch beneath her wheels and felt the thrill of being the first to mark it. The centre didn't officially reopen until tomorrow so she was quite sure no one else would be in.

She thought, with a pang of envy, about Tina's plans to entertain Gabriel for the day. She had been regaling him with tales about the thrill of skiing and planned to build a little mound in the snow-covered yard behind the apartment, so he could experience the joy of sliding on snow.

She walked as quickly as she dared from the car to the door and stood shivering as she tapped the code onto the pad. The lock seemed to have frozen and it took several attempts for the mechanism to give way, but at last the door opened and she stepped inside.

She pressed the code into the alarm and flicked all the light switches on. As she strode through the silent corridors, she spotted a tinselled decoration still dangling from the ceiling, a remnant of the efforts made for the children's party.

Despite her wariness of Christmas fever, Eleanor had found herself thinking fondly of Christmases past. She felt sorry that her mother had missed Gabriel's first Christmas and his first birthday. At one point, she'd thought she might arrange a holiday for her to come and visit them in Vancouver, but soon realised this wouldn't be possible. There would be no way to prepare her for the grandchild she would now see. How could she begin to explain his growth and development? And although she could easily spin the same yarn of the brain tumour, she knew how much distress this would cause her mother and decided the transient joy of seeing her grandson would in no way compensate for the endless hours of sadness and anxiety which a lie about a tumour would create. And yet, it would be years before Gabriel's appearance would in any way match his apparent age. Eleanor sighed at the thought of the lies and disappointments that lay ahead.

Settling herself to work, she tried to focus on the task in hand, blotting out the outside world. She was looking forward to having something constructive to add to the Lillooet puzzle and hoped a few more hours in the lab would yield results. She was meeting with Simon and Allen in a few days so she wanted to complete the task she'd started several times now and have the main findings ready to present.

As the day outside grew brighter then receded once more into darkness, Eleanor remained absorbed in her work and it was with irritation that she was called back to the moment by the shrill ring of her mobile. She was at a critical stage; she had completed the statistics and was just about to read off and interpret the final results. She thought about ignoring it but then glanced at the caller display and reached immediately for her phone.

'Tina? Is everything all right?'

'Eleanor, so sorry!' Tina sounded distressed.

'What's happened? Has something happened? Is Gabriel all right?'

'He fell on snow. He was unconscious.' Tina's voice was shaking.

'My God! Where are you now?' Eleanor felt her throat tighten.

'I call ambulance.' Tina was crying. 'They come now.'

'Is Gabriel all right?' Eleanor was pulling on her coat as she spoke.

Tina replied but it was difficult now for Eleanor to make out what she was saying through her sobs.

'I'll come to the hospital straight away.' Eleanor snatched up her handbag and headed for the door.

In a blur of terror, she ran from the building, rummaging for her car keys as she struggled to hold her coat tight against the blast of icy wind. Beneath her, she could feel her feet slip, but she could not slow down. She had to go to Gabriel.

'Which way, which way?' She heard the tremor in her voice as she spoke the words aloud and started up the engine. The wheels spun as she skidded her way across the untreated car park and pulled into the deserted road.

She had noticed the signs to the children's hospital before and had even thought of rehearsing the route, just in case. But now she needed to get there quickly. Her hands trembled on the wheel as she raced onto the main highway and, disregarding the speed limit, accelerated towards the hospital.

Abandoning her car at the entrance, she sprinted towards the emergency department and, bursting through the double doors, found Tina slumped in a chair, sobbing.

'I so sorry,' she cried as she ran towards Eleanor.

'Where is he? Where did they take him?' Eleanor shouted at Tina as she rushed towards the reception desk.

'I'm looking for Gabriel Bartlett,' she gasped at the receptionist.

'He had an accident, a fall? Please?'

The receptionist consulted a screen in front of her.

'It happened so—' Tina started.

Eleanor flapped a silencing hand towards her without taking her eyes off the receptionist. 'Can I just see him, please?'

'Eleanor, I just want to say—'

'Leave it, Tina,' Eleanor snapped. 'I can't listen to excuses at the moment. There's one of you and one child, surely a manageable ratio!'

A young woman in green scrubs approached.

'Are you Gabriel's mother?' She placed a hand on Eleanor's arm.

'Yes.' Eleanor panicked that the physical contact was meant to soothe her, to prepare her for bad news. 'What's happened? Is he going to be alright?'

'He's fine, Mrs Bartlett. Come this way.'

A wave of relief swept through Eleanor's body. She read the badge pinned to her chest. *Dr Ashley Pearson.* She had glossy dark hair tied back in a ponytail and even in her distraught state,

Eleanor found herself thinking she looked too young to be a doctor.

'Is he badly hurt?' Eleanor asked as they made their way along a wide corridor. Doors on either side opened into small rooms, offering glimpses of children and their parents. She could hear voices, the clatter of trolleys wheeled in and out of rooms, the occasional tears of a child.

'No broken bones as far as we can see.' The doctor paused outside a door marked Treatment Room 7. 'But he is concussed, so we'd like to keep him overnight for observation, if that's okay?'

'Of course,' said Eleanor. 'Can I see him?'

Dr Pearson led Eleanor into the small room then stepped aside. There, on the bed, lay a very still Gabriel. Eleanor rushed to him and leant across the raised side of the bed. She stroked his forehead and bent down to kiss his cheek, searching for signs of injury, but apart from a graze on his chin, he looked okay.

But as she gazed at her son, a new feeling of panic welled up within her.

'He looks too still…' She looked up at the doctor. 'Don't you think? Like he's, he's unconscious…'

'He's doing all right, Mrs Bartlett. He has suffered a moderate concussion and is sleeping it off.'

'How can you be sure… I mean, did you do a scan?' Eleanor was trying to balance her desperation for his return to good health with her fear of unwelcome assessments.

'No, we don't think that's necessary. There's no sign of a skull fracture, no black eyes or bleeding. CAT scans aren't risk-free, so we don't do them routinely.'

Eleanor nodded and her sensation of relief intensified. 'So, no further tests?' She kept her eyes on Gabriel as she spoke to the doctor, anxious not to betray her delight.

'Well, we'll do a rerun of the admission assessments when he wakes up…'

'A rerun?' Eleanor turned sharply.

'Yes. We'll ask again about the accident, make sure his memory and concentration are fine and assess his balance. Nothing too demanding,' she said, smiling.

'So, he was talking when he arrived?'

'As I said, Mrs Bartlett, your son has suffered a moderate concussion and was only briefly unconscious. And while we can't treat it lightly, there usually is no cause for alarm. The monitoring we do is more precautionary than anything.'

'Thank God!' Eleanor exhaled heavily.

'Try not to worry. He's in very good hands here. He's actually the fifth child today with a snow-related injury. He'll soon be boasting about it in the schoolyard.' She smiled. 'One of the nurses will see you shortly to take down some more details. I'm afraid your babysitter was too upset to give us much information.'

A shaky voice called out from the doorway. 'Eleanor?'

Eleanor turned to see Tina, trembling, her face blotchy from crying.

'Gabriel, he will be okay? It happened so quick, I was right there but…'

Eleanor glared at her. 'We'll talk about this later. I need time to deal with this, *please*.' She turned back to face Gabriel, then remembered Tina was probably stranded at the hospital. 'You go home.' She rummaged through her bag and pulled out some notes. 'Call a cab at reception. We'll talk tomorrow.'

'Th-thank you,' Tina stammered.

Eleanor sank into the chair at the top of the bed and placed a hand on Gabriel's still body. She would have to prepare herself for questions the nurse might ask and create a backstory that wouldn't raise any eyebrows. With any luck, Gabriel would make a speedy recovery and they would be allowed home early the next morning before too much embellishment was required.

A short time later, Gabriel was transferred from the treatment room to a slightly larger one. There was a chair that pulled out to a makeshift bed so parents could stay if they wished. A friendly nurse demonstrated how it could recline and produced a couple of thin blankets.

'Would you like to pop down to the canteen for something to eat?' he asked when she'd folded the chair back into place. 'I'll keep an eye on things for you. He'll probably sleep for a while yet.'

'No, I'm fine, thanks,' replied Eleanor. She was determined to maintain her bedside vigil but was very grateful for the tea and toast he returned with some time later.

Eleanor stared at her little boy. He was so perfect. She recalled her first vision of Lillooet and was again struck by their similarities. They both had a kind of nobility about them. Their skin tone and features were so similar; they even shared the same expression. It was the look of those who saw beyond the common vision, who knew things of which others were unaware, truths hidden from known wisdom. Gabriel was Lillooet's son, not hers, and despite always having accepted this fact, Eleanor had never before felt it so profoundly.

Gabriel gradually became more restless, rousing each time the nurse returned to take his temperature and monitor his progress. Eventually, his eyelids flickered and he murmured a few words. Eleanor leant over him to hear what he was saying and immediately, his eyes opened and a smile spread across his face.

'Mummy.' He stretched a soft little hand to her cheek. 'Don't worry. I'm going to sleep for a while. Are you going to sleep here too?'

'Yes.' Eleanor's heart soared with gratitude. Gabriel was fine. Everything in her world felt right again.

***

By the time the rattle of breakfast trolleys could be heard travelling the length of the corridor, Gabriel was seated upright in bed, delighting in the novelty of his surroundings and chatting to Eleanor about the previous day's drama. When his breakfast tray arrived, Eleanor slipped away to call Allen. She was worried she'd gone to the hospital in such a hurry that she might have left the centre unlocked overnight.

A short time later, as she hurried back to Gabriel, she was dismayed to hear gales of laughter as she approached his door.

'How do you know so many Slovakian words?' she heard a nurse ask.

Eleanor slowed her pace and walked into the room.

'Is his father Slovakian perhaps?' The nurse turned to Eleanor. 'My family's from there originally. It's a treat to hear my mother tongue again!'

'Our nanny is Slovakian,' said Eleanor, shocked she had been unaware of this aspect of Gabriel's linguistic skills.

'Has your nanny been teaching you to speak Slovakian? What a good idea,' said the nurse. 'What a clever little boy you are for…' She paused and scanned the information sheet Eleanor had completed the night before 'Five years old.'

Eleanor looked to Gabriel and noticed his surprise, but he seemed to understand her unspoken appeal for collusion and simply nodded. She would have to find some way to help him make sense of all of this, but for the moment, she just wanted to take him home before anything else could unravel.

Dr Pearson eventually returned and gave Gabriel a clean bill of health. Eleanor helped him to remove the hospital gown and put on the clothes he had arrived in. They said goodbye to the nursing staff and made their way along the corridor. But just as they neared the exit, they heard a call from behind them.

'Just one thing.' Dr Pearson was running towards them. 'Could you bring Gabriel back to outpatients next week?' She handed Eleanor a green card.

'I thought you said everything was fine?' Eleanor studied the doctor's face for signs she was hiding something from her.

'I'm sure it is,' she said, 'But there were just a few anomalies regarding Gabriel's blood that we need to take a look at. Probably a procedural error, but we'd just like to check it out, if that's alright with you?'

Eleanor felt sick. 'What do you mean?' She searched her expression. 'Is there something you're not telling me?'

'Not at all, but we couldn't identify Gabriel's blood group. Maybe we could take a few samples, from Gabriel, you and his father too? As I said, it's almost certainly a procedural error or the sample got contaminated in some way, but it's more for future reference, you know, in case he needs a transfusion one day.'

'Of course.' Eleanor clutched the card in one hand and held tightly to Gabriel with the other. 'I understand.'

As they walked back to the car, Eleanor crumpled the appointment card in her palm and slipped it into one of the bins that lined the path. *I don't think so*, she thought as it tumbled into a mix of greasy food wrappers and stained paper cups. She congratulated herself on the false details she had given; they would never track her down.

'Blood groups,' she mumbled as she pulled out onto the main highway. 'Of course!'

Eleanor remembered it was one of the results Allen's tests had thrown up as unorthodox. They planned to repeat it at Gabriel's next assessment session. She searched her memory for the details but she felt hot and confused and couldn't seem to follow a single strand of her own thoughts. *I got lucky this time,* she told herself, *but maybe not the next.* She would have to be more careful.

***

Eleanor took Gabriel into her own bed that night and didn't sleep a wink, gazing at him and listening to every breath he took, but despite her fatigue the next day, she was keen to meet up with Simon and Allen as arranged.

Gabriel seemed perfectly well and waved happily from his spot at the window as usual. Tina stood at his side; her arm wrapped tightly around him. She had been quieter this morning and avoided eye contact. *Shit,* thought Eleanor as she made her way to work through a flurry of snow. *I hope she doesn't hand in her notice.*

As soon as she entered the centre, she began to recall what she'd been doing before the phone call. She really wanted to print off her results and formulate some initial hypotheses regarding their possible interpretation, then at least she would have something concrete to put before the others.

Once settled at her desk, Eleanor flicked open her laptop, turning first, as always, to her emails. She was heartened to find one from her mother but was surprised by the pang of sadness she felt at seeing it and realised she had never really *missed* anyone before, she had only missed things: her home, her comforts, her privacy. But lately, she'd felt somehow more aware of her feelings and connections with people.

She scanned the page, imagining her mother's gentle voice telling her all the latest snippets of family news.

Suddenly, her attention was caught by an email from Carl:

Eleanor,

Attached is outline of paper I've been invited to present at Paris Conference. Keen to avoid overlap with whatever you're up to. Comments helpful.

Carl.

Eleanor clicked on the highlighted text.

Looking Forward to Looking Backwards: Genetic Archaeology, the Next Frontier.

'What?' She skimmed the vague sentences that followed, Carl's unmistakable style asserting itself with its customary bluster: an eye- catching headline followed by insubstantial waffle.

What the hell is he playing at? Eleanor closed her emails. *Genetic archaeology?* If he was trying to trespass into their research then she needed to know. But how could he? He had no idea what they were doing and he had no access to their data. Surely to God he wouldn't consider even a vague reference to Lillooet?

Eleanor turned to the results she'd been working on. Her heart was racing. She would need to get moving and try to get a grip on this material. She'd have to find something to ensure Allen and Simon remained keen to make sure Gabriel continued to thrive before Carl lit the fuse on a trail that might lead to them and have them running scared.

***

Some hours later, when Eleanor took her place in Allen's room waiting for the meeting to start, the pounding of her heart was so loud it drowned out whatever it was Allen was saying. But she didn't care, because she had no interest in anything at the moment, other than the facts now crashing through her normally well-ordered thoughts, facts freshly gleaned from her own research. Facts about Gabriel, her precious boy. She stared straight ahead, to a future she could no longer imagine and a past she could not understand. She felt stunned, immobilised by her own fragmented thoughts that swirled around her like an ever-shaken snow globe, Gabriel's image amongst them. Nothing seemed real.

Surely, I've got this wrong. She crushed the corner of the single A4 sheet she held on her lap. *A stupid error that the others will spot? Dear God, I hope so…*

'You okay?' Allen suddenly stopped in front of her.

Eleanor stared back at him, but found she was unable to speak. She lifted her hands towards him, fingers cupped around an invisible burden, an idea too heavy to hold.

Before she could speak, Simon entered the room.

'Ah, Eleanor, that was quite a drama for you…' He stopped when he caught sight of Eleanor's expression.

'What has happened? Is Gabriel… is he all right?'

'Should we be worried?' Allen asked.

'Did they find something?' demanded Simon.

'No, well, yes, but that's not it…' Eleanor started.

'So, what *is* it then?' Allen sounded impatient.

'Look, I… this is new to me too, it's…'

'For Christ's sake, spit it out!' Allen demanded.

'Shh!' Simon shot a glance at his colleague. 'There is no need for that.' He shuffled his chair closer to Eleanor. 'What has happened, Eleanor?'

'My research,' she eventually blurted out.

'Yes?' Simon encouraged her.

'I've just printed off the results… I need you both to double, no, triple-check everything.'

'Of course,' said Simon, 'But what is it you have found?'

'Well,' Eleanor started, 'There's a lot more to it, for sure, but what I've got so far is enough to be going on with.'

'And that is?' Allen glared at her impatiently.

'The results of the comparative analysis of Lillooet's mitochondrial DNA with the range found worldwide today…' She paused and shook her head. 'Seem to indicate that…' She stopped again and took a deep breath. 'When I compared Lillooet's mitochondrial DNA with every other file in the archives… I found traces of her genetic imprint on every species. And I'm not just talking here about anatomically modern man… the Archaics too… but none of their DNA is present in Lillooet's.'

'Okay, so she has passed her genes on to them, but not vice versa?' Simon shrugged. 'How could that be?'

'Fucking hell!' Allen's jaw dropped. 'One-way traffic? That can only mean one thing!' He fixed on Eleanor.

She nodded.

'What are you saying? *What* does this mean?' Simon had paled.

'It means, Simon, that she is older than all of them.' Allen's voice quivered as he spoke.

'Older than who?'

'Sapien, Erectus, Neanderthal, Denisovan… need I go on?' Allen shivered. 'Fuck…'

'But surely that is impossible!' Simon exclaimed.

'Exactly what I would say too, but the results…' Eleanor started.

'How many times have you run through the matching process?' Simon asked.

'Not many, I agree. But on each occasion, I've processed many separate pairs.'

'And nothing of them in her?'

'Nothing. It appears Lillooet and Gabriel are completely different people from you or me or anyone else walking this Earth.'

The two men sat in silence.

'He is an entirely different sort of human,' Eleanor continued.

'What the fuck?' Allen clamped his hands on his head.

'How can that be? It is preposterous, surely…' said Simon.

No one spoke. The stillness hissed around them. Suddenly, Allen snatched up the document Eleanor had placed on the table. He scanned the results and then dropped them back down.

'So…' Simon paused before continuing. 'If Gabriel has not developed from the same line as we have, where *has* he come from?'

'I have no idea,' said Eleanor, 'I can only imagine he is from a separate, distinct group, that for some reason died out.'

'But intuitively, that seems so unlikely, don't you think? I mean, if they were anything like Gabriel, why on earth would they have died out while we survived?' Allen stared at Eleanor. 'He's so…'

'I don't know,' replied Eleanor, 'Perhaps the competition around at the time was even more advanced…'

'Or more aggressive?' suggested Simon.' It is not always the worthy that win.'

'True,' said Allen, 'There's plenty of evidence of that in every walk of life.' He stood up and paced the room.

'So, what does this mean for Gabriel?' Eleanor asked quietly, as if in rhetoric.

'And what does it mean for us Sapiens?' Allen inhaled sharply.

Eleanor regarded the two men, neither of whom was now looking at her. They were scared, she knew that; she could see it, smell it. Simon's face had drained from pale to ashen and she could see his fingers tremble as he swept them through his hair.

'At the moment, I have absolutely no idea.' Eleanor's voice sounded suddenly stronger. 'The best way forward, I believe, is to mount the most thorough and comprehensive investigation of Gabriel we ethically can, examining as much of him as possible, body and mind. And while this might take some time and effort, it will be a wise investment. Gabriel, and Gabriel alone, holds critical clues to the rise and fall of human life forms on Earth and to understand this will be to unlock a treasure trove of genetic data.'

'And then?' Allen lifted his eyes and stared solidly into Eleanor's.

'Then we'll have to do what we have to do,' she declared.

***

It was pitch dark by the time Eleanor walked from her car to her apartment block. She knew her revelation today did not make her son any safer, but she hoped the promise of future glory would be enough to silence calls for his termination. Eleanor shivered. She would have to get him out of here, but to avoid arousing their suspicions, she would need to plan meticulously and move with a stealth that kept her safely below the tripwire of Allen and Simon's radar, and that would take time.

Looking up, she saw Gabriel at the living room window and felt the joy in his smile as he spotted her. She had worried that her discovery might alter her sense of attachment to him, and make her feel wary of him, or a bit afraid. But she felt neither of these things. She couldn't stop loving this little boy, no matter where he came from. And she knew he felt the same attachment to her.

'Hi.' Eleanor half-smiled in Tina's direction, but her greeting was not returned. 'How was the day?'

Eleanor found herself irritated not only by Tina's silence but also by her very presence. But she didn't want to lose her yet, not until she'd been able to make alternative arrangements.

'Hey!' She threw her arms around Gabriel, who had run towards her, burying her head into his thick, glossy hair, breathing him in. 'Could you play in your room, darling, just for a little while? Mummy and Tina need to talk.'

Gabriel looked at Tina, whose mouth was twisted into a weak smile, a faux fervour challenged by her dull eyes. He nodded slowly and walked to his room. Eleanor knew he sensed something.

'Look, Tina; I was upset yesterday…'

'And so was I… I did my best. I always do—' Tina started.

'I know that,' Eleanor interrupted. She was keen to avoid hearing a rehearsed speech. 'But the fact remains, he ended up in hospital. No broken bones, thank God, but things could just as easily have gone that way…'

'But Eleanor, he is a child, he wants to play… he *needs* to play. And sometimes children get hurt when they play, but that is normal.' Tina had walked a few steps closer and Eleanor noticed the dark hollows beneath her eyes.

'Exactly, Tina, that is normal. But as I've explained to you, Gabriel isn't normal; he's… fragile.'

'For how long will he have to live like this? I sometimes wonder *does* he have to live like this? It seems unfair, cruel…' said Tina, her voice now firm as she stared Eleanor in the eye.

'Cruel?' Eleanor gasped. 'I can't believe I'm hearing this. You know he needs protection, that he is not well…'

'*Is* he? I'm not sure.'

Eleanor felt a swell of rage course through her. *How dare she? How the fuck dare she?* She felt the sharp edge of her nails cut deep into her moist palms. But then she thought of Gabriel and held herself in check.

'Let's both calm down and try to talk this through again tomorrow.' Eleanor's words now sounded measured and tightly controlled.

Tina said nothing, but nodded, then scooping up her rucksack from the floor, she walked to the door.

***

That night, Eleanor was keen to settle Gabriel to bed as quickly as she could. She wanted time to research all the possibilities that might be open to them.

'When are we going back to the hospital?' Gabriel asked as Eleanor turned down the nightlight beside his bed.

'Oh, I'm not sure that it will be necessary. Why?'

'The kind doctor said she wanted to take blood from my father. Will he be there? I'd like to meet him,' said Gabriel.

'No, Gabriel, I'm sorry. I should have explained that to you. He can't be there.' Eleanor sat on the bed beside him and held his hand.

'Why not? Where is he? Who is he?' He gazed into her eyes.

Eleanor took a deep breath. She had known this question would come one day, but she hadn't expected it just yet.

'Well, this might seem rather strange to you, Gabriel, but the truth is, I don't know.'

Gabriel stared in confusion. It was only recently that he had quizzed Eleanor about how babies were made.

'You see,' she continued, 'Sometimes doctors help babies grow in a mummy's tummy even when a daddy isn't there. So, the mummy and daddy might not know each other.'

'So, you have never met my father?' Gabriel sounded disappointed.

'No,' said Eleanor, 'But I'm sure he was a very special man, just like his son will be one day.' Eleanor tucked Gabriel's favourite teddy under his arm.

She felt guilty that what she had told him was not the full truth but knew she couldn't possibly explain any more than that to him. Not yet. But she had betrayed his trust. She rushed to leave the room before he could see the tears roll down her cheeks.

Chapter 26

The next morning, as Eleanor drove away from the apartment, she turned left at the junction rather than right, her normal route to work. She had been surprised to receive such a prompt reply to the enquiry she had made only the night before and was delighted when the principal had scheduled their meeting straight away. Her internet search had thrown up several promising schools within reasonable travelling distance, but there was something about this one, April Springs Elementary, that had drawn her back to it several times.

As she pulled into the school's tree-lined driveway, a single-storey modern building came into view. There was a generous car park a little distance from the school itself and a smooth ribbon of concrete that led visitors to its main entrance.

There was snow on the ground swept into still waves on either side of the glittering path, like a frozen sea parting to herald her arrival. A bright, low sun played on the huge wall of windows that ran at right angles away from the main doors. Eleanor felt a flutter in her stomach as she pressed the buzzer, summoning a black and white image onto the small screen at its side.

All the way there, she had rehearsed Gabriel's story. She had written it down to help her absorb the details and elaborate if need be as time went by, practising his *date of birth*.

As she entered the reception area, Eleanor was greeted by a tall, slim woman aged around fifty, she guessed, whose colourful, airy clothes seemed to defy the season.

'Mrs Bartlett?'

'Yes,' replied Eleanor, 'I have an appointment with the principal, Mrs Quinn?'

'That's me. I'm so pleased to meet you.' Mrs Quinn shook Eleanor's hand. 'Shall we talk in my office?'

The room was as bright as the principal herself. An entire wall was covered in children's paintings and drawings, a kaleidoscope of colour, a mosaic of form and mood. *Olivia would love this.* Eleanor surprised herself with her own train of thought.

From beyond the door, she could hear children talking and laughing as the school day started, and she watched as the principal placed a jug of iced tea and two glass mugs on the table between them.

'So…' She smiled at Eleanor as she poured the drinks. 'Tell me about Gabriel.'

Eleanor assembled the facts of Gabriel's story and began to breathe life into the fiction she had scripted the night before. Forming clay from the earth of her imagination and flesh from the clay, a new Gabriel was born.

'He's just turned six,' Eleanor explained, 'But hasn't attended school yet because of the uncertainty of where we would be living. He's curious, kind and extremely bright, something of a prodigy I've been told, although I'm sure lots of parents tell you that about their precious child! He is very sociable, and I think he should settle quite easily.'

'So, he's been assessed, but not been in the school system?' Mrs Quinn asked.

'He attended Glasgow University's preschool facility.' Eleanor had been expecting this question. 'They flagged up his advanced development and organised psychometric testing.'

Mrs Quinn nodded. 'I'm sure we can keep him busy. We have quite a range of abilities here and we encourage the more able children to do as many extra-curricular activities as possible. The current thinking on supporting such children being that peer bonding is more successful if their talents are allowed to develop laterally rather than vertically. It reduces the sense of distance between them and their peers.'

Eleanor nodded. She liked the philosophy, even though she guessed Gabriel would have little difficulty fitting in socially. The main problem would be his rapid growth, but that was next term's problem, she reminded herself, realising she'd stopped listening to Mrs Quinn.

'So, when would you like him to start? Tomorrow?'

'*Tomorrow*?' Eleanor could hear the surprise in her own reply. 'Yes, of course,' she rallied, 'That will be perfect.'

'We always recommend a trial period of one week, to ensure all parties wish to proceed with the placement. How would that suit you?' Mrs Quinn handed her a colourful brochure as she spoke.

'Perfect.' Eleanor glanced at the booklet, its front cover filled with smiling young faces and felt a pang of excitement at the prospect of Gabriel becoming one of them.

'I know much of the information is available online, but there's a useful section at the back, outlining clothing recommendations, lunch options and so on.'

'Thank you.' Eleanor slipped it into her bag.

'Shall we say ten o'clock tomorrow?'

Eleanor nodded. 'I shall look forward to that.'

Mrs Quinn made her way to the office door and Eleanor followed. She walked back to the car in a daze, proud of her performance and not quite believing it had gone so well.

As she drove back to the office, she talked herself through the approach she planned to take with Simon and Allen. Ideally, she would already have laid some groundwork on manoeuvring them into suggesting a move to school, but there had been no time for that. She knew she would have to play a crisis card and scare them into going along with it and braced herself to deliver the acting performance of her life.

'Are you off your fucking head?' Allen tossed the glossy handbook onto the floor as Simon shook his head in disbelief. 'Jesus Christ, Eleanor! One minute you're telling us *he's not human* and the next you're punting him out into an elementary school?'

'I didn't say he wasn't human,' Eleanor reasoned, 'Just not human as we know it. There are already traces of Lillooet's DNA in us—'

'Stop splitting fucking hairs! You know exactly what I mean,' he shouted.

'Shh,' warned Simon, 'Keep it down. But he has a point, Eleanor, this sounds like a reckless idea to me. What is wrong with keeping things as they are?'

'Tina's on to something, asking questions about why Gabriel's not on medication, doubting the whole brain tumour thing.'

'So?' challenged Allen. 'Get rid of Tina and hire someone else!'

'That's not so easy. She's accusing me of cruelty regarding his condition, some kind of Munchausen by Proxy.'

'What?' Simon was aghast.

'I know, it's nuts. But she's threatening to go to the authorities,' Eleanor explained, amazed by the clarity of her thinking as she wove the story. 'I can't risk crossing her.'

Allen covered his face with his hands. 'Okay, I see. So, the solution to Tina's awkward questions is to place Gabriel in the spotlight for all the world to scrutinise? Brilliant, Eleanor! Just fucking brilliant! Whatever happened to joint consultation? Since when do you have sole charge of this project?'

'Since I became his mother!'

'But that's just it, Eleanor. You are *not* his mother, no more than I am. Gabriel is an experiment! And if you can't handle it anymore then maybe one of us should take over,' Allen seethed.

'Don't threaten me,' Eleanor fired back. She stood up and paced to the window, frantically searching her mind for some sort of escape route which would pacify them and keep her story intact.

'Look.' She finally turned back to face them, her tone subdued. 'You're absolutely right… and I'm sorry.' She returned to her chair. 'Let's get this back on track.'

Allen stopped pacing.

'I panicked… probably when Tina mentioned reporting me to… whoever deals with these things. I am sorry, let's start again.'

They sat down and were silent for a few moments.

'Okay,' said Simon, 'Let us consider the actual problem.'

'Tina,' replied Eleanor.

'Fire her, just fire the bitch!' Allen erased her with a swipe of his hand.

'And if she reports me?'

'No, no,' said Simon, 'I thought you got on well with her? Why did she not just discuss it with you?'

'Probably because she was still angry with me,' Eleanor replied, 'For blaming her for Gabriel's accident.'

'Ahh!' Simon exclaimed. 'You see? There is always another layer. Revenge anger! Okay, so that is simple then, just apologise and move on?'

'No, we're past that. She's realised she's on to something.'

'I agree,' snapped Allen, 'Better to meet like with like. Tell her you'll report *her* for gross negligence. Could even slip in that you might flag up her visa status somehow... She is a visitor, isn't she? That should shut her up.'

Eleanor bristled inside at the racist undertones of Allen's suggestion but merely nodded. She needed him on-side.

'Okay. I just need to find someone else now. I might be off for a day or two, and if you don't mind, I think I'd better go straight away.'

'So, enough of this crap, right?' Allen picked up the glossy handbook from under the table and tossed it into the waste-paper basket. From where she sat, Eleanor could still read the bold red print: White Peaks Elementary, the prospectus for another local school some distance away from April Springs. There was no way she was letting them know exactly where Gabriel would be, not while they were making remarks about her fitness as his parent.

Shaken by the standoff, Eleanor slipped into the ladies' washroom next to Allen's office to gather herself together before going home. The last thing she wanted was for Gabriel to pick up any sense of her distress. She stood in front of the mirror and did the breathing exercises she had trained herself to do. Looking directly into her own tired eyes, she took a deep breath, held it for ten and released slowly. She repeated the exercise several times before turning on the tap and cupping her still shaking hands to gather cool water to sprinkle onto her burning cheeks.

It was at this moment she thought she heard the faintest of noises from the cubicle behind her. She turned off the tap and listened again. Nothing. Turning the water back on, she slowly lowered her head to floor level and peered through the gap below the door, instantly recognising the shoes.

'Sophie?' she exclaimed.

There was no reply.

'For God's sake, Sophie, I can *see* you're in there!'

Eleanor heard the scrape of the opening lock and waited with bated breath as the door slowly opened, revealing a startled-looking Sophie, who placed a finger against her lips.

'Shh.' She pointed behind her.

'What… why?' Eleanor whispered back.

'I just popped to the washroom and I heard raised voices from Allen's room back there. Poor sound insulation.' Sophie blushed. 'Are you… okay?'

'So, what, exactly, did you hear?' Eleanor suddenly felt sick.

'I wasn't trying to listen, honestly. I just heard shouting, you and Allen… I was worried, that's all.'

Eleanor studied Sophie's expression. It didn't look like she was lying, and it certainly didn't seem like she had heard anything shocking.

'But why were you hiding in there, listening?' Eleanor whispered angrily.

'I didn't want to embarrass you. I thought you might be upset, needing a bit of time alone…' she tailed off and shrugged.

Eleanor nodded. Maybe this would be okay.

'I *am* sorry, really,' Sophie repeated. '*Are* you all right? Do you want to talk…?'

'No, I'm fine. Just taking a moment to calm down. Academic disputes can be heated… like domestic ones. Sometimes you get to know each other too well when you work in close quarters.'

Sophie nodded.

'I need to go.' Eleanor swept her hair from her face. 'Things to sort out at home.'

Back in the car, Eleanor prayed Sophie was telling the truth and that no key words had slipped through the general noise of the exchange. But right now, she had to clear her mind and get in role for the next drama back home, featuring Tina.

***

'Hi!' she called out as she opened the door into the apartment.

A pale-faced Tina appeared. They hadn't talked that morning when Eleanor was leaving so the mood between them was tense.

'Hi,' Tina whispered.

Eleanor noticed the young girl's furrowed brow and the limp hair that was normally pinned up in a 'ready for business' fashion. A wave of compassion convinced her that her new plan was the right one.

'Let's have a chat.' She reached out to Tina and hugged her.

The young girl began sobbing as she allowed herself to fall into Eleanor's embrace.

'I am so sorry…' Tina began.

'No, no, no.' Eleanor guided her into the living room and sat beside her on the settee.

Gabriel slipped quietly away to his room.

'I'm the one who should be sorry, Tina. In saying what you said, you were voicing my own fears and that made me feel guilty and lash out at you.'

Tina gazed up in confusion, wiping her nose on the cuff of her cardigan. Eleanor offered her a tissue.

'You're absolutely right, Tina. It's not fair to keep Gabriel at home. He does have… special needs.' Eleanor pretended to swallow back tears. 'I think I told you it wasn't a straightforward pregnancy and that has probably made me overprotective.'

'No, it none of my business…' Tina whispered.

'Well, I think it is your business and what you said to me was brave. It got me thinking… and this morning, I went to visit a school.'

'Oh.' Tina's eyes widened. 'That's… good.'

'It was lovely. In fact, they suggested he starts tomorrow. No time like the present, I suppose.' Eleanor feigned a brave smile.

'I understand. I will miss him.' Tina's lip was trembling.

'And he will certainly miss you.' Eleanor stroked Tina's arm. 'Why don't we call Gabriel in and tell him the news together? I'll get the kettle on.' Eleanor rose to her feet, lifted an envelope out of her bag and placed it on the table in front of Tina. 'This is for you. It should keep you going until you find another position.'

***

Gabriel was up early the next morning. He had been thrilled at the news he was to start school and as soon as they left the apartment, he raced ahead of Eleanor and jumped up and down at the car door, desperate for his mum to catch up with him. He wriggled so much Eleanor struggled to do up his seatbelt.

'Excited?' She kissed Gabriel on the nose once he was securely strapped in.

'Yes!' He kicked his legs. 'Will the party children be there?'

'Who?'

'The children at the Christmas party, remember?'

'Oh, I really don't know.' Eleanor's heart sank. *Hopefully not*, she thought; she'd added two years to his age since then.

'What will Tina do now?' Gabriel asked. He had accepted Tina's departure remarkably well, especially given her promise she would keep in touch.

'She'll look after another little boy or girl who's not old enough for school yet,' said Eleanor.

'Am I old enough for school?'

'Yes, you are,' replied Eleanor.

'What makes you the age you are?' Gabriel screwed up his nose.

Eleanor was quiet for a moment as she considered how best to answer the question.

'Age is a funny thing, Gabriel. In one way, it's a number that tells you how many years have passed since someone was born. But sometimes, people use it as a sort of description of someone's maturity and abilities.' She paused to assess his understanding of what she was trying to explain.

'Yes?'

'It can be quite confusing for people when they hear that someone is, say ten years old, but then find they can't read or don't understand things in the way that ten-year-olds usually do. Saying they are ten might make people expect the wrong things of them,' Eleanor continued.

Gabriel nodded as she spoke.

'Well, in the same way, people don't usually expect young children to be able to do some of the things that you can do, like read or count…'

'Or speak in another language?' Gabriel cut in.

'Exactly.' Eleanor delighted in his grasp of her explanation. 'So, sometimes, to save all that confusion, it's simpler to describe a person by what is called their mental age. That's sort of like their thinking and understanding age.'

'So, how old would you say I am now?' asked Gabriel.

'Let's just say for the moment, that you're six?' She turned and looked at him to gauge his response to her suggestion.

He nodded. 'Today, I'll be six. Look! April Springs Elementary!' Gabriel giggled and bounced up and down in his car seat, thrilled to have spotted the sign while it was still too far in the distance for Eleanor to read.

'Yep, we're nearly there.' Eleanor watched through the rear-view mirror as he twisted to the right and left, taking in as much of his surroundings as he could.

There were plenty of free places in the car park, most of the parents having dropped their children off an hour before. Eleanor rolled into the space closest to the path and brought the car to a slow halt. Her heart was racing and she could see her hands trembling as she reached for her bag.

'So, what do you think?' She tried to keep her voice as normal- sounding as possible.

'I like it.' Gabriel undid his seatbelt and reached for the door handle.

Eleanor joined him at the side of the car and took hold of his hand. She took in a deep breath of the fresh air. It was the smell of playing outside, of childhood, of freedom. Despite her nerves, she felt a thrill of excitement for her little boy at the thought of the joys and discoveries that lay ahead of him.

'This place feels happy,' Gabriel said, smiling up at his mother.

'Yes, it does,' replied Eleanor, in a faraway voice.

They paused at the entrance.

'Don't worry, Mum. I'm going to have a great time.'

Mrs Quinn was waiting to greet her new pupil and held the door open for them before Eleanor could press the buzzer.

'Good morning!' She smiled. 'Welcome to April Springs, Gabriel.'

Eleanor watched as Mrs Quinn looked into Gabriel's eyes. She saw that look she had seen so often now in those meeting him for the first time. It was a look of surprise that soon became enchantment, a look that lingered. She glanced up at Eleanor, as if reviewing in her mind the description of the child she'd heard the day before. Eleanor nodded her response.

'Would you like to see my office, Gabriel?' The principal's tone had altered since her effervescent greeting, becoming quieter and more considered.

'Yes please.' He took the principal's outstretched hand. 'Mummy too?' He looked back at Eleanor.

'Of course.' Mrs Quinn laughed gently as she led the way.

From beyond a closed door at the far end of the corridor, Eleanor could once again hear children's laughter rise and fall in waves of delight. This was exactly the sort of environment Eleanor wanted for her son. Yet, at the same time, she felt suddenly blindsided and powerless. Something deep within her wanted Gabriel to turn from it, refuse to go, to need her more than anything or anyone else. She had to fight hard to quell a huge wave of sadness that threatened to overwhelm her as she took the seat beside Gabriel's and clenched every muscle in her aching throat to reduce the chance of breaking into sobs.

'So, Gabriel, are you looking forward to starting school?' Mrs Quinn asked, smiling kindly at him.

'Oh yes!' he replied, without taking his eyes off the wall of pictures.

Eleanor tapped his knee, gently calling his attention back to the conversation.

'Don't worry,' Mrs Quinn said, smiling, 'I take that as a good sign.' She looked back at the little boy. 'What are your favourite things to do?'

'I like drawing and books and playing games and puzzles and making things and listening to stories and…' Gabriel listed his interests as if he would never stop.

'Gee, you like to keep busy, don't you? Well, we do all those things here, and maybe even things you haven't ever tried before, like swimming, music, dancing…'

Gabriel grinned with delight.

'Why don't I take you straight to Miss Hunter's room and you can meet your new friends? She'll show you where to hang your coat and bag and you can change into your indoor shoes. Would that be all right, Mom?'

Eleanor's heart lurched. It was time. 'Now? Oh… of course,' she replied.

Gabriel raced to the door, but just as they were about to leave, he ran back to Eleanor and threw his arms around her neck. 'I love you so, so, so, so much,' he whispered before returning to the principal's side.

Eleanor could feel the dam of tears was ready to breach her weakened defences. She stood up and followed them into the corridor, watching as they made their way to the door that separated the children from the outside world.

'Don't worry, Mummy, I'll be fine!' Gabriel called over his shoulder to her once they reached the door.

'Well, aren't you a sympathetic young man?' Mrs Quinn exclaimed.

Gabriel took her hand again and, together, they walked out of sight.

He was gone. Eleanor stood alone on the polished tiles. No longer able to restrain the salty torrent another second, she began to cry.

'He'll be fine,' the receptionist said. 'It's usually harder for the parents than the children. Here.' She offered a tissue, clearly accustomed to reactions like these.

'Thanks, I'm sorry.' Eleanor felt foolish and annoyed with herself. She wiped each cheek and then her nose and forced a smile. 'Pick-up at three then?' She just managed the words.

'Yes,' the receptionist replied. 'Most of the moms wait at the gate over there.' She pointed through the front door.

Eleanor got into her car and rubbed her face with her hands. She'd thought about this moment so much, the moment she left Gabriel exposed to the world, at the mercy of people who knew nothing about him. She had desperately wanted this normality for him but now it had happened, she felt bereft of all purpose. *Please God,* she thought as she sat weeping at the wheel of her stationary car, *I hope I've done the right thing.*

***

That afternoon, she tried to work at home but it was impossible. Her mind was fully taken up with replaying the Sophie encounter and worrying about her son. She checked her watch constantly, willing it to be time to collect him and finally, unable to sit still, left to pick him up much earlier than was required.

She parked on the tarmac beside the playing fields and waited. More cars began to arrive, filling the spaces around her until parking spots were scarce and drivers circled slowly, like birds of prey.

Women, mostly younger-looking than Eleanor, gathered in groups along the fence, chatting and laughing. Many held babies in their arms or held tightly to toddlers, determined to free themselves of their mothers' grasp. Eleanor watched from her car; she wouldn't go and join them, not today.

Instead, she peered through her windscreen, beyond the chatting parents, to the glass doors that led from the classrooms onto the playground. At last, she saw them open and her heart leapt. She got out of the car and hurried towards the pick-up point. No children appeared for a while but she could see an adult beyond the doors, helping with coats and shoes.

Suppose they notice something unusual about him? Eleanor worried. *What then?*

Children began to wander out, just a few at first, then a large group and finally, the stragglers. But there was no sign of Gabriel. Eleanor felt her breathing become shallower, faster. There were only two other mums still at the gates and they were just chatting, their children already by their sides.

Unable to bear the suspense, she opened the gate and entered the playground. The mums stopped talking and watched as she walked across to the classrooms. She guessed she was breaking a rule, but she had to find out what was going on.

When she reached the open doors, she tapped on them with the back of her hand, but there was no response. She stepped inside and found herself in an open hallway. Around the bright red walls, coloured pegs at the level of her waist were fixed, each with a picture card and a name in bold letters above it. Her eye was drawn to the only one still holding a jacket: Gabriel's.

Then, from a door to her left, she heard his voice. *Thank God*, she thought, and hurried towards it.

'Don't worry, you're safe now,' she heard a woman say, 'No one is going to hurt you.'

Eleanor's heart lurched. What on earth had Gabriel been telling her?

'We're here to help you, to set you free.' The voice was gentle, encouraging. Was it his teacher? *What in God's name?*

'Such a little thing, but, with any luck, you can find your way back home…'

Eleanor clutched onto the door frame.

'Is everything all right?' she heard a familiar voice from behind her.

She turned sharply, clutching her chest.

'I'm so sorry, I didn't mean to alarm you,' Mrs Quinn apologised. 'Gabriel… he didn't come out… I panicked…'

'I quite understand. One moment.' The principal stepped into the classroom.

Eleanor heard a whispered interchange, too soft for her to pick out words.

'Mrs Bartlett?' The principal beckoned to her. 'Come.'

Eleanor walked towards the room. The rush of blood through her ears was deafening, the putrid taste of fear. At first, she could see no one, apart from Mrs Quinn, but then she heard Gabriel's voice, low and gentle, murmuring, 'Come and see.'

Then she spotted him, crouched on the floor, Miss Hunter kneeling by his side.

'It was trapped and really scared, but we managed to catch him. I hope he's okay.'

Leaning forwards, Eleanor saw Gabriel cradle a small bird in his cupped hands.

'Oh my,' she managed to mumble, before sinking to the floor beside him.

'Poor little thing, it must be terrified,' Mrs Quinn said.

'Actually, it's been quite calm since Gabriel picked it up,' Miss Hunter said, shrugging.

Eleanor said nothing; she could only feel relief.

'You'll be okay, won't you?' Gabriel whispered and smoothed his thumb over the tiny creature's head.

'I'm sure he will be,' Miss Hunter replied. 'We've had little visitors like this before, and they always fly off just fine. But he wouldn't leave Gabriel's hands.'

'He landed right in front of me, Mummy. I think he's a winter wren.'

'Really?' Mrs Quinn swallowed back her surprise. 'How do you know that?'

'Tina and I used to look at lots of bird books.' Gabriel didn't raise his eyes from his feathered treasure.

Both teachers stared at Eleanor.

'Of course,' she responded brightly, 'Tina was our nanny and her partner is a keen ornithologist…'

'I see,' said Mrs Quinn, her voice sounding more curious than convinced.

Miss Hunter stood up. 'I think it's time we helped him on his way. Perhaps he'll fly off if I hold him?' she asked Gabriel.

He nodded and kissed the bird on its feathered head. 'Come back any time,' he said, passing it into Miss Hunter's hands. 'He should leave the way he came in,' the little boy said as his teacher approached one of the windows. 'That will make it easier for him to find his way home.'

'Of course.' Miss Hunter joined Gabriel at a neighbouring window.

Slowly, she unfolded her fingers, but the bird did not move.

'Fly home,' Gabriel encouraged, 'Your mummy is looking for you.'

At last, the little bird flapped its wings and in an instant was gone, up into the nearby trees.

'Well done,' said Miss Hunter. 'You have a way with animals. Do you have any pets at home?' She turned to include Eleanor as she spoke.

'No,' Gabriel answered before Eleanor had a chance, 'We live in an apartment. It wouldn't be fair, would it, Mummy?'

Eleanor shook her head. 'No, it wouldn't. So, have you had a good day?'

'It's been great fun,' said Gabriel, 'And I've got homework!' he added proudly.

'Gabriel has settled in very well. I can't believe he's only been here for one afternoon. He already feels like part of the class. And tomorrow you'll be here for the whole day.'

***

The following Monday afternoon, Eleanor flicked through Sophie's assessment report on Gabriel while she waited for the others to arrive. It was well-written but meaningless. Sophie had no direct contact with Gabriel and believed the assessments were carried out by Eleanor at home. It was Sophie's job to analyse and interpret the data she was given, but the results were a fiction of Eleanor's making and while they continued to reflect his gifted nature, they considerably understated his true progress.

'What the fuck is he playing at?' Allen slammed into the room, Simon at his heels.

'Who?' Eleanor was brought abruptly back to the present.

'Who do you think?' Allen opened his laptop and clicked on his emails.

'Carl, of course.' Simon sighed heavily.

'That man has one hell of a nerve!' Allen's face was flushed. 'I've been asked to provide a reference in support of *his* application for a research grant to fund some project or other on genetic matriarchy: *The Might of Mitochondria*. That's our field, not his. What's he playing at?'

'Power games,' Eleanor snapped, silently recoiling at Allen's assumption of *his* part ownership of her research. 'He's always been like that, desperate to link his name with anything new. He's scared we'll come up with something, so he's allying himself to the subject area in general. It's a sort of insurance policy with a very low premium, because I'm quite certain he has no intention whatsoever of investing any time or effort into this. He has no data and no involvement in what we're doing in any way. He's just planting his flag in the academic soil. I've seen him do this before, many times.'

'He doesn't have any samples, does he?' asked Allen.

'Unlikely.' Eleanor paused. 'Although he did, of course, have access to everything while we were still in Glasgow.' She drummed her fingers on the table.

'And he was a party to many of the discussions then too,' said Simon. 'I suppose we will just have to wait and see.'

'Anyway, how did your showdown with Tina go?'

'Messy,' Eleanor grimaced, 'But it's sorted now, thanks to your genius idea, Allen.'

'Which one would that be?' He half-smiled with satisfaction.

'Fighting fire with fire.'

'Ahh,' Simon joined in, 'Scared her away?'

'Absolutely. Ended up feeling quite sorry for her,' Eleanor said, sighing.

'So, who has an eye on the kid now?' asked Allen.

Eleanor felt her anger swell at Allen's words. She despised the way he now rarely mentioned Gabriel by name.

'It was no big deal,' said Eleanor. 'I got a temp in for this week and a new nanny starts next Monday.'

'And Gabriel, he's okay with that?' asked Simon.

'Surprisingly, yes. I think I underestimate his resilience,' offered Eleanor. She glanced at her watch. 'I'd better go, the agency could only offer part time nannies at the moment, I'm afraid.'

'Sure,' said Simon, 'See you tomorrow.'

***

When she collected Gabriel from school that afternoon, Eleanor delighted in hearing the details of his day.

'What do you like doing best of all?' she asked him as they made their way back to their apartment.

'I love it all,' he announced, 'But probably most of all, I like being with my friends. They're very good fun, although Elizabeth can be unkind when she is having a sad day.'

'Oh dear, is she mean to you?' Eleanor half-listened as she concentrated on a four-way stop.

He shook his head.

'So, what does she do?'

'She doesn't do anything, she just thinks things that aren't very kind,' said Gabriel.

'And does she tell you what she's thinking?'

'No, she wouldn't do that. And it's not her fault she can't do her work very well, but it's not anyone else's fault either. She's just frightened, and I try to help her, but sometimes she's too sad to see that.'

'And do the other children try to help too?' Eleanor slowed her pace to concentrate on Gabriel's words.

'Sometimes. Nathan tried to make her laugh, but she thought he was laughing at her and she felt really sad, and so did Nathan. That's why he didn't eat his lunch...'

'Did he tell you that?'

'No, he wasn't at my table, but I could feel it.' Gabriel sighed. 'I tried to explain it to him at craft time, but he wasn't listening well enough, although Miss Hunter was and she said that was very interesting.'

Eleanor pulled into the car park of a local store and turned to look at Gabriel. She stretched towards him and stroked his knee as she spoke.

'You know, darling, it can be quite difficult being with other people, especially if you are kind and care about them.'

Gabriel nodded.

'And some people are better at understanding these things than others. You are very good at it, you're sensitive.'

'So are you, Mummy.'

Eleanor smiled. 'Not as much as you are, my lovely, but I'm working on it.'

'So, is it a good thing?'

'Yes, it's a lovely thing, but… for some people, it can be a scary thing, if other people are sensitive and they are not.'

'Why?'

'Because… well, it's a bit like being with people who are speaking a language you don't understand. And they don't like it.'

Eleanor examined Gabriel's expression, trying to assess his grasp of what she was saying.

'I see,' he said, 'So, should I try not to feel things?'

'I don't think that's possible, darling, and it's good to understand people, it makes us kinder to each other. But it's better not to tell people what you know about *them* unless they tell you first.'

'All right.' Gabriel nodded but she could see confusion in his eyes as he turned away from her.

All the way home, he was quieter than normal, as if his exuberance had been blunted. But for his safety, he had to learn what not to say. She just hoped he would understand that, without being frightened.

***

Eleanor found it difficult to sleep that night. Gabriel's words replayed in her head, a verbal backdrop to the collage of images that raced before her each time she closed her eyes. Time and again, she awoke abruptly only then realising she had slipped away. At last, sleep descended, and in her mind, she found herself strolling through a meadow.

It was filled with wildflowers that swayed effortlessly, casting their scents to the wind. Gabriel was by her side, skipping and smiling as they sauntered through this paradise. He took her hand and squeezed his love into her palm. Never before had she felt such contentment.

Then, sitting beneath a great oak, she opened the basket by her side, lifting out the sandwiches and strawberries that were to comprise their picnic lunch. They sipped cool drinks from plastic cups and listened to the sounds of nature all around them.

Eleanor watched as Gabriel splashed in a nearby brook. He was safe; she need not worry. In her dream, she rested her head on a pillow of moss and allowed herself to slip into a balmy haze. Then, rousing to the chill of a sudden breeze, she looked to the stream and saw Lillooet on the opposite bank, beckoning to Gabriel. He waved to her and looked excited to see her. Eleanor called to him and as he turned to face her, she saw the baby become a child and then a man. He smiled at Eleanor and blew her a kiss before turning back towards the brook and the stepping-stones that lay across it.

'No!' she shouted, waking herself up from her dream. 'Please, no!' she said more quietly, into the darkness.

And instantly, from Gabriel's room next door, she heard him wail his reply.

Chapter 27

Eleanor sat close to Allen and Simon. Against her better judgement, her colleagues had pressed her to call Carl and find out more about the research behind the paper he was due to present in Paris. She held her breath as the tone rang out for longer than she'd expected and looked to Simon and then Allen, glued to either side of her, having insisted the call was conducted on loudspeaker. She wondered if they were checking up on *her* as much as anything.

With some relief, her finger dropped towards the red circle, when suddenly they heard him pick up.

'Yes?' he barked.

'Carl, it's Eleanor here…'

'I gathered that. Caller display is a marvellous invention.' There was a lot of background noise and it was difficult to make out his words, but his tone was crystal clear.

'Sorry, are you still at work? What time is it there, just after five?'

'Yes, it is and I am. What do you want?' Carl's tone was exactly as she had anticipated.

'Just wanted a chat about the subject of your paper… genetic archaeology… but is this a bad time?'

Allen glared at Eleanor; she knew he was desperate to hear what he had to say.

'What about it?' Carl seemed to have acquired a new economy with words.

'I'm curious, Carl. This isn't your area—'

'*Wasn't,*' he corrected her.

'So, have you been researching this for long? How on earth did you amass enough data to sustain a publication in so short a time?'

They heard music in the background, then a voice, a female voice, call to him.

'I'm going to have to go, Eleanor, got a lot going on here. Talk later.' He ended the call.

Sounds like we were intruding on someone's social life,' Simon said, tutting.

Eleanor felt a wave of shame wash over her as she recalled being that voice in the past, while Carl fended off calls from his *crazy* wife. How she had laughed at his antics in those days.

'Bastard. We've got to find out what he's up to,' said Allen.

'We do,' said Simon, 'You need to get over to Paris, Eleanor. Applications to attend must be submitted by the start of summer break.'

'When is that?' Eleanor's heart plummeted at the thought of making new childcare arrangements.

'The end of next week,' said Simon. 'I *know* Carl is not up to date with our project, but from my reading of the abstract, he seems to be asking exactly the sorts of questions thrown up by our work with Gabriel. And we all know how he likes to make a splash.'

'Absolutely. And we need to make sure this one doesn't turn into a tsunami,' said Allen.

'I'd love to go, but I can't imagine I'd be a popular choice round here for attending,' said Eleanor, 'Last into the department and all that.'

'Do not worry about office politics, I can deal with that,' said Simon. 'I think it's important that you *both* go. Carl will not be expecting you to be there, and Allen is the only other person who knows what is going on, so if any questions are asked, he will be there as… backup.'

Allen consulted the diary on his phone. 'Last week in July, isn't it?'

'Yes.' Simon pushed a programme across the table. 'Will that be a problem for you, Eleanor?'

'I shouldn't think so,' she replied with much more confidence than she felt. 'I'll see what I can do.'

***

For the remainder of the day, Eleanor was preoccupied with the problem of what to do with Gabriel while she was in Paris. She had never left him with anyone for any length of time apart from a few overnight stays with her mother when he was a baby. By the time she arrived at April Springs that afternoon, she was no further forward and was looking forward to the distraction of spending some quality time with her son.

She parked her car and strolled down the path to where mothers were gathering. But before she reached them, she saw the receptionist standing at the main entrance, beckoning Eleanor towards her.

'Mrs Bartlett, would you have a few moments to speak with the principal?'

Despite the warmth of the day, Eleanor felt her skin chill.

'Of course, is everything all right?' she asked.

'I'm sure it's nothing to worry about. Mrs Quinn often tries to catch a few minutes with the moms like this. Saves them taking time off work.' She stepped back, inviting Eleanor to enter. 'Do have a seat, she won't be a moment.'

Eleanor sat in the corner chair and picked up a magazine from the coffee table. She could see the paper tremble between her fingers.

Dear God, she thought. *What am I going to hear?* Eleanor stared at the page ahead of her without trying to read it.

After a few minutes, a door opened and Mrs Quinn appeared in the corridor, beckoning Eleanor into her office.

She had been dreading this moment since Gabriel had started at April Springs. The silence from the school had already been longer than she'd expected. She knew this would happen at some point but nonetheless, she felt her mouth go dry as she waited for Mrs Quinn to speak.

With a practised professionalism that made it impossible for Eleanor to guess what was to follow, Mrs Quinn finally opened the meeting with a question.

'So, how do you think Gabriel has enjoyed his time with us so far?'

'He seems to be very happy here,' Eleanor replied.

'Yes,' the principal said with a smile, 'But I'm sure you must be aware of his outstanding abilities. He is quite the most remarkable child we have ever taught.'

Eleanor nodded and waited for what was to follow.

'We're only a few weeks away from summer recess, so I'm thinking now of what would be best for Gabriel next year.' She paused. 'I'm sure you'll agree with me that grade two would not be appropriate. Not that Gabriel would make things difficult, he's always so… accommodating.'

Eleanor nodded again.

'How would you feel about Gabriel moving up to grade three, or perhaps even four? He's become such a tall boy, I'm sure he wouldn't look out of place. And he seems to have made friends throughout the entire school, so I imagine he would settle anywhere.'

Eleanor hesitated as she considered the year ahead. Gabriel was certainly very happy at the school, but with each month that passed, his anonymity would be increasingly threatened. She couldn't imagine how mature he would look by the start of the next term, never mind the end of the next academic year. She knew also that, once observed by the school in real time, she would have great difficulty warding off questions and investigations.

'Actually,' said Eleanor, 'I've been deferring making plans for next year because of the fluidity of my own arrangements and, well, it now seems quite likely that we will be returning to Scotland in the autumn. So, thank you for giving this matter your attention, but we will probably be gone by the start of the next session.' Eleanor surprised herself with the ease with which she delivered her response.

Mrs Quinn's face fell. 'Oh, I am sorry to hear that,' she said, 'It has been such a pleasure to have Gabriel in the school.'

'And I'm grateful to you for making him so welcome. I haven't told Gabriel about the move yet,' Eleanor added, 'So I'd appreciate it if we kept this between ourselves for the moment.'

'Of course, naturally.' Mrs Quinn stood up and walked to the door. 'Thank you for letting me know, I do appreciate it.'

Eleanor walked into the playground just as the children began to emerge from their classrooms. She would have to find a new placement before she could break the news to Gabriel.

***

That evening, the sun poured into the apartment as Eleanor sat with her laptop on her knee. She had a backlog of emails to deal with but was struggling to stay focussed on the task.

Gabriel looked up from his drawing. 'What are you thinking about, Mummy? You look worried.'

'Do I?' Eleanor startled to attention. 'Not worried at all, darling, just thinking.'

'What about?'

'The summer holidays, weeks and weeks of no school, and I will still have to work…'

'Tina?' Gabriel leapt to his feet and jumped up and down.

'Oh, darling…' She felt so guilty looking into his hopeful eyes. 'That would be perfect, but Tina is working somewhere else now.'

The little boy looked disappointed for a moment, then announced, 'I know…' He ran off to fetch his school bag. 'I could always go to summer camp.'

'What was that, darling?'

'I was thinking that perhaps I could go to summer camp?'

Eleanor closed her laptop and stared at the boy, unsure what to say.

'We were given some information about it today.' He pulled out a bundle of brightly coloured fliers and a letter printed on an A4 sheet of white paper from his bag.

'Summer School: Day and Residential classes,' Eleanor read. She glanced at a few of the sheets. 'These look very interesting.'

'And I think it would be fun.' Gabriel's face glowed as he spoke.

'You're right, these look great!' said Eleanor. 'Which ones do you like the look of?' She read each sheet in turn then passed them back to Gabriel.

He flicked through the small pile, reading aloud the headline on each.

'Multi Activity, French Immersion, The Great Outdoors, Maths is Fun…' He paused to read more of the blurb on the maths sheet.

'Perhaps something more entertaining than academic?' Eleanor suggested, calculating that artistic activities might offer less risk of Gabriel being noticed as a prodigy. 'In fact, I may have to be away for a week or so at the end of July. How would you feel about trying out one of the residential courses?'

'Cool,' said Gabriel. 'So, how old do you think I'll be by then?' He held a sheet in each hand, one headed five to eight years and the other, nine to twelve.

'I think you'll find those activities more interesting.' Eleanor waved in the direction of the latter sheet.

'So do I, Mum, just checking.' A cheeky grin had spread across his face.

***

The long summer recess had finally begun and there were fewer students to be seen around the research centre as Simon, Eleanor and Allen met to discuss their Paris strategy.

'I still can't believe we've both been given the green light to go,' Eleanor said grinning at Allen.

'Childcare sorted?' asked Simon.

'Yes, no problem. The nanny was more than happy to stay over, said she needed the money.'

'Perfect.' Simon nodded.

'So long as she doesn't cancel or end up in the emergency room with him again,' Allen quipped.

Allen didn't trust her anymore, she knew that; since she had gone behind their backs about Gabriel's schooling four months before. *Dear God,* she often thought, *what would he do if he knew the truth?*

But as for Simon, she wasn't sure where she stood with him.

'Let's hope not,' Eleanor commented calmly, but her stomach turned at the very thought of being so far away and unable to protect her boy.

Allen was flicking through a pile of papers on his desk. Suddenly, he snatched one of them and marched towards the other two, tossing the document onto the table.

'What is this?' Simon picked it up.

'It's a golden opportunity, Simon, that's what it is! A way for us to get some idea of what Gabriel's rapid growth means for his life expectancy.'

'That would be helpful,' Eleanor said mildly, determined not to become the audience.

'Absolutely,' Allen continued. 'Are we looking at a *creature* that runs the course of its life in tune with its accelerated development, and therefore will die sooner than a *normal* person would…'

'Or,' continued Eleanor, ignoring Allen's cold portrayal of her son, 'Will he reach maturity early and remain there for—'

'Christ knows how long!' Allen talked over her.

Simon picked up the paper and read the introduction.

'DNA Transfer in Mice?' He peered over at Allen. 'How can this help?'

'It's a technique for introducing sections of DNA into colonies of mice and observing the effects,' Allen replied. 'If we were to graft part of Gabriel's DNA, those sections known to be associated with longevity, onto mice then we could observe their rate of development and any changes to expected lifespan,' said Allen.

Eleanor winced.

Simon continued flicking through the paper. 'But this research, it was done using mice DNA only,' he said. 'You cannot just insert human DNA into mice like that.'

'Can't? Or *shouldn't?*' urged Allen. 'Of course we can! We've all seen those pictures, grotesque though they are, of a mouse with a human ear growing on its back…'

'That's hardly the same thing,' Eleanor jumped in. 'That wasn't DNA transfer; that was—'

'Whatever. It's the same principle.' Allen waved away their objections. 'Ethically the same and…' He brandished the paper. 'Scientifically just as doable.'

Eleanor was reeling at the thought of what Allen's plans might mean for Gabriel. He was growing incredibly rapidly; most people would probably guess he was around nine or ten now. But he had only been alive for eighteen months and to Eleanor, he was in so many ways still the infant she cradled and caressed just last Christmas in her apartment, who had by some miracle, navigated his unlikely route to life and who had lain in her arms, staring into her eyes.

She was brought back to the moment by a knock on the door.

'We need to do this,' Allen insisted, his voice quieter than moments before. 'Come in.'

The door opened slowly and Sophie peered around it. 'Sorry to interrupt. I just wondered if you still need a lift home tonight?'

'Ah, yes, that would be great,' Allen replied.

'Sure.'

'Hang on, Sophie. Do you have a minute? I'll print off the most recent results for Gabriel. Might give you a break from admin duties.'

'Of course.' Sophie closed the door behind her and sat down.

'We have not seen you for a while,' Simon said, smiling at Sophie.

'Yes, poor Sophie's been press ganged into updating my *finds* catalogue. Not too exciting, I'm afraid.' Allen didn't take his eyes off his laptop as he spoke.

'It's fine,' said Sophie. 'It's certainly not as entertaining as assessing the infants, of course, especially Gabriel. How is he doing at the nursery?'

Eleanor had almost forgotten the lie they'd used to terminate Sophie's front line role. She froze for a moment, fearing Sophie somehow knew about April Springs. But neither Allen nor Simon seemed perturbed; they had fewer threads of deceit to hold together.

'He's fine.' Eleanor nodded slowly as she fought to maintain her composure.

'I imagine he's a bit of a star there already,' she continued.

'He's settled well.' Eleanor hoped her tone would encourage Sophie to drop the topic.

'I mean, we've all just got so used to him,' Sophie said, almost to herself, 'But it must be harder for other people. You know, people who don't know him. I wonder what they'll make of him?'

'True,' Simon mumbled, glancing at Allen to hurry him up. But Allen did not appear to be listening.

'It must be so much harder for someone like Carl too. I wonder if he thought the data was wrong? I found it hard enough to believe and I was the one gathering it. But it must all seem even stranger when you're so far away…'

'Carl?' Allen looked up sharply. 'What's this got to do with Carl?'

Sophie looked startled. 'Well, you know, the whole Gabriel thing,' she said.

'Yes?' He pulled himself upright. 'But what has *that* got to do with Carl?'

Sophie was silenced by the urgency in Allen's voice.

Eleanor didn't move, all her senses focussed on Sophie.

'Have you been in contact with him recently?' Allen rose to his feet.

'Recently?' she faltered. 'What do you mean?'

'I mean, since you came back from Glasgow. Has Carl made any contact with you?'

'No, not really,' said Sophie, 'He doesn't even acknowledge that he's received my reports.'

There was a moment of stunned silence.

'Sophie!' Allen slammed his fist against the wall. 'Who in God's name told you to keep Carl in the loop?'

Eleanor gasped.

'What do you mean? Nobody ever told me he was out of it!' Sophie turned to Eleanor and then Simon, whose white-knuckled hands covered his mouth.

'Wasn't it obvious?' Allen shouted.

'Why would it be obvious?' Sophie snapped back. 'I have no idea what you're talking about. And if I've made a mistake, then I'm sorry. But maybe if you guys weren't so secretive about everything to do with Gabriel, maybe if you'd trusted me a bit more from the start, then this… whatever it is I'm supposed to have done wrong… could have been avoided!' She rose sharply and slammed out of the office.

'Fucking, stupid, fucking idiot!' Allen scattered the thin sheets from the printer tray onto the floor, the fake Gabriel data now strewn at their feet.

'At least now we know where Carl is coming from,' Simon said, sighing heavily.

'Perhaps,' seethed Allen, 'But that doesn't mean we know where he is going.'

Chapter 28

Arriving in Paris with Allen, Eleanor was disappointed to step from the plane into a cold, damp morning, having become accustomed to the more comfortable climate of British Columbia and the assumptions she had learnt to make about the weather.

As she and Allen made the short journey in the cab around the outskirts of the city to their hotel, she thought only of Gabriel, calculating, as she had done throughout the flight, what time it would be back at home and wondering what he would be doing and how he was feeling without her. She recalled how thrilled he'd looked as they were shown to his dormitory at summer camp and how easy it had seemed for him when they said their goodbyes.

'Have a great time in Paris, Mum,' he had said before she hugged him, 'And please don't worry about me. I know this is going to be fun.' He kissed her moist cheek and waved her off with a smile.

'You been to Paris before?' Allen's question snapped her out of her reverie.

'Yes,' said Eleanor, 'But it was a while ago now. We passed through briefly on a family holiday. I was a teenager, still at school.' She smiled at the recollection. 'What about you?'

'No,' he replied, 'This is my first time. Sure looks busy. Would like to look around a bit but I don't imagine that'll be possible. Want to keep my eye on things.'

'You mean Carl?'

Allen nodded.

'That might be harder than you'd think,' Eleanor warned. 'If he's true to form, he'll be following his own agenda and that tends to have little to do with any conference.'

***

'Thank God,' she breathed, letting the door of her hotel room close heavily behind her.

It was a dark room and when she pulled the curtains open, she found herself peering down into a drab service area, crammed with bins and crates.

With a sigh, she closed the curtains again, turned on the lamps and looked at her watch. It was eleven in the morning. She pulled her phone from her bag to call Gabriel. She couldn't wait to hear his voice again but then, with a muttered curse, she dropped the phone onto the bed. *It's the middle of the night there,* she sighed to herself. She gazed around the room, yawned and wondered if she should sleep a while. She flicked through the conference welcome pack and scanned the day's programme of events, deciding there was nothing that couldn't be missed. She'd sleep until lunch.

But then her phone beeped. Picking it up, she found a message from a number she did not recognise. She opened it.

Where are you? Need to talk. I'm downstairs. Carl.

Eleanor tossed the phone back onto the bed. *No!* she thought. But then, she took a deep breath and picked it up again. This was why she was here. It was as good a time as any to get their first encounter over with.

She glanced at her bedraggled image in the mirror. *So?* She flicked her hair defiantly. *I'm not putting on a show for him!* She threw her phone in her bag and marched to the door. But just as she reached for the handle, she stopped. Why on earth should she make it so easy for him to act detached and uninterested? She strolled back to the mirror. Smiling at her image, she selected one of her more tailored outfits from her suitcase and headed for the shower.

***

Entering the foyer, Eleanor could see quite a number of the delegates already mingling. She recognised many of the faces but couldn't see Carl amongst them. She hadn't seen him since she'd stormed out of his office nearly a year before and despite herself, her stomach churned at the thought of facing him again.

But she knew Carl would not bring up anything contentious here. He would never cause a scene in public; he cared far too much about impressing others.

Suddenly, she heard him. She turned to see a group of four sitting at a table near the bar with Carl, holding court as ever, his voice ringing out. She studied each member of his audience, all female, their eyes fixed on him, and the smiles with which they rewarded each fleeting moment of attention he gifted them.

'Old flirt,' she muttered. 'Why the hell are they falling for it?'

He did have a way of making people feel special, she conceded. At least, those he singled out for his attention. She recalled how flattered she had felt in those early days of their acquaintance, when he chose to sit beside her in meetings or asked for her opinion on matters of importance. But that was years ago and now that Eleanor had seen him work on others in the same way, all those pretty research assistants and wide-eyed undergraduates, she felt foolish that she, too, had been so taken in by him.

'My lips are sealed,' she heard him say to the three women who laughed and smiled back. 'You'll just have to come and hear the full story at my presentation tomorrow. At least I'm one of the first up, so you won't have to wait too long.'

He spotted her. 'Eleanor!' He beckoned to her from the midst of his entourage. The three women in his company were all about Sophie's age and they all turned to watch her as she approached.

Carl stood up and held out a welcoming arm. Eleanor found herself placing a kiss on his cheek, before sitting in the chair he pulled over from a nearby table.

'A most welcome addition to this delightful company,' he boomed, 'Estelle, Claudette and Eloise.' He waved his arm towards each of the trio. 'They all work for the *Institut de Reserche de Paris*,' he said with an exaggerated French accent.

Eleanor smiled, suppressing her urge to laugh.

'And this, ladies, is Eleanor Bartlett, formerly of the research institute, Glasgow, now cutting about in North America, no less.

Eleanor was my research assistant for a while, amongst other things.' He smirked as Eleanor rolled her eyes. 'So, how are things across the pond?'

Eleanor watched as his eyes scanned her, first from face down, then on a slow return, resting briefly on her cleavage.

'Good.' Eleanor nodded, her fists clenched.

'Are you here on your own?' Carl continued, knowing full well, Eleanor guessed, she was not.

'No, Allen's here too,' she replied, meeting his gaze.

Carl smiled but said nothing. Eleanor thought she saw one of the young women smile too.

'How are Lydia and the girls?' asked Eleanor, hoping that reminding him of his family might dash his swagger a bit.

'Fine.' He caught her drift and paused to sip his drink as the women began to strike up a conversation amongst themselves.

'I didn't ever get the full copy of your paper,' Eleanor went on, relieved to find she felt a little calmer. 'Looking forward to reading it.'

'Yes, it's fascinating stuff. Would be interesting to have a proper chat with you about it sometime.'

'What about dinner, tonight?' Eleanor held him with a fierce gaze.

'I'm not sure I'll be up for anything tonight,' he replied, 'I'm rather tired.' He stretched with exaggerated weakness.

'Tonight, Carl,' Eleanor repeated, 'It's important.'

'What about tomorrow?'

'Can't do.' Eleanor shook her head. 'Anyway, I rather think you'll be too busy with the post-show fan club.'

'Oh, very funny. I see the Canadians haven't tamed you yet.' He straightened his already perfect tie. 'Actually, now that I think about it, tomorrow might not work. I might have to go back shortly after my presentation. I've got rather a lot going on back at the institute, so this is very much a flying visit for me.'

'I see.' Eleanor found it difficult to disguise her surprise. Carl usually made the most of these away trips. 'Well then, tonight it must be,' she said firmly.

'And does the invitation extend to Allen?' Carl asked.

'No.' She offered no explanation.

'Okay then.' Carl finished his drink and studied his watch. 'Here at, say, seven?'

'Fine.'

Carl stood up to leave then turned back to the three young women he had been talking to earlier.

'See you charming ladies later. Lovely talking to you.'

Eleanor watched him stride through the crowd as he headed for the main door. Some of the delegates turned to watch him as he passed. She could see them lean closer to one another, exchanging words about him; he was still quite the celebrity within the conference circuit.

Eleanor felt uncomfortable about her decision not to include Allen. She knew she was taking a risk and if he ever found out, his trust in her would be lost. But this was not about deceit, she told herself. It was vital she heard whatever Carl had discovered before any hint of it became public. Only then would she have time to come up with a strategy that would keep the others at bay, while she figured out how to get Gabriel away from all this; how to save his life.

***

Despite the brightness of the early evening, the restaurant Carl suggested for their rendezvous had the glow of a cosy, rustic cave. High-backed wooden benches faced each other across sturdy tables, promising intimacy. Candles flickered in raffia-wound carafes, adding more atmosphere than light to the low-ceilinged booths. Carl studied the wine list before ordering a bottle of Pinot Noir. They sat in silence as the waiter polished the glasses with his starched white cloth and placed them on the table. He poured a centimetre of wine into Eleanor's glass and slid it towards her.

She drank the offering. 'Lovely,' she said.

The waiter poured two glasses without a word and left.

'So, what's with the cloak and dagger?' Carl asked.

'No cloak, no dagger, Carl. I just need the facts.'

'I'm not sure I have any to offer.' He swirled the wine around the bowl of his glass. 'None that you don't already know yourself, that is.'

'And how would you know what I know? Oh, hang on.' She clicked her fingers. 'Maybe that has something to do with the theft of our research data.'

'Theft? I beg your pardon. I've only used what I've been freely given—'

'By mistake,' cut in Eleanor, 'And don't pretend you didn't know that!'

'Give it a rest, Eleanor. You're hardly the paragon of virtue when it comes to professional ethics. And anyway, if you know that much, what can I say? We're on a level.'

'I don't think so. What's this paper about? I want to know what you've made of all *our* data, especially given that you'd written this whole thing off as nonsense.' Eleanor glared at him.

'Correct. I had,' he said. His voice sounded suddenly more serious, stripped of its usual bluster. 'But Sophie's reports rekindled my interest. And just as well they did too because it sounds like your guys in Canada are being a bit slow on the research front. Unless, of course, there are projects on-going of which you are unaware?'

'Absolutely no way,' said Eleanor. But in her heart, the seed of a new fear had been planted. *What if he was right?* Perhaps Allen and Simon did know things they had decided not to share with her.

'I was curious about Gabriel's developmental rate,' Carl went on, 'So I decided to use the samples still in storage in Glasgow to study the impact of key sections of his DNA associated with the rate of physical growth on a colony of mice.'

'Oh.' Eleanor stared at Carl. 'And?'

'In brief,' he continued, 'The treated mice matured significantly more rapidly than the untreated controls…'

'At a rate of?'

'Probably around seven times the norm.'

'Did you replicate these results?' Eleanor demanded.

'Several times, and always with the same outcome,' said Carl.

'And in all other respects, did they match the controls?'

'No. The treated mice had a much higher rate of survival, appeared healthier and rapidly produced larger litters, each around twice the size one would expect.'

'And longevity? They matured quickly; you said…' she tailed off, before steeling herself to complete the question. 'Does that mean they also died prematurely?'

'No. We haven't had one of the treated group die naturally yet. They're outliving all the controls.'

'Good God!' Eleanor gasped. 'That means an incredible reproductive capacity!'

'But even more interesting than that,' he said, 'was the social response of these mice to the overcrowding that ensued.' Carl's words were now tumbling out and he was leaning closer to her as he spoke.

'Go on,' she urged.

'Instead of the usual increase in aggression...'

'Of course, the inverse relationship between population density and social cooperation,' Eleanor muttered, as if recalling the title of a paper.

'Exactly, but in this case quite the opposite happened. The mice became more tolerant.'

Eleanor frowned. 'But that's unheard of, surely, even in the plant kingdom? It's nature's way of maintaining an equilibrium.'

'But these mice did no such thing. Parents shared care for offspring and reduced their food intake if required.' Carl shook his head. 'Truly, I've never seen anything like it before. Quite a remarkable degree of... of...'

'Altruism?' suggested Eleanor.

'Yeah, something like that.' Carl nodded.

'What did you do with the offspring?' asked Eleanor.

'Killed them, mostly. There were so many. I tell you, if they'd escaped, we would have had quite a rodent problem in no time at all. I kept a few, a small sample only, each caged in isolation.'

Eleanor sank into the back of her chair. For a while, she and Carl just stared at each other.

'So, what about your side of the story?' Carl eventually said. 'What about the boy himself? I can't begin to imagine.'

'Okay,' she said after a long silence. *What did she have to lose?* She decided she might be able to buy back a little of the goodwill lost between them and to build a bridge that might one day become a critical part of Gabriel's escape route. But she would only tell him as much as he could easily observe for himself were he in Canada.

'Here are the headlines. His nature is unfailingly kind and his sensitivity to and concern for the wellbeing of others exceeds anything I have seen in any other human being. His capacity for learning seems on a par with his rate of growth, his memory is flawless and his ability to apply what he knows to new situations is… inspiring.' She paused to assess Carl's reaction and noted the intensity of his fascination for what she was saying.

'Socially?' he asked.

'Exceptional. He seems to draw people to him effortlessly. He's a favourite wherever he goes.'

'And his rate of growth, of maturation? Would you say it's at a constant ratio to our own, say five years to one, ten to one?'

'That's hard to say. I've tried to think up a formula like that to transfer Gabriel years to more conventional ones, but it's not that straightforward. But as a rough estimation, I would say he seems to advance around one year every seven or eight weeks.'

'Fucking hell!' Carl took a large gulp of wine.

'Longevity plus rapid reproductive capacity.' Eleanor leant her head on her hands.

'We have to be careful, very careful.' Carl stared directly into Eleanor's eyes.

'*We*?' Eleanor sat bolt upright.

'Yes, Eleanor. We! Forget the politics. I need to be back on board. Sounds like your *team* could do with a bit of assistance.'

Eleanor glared at him. She resented his assumption that he could simply step back into the project, but she had to acknowledge he had made headway with critical research.

'We all agreed at the start to *limit* this experiment to a pre pubertal stage of development.' He fixed his eyes on Eleanor as if pinning her down.

'I don't recall anything so specific,' Eleanor snapped back.

'Come off it, Eleanor. You got the drift...'

'Did I, indeed? Perhaps your powers of telepathy let you down on that occasion!' she said through gritted teeth. 'We said we'd need to keep an eye on the situation. And that is what we are doing.'

'Don't do this, Eleanor. There's much more than one person at risk here, you know.'

'Jesus, Carl, don't you think I've already worked that out?' He leant closer to her. She had never seen him look so serious.

'I'm sure you'll agree, Eleanor, that in the light of my findings, the time for serious intervention has arrived.'

'Intervention, perhaps, but that doesn't mean murder!' She dropped her voice to barely a whisper.

'No need for drama, Eleanor, this is an *experiment*, remember? An experiment that we need to terminate and we need to do it now.'

Chapter 29

Eleanor met Allen outside the main auditorium just before nine. Carl's presentation was to be the first of the day and she knew his talk would be well attended. As they made their way to the front of the lecture theatre, Eleanor could still hear Carl's chilling words from the night before. She wondered when she should discuss it with Allen. Soon, probably. If he spoke with Carl today and realised Eleanor had held information back from him, there would be trouble. And any hopes of buying time to make plans to protect Gabriel would be dashed.

By ten minutes after nine, Carl had not yet made his entrance and there was an impatient buzz in the room. But then a moment later, one of the organisers stepped onto the podium and unfolded a slip of paper which he held unsteadily in his hand.

'Dear fellow delegates,' he began.

The audience grumbled to a hush.

'I'm sorry, and disappointed, to announce that our first speaker was obliged to return home in the early hours of the morning. Professor Carl Thornton, Glasgow University, sends his sincere apologies. He will endeavour to upload his presentation on the conference website as soon as possible.'

'Pfff! I wouldn't hold your breath for that one!' Eleanor scoffed.

All around her, she heard a wave of muttered reactions rise and fall and when she glanced at Allen, she saw him clench his jaw as he pounded his white knuckled fist into his palm.

Eleanor was not surprised by Carl's no-show. She had marvelled for years at how this man had managed to maintain such high regard in all quarters, when time and again, deadlines were missed and his excuses for non-appearances at events were inventive and plentiful. But at least this time she knew why he had bothered turning up at all.

'I suggest,' the speaker continued over the gathering rabble, 'That we break for thirty minutes to allow the next presenter to set up.'

Allen was aghast. 'We've come all this way to hear *that*?'

'Could be worse,' said Eleanor, 'He could have presented his paper and dropped a bombshell or two, raising questions we'd rather he didn't try to answer.'

'True,' Allen said, sighing, 'But still, it feels like a colossal waste of time and money.' He folded the day's itinerary and pushed it into his jacket pocket. 'There's nothing else on the programme that has any relevance for our work whatsoever. So, I think I've got some serious sightseeing to do. Care to join me?'

'We can't just become tourists, Allen!' Eleanor feigned surprise at his suggestion.

'You feel free to attend everything, Eleanor, but really, there's no need. Our brief here was simply to keep an eye on Carl and he's on his way back to Glasgow now, so…' Allen checked his watch. 'I think I'll see if I can snap up a spot in a particularly inviting-looking cheese and wine tasting lunch I was reading about last night.'

Eleanor paused. This could be the ideal opportunity to tell Allen about last night, drip-feeding him just enough information to keep him on-side.

'Sure you don't want to join me?'

'No thanks,' she eventually replied. 'I think that's the last thing I need when I'm jet lagged. *Bon appétit*!'

Allen left and Eleanor sat blankly through the next session, barely taking in a word of what was being said. Her conscience was nagging her about her decision not to share Carl's findings with Allen but now there was no chance of the two men meeting to talk, the need to do so had become less urgent. This was a gift she would happily accept: some time to think things through.

She pictured Carl in a taxi, taking him from the airport back to the institute in Glasgow and felt a pang of jealousy, feeling suddenly overwhelmed by sadness and a longing to see all the people she had left there.

She had never been an impulsive person and so found herself smiling in giddy surprise as she stood up and made her way out of the hall. She took the lift to her room and placed some clothes and toiletries into the smaller of the bags she'd brought with her to Paris. Then, making her way to Reception, she ordered a taxi to the airport. She had no difficulty securing a seat on a plane bound for Glasgow and, by early afternoon, found herself airborne, gazing out of the window, marvelling at the brilliance of the sun once they were above the heavy canopy of cloud cover.

She had missed her mother's gentle smile and wise, softly spoken words. She even missed the old furniture in her childhood home and the smell of lavender polish that hit you as soon as you walked in the front door.

In the ten months since her departure, they had spoken only occasionally on the phone, tending instead to communicate by email. Eleanor had carefully avoided FaceTime, Zoom, and Skype, knowing she couldn't possibly let her mother see Gabriel, and counted her blessings that her mother hadn't expressed any interest in them in any event. She had seemed mercifully content with the photographs which Eleanor had taken months before and drip-fed to her mother in a carefully orchestrated and entirely fake timeline.

When at last her taxi was pulling out onto the motorway towards Glasgow's West End, everything she saw brought a smile to her face: the houses that looked small and neat compared with Vancouver's high-rise apartments and ranch-like dwellings, washing flapping in the breeze, the lesser scale of the motorway compared with Canada's highways and the majesty of the cranes along the Clyde.

But as the taxi approached her mother's neighbourhood, Eleanor began to worry. Miriam did not care much for surprises, preferring the anticipation of an event and the smooth management of all the emotions around it to the fizz and froth of the unexpected. But it was too late. She had arrived.

Brightly coloured pots displaying sprays of summer flowers lined the path to the front door, and two scooters lay abandoned on the front lawn.

After several unanswered rings of the bell, Eleanor peered through the living room window. There was no one to be seen, but the house oozed that indefinable sense of being occupied, and so she followed the path around the side of the red sandstone semi to the garden at the back.

It was late afternoon. The clouds had drifted off, and the warm summer sun was beating down upon her head. Washing danced idly on the line that stretched from the kitchen wall to the pole beside the garden hut and in amongst the hum of bees, she heard the unguarded lilt of children's voices and the attentive responses of their grandmother.

'Hello-o!' Eleanor swept a damp bed sheet to the side, like a stage curtain. 'Anyone at home?'

'Aunty Eleanor, it's Aunty Eleanor!' Beth and Hannah ran towards her and jumped up and down in front of her.

Eleanor bent down and gave them each a hug and a kiss on the forehead.

'Hello, girls. My, don't you look very summery?' she said.

Eleanor could see her mother now, sitting on an ancient deckchair, its striped cloth sagging behind her. The bright afternoon sun gave highlights to her hair, making it look greyer than Eleanor recalled, and her face was thinner, older. Miriam stared up at her daughter, dropping her cross-stitch embroidery onto her lap.

'Eleanor, darling! There's nothing wrong, is there?' Miriam rose to her feet, her sewing falling to the grass.

'Of course not.' Eleanor hugged her mum. 'I'm attending a conference in Paris at the moment but got a bit of time off, so I thought I'd pop over for the night.'

'You should have called, darling; I would have been more organised…'

'It was a spur of the moment thing. Anyway, the last thing I wanted was for you to be running around making loads of preparations. I hope that's all right?'

'Of course, this is wonderful — look at you!' Miriam clapped her hands in delight. 'You're looking marvellous, Eleanor. Oh, what a wonderful surprise!'

'Where's Gabriel? Is he here too?' The girls looked around for their cousin.

'I'm afraid not. He had to stay in Canada. I'm only over here for a short while. It's a work trip and it would've been very difficult to bring him.'

'Aw,' said Beth, 'I wanted to take him to the park.'

'And push him in his buggy,' Hannah added.

Eleanor winced, feeling sick at the contrast between the little girls' open honesty and the complex knot of lies within which she now lived.

'And he would just love to see you girls too. Don't you look pretty in your summer dresses?' she said, swiftly changing the subject.

Miriam went to the garden hut and returned with a second deckchair.

'Here, dear, sit down. You must be tired.'

Eleanor eased herself into the low dip of the canvas chair.

'Who is looking after the baby?' Hannah plonked herself down on the rug at Eleanor's feet.

'He's quite a big boy now.' Eleanor stroked the little girl's hair.

'Is he with… what is your nanny's name again? Christina?' Eleanor's mother asked.

'Yes.' Eleanor decided to accept the easy explanation offered. 'But it's only for a couple of days. He'll be fine.'

'Of course he will,' said Miriam. 'And I'm sure Aunty Eleanor will come back soon with little Gabriel.'

'Can you phone home so we can see him?' Beth suggested.

Dear God, Eleanor faltered, then thought fast. 'It's the middle of the night there; he'll be fast asleep.'

'Really?' Beth screwed up her nose and giggled.

Eleanor nodded.

'Can we see pictures then?' Hannah continued.

'Of course.' Eleanor could think of no other reasonable response. 'But I'll need to charge my phone a bit. I'll do that later.'

The girls skipped off to resume their game.

'So, tell me all your news, dear.' Miriam turned to face her daughter. 'How is life in Vancouver?'

'Much the same as over here actually, Mum. Except it's a bit warmer.'

'What an unexpected delight. I can't believe you're here!' Miriam's face glowed, but then suddenly, her expression changed. 'There really is nothing wrong, is there?'

'Absolutely nothing, I promise you. The presentation I'd gone to Paris to see was cancelled at the last minute, would you believe, so I had a bit of time on my hands, and Paris is much closer than you'd think.'

'I suppose so,' said her mum, 'Especially if you're used to being on the other side of the Atlantic.'

'So, what's the news here then? Have I missed much in the past ten months?' Eleanor adjusted her chair to a reclined position.

'Surprisingly little.' Her mother scrolled through the highlights of the previous months. 'The Thompsons next door have moved, and a lovely young family live there now.' She resumed her sewing. 'Grant's greengrocers have expanded their premises, and they've opened a sort of deli next door.' She paused for thought. 'Oh, and the vicar is retiring next month, leaving us with a temporary fellow. Seems there's a bit of a shortage. That's about it, I'm afraid.'

'What about Olivia?' Eleanor asked in a lowered voice. 'How's everything going there?'

'Actually…' Miriam cast an eye behind her to make sure the children were not within hearing range. 'Olivia is very happy. I don't think I've seen her so content in such a long time.'

'Uh huh?' Eleanor awaited the explanation, but her mother seemed engrossed in counting threads. 'Is there a particular reason, or is she just suddenly happy?'

'I think she's sorting herself out, Eleanor. Finding herself, as you young ones might say.'

'What's she doing, then?' Eleanor sat up. She was more intrigued by her mother's apparent playing down of things than by the subject itself.

'She's made herself busy, doing so many things. She's joined a gym and goes to various exercise classes there. She's become involved with a book club, and they meet up every now and again to discuss what they've read, and she's been attending a pottery class at her local college. She's very good, apparently.

She's having a few pieces displayed at some exhibition in town in a few weeks' time.'

'Jolly good!' said Eleanor delightedly. 'It's wonderful to think she must be getting over Charles. He always seemed to dampen her spirits. She would never have done anything arty when he was around. Can you imagine?'

'Mmm,' her mother replied, 'I'm not sure your father and I were much better.'

'What do you mean? You and Dad only ever encouraged us.' Eleanor was startled by her mother's self-blame.

'Yes, but to do what? Olivia was such a sensitive child. She was always artistic and I know she resented us pushing her towards university. She would much rather have gone to art school and I think it crushed her to have to turn that offer down.'

'Which offer?'

'Some art school in London, I can't remember the name now.'

'Really? Wow!' Eleanor shot up and turned to her mum. 'Why didn't she go?'

'Lots of reasons, I suppose, but it would have cost so much and…'

'But you let me go to Edinburgh, that wasn't cheap!'

'We couldn't do both, Eleanor.'

'Please don't say she didn't go so I could, Mum?' Eleanor's heart was pounding. 'Mum?'

'We did our best, Eleanor. Sometimes parenting is about making difficult decisions… choices…'

'Do you think I don't know that?' Eleanor's voice was growing sharper.

'Shhh.' Her mum glanced over to where the children played.

'Mum, this is important! I can't believe this…'

'I don't know why you're so upset, Eleanor. Especially with the way things have turned out for you…'

'But that's just it, Mum. I'm upset *because* of the way things have turned out for me… and not for Olivia! No wonder she hates me!'

'Don't say that!' Miriam said firmly. 'She does not hate you.'

'Dear God, Mum! I can't believe I'm hearing this… and that you don't seem to get why I'm so angry. I had a right to know!'

'We thought we were protecting you…'

'From what? The truth? The chance to discuss this openly, as a family? That's not protection, Mum, that's… denial! Kicking dust over facts and feelings. But when we bury emotions like that, we bury them alive and they'll always fight their way to the surface…'

Eleanor leapt from her chair and marched indoors, slamming the bathroom door behind her.

'Dear God!' She paced the small floor space. 'Why didn't I realise what was happening?' She shook her head at her own reflection. 'Poor, poor Livy,' she whispered, using her sister's childhood name for the first time in decades.

***

When Eleanor returned to the garden, she could see her mum had been crying.

'Mum…' She approached and sat on the rug at her side. 'I'm sorry I lost my temper. I know you did your best, but I need time to take this all in… I'm surprised… shocked.'

Miriam pulled a handkerchief from her cardigan pocket and wiped her eyes.

'I know, darling. To be honest, I'm angry with myself… all those years of compensating, making allowances for Olivia's behaviour because I felt guilty. It hasn't done any of us any good.'

'We all learn from our mistakes, Mum. We do what we think is best at the time.' Eleanor felt her throat tighten as she spoke, visions of Gabriel flashing before her. 'And if I can be half the mother to Gabriel that you have been to me, I will feel very proud of myself.'

'Thank you, dear.' Miriam took a deep breath and looked into Eleanor's eyes. 'That's a comforting thought.'

Eleanor left her mother to gather herself together and went to the kitchen to put the kettle on.

'You want a cool drink?' she called back through the open door to where the girls were playing.

'Yes please,' said Beth.

'Me too,' called Hannah. She was dragging a chair from the garden playhouse to the low wall around the lawn where they had set up shop. Rows of leaves were piled into bundles and petals, fallen from their gran's rose garden, were ordered by colour.

'So, who's in charge of this shop?' Eleanor walked towards the game.

'I'm the shopkeeper.' Hannah sat on the chair.

'And I'm the customer,' said Beth.

'Oh, these look lovely.' Eleanor picked up one of the soft, shell shapes and held it to her nose. 'So silky and the smell is… *magnifique*!'

The girls giggled.

'Would you like to buy one, Aunty Eleanor?' asked Hannah.

'I think I would. Could you choose one for me please, Mrs Shopping Lady?' She turned to Beth.

The six-year-old studied the display then selected the largest petal on show and handed it to her aunt.

'You can have this one.' She held it up to her.

'Perfect. That's my favourite.' She crouched down beside Beth. 'How much do I owe you?' Eleanor asked Hannah.

'Ehhh. How much have you got?' she replied.

'Hang on.' Eleanor stood up. 'I know how to pay for it.' She walked back into the kitchen and returned a few moments later with a tray holding two plastic beakers of juice and two chocolate biscuits. She sat it on the ground beside the goods on display. 'Will this do?'

'Oh yes,' said Hannah, smiling up at her aunt.

'I love you, Aunty Eleanor,' said Beth, throwing her arms around Eleanor's waist.

'And I love you too, very much. Both of you.' Eleanor held them close to her and, breathing in their outdoor freshness, she felt suddenly brimming with gratitude for their easily won affection. Why had she hardly noticed them before? She felt sad for all the opportunities she had let slip to be with them, to get to know them, to love them.

Eleanor returned to the kitchen and finished making the tea. She walked back out to where her mother was sitting and placed the tray with tea and biscuits on the ground between them.

'I'm glad I came over, Mum. I've missed you so much.' She kissed her mum on the cheek then sat back in her chair.

There were no traces now of Miriam's tears and when she smiled back at her, Eleanor knew she had recovered.

'All will be well.' Miriam sipped her tea. 'And before we know it, you will be back home and Gabriel will be playing in the garden with his cousins.'

Tell her. Tell her now! Eleanor's mind was racing. *Such a hypocrite,* she chastised herself, *with all my talk of truth.* She shook her head.

'What is it, dear?' Miriam placed her hand on Eleanor's. 'There *is* something wrong, isn't there?'

Eleanor felt she might cry. She wanted to let it all out, to be a child again and have her mum wrap her arms around her and let the world take care of her problems. Perhaps she would understand? Maybe she could even help?

'Aunty Eleanor, look!' Hannah had run to her side. 'It's working now! Look!'

Eleanor could see Hannah had brought something to show her and when the little girl held out her hands, Eleanor's phone was there.

'Can we see some pictures of Gabriel? Please, please?' She jumped up and down.

'Not now!' Eleanor snatched the phone from her hands.

Hannah stopped jumping and fell silent. She stood blinking for a while then turned to her gran.

'Maybe later, darling.' Miriam stroked her hair. 'Aunt Eleanor and I are talking about something important right now.'

Hannah walked slowly back to her game.

'What is going on, Eleanor?' Miriam glared at her daughter.

Eleanor placed her head in her hands.

'It's about Gabriel, isn't it?'

She was unable to reply.

'I think you should tell me.'

Eleanor kept her eyes fixed on Miriam's hand. If only she could find the words, a way of making it all sound normal. But then, she noticed for the first time the loose skin of her mother's hands. She was getting older. She could never understand what Eleanor had done and what she had agreed to.

No. She was going to have to deal with this herself. She might never be able to live a normal life with Gabriel, but that didn't mean she couldn't have a life with him at all. She'd just have to find a way, *any* way, of getting out of this mess and keeping her son out of reach of anyone who might want to harm him.

Chapter 30

As Eleanor stepped out of her car, she could not recall having felt such excitement since her childhood. She scanned the clusters of parents and children calling to one another, hugging and celebrating their reunion.

'Mum! Mum!' She turned and saw Gabriel charging towards her.

'Hello, you!' Eleanor opened her arms wide and wrapped them tightly around him as he threw himself into her embrace. 'How are you, my darling? I've missed you so much!'

She held him to her, feeling his chest heave as he caught his breath. She buried her face in his thick tussle of hair, enjoying its familiar smell and texture.

'I'm great, Mum. I've had *so* much fun!' He beamed at her.

She cupped his face in her hands and kissed his forehead. 'I can see that!'

'We need to hurry though.' He grabbed her hand and pulled her towards the auditorium. 'The performance starts soon and I don't want you to miss a single thing! I'm on three times!' he said, grinning.

Eleanor felt grateful for the cool, conditioned air that lent the theatre a sense of calm, a reprieve from summer's crushing heat.

'Wow, it's packed!' She looked around for a vacant seat.

'Don't worry, Mum. Follow me.'

He headed off towards the front, stopping close to the rows reserved, she guessed, for local dignitaries and invited guests.

'Excuse me,' Gabriel addressed the occupant of the aisle seat. 'Do you mind if my mum slips past you?' Then he turned back to Eleanor. 'Your seat is near the middle, Mum. It's the only empty one there. I'll need to run now. See you later. Oh, and enjoy the show!' He turned and ran to the back of the theatre.

When Eleanor arrived at the vacant seat, there was a small bag on it, with her name written in Gabriel's hand. Inside was a bottle of water, Eleanor's favourite mints and a note, saying, *Love You Mum xxx.*

'What a polite young man,' the elderly lady to her right commented as soon as she was settled.

'Yes,' agreed Eleanor, distracted a little by her reference to him as a young man. 'Thank you.'

'Do you know, he sat in this chair for such a long time, told me he was reserving it for you. He gave me a bottle of water too!' She lifted it out of her bag to show it off. 'Do you have a programme?' she continued.

'No, I don't. In too much of a hurry to pick one up.' Eleanor hadn't given much thought to the performance itself, she realised. She just wanted it over with so she could take Gabriel home.

'Here.' Her neighbour handed her one from the bundle on her lap. 'I always pick up a few.'

'Thank you.' Eleanor accepted the offer and turned the booklet in her hand. 'This looks very professional.'

'Yes, doesn't it? The pupils do it all themselves; they're very accomplished. My niece designed the cover this year.' Her face glowed with pride.

'That is impressive.' Eleanor smiled.

'Wait till you see the show. It's always excellent.' She nodded to the stage. 'Here we go. That's Mr Wallace, one of the school governors. He's a sponsor too. Puts a lot of money into the school.'

Eleanor nodded and turned her attention to the stage. A middle-aged man was standing in front of a heavy red curtain. He smiled out at the audience and tapped the microphone on the stand in front of him.

'Ladies, gentlemen… and parents!' He paused, giving the audience time to laugh. 'We meet again to savour the delights of Cardinal's Summer Review. As you know, the talented children of Cardinal College have worked tirelessly throughout the year to create this wonderful show. And as usual, we are joined today by our friends from summer camp in bringing this event to you. So, let's give them all the welcome they deserve!' He started to clap, the audience joining in with him as the curtains behind him drew open.

Only once before had Eleanor attended a school performance, having by chance found herself at her mother's house on the afternoon of Bertie's first nativity display. Charles had called from work at the last minute to say he would have to miss the show. Bertie was upset and Eleanor had been persuaded by her mother to take his place.

She winced as she recalled the event. Huddled in the cramped assembly hall, Eleanor had strained to understand the sometimes whispered, sometimes bellowed lines of the painstakingly coached infants. Miriam, on the other hand, had smiled upon the proceedings, bouncing Hannah on her knee in time to the faltering piano accompaniment while Olivia beamed as she balanced her once-more pregnant body on the edge of her seat. Like all the other parents, she was eagerly awaiting her child's contribution, camera at the ready.

What spell, Eleanor wondered at the time, *had come over these people, to turn them from rational, discerning adults into narcissistic sentimentalists?* For she was quite sure, back then, that it was this emotion which powered parenthood: a self-love, skilfully projected by some underhand force of nature onto their offspring, crafting a bond that drew from its hosts all the fervour of their own vanity and grafting it seamlessly onto their progeny. Embarrassed by her sister's show of pride, Eleanor had vowed she would never put herself in that situation again.

But now here she sat, of her own free will, unashamed in her joyous anticipation. And while she often wondered at the depth of her attachment to Gabriel, she had not yet been able to fully account for it. Gabriel was not her flesh and blood. She did not, *could not*, see anything of herself in him. He was in no way an extension of her own ego from which to draw vicarious glory. True, he had grown within her, he had come from her, but he was not *of* her. She had only provided the environment necessary for his development. Could that, in itself, account for the instant pull she had felt towards him from the moment of his birth, her overwhelming drive to protect him, her terrifying love for him? Was that possible?

She thought of the article she'd read on the long flight, offering evidence that the cells of a foetus migrate into the mother during pregnancy. Perhaps, she hypothesised, that even though she had made no contribution to Gabriel's genetic profile, he had to hers? Could *this* be the physical basis for attachment?

A reverential hush fell upon the audience and Eleanor came back to the present. She sat poised to applaud whatever efforts unfolded before her. While clearly the work of amateurs, the painted scenery was of a high standard and Eleanor was impressed, upon consulting her programme, to discover that it, too, was the work of the youngsters attending the college.

The show consisted of a series of brief sketches, varying in style from contemporary humour to historical drama. Each performance was to be a subtle development of some aspect of the preceding skit. Eleanor found herself sufficiently engrossed to forget her focus on Gabriel and to sit back and enjoy the performances, to such an extent she was slightly surprised by his eventual first appearance on stage, some twenty minutes into the show.

He stood towards the back of the stage, dressed as a gladiator. He was not required to speak, but stood silently, in his dazzling attire. Eleanor could not take her eyes off him; he did not look at the audience but stood firmly in role. She did not hear the words his peers recited, nor did she notice the others pace the stage; her eyes were fixed on Gabriel. When at last the act came to an end and Gabriel left the stage, Eleanor felt shaken and confused by the experience. She had been transfixed. But why? He had just stood there…

Eleanor sat motionless, unaware of the applause around her, cocooned in a halo of tingling warmth that seemed to come from deep inside her, reminding her of something she had forgotten and could not yet remember. She heard herself sigh, much louder than she had intended.

'Very good.' Eleanor's neighbour leant towards her. 'Your boy makes a dashing young Roman.'

'Thanks,' Eleanor whispered and, embarrassed she might have made her favouritism too obvious, stared down at the programme. There were three more acts until he appeared again. Would he have the same presence? She forced herself to attend to the intervening performances.

When he next appeared, dressed in a formal black suit and starched white shirt, silver tray beneath one arm, it became clear he had been well cast as the butler, Jeeves. Eleanor could tell Gabriel captivated the audience, playing out his character with maturity and a degree of understatement that rendered his well-articulated lines all the more amusing. Even his delivery of single word utterances, such as 'Perfect!' prompted gales of laughter.

Relieved she wasn't the only one transfixed, Eleanor soon forgot her inhibitions and laughed heartily with the crowd.

The last item mentioned on the programme was described simply as 'Solo Performances' and listed four names, of which

Gabriel's was the last. Wiping moist palms on her linen trousers, Eleanor tried to still the pounding in her chest. It was the final act of the show and people were becoming a little restless. Anxious for her son, she hoped they would tolerate just a few more minutes.

When at last he made his appearance, he did so with such confidence that Eleanor felt herself relax. A few voices nearby whispered their recognition of the boy who had been Jeeves.

Gabriel stood alone, head slightly bowed then, looking up, he focussed sincerely and profoundly upon his mother's gaze and began to sing.

'*In paradisum.*' His pure voice resounded throughout the auditorium.

Eleanor gasped and clutched her chest.

'*Deducant te angeli.*'

The audience fell silent, mesmerised.

'*In tuo adventu, suscipiant te martyres.*'

Eleanor made no effort to stop the tears that fell, knowing Gabriel would feel them for what they were: tears of love.

'*Et perducant te, in civitatem sanctam.*'

Still focussing solely on his mother, he smiled with sheer joy.

'*Jerusalem, Jerusalem, Jerusalem,*' he sang, his faultless voice resonating throughout the cavernous room.

Overwhelmed by a gratitude she could not comprehend, Eleanor closed her eyes and felt the scene before her melt away as Gabriel's face, persisting like a dim retinal after-image, superimposed itself upon other scenes that played themselves out before her: her childhood, her sister, wintry landscapes, his birth, the blue of his honest eyes, her love for him. In an instant, they all seemed to come together to form part of a coherent wholeness, an emotional Pangea that embodied the totality of her experience.

'Well done!' the elderly lady beside her called out as Gabriel bowed and walked modestly from the stage.

'What a voice!' she heard one man exclaim over the deafening applause.

'Yes, very talented,' gushed another.

Pushing a path through the crowds to the exit, Eleanor followed the queue to the refreshment tent that had been erected on the playing fields. It was not long before she spotted Gabriel, smiling and nodding attentively to the man who stood by his side.

'Aha, you must be this young man's proud mother!' A tall gentleman wearing what looked to Eleanor like a safari suit and a Panama hat approached. He grasped her hand in both of his, holding it as he spoke. 'Jonathan Tate, Cardinal's principal.'

'Of course, lovely to meet you.' Eleanor nodded. 'Eleanor Bartlett.'

'I hope you enjoyed our efforts?'

'Absolutely,' Eleanor replied, withdrawing her hand. She didn't want to become involved in any lengthy conversations, preferring to pack up Gabriel's belongings and head for home as soon as possible.

'It's such a pity Gabriel's singing teacher couldn't make it today to hear that performance, it would sure have made her proud.' Mr Tate looked to Gabriel, who smiled knowingly at his mother.

'Yes,' said Eleanor, gratefully reading the message in her son's eyes. 'I really enjoyed the whole performance.' She widened the discussion. 'These children have certainly been busy this week, I'm very impressed.'

'Of course,' the principal continued, 'But many of these kids have been working hard towards this all year. It's one of Cardinal's highlights. And we're always looking for fresh talent.' He smiled towards Gabriel again. 'It is unusual for one of our summer camp children to feature so prominently in the show, you know.'

'Really?' said Eleanor.

'Yes. Your son is a talented boy, Doctor Bartlett.'

'Thank you.' Eleanor smiled.

The principal had clearly consulted the details on Gabriel's application, she calculated; this was no casual chat. She glanced towards the car park, hoping to make a quick getaway to beat the queues.

'Many of our students come to us as a result of our summer schools.' His tone settled to something more business-like. 'We do offer bursaries, you know,' he continued, 'And I don't think Gabriel would have any difficulty in securing one, were you interested. How old is he?' He turned to look at Gabriel. 'Ten, eleven? Best age to get them started, I should say.'

'That's very kind of you,' Eleanor said smoothly. 'I'm so sorry if I seem ungrateful, it's just all a bit of a surprise. We only saw this as an enjoyable way to pass a bit of time in the summer.'

'That's often the way,' he said, 'But it doesn't mean it needs to stay like that.'

***

When at last they were free to go, Eleanor watched as Gabriel said his goodbyes to countless other young people. Everyone knew his name. She didn't want to hurry him, but she was grateful when they were finally in the car and driving away from Cardinal's.

'I missed you so much,' she said.

'I know, and I missed you too, Mum.' Gabriel placed his hand on Eleanor's. 'You weren't too sad though, were you?'

'No, not at all.' She regarded him curiously. 'I thought you sang beautifully, Gabriel. What a wonderful surprise.'

'Thanks. I sang it for you. It is your favourite, isn't it?'

'Yes, it is.' She paused. 'I wasn't expecting it at all. I didn't even realise that you knew it. Who taught you it?' She tried to make the enquiry sound casual.

'I learnt it from you,' he replied.

'I can't remember playing that song for such a long time,' she said. 'You have a very good memory.'

'Perhaps,' he said, 'But I don't need to try to remember it, because you already know it.'

'So…' Eleanor hesitated, jolted by the recurring thought that he could read her mind. 'Do you know everything I know, every thought I think?'

'I couldn't tell you.' He laughed. 'I have no way of knowing that.'

***

When they arrived back at their apartment, Eleanor was keen to return to their normal routine as quickly as possible, emptying Gabriel's bag and sorting piles of washing. She felt thrilled just to be back at home, doing ordinary things.

She had given little thought to her work since her return, having been consumed by her desire to see Gabriel. But now she began to think over her schedule, the problem of what to do about school after the vacation and the information she would have to share with Allen and Simon. She dreaded their meetings and found the rapid censoring of every word she planned to say utterly exhausting. But it had to be done, and she would keep doing it until she had wrenched Gabriel, and herself, free from this Gordian knot of her own making.

Gabriel was exhausted and after eating, settled quickly to bed. Eleanor set up her laptop on the table beside the living room window. It was a beautiful night, one that called for a walk in the woods to listen to the evensong of its winged choir or a stroll along a twilight beach.

She wanted out, into the fresh, evening air, into a life that did not require constant surveillance. But she wanted Gabriel with her in that life. She wanted him to be free from scrutiny, beyond the reach of others.

Replaying his accomplishments of the day in her head, she wondered, yet again, whether Gabriel, the young, angelic, delightful performer, could in any way pose a threat to modern man. Surely a few more of him on the planet could only be a good thing? She knew of no one who thought anything bad of her son and she had only ever witnessed in him the most altruistic and selfless behaviour.

She needed time to build the case for his defence, to persuade the others there was nothing to fear in simply letting Gabriel be. But so much had happened to put her objectivity in doubt, she wondered if Allen, Simon and Carl could ever see such an appeal as anything other than the consequence of her unwelcomed attachment to Gabriel.

She needed an ally, another voice to add to her own, to disrupt the polarisation of opinions that had created so much distance between her and the others. But she could think of no one and she was running out of time. How long now, she worried, before Gabriel reached puberty

The principal's assumption of his being around ten or eleven years of age was not a preposterous one. Allen and Simon, of course, might be panicked by his appearance over the next few months and now Carl was determined to scramble back on board, the odds against her point of view prevailing were only increasing.

Going back to Glasgow was, of course, out of the question. Her mother was already alert to something being not right about Gabriel and Olivia would not help matters.

Would he be safer, she wondered, if he was out of sight? If she made sure her family did not see Gabriel and if she took him out of her colleagues' reach? Or would that just make it easier for them to detach further from him and stick to the plan?

She opened her laptop and started her search: *Residential Schools, British Columbia.* She would find somewhere safe for him, somewhere they could not find him. It wouldn't be a permanent solution, of course; he would mature too quickly to be able to stay for more than one term. But that would buy her time to plan her next move.

She would do it right now, before any questions could be asked or objections raised. She could wait no longer. If she wanted to save Gabriel, she would have to let him go. At least for a while.

Chapter 31

Eleanor decided to stay at home the next morning. She had spent much of the previous night on the internet and was struggling to find the energy to face the new day. The last thing she needed was a probing conversation with Allen and Simon when her defences were low.

Flipping open her laptop, she quickly composed an email sending her apologies for the meeting they were due to have that morning and excusing herself from work for the next week. *Childcare problems*, she had put. Then, pressing 'send' before having second thoughts, she consulted again the shortlist she had drawn up in the early hours of the morning.

There was no shortage of residential schools, each offering its own brand of *unique experience*. The choice felt overwhelming but she was determined to find the right one.

She no longer felt grief at the thought of separation from Gabriel because a sickening fear for his safety had taken its place. She could see he was fast approaching puberty and the normally rapid changes of adolescence would be even apparent in her son.

Exhausted, she snapped her laptop shut and looked out of the window. *How different from the Glasgow sky*, she thought, *that fell dark and grey upon its subjects.*

'Let's go!' Eleanor suddenly stood up and marched through to Gabriel's room.

'Where to?' He closed his book and bounced from his bed with ready enthusiasm.

'Anywhere.' She smiled, her mood instantly lifted by Gabriel's delight.

She went to the kitchen and opened the refrigerator, searching the shelves for whatever items she had that could be used for sandwiches, and hastily put together a picnic lunch.

***

The heat of the morning sun was tamed by a gentle breeze, so Eleanor agreed to Gabriel's plea to drive with the car roof down. Laughing at the tangle of each other's wind-tousled hair, they made their way out of the built-up district. Not far from their suburban enclave, acres of open fields unravelled before them, shades of green and golden yellow spilled out like spools of bright ribbon, running paths into the distance.

In this ocean of open land, a Mayan blue sky stretching high above her, Eleanor felt a new sense of freedom and she began to realise how hemmed-in her life had become. In her mind, she saw herself, arms tight around her son, trapped in a room, its towering walls moving in closer and closer towards them. But out here, as they sailed through the seemingly endless expanse, it seemed freedom was theirs for the taking and everything was possible again.

They drove on and on, away from the wide lanes of the highway, down narrow, unfamiliar roads. Eleanor had no route in mind; she turned at random onto tracks that bordered swathes of land scattered with small farm buildings and bursting with summer crops in full sway, ripe for harvesting.

Gabriel switched the playlist to *shuffle* and they amused themselves by guessing which songs the other would like to skip, Gabriel easily outperforming his mother. Singing along to their favourites, they threw themselves into the sheer delight of the moment.

'Hungry?' Eleanor eventually yelled over the noise.

'Yes,' he replied, though she could hardly hear him.

She turned onto a rough road that led into a meadow. Parking the car beside an empty water trough, they stepped out onto the dry grass. The sun had risen to its highest point and would soon begin its descent. Gabriel carried the picnic bag to a spot at the far end of the field, where a great oak offered shade. Eleanor followed, clutching some rugs. They spread the blankets in the cool shade and unpacked the food, then sat in comfortable silence as they ate.

Bees hummed and from the lush green of the tree above, birds chirruped. There was no need to talk. When they'd finished eating, Eleanor gathered up the empty snack bags and pushed them back into the carrier.

'This is such a brilliant day, Mum.' Gabriel tumbled closer to her and placed his head on her lap.

'Yes, it's just perfect,' she said. 'This will definitely be filed under *favourite moments.*' Then she sighed, resisting her mind's dark drift towards thoughts of Gabriel's uncertain lifespan.

'Mine too.' He closed his eyes.

'You know, Gabriel…' Eleanor hesitated. 'Things might have to change for a while, in a way that neither of us would ideally want.'

'I know, Mum, don't worry.'

'You do?'

'Everything will be fine. Change doesn't upset me. It's exciting. New opportunities,' he said drowsily.

'But this will be a bigger change than usual, one that will alter the way we live on a daily basis,' said Eleanor.

Gabriel opened his eyes. He sat up and looked at his mum.

'I think it's time to move to another school. But it might be better for you to go to one that would look after you as well as educate you.' She took a deep breath. 'Boarding school.'

Gabriel nodded. 'It's okay, Mum, really. I know you're doing your best for me. I think boarding school is a great idea. I loved summer school, didn't I?' He smiled and reached for her hand. 'So, when do I start?'

A wave of relief washed over Eleanor's body. 'Oh, I've nothing that concrete to tell you yet, Gabriel. In fact, I'm still searching for the school that ticks all the right boxes.'

'What about Cardinal's? I really liked it there and it's not too far away. Surely that ticks a few?'

'But is Cardinal's academic enough, Gabriel? I'd be worried you might get bored.'

He laughed. 'Oh, Mum, please don't worry about that sort of thing. Really, I'll be fine. I'm sure they'll do all the regular school stuff too,' he said, then leapt to his feet. 'Is it alright if I explore a little?'

'Of course! Off you go. I've got plenty to think about.'

Eleanor folded her cardigan and placed it on a mound of grass, then lay down and closed her eyes. She knew Cardinal College could solve a few problems, not least the financial one. The possibility of a bursary was certainly attractive; she'd been unsure how she would afford boarding school fees without putting herself heavily in debt. Then there was the advantage that the school already knew Gabriel, so there would be little to do by the way of engineering expectations. His rapid growth would still come as a surprise to them, almost certainly too much to pass off as an adolescent spurt, and the brain tumour *explanation* had caused as many problems as it solved when she'd tried it before. She could see no way of pre-empting the inevitable enquiries. No doubt another move — perhaps many moves — would be required at some point.

She settled into a more comfortable position and willed her worries away. In the near distance, she heard the comforting trickle of a stream and imagined Gabriel by its side. A feeling of contentment fell upon her. The tension that had gripped her shoulders seemed to have lifted, leaving them free and light as air. Her breathing slowed and deepened. She felt at one with her surroundings, so far from her normal sphere of existence, yet unaccountably, on familiar ground.

She closed her eyes and soon found herself drifting down the meadow towards the stream. Its lazy gurgle had grown to a raging torrent. Her pace quickened in response to what she felt sure were cries for help. As the soft grass of the meadow gave way to prickly gorse, she found she had to fight her way through, her feet entangled in its tough snares.

In the distance, she could see two men, their backs towards her. They stooped above the riverbed, arms rigid with sustained effort. She saw their sweat-drenched shirts and heard their muted groans, before they waded heavily to the farther bank and fled. A child's body, freshly limp, half-floated in the newly corrupted stream, his face turned towards her, tossed by the water's rush.

'Gabriel!' she gasped, sitting bolt upright and looking frantically about her.

'It's all right, Mum!' Gabriel ran to her side. 'Don't worry, I'm right here.'

Fully awake, Eleanor knew immediately what she had to do. The vision, the murdered child, wouldn't clear from her mind. There wasn't a moment to lose. She took her phone from her bag and scrolled through her list of contacts, pausing at one name before pressing the call sign. Gabriel sat by her side, listening as the tone rang out. A woman answered.

'Hello, this is Eleanor Bartlett speaking, Gabriel Bartlett's mother. Is Mr Tate available?'

'One moment please,' the receptionist replied.

It wasn't long until she heard the principal's voice. 'Doctor Bartlett, what a pleasure to hear from you! How can I help?'

'We've been discussing your offer, Mr Tate, of a place at Cardinal's for Gabriel?' Eleanor felt suddenly anxious she'd made a mistake. Had she misunderstood him? Perhaps he made these offers light-heartedly to all the parents, hoping to prompt a flood of applications?

'Splendid. I was hoping you'd give the matter some thought. That young man of yours sure is talented and I'm confident Cardinal's can bring out the best in him.'

'I think you're right. Gabriel and I would be thrilled to apply.'

'No need for all that. As I mentioned to you at camp, we use these events as informal auditions. Gabriel already has a place if he wants it, approved by the Board, fully funded.'

'That's wonderful news.' Eleanor looked to Gabriel who grinned and gave his mother a double thumbs-up.

'Just one possible problem,' Eleanor went on, 'I know the term doesn't start for another two weeks, and forgive me if I'm pushing my luck here, but I'll need to have Gabriel settled before that. I've been called away on urgent business next week and I won't be back by the start of term.' Eleanor looked again to Gabriel; she hadn't yet raised this with him.

'That'll be fine. Junior camp is next week so Gabriel could come along and help us out with the young ones. He'll love it.' Mr Tate sounded as determined as Eleanor that the plan would succeed.

'I think he would enjoy that.' She looked at Gabriel. He was still smiling and nodding back to her. 'You've been so helpful, I can't thank you enough.'

'It really is my pleasure, Doctor Bartlett. I'll have my secretary email all the details. You can discuss arrival dates and whatever with her.'

'Thank you, I'll do that.'

The call ended.

'That was surprisingly simple.' Eleanor turned to Gabriel.

'Good work, Mum.' He reached out to hold her hand.

'We're going to have one very busy week, my darling.' She kissed his forehead then turned away. A wave of sadness had caught her unawares.

'Don't be sad, Mum. I'm looking forward to it. Honestly.'

'I know. You'll have a great time.' She brushed her hand down the side of her eye then turned back to face him and hugged him close. 'And it's not too far. Heaven knows, plenty of children go to boarding school. It's not the end of the world.'

The sun was cooling and a cloud gathered overhead. Eleanor looked at the sky then across to the stark mountains silhouetted in the distance.

'Time to go home,' she said.

***

Once Gabriel was asleep, Eleanor braced herself to check her emails. She had little doubt there would be a withering one from Allen. But the first message that caught her attention came from Sophie.

Eleanor opened it. Sophie rarely contacted her nowadays and she was curious about why she would today.

We need to talk. Urgently.

Eleanor shot to her feet and paced between the table and the window. Outside, the sun was setting and within her, a dark cloud was gathering.

She returned to her laptop and pressed reply.

Is everything okay, Sophie?

Sophie responded immediately.

Can I come round to see you? I'm not far away. I can be there in ten minutes.

There had been no visitors to the apartment since Tina had left. This was their safe zone.

Maybe I could call you? Eleanor replied.

No. This is too important.

It had been almost a year since Sophie had set eyes on Gabriel and he had changed beyond all recognition. Eleanor looked towards the closed door leading to his bedroom. Only that would separate him from discovery, chaos, who knew what? But Sophie seemed insistent. Eleanor had to hear what she was so determined to tell her. She looked again to Gabriel's door. He rarely woke in the night. She would take the risk.

Okay, but don't press the buzzer. Text when you're here. I don't want to wake up Gabriel.

Of course, was all Sophie said in response.

***

When Sophie's text arrived to say she had arrived, Eleanor crept to the front door and eased it open. Sophie's pale face looked older. Eleanor led her to the living room, gently closing the door behind her.

She wanted to say, *sit down, what's going on*? But when she opened her mouth to speak, not a sound came out, not even a whisper.

Sophie took her place on the sofa. Eleanor sat inches away, fixed on her guest's eyes. She could see the remnants of mascara streaks beneath them.

'Well?' Eleanor eventually found her voice.

'I don't know how to say this…'

'What?' Eleanor's fear gave an edge of anger to her voice.

'Remember the day we met in the washroom, and you thought I was spying on you, and I explained about hearing shouting from—'

'Of course.'

'Well, it happened again today...' Sophie covered her mouth with trembling hands.

'*And?*' Eleanor groaned at the stress of managing her suspense.

'I heard them, Allen and Simon. I heard them say they were going to kill him!'

'Who?' Eleanor demanded.

'Gabriel!' she sobbed.

'What?' Eleanor exclaimed, her voice quaking.

'I didn't mean to hear it, but Allen was angry, very angry. Simon kept telling him to quieten down. I heard everything.'

'Everything?' Eleanor's heart was thumping. *What else did she know?* 'You mean, there's more?'

'Allen was raging about trust and you and Carl... it was awful... I've never heard him sound so furious.' Sophie pulled a bundle of tissues from the box on Eleanor's coffee table.

'Stop, Sophie! Stop right there!' Eleanor raised her hands. 'How did this all start? You'll need to go back to the beginning and tell me word for word. What *exactly* did you hear?'

Sophie blew her nose loudly.

Eleanor cringed and looked towards the door to Gabriel's room.

'It was this morning, first thing.' She took a deep breath before continuing. 'At first, I couldn't hear any words, just sharp voices, like they were having an argument. But then Allen shouted. He sounded so furious.'

'What did he say?'

'He was shouting at Simon, calling him naïve, stupid… something about sleepwalking into disaster…'

'Okay, then what did Simon say?'

'I couldn't hear. He wasn't shouting yet.'

'Then?'

'Allen said the email was no surprise. Then there was a loud noise, like he'd slammed his fist or something and started bawling at Simon, saying, "I told you she's not to be trusted!" And then Simon's voice got louder, saying something like, "Give Eleanor the benefit of the doubt."' Sophie paused and looked tearfully up at Eleanor.

'And? Please, Sophie, if you can, I need to hear everything.'

'Well, then, it was awful! I heard Allen rage about lots of things I couldn't catch until he stopped for a while and then said very clearly, 'He has to go. Now. He's a ticking bomb.' Simon seemed to agree. He added something like, 'No time for subtlety or discussion. She'd sniff us out and run off with the boy.'

Sophie buried her head in her hands and let her tears fall freely.

Eleanor rose to her feet and paced the floor, trying to maintain a calm exterior whilst desperately trying to form her next words in her head. It was some minutes before she took her place beside Sophie again, put a hand on hers, and gave a small smile.

'Sophie, you poor thing, don't be so upset. Look, think back over everything you've just said, everything you heard. It sounds to me that they didn't actually mention Gabriel's name, did they?'

'But it was obvious… who else could they mean?'

'I have no idea.' Eleanor felt she may have found a way through this disastrous turn of events.

'Eleanor, believe me, please don't brush this off…'

'But Sophie, think about it! No one mentioned him. Kill Gabriel? Can you hear yourself? Kill a tiny child? Allen and Simon would never even think such a thing. In fact, it seems to me that the idea they want to kill Gabriel… is coming from you.'

'What?' Sophie gasped, her eyes suddenly huge.

'Look, Sophie, relax. I'm just saying you must have misunderstood. It's easy to get the wrong end of the stick, especially when you can only hear words and not see the people saying them…'

'No! I heard them. Allen, he said it would be dangerous to postpone things, and Simon agreed. He said it was better to get rid of him when he was still too young to understand…' Sophie was shaken by a fresh wave of tears.

Shit! Eleanor's mind was racing. She desperately wanted to hear more, to know exactly what they were planning, but she couldn't risk giving herself away. She had to put her off the scent.

'Are you… feeling alright, Sophie?' Eleanor forced out the words in the calmest voice she could muster. 'This isn't like you. And, well, what you're saying's just… not quite right, is it? Do you think you maybe need a rest, should go and see your doctor, perhaps?'

'Fuck off, Eleanor!' Sophie jumped up. 'Don't patronise me! Do you really think I'm stupid? That I haven't worked out that something very odd is going on?'

'No, not at all.' Eleanor recoiled, surprised by the strength of Sophie's reaction.

'From the moment you turned up at the conference, nothing has felt right. You might think you're a good liar, Eleanor, but you're not. I can see right through you. You are as transparent as Allen is dishonest.'

'It's not like that, Sophie. You're right, I have kept things from you, but only because I don't want you to worry…'

'You mean, *meddle*.'

'Trust me, Sophie. You've got this wrong, all wrong.'

'Trust you? Trust *you, Eleanor*? Maybe you're the one who's got it all wrong?' Sophie marched to the door. 'Well, on your head be it,' she hissed. 'I came here to help you, to support you, to protect Gabriel. But if you can't see that, then there is no more I can do.'

***

When Eleanor arrived at work the next Monday morning, she headed straight for the usual meeting in Simon's office. She knew they would be waiting for her. She had some explaining to do about not showing up the previous week and she was still worried about whether Allen had found out about her meeting with Carl in Paris. She knew not telling him was a risk but had decided it was one worth taking; her silence had bought her time. All night she'd lain awake, planning how to manage this day, this critical conversation.

'So sorry about last week.' Eleanor walked in calmly and took her place in her usual chair. 'Our nanny was unwell, a tummy bug.'

'Do not worry about it,' Simon replied. 'It does not seem so long ago that I was dealing with the very same problems.' He smiled at Eleanor, but she could see his eyes told a different story. 'How is Gabriel? Not unwell, I hope,' Simon went on.

'He was a little out of sorts, but he always seems to shake these things off quickly. In fact, I think that would be something worth looking into, the rapid response of his immune system.'

'Perhaps,' said Simon. 'When do the schools go back? Strange how you get out of touch with these things. For years your life is all about school timetables and then suddenly, none of that matters to you anymore.' He forced a laugh.

Allen stood up and strode over to the window.

Eleanor's heart sank. She knew Allen would not be won round easily. There was no time to lose. She would have to play the first card rather than wait to fight defensively.

Allen was staring into the distance; his hands pushed into his pockets, his jaw rigid.

'Actually,' she announced, as confidently as her nerves would allow, 'We need to talk about that.' She waited until she knew both men were looking at her. 'You were right about April Springs.' She sighed heavily. 'I should have listened. There is no way Gabriel can go back there.'

Both stared at her. She knew she had disarmed them.

'He is maturing so quickly,' she continued, her voice faltering, 'The changes he's undergone over these summer months alone would be bound to attract a great deal of attention. He seems to be hurtling towards adolescence and God only knows what kinds of challenges that will throw up.' She shook her head.

Neither Allen nor Simon spoke a word.

'I can't bear to think about it, but…' She paused and took a deep breath before continuing, 'We need to do something… to put an *end* to…'

'*Wow!*' Simon gasped. 'You have courage, Eleanor. This cannot be easy for you!'

'I can't deny I've become so much more attached to Gabriel than I ever expected, and I know this has made me evasive… defensive. I just needed time to think it through and…' Her voice dropped to a whisper. 'That's really why I stayed away this week.'

Out of the corner of her eye, Eleanor saw the two men glance at each other and sensed her strategy was working.

'I can hardly believe I'm the first to suggest it, but I don't see another way. We have to… *dispose* of him.' She allowed a single tear to crest and fall.

Allen nodded and Eleanor thought she saw his shoulders relax.

'I hadn't expected this day to come so soon,' she went on, as if trying to sound strong again, 'But given what Carl told me in Paris, I've been forced to reassess things.'

'What Carl told you?' gasped Simon.

Eleanor could hear the surprise in his voice. Perhaps they knew nothing of her meeting with Carl after all but there was no going back now.

'Yes. We met briefly for dinner that first night. Sorry I didn't tell you, Allen. But Carl insisted he met with me alone and I needed to hear what he had to say.'

'Carl? Cutting me out? How surprising!' Allen made no effort to disguise his contempt. 'So, what *did* he have to say?'

'Apparently, he's been working with some samples still available to him. I'm not entirely clear about his experimental approach but he seems to believe there might be some evidence to suggest that Gabriel, once mature, will be particularly sexually active and fertile.'

'What was his method?' Allen's eyes looked keenly at Eleanor. 'Mice, injected with Gabriel's DNA,' she replied. 'He devised some technique or other and seems convinced by his preliminary results.'

'*Replicated* some technique you mean,' sneered Allen. 'But regardless, I don't think this is something we can ignore, given the implications.' He leant towards her as he spoke, and Eleanor could hear his words had lost their sharp edge. She knew she had him back on side.

'We do need a plan, Eleanor.' Simon placed his hand on Eleanor's arm.

'Although I'd like to get over there and see what Carl's up to for myself first.' Allen chewed on the tip of his pen.

Eleanor winced. Somehow, the word 'first' had pierced her heart. But she steeled herself to complete her plan.

'That would be helpful, of course,' said Simon, 'But you would have to fund the trip yourself.'

'But what about Gabriel?' Eleanor fixed Simon in her gaze. 'What are we going to do with him?' She saw the fear in his eyes. He turned to Allen. She knew then, she had been wise to take this tack.

'Okay, well, under the circumstances, my guess is we could have a few months more before we need to take action as far as Gabriel is concerned,' he said, 'And I'd like to reflect a bit on Carl's research before we do anything… irreversible. We'll also want some more samples from Gabriel, before it's too late.' He snatched a notepad from the table and scribbled out a memo to himself.

'This will be hard on you, Eleanor.' Simon reached across the low table and squeezed her hand. Eleanor seized the moment.

'I do feel guilty every time I see him, and I try not to think about what lies ahead. I'm worried he'll pick up on it. He seems to know exactly what I'm thinking.'

Eleanor watched in satisfaction as the men exchanged thoughtful glances.

Simon sighed.

'What happens if he senses this? What would he do? Run away? Then what?'

'That hadn't crossed my mind,' said Allen. 'That *would* be a problem.'

'Perhaps we could send him away for a while?' Simon had the brightened air of a man who had just come up with a solution. 'It would give us the time we need to think things through and it would let you step back a bit, Eleanor, become more detached.'

Eleanor nodded slowly, as if considering a novel idea. 'But where?' she questioned, feeling hugely relieved she had steered them onto this path.

'What about sending him to a boarding school, Eleanor? I know you probably won't want to, but it would give us time to do all the things we have to do and for you to prepare yourself for the next phase?'

Eleanor noticed Allen could not meet her eyes as he made this suggestion.

'Yes, perhaps,' she replied. 'That's a good idea. That could solve a few problems. Boarding school! I'll get on to it immediately.'

She gathered her belongings together, walked briskly to her car and headed for home. *Thank God everything went to plan*, she thought. And as she drove along the freeway back to her empty apartment, she smiled at the thought of Gabriel, a residential pupil in Cardinal College, already safely out of their reach.

Chapter 32

The first night she spent on her own, Eleanor felt only relief that she'd managed to outwit Allen and Simon. Gabriel was safe, at least for a while. And she knew he was happy. When he waved her off from the front door, his eyes were shining, and his broad confident smile reassured her. Returning to Cardinal's seemed comfortable and natural for him.

Eleanor could hardly remember the journey home. She felt exhausted by the rush of all the preparations and overwhelmed by the panic she felt when it had been time to say goodbye. She would visit soon, she'd promised, but knew the school preferred parents to stay away for the first few weeks to allow the children to settle.

She didn't expect the transition to be easy, even though she'd lived on her own for most of her adult life. But she would have to adapt. Gradually, she began to take on more responsibilities at work, arriving early and leaving late most days.

It was the evenings and the weekends that unsettled her. Once back in the apartment, *their* apartment, she felt Gabriel was all around her. But his bedroom door remained firmly shut. Eleanor didn't want to see his shelves, laden with the toys that marked out his rapid progress from toddler to middle childhood. She ached to hold him again and to hear him laugh.

The nights felt endless. Eleanor tossed in bed, snatching only moments of sleep before shuddering awake, wishing he was in the room next door. Sometimes she imagined she would sleep better in Gabriel's room, lying between the sheets she had chosen not to change. But she resisted this, knowing it would only lead to further pain.

This evening, she flitted from one activity to another, searching for something to distract her from the loop of her own anguish, although nothing worked for long. But then, startled by the shrill call of her phone, she leapt to attention.

'Yes?' she barked, alarmed by the sharpness of her own voice.

'Eleanor?' It was her mother.

'Oh, Mum, sorry, it's so good to hear you.'

'Are you all right, dear? I hope this isn't a bad time,' said Miriam.

'Not at all.' Eleanor tried to make her voice sound cheery. 'This is a perfectly good time. I was just away in a dream.'

'I take it that means you're not still running around after Gabriel then?' Her mother laughed.

'Oh no, he's fast asleep.' Eleanor bit her lip.

'Perfect, dear, because I want your full attention for some marvellous news. You will never guess what?' She barely paused for a response. 'Olivia is getting married!'

'Really? Well, that is a surprise!' Eleanor exclaimed. 'When did all this happen? And the children, how are they taking it?'

'Oh, they've just taken to Kit so well. He's such a lovely man, as I hope you'll see for yourself. Not a lot of notice, I'm afraid, the wedding's in four weeks' time. But I do hope you can both make it, Eleanor. I know Olivia would be really touched.'

'Gosh, that is quite soon, Mum. But I promise, I'll see what I can do.'

'Thank you, dear.'

'Hang on, Mum. That's Gabriel crying, I'll need to go, sorry.' Eleanor couldn't face a long chat. She felt bad about cutting the conversation short, especially with a lie, as she knew her mum would be excited about the news and keen to talk. But she didn't feel strong enough to put on an extended performance of happiness.

'Not at all, darling, you go and settle that little one. Give him a great big hug from me, will you? And tell him Granny just can't wait to see him.'

***

'I think it would be good for you to see the family again,' said Simon. 'You could do with a bit of normality and some looking after, Eleanor. You look worn out.'

Eleanor wasn't sure if this was the response she'd hoped for or not. In many ways, it would be so much easier to swerve the wedding altogether. But she knew that would be a betrayal too far.

'You're right, Simon. I am. And I should go to the wedding. Olivia will be hurt if I don't. And it did also occur to me that I could drop into the institute, maybe get more information from Carl?'

'Definitely!' Allen nodded enthusiastically. 'See what he's willing to divulge.'

'Then I'll organise it, ASAP.'

'And, for once, you need not worry about childcare,' added Simon

'Of course,' added Allen. 'What's the name of the school again?'

'Hamilton Academy,' Eleanor replied, looking directly into Allen's eyes.

'Must look it up. Good to get your freedom back, I imagine.' Allen checked his emails as he spoke.

'Yes. Not sure what I would have done with him otherwise,' said Eleanor. 'I could hardly spring him on the family on my sister's wedding day.'

'Well, it is settled! And do not worry about your students. It is only for a few days,' said Simon.

'Perhaps you could do me a favour while you're there?' Allen looked up from his phone. 'I wouldn't mind a copy of Carl's report on those experiments you mentioned, if you can prise one off him. I have asked a few times, but nothing's come back yet.'

'I'll do my best,' said Eleanor, 'But I rather doubt he will have written anything up.'

***

Four weeks later, Eleanor stared out of the window of the black cab as it sped along Glasgow's dull October streets. The laden clouds pressed upon the rows of low, slate and tiled roofs, like tyrants oppressing their subjects. But despite the weather, Eleanor was glad to be home and felt more interested in the wedding the next day than she had expected. She only wished Gabriel could be with her. She longed for him to be a normal part of her life and was tired of having to think up reasons why her family didn't see him; the endless mess of lies she had to tell to cover her tracks.

As the taxi turned into her mother's street, she spotted Hannah and Beth standing at their granny's gate, looking out for her.

'Eleanor's here!' She heard their excited calls as she paid the driver. The girls ran back down the path to the open front door and reappeared with Miriam.

'Come in, come in!' Her mum held her arms open to greet her daughter. 'You must be exhausted, dear. It is so good to see you.'

'Where's Gabriel?' Beth came rushing towards her.

'I'm so sorry.' Eleanor crouched down to break the news. 'Gabriel couldn't come.'

'Not again!' Hannah was now at her side too.

'He's not well, I'm afraid.'

Miriam sighed.

'We never get to see him!' Hannah stomped off with Beth at her heels.

'Eleanor.' Olivia appeared from the kitchen and walked to her, with her arms open. 'Thanks for coming.'

'I wouldn't have missed it for the world.' Eleanor hugged her sister, enjoying the feeling of their closeness. She couldn't remember the last time they had embraced. She could feel the steady rhythm of her older sister's breath brush across her cheek and leant closer towards her, resting her head, lightly, against hers.

Over Olivia's shoulder, Eleanor could see her mother at the kitchen door, watching them. Miriam turned quickly, taking the girls with her out to the garden. Eleanor pulled back and looked deeply into her sister's eyes.

'I'm so sorry, Olivia. I've wanted to talk to you since I was last here. Mum and I had a long chat, about… everything that happened back then. You know… art school… and Dad. I had no idea…' Eleanor searched her pockets for a hankie.

'Shh,' her sister replied in her kindest voice, normally reserved for the children. 'You have nothing to be sorry for. Mum told me all about it too — we put things straight, or at least, as straight as we could. None of it was your fault. I know that.'

'I didn't exactly do anything to help though. You must have been livid…' Eleanor sniffed.

'You were a child. And so was I, for that matter. But yes, I was furious at Dad for stealing my dreams from me, at Mum for going along with it… and even at you. Maybe even especially at you, because your life just seemed to skip along as if nothing was wrong.

'I was so… *angry* that I had to turn down my place at art school, and so jealous that you were being allowed to live the life you wanted, and I wasn't. And somehow or other, those two emotions merged into one… and I became angry with you too.'

Eleanor hugged her sister again. 'I'm so happy to have you back, Livy. I've missed you.'

'Hi.' They were interrupted by a voice at the front door; a deep voice Eleanor did not recognise.

She turned and was astonished to see Bertie standing there. He had been a boy of twelve when she last saw him but now, as he approached fourteen, he looked very much like a teenager. Eleanor gave him a hug.

'Bertie?' she said, surprised to discover their eyes were now more or less on the same level. His dark hair was styled, and his skin felt rougher as she kissed him on the cheek. 'Good heavens, I go away for a year, and look what happens!'

'That's life.' He smiled bashfully, a crimson flush rising from his neck.

'And he has a girlfriend now,' Olivia teased.

'Mu-um,' groaned the teenager.

'Would you do me a favour, Bertie, and take my bag upstairs?' Eleanor rescued her young nephew.

'No problem.' He lifted it effortlessly and made his escape.

'Poor soul, he's at that awkward stage,' said Miriam as she joined them in the hallway.

'We all have to go through it,' said Olivia. She sounded happy and accepting of her son's adolescent awkwardness. 'And I think it's good to help them not take themselves too seriously and become all tense and introverted. At least you don't have that to worry about for a while, Eleanor.'

Eleanor tried to smile through her misery.

'You don't need to think about that today, darling, and every stage brings its highs and lows,' said Miriam. 'You should just try to appreciate each moment as it happens, because the only sure thing on this Earth is that it will pass.'

***

Despite enjoying the company, Eleanor was more than ready at the end of the evening to make her excuses and escape to the sanctuary of her childhood bedroom. She had never seen her sister so happy, not since they were small at least, and she knew this was a time for them to heal old wounds, maybe even to start again. But her heart was elsewhere, with Gabriel, who was thousands of miles away and more vulnerable than she would ever want him to know.

'Sorry to break up the party,' she said, rising from her chair, 'Jet lag's a pain.'

'Of course,' said Olivia. 'I'll go soon too, Mum. Still got a few things to organise before it all kicks off tomorrow.'

Eleanor left her mother and sister saying their farewells and made her way upstairs to her beloved room. She closed the door firmly behind her and leant against it, feeling exhausted by the effort of appearing happy and answering questions about her son as if he was a normal toddler. She had shown them photos of Gabriel taken shortly after they arrived in Vancouver and easily passed them off as recent snaps. But she was worried that her mum seemed to be paying a lot of attention to background details. She had done her best to avoid any tell-tale signs of real time, but they could be easy to miss. Olivia and her mother had delighted in the pictures, but to Eleanor each one was a reminder of an era long past, of a child she felt she had abandoned and of the dreadful lie they were now forced to live.

Sleep did not come easily that night. *There's got to be a way out of this;* she thought as she shifted restlessly upon the narrow bed. She would call in on Carl and check up on what he'd been doing. Perhaps there would be good news. He could have made a mistake in his findings, perhaps even uncovered something new about Gabriel which would give everyone a reason to keep him alive.

***

Eleanor woke early the next morning. She could hear her mum moving around downstairs, preparing for the wedding. She pulled on her old dressing gown and made her way to the kitchen.

She had been intrigued, the night before, by the few details she had picked up about Olivia and Kit's plans for their ceremony. She wondered if her mum was disappointed that it was not to be a church wedding, but soon saw the spring in her step as she bustled around the garden.

Miriam had confirmed it was to be an informal affair with only the closest of family and friends present. Kit, who Eleanor had yet to meet, had dropped off a stack of folding wooden chairs from his workshop, and as Eleanor gazed out of the kitchen window that morning, she smiled as she watched her mum lovingly tie ribbons onto the back of each.

It was a beautiful morning, and although the garden was in the shade now, Eleanor knew it would be full of warmth and light by the afternoon, if the weather held up.

'Can I do anything to help, Mum?' She strolled outside, coffee in hand.

'Actually dear, that would be wonderful. I know Olivia doesn't want to make a fuss, but I do want the garden to look its best.'

'Of course.' Eleanor placed her mug on the table. 'Has Kit been involved much in the planning?'

'Oh, yes, they seem to do everything together.' Miriam smiled broadly. 'And he made these for the occasion, look.' She lifted two delicately crafted ceramic bowls from the small table that stood in front of the chairs.

Eleanor inspected them. *Olivia* was inscribed on one, *Kit* on the other.

'These are beautiful.' She turned them carefully in her hands. 'What are they for? Communion?'

'No... they don't want any of that. It's going to be a humanist service, all the rage, apparently. One of Kit's friends is a humanist and she's been authorised to solemnise the wedding. I haven't met her, but she sounds lovely.'

'I see,' said Eleanor. 'So, what will these be for?'

'They're for wildflowers, that Hannah and Beth are to scatter as they lead Olivia to the... table.' Miriam patted the slatted wood surface.

'And Bertie?'

'He's on meet and greet duties.' Miriam smiled. 'Escorting people from the front gate to their seats.'

'Very good!' Eleanor rubbed her hands together. 'How can I be of most help here?'

'If you could arrange the crockery, the good stuff obviously, cutlery and glasses on the sideboard, we'll be organised by the time the caterers deliver in about an hour. They've gone for a cold buffet.'

'Very sensible, will do.' Eleanor turned to go.

'Oh, and Eleanor?' Miriam's voice had lost its business-like tone. 'I just want to say… thank you.'

Eleanor swung round. 'What for? I've done nothing.'

'No, darling, you've done everything, you *and* Olivia. Your friendship reinstated is the greatest gift you could ever give me. Thank you.'

***

When Olivia and the children arrived around midday, Miriam helped her daughter prepare while Eleanor took charge of organising the excited girls.

Later, when the guests started to arrive, she retreated to her bedroom and watched from her window as they took their seats. Tubs of flowers framed the garden, creating a kaleidoscope of living colour, while at the back of the lawn, in front of the old hut, she could see a linen-clothed table that held shimmering trays of sparkling champagne glasses.

Eleanor studied each guest in turn and was relieved to find she didn't know any of them. She made her way downstairs just before the ceremony was due to start, taking Bertie's proffered hand as he led her solemnly to her seat in the front row, beside Miriam and the girls.

The chattering behind Eleanor quietened to a whisper. *Please God,* she thought with a sudden rush of dread, *no New Age music on panpipes, please…* but as Hannah and Beth cast handfuls of dried cornflower and lavender petals the length of the short path to the front of the crowd, the only sounds to be heard were the soft applause from the small gathering and the chattering of birds.

When the couple arrived and took their places in front of their guests, the girls ran back to their seats.

Eleanor caught her breath when Olivia turned to face the small gathering.

She saw instantly a new peacefulness in her sister's demeanour and a glow of contentment she thought her sister had lost somewhere in her childhood. She had the aura of one who had nothing to prove, no need to seek approval, one who knew she was loved.

Eleanor swallowed hard against the tears that threatened to surface, though not out of self-consciousness. She held back because she felt suddenly unnerved, unsure of what she was feeling, afraid her tears were those of sorrow for herself rather than joy for her sister.

Kit looked nothing like she had expected. A handsome man of medium build, he was not much taller than Olivia, his shoulder length hair pushed back from his face. As he looked around at his guests, his eyes sparkled with an open and honest vibrancy, his chinos and loose, white cotton shirt suggesting to Eleanor he was a man without vanity.

She immediately warmed to her future brother-in-law, so far removed from Charles with his sneering superiority and his meticulous attention to the details of his appearance. How one woman could have been attracted to two such wildly different men puzzled her.

The ceremony, which was light-hearted and brief, was rounded off by Kit wrapping his arms around his new wife and kissing her tenderly, first on her forehead, then her nose, and, finally, her lips. The girls giggled. Eleanor was struck by this show of affection. In all the years of Olivia's previous marriage, she had never seen Charles act with such warmth.

The guests rose to their feet and cheered. But before the newlyweds walked back along the petal-strewn path to the chilling champagne, Kit urged the guests to hush.

'Thank you, everyone, for coming here today and sharing with us our great good fortune. Thank you to the amazing Miriam, who has managed to create this magical venue for our very special day. Before we party, though, my wife…' He beamed and paused to allow more applause to burst forth, before continuing. 'My *fabulous* wife wants to say a few words.'

Eleanor sat up in surprise. This was not the sort of thing Olivia would normally do.

'While words are not required to express the great joy I am feeling, I do want to say a few things at this important corner of my life. In so many ways, today marks a new beginning.' Olivia smiled up at Kit. 'And I can honestly say, I've never felt happier.' She took hold of his hand.

'Kit is part of our family now, a family which, like any other, has seen its fair share of turmoil over the years. But if there is anything I have learnt, it's that family is more than a group of people who happen to live together. It's not even just about shared genes.'

She smiled at Eleanor before continuing. 'When we become part of a family, we share our lives' journeys. We are travelling together, across an ocean unknown to any one of us, in a vessel of our own making. Inevitably, there will be disagreements and tensions, but we must learn to pull together, or our poor little boat will go round in circles. We try to understand each other, to learn the difference between an explanation and an excuse, and to be courageous enough to forgive.

'Everyone here knows me pretty well, and so I'm sure you'll agree that these are probably not qualities that spring to mind when my name is mentioned.'

A warm ripple of laughter swept round the sunlit garden.

'But forgiveness starts with the self, and the untangling of old misunderstandings goes a long way in helping this process. To all of you who have had to put up with me over the years, I'm sorry. Especially to my mum, whose patience knows no bounds, and to my darling sister, Eleanor, who has often, unfairly, been the focus of my unhappiness.'

Eleanor put her arm around her mum, who was crying, and smiled at Olivia.

'So now, I feel excited about tomorrow — and all my tomorrows,' Olivia continued, 'And I feel so very grateful for my life and for everything, and everyone, that has brought me to where I am today. I have the most wonderful children that any parent could ever dream of and, as of today, a very talented and caring husband.'

The guests cheered and applauded, and the children beamed with joy.

'Champagne is now served!' Miriam announced, once her tears had subsided.

***

The next morning, Eleanor rose early and made her way to the institute. The sun was out, and the streets were packed with students, parents, pensioners, and children, that fabulous fusion of people and purpose that characterised Glasgow's West End. Eleanor loved it.

She felt her stomach churn as she entered the building, dreading queries about Gabriel. In the past, she had had little difficulty putting up a convincing front, giving little or false information as the occasion required. But things were more complicated now, and she found it increasingly difficult to remember the details of what she had said before and to be consistent in her deceit. But she had to speak to Carl, to find out if there was any way he could help save Gabriel. He was a persuasive man, and if she could get him on her side, perhaps he could argue Gabriel's case to Allen and Simon. She would do *anything* to improve his chances. She smoothed down her tight-fitting dress and quickened her pace.

She noticed how shabby the place was looking. Paint was peeling from the walls, and there was an ugly yellow damp patch on the ceiling of the foyer. She made her way to her own department and prepared herself to be greeted by Jane.

'Can I help you?' a new face asked.

'Oh, has Jane left?'

'She's on maternity leave. Do you have an appointment?'

'Not as such. I've just popped in to see Carl,' said Eleanor.

'Professor Thornton's not here, I'm afraid. Can I take a message?'

'That won't be necessary, thanks.' Eleanor glanced at her watch, wondering where Carl might possibly be. 'I work here,' she went on. 'We haven't met because I'm on sabbatical at the moment. Eleanor Bartlett.'

'Oh, hi.' The secretary offered her hand.

'I'll just go and see who else is around.' Eleanor walked through into the main office, seeing no one. Her desk was still free, awaiting her return. There was no one around, so she sat in her old seat and gazed around. Carl's office door was closed, but within moments, she heard footsteps from within. Rolling her eyes, she stood up and marched in.

'Good God, Eleanor!' Carl placed a hand above his heart. 'You could have given me some warning!'

'I thought you weren't in?' Eleanor nodded in the direction of reception. 'You've got the temp well trained.'

'Oh, you know how it is. Impossible to get peace to do any work done when people know you're available.'

Eleanor sat down without waiting to be asked.

'What on earth are you doing here?' he asked.

'It's just a brief visit. My sister got married yesterday, and I'll be flying back tomorrow. Just thought I'd drop in and see how things were going.'

'Well... wonderful. Although you will soon be back for good, won't you? How long will it be now?'

'No firm timescale yet, but it should be within the next six months. We still have a couple of things to round off.' She stared intently at him.

'Quite.' He raised his eyebrows. 'Any concrete plans?'

'We're getting there. In fact, one of the reasons I'm here is to find out if you've managed to get any further with your research. Is there anything else we should know? Anything that might *alter* our plans?' Eleanor was struggling to keep up her confident facade.

'Funny you should ask. I was just going to get in touch with you,' he said.

Eleanor doubted that. 'Really?'

'Yes. I'm still trying to figure it all out myself.' He reached into his top drawer and pulled out a bundle of papers. 'I can't account for the latest batch of results.'

'Results from what?' Eleanor felt her heart begin to race.

Carl leafed through the papers in front of him. 'Remember I told you the injected mice reproduced at a rapid pace?'

Eleanor nodded.

'I was worried about overproduction and destroyed the offspring, then separated the adult mice to avoid repeated impregnation.'

'I remember.'

'Well, I decided to see what would happen if I allowed some of the mice to mate for a second time. I wanted to test whether the outcome would be the same or whether the bumper yield was just a one-off thing. I thought it may have been a phenomenon that only occurred when carrying a first litter, in which case it would have less of an impact on the wider population, obviously.'

'And?' Eleanor braced herself for whatever was coming next.

'What occurred was incredible. Cataclysmic, in fact.'

'Carl...'

He pulled out a sheet of figures and turned it towards her. 'When allowed to mate for a second time, all the pregnant females died early in the pregnancy.'

'And the adult males?' Eleanor pulled the data sheet towards her.

'They seemed fine. But there was more than that,' Carl said. 'If the males were allowed to mate with other virgin females, they too would die in early pregnancy.'

Eleanor squinted at the data. 'Stop. I'm getting confused. You're saying then that females were programmed to produce one litter only?'

'Yes. One large litter,' said Carl. 'Another impregnation always resulted in their death.'

'But the males survived?' Eleanor pressed.

'They did. But if that male mated again, even with a virgin female, then that female died.'

'That doesn't make any sense!'

'Tell me about it.' Carl sighed.

'Are you sure?'

'Perfectly,' he said curtly.

'So, whatever these mice are carrying is linked to the male of the species,' said Eleanor.

'It would appear so.'

'And only a male's *first* partner will survive?'

Carl nodded.

'Any subsequent partners will die…' Eleanor shook her head.

'Correct,' said Carl. 'I can't see how it works, or what the evolutionary advantage might be.'

'But it's so… bizarre! Have you replicated it?'

'Several times,' said Carl. 'It seems like some drastic form of birth control. A sort of punitive tax on infidelity, if you like.'

'I don't think we're looking at a genetically encoded morality check, Carl, as attractive as that might seem to some.' Eleanor studied the data in more detail. 'Surely it's more likely that the males are the carriers of some destructive element — a virus, perhaps — that only becomes active once they have reproduced?'

'But how could that work? How does the male of a species know it has successfully reproduced?'

'I have no idea. But on a superficial level, it could account for these results, don't you think? Have you repeated this work with any other species?'

'How could I, Eleanor? It's been hard enough keeping the mice under wraps.'

'There's got to be some way of testing this more fully. You might even have been working with a batch of contaminated mice!'

'Pfft, come on, Eleanor. I know you don't really believe that. I suppose our controls all happened to be fine?'

Eleanor could think of nothing to say. If Carl was right, if his findings were accurate, then he had no new information that could be used to help Gabriel. Quite the reverse, in fact. She noticed his gaze loitering on her cleavage. Her stomach heaved, but she knew she had to think of something to say to keep him sweet.

'Can we go over this again? Together?' she asked.

'No time, I'm afraid. I'm flat out all week.' He stood up and placed a hand on her forearm. 'I'm sorry it's all worked out like this, truly,' he said. 'Despite your best attempts to pretend otherwise, Eleanor Bartlett, I do know you're looking for an escape route for Gabriel. But I haven't found one. And these results are worrying.

'A sexually active Gabriel might produce several others of his kind in the first instance, then kill off every other partner he encounters. How many generations would it take to cause mayhem? I don't know. But with his accelerated rate of development, it might not be too long in our years. Eleanor, Gabriel *must* be stopped.' Carl pushed the papers into his bag. 'And as far as I can see, the sooner the better.'

***

The next morning, Eleanor had to rise early to catch her flight from Glasgow back to Vancouver. She had made her mum promise to stay in bed for a rest but was not at all surprised to find her waiting in the kitchen, a teapot and two cups on the table in front of her.

'Your taxi will be here in ten minutes, darling.' She poured tea into Eleanor's cup.

'Thanks, Mum.' Eleanor reached for her hand.

'Whatever for, darling?'

'For tea, the taxi, the wedding… and for looking after me so lovingly all these years.'

'I wouldn't have had it any other way. But there is one thing you could do for me?'

A horn beeped as the taxi drew up outside.

'Anything, Mum.' Eleanor pulled on her coat and took one last sip of tea.

'Gabriel,' she replied, 'Bring Gabriel to visit, please?'

The longing in her mother's eyes as she grasped Eleanor's hand at the door spoke of an aching heart, suffering from a wound *she* had inflicted and one she was powerless to heal.

'Of course, Mum,' she lied. 'Soon, very soon.' She hugged her tightly then ran to the waiting cab, the happiness of the wedding now smothered by her own, suffocating sadness.

Chapter 33

Eleanor was exhausted. Dragging her bag from the carousel at Vancouver International Airport, she headed for the exit. She would go home briefly, shower and head straight for the research centre. Either Allen and Simon knew about Sophie or they didn't and either situation would be a clue to solving this new twist.

Ahead of her, the doors into the arrival lounge swept open and shut as each traveller was ejected into the crowd, some hailed by whoops and hellos, others by silence. As Eleanor approached, the doors whipped open briefly for the man in front of her. She glanced over his shoulder towards the throng in the arrivals lounge and in the glare of the artificial light, she thought she spotted a familiar figure. Her blood ran cold. Suddenly more alert, she took her turn to enter the bustling hall.

There, before her, at the front of the barrier, stood Sophie, glaring at Eleanor as she made her way forwards. Dangling from Sophie's travel bag, Eleanor spotted the luggage label of another airline. *Glasgow to Vancouver*, it read.

'We *need* to talk,' Sophie said.

Eleanor halted, unable to speak.

'What in the name of God are *you* doing here?' she eventually stammered.

Sophie ignored Eleanor's question. 'We can talk in your car.'

As they walked side by side out of the terminal building towards the car park, Eleanor began to feel her shock turning to anger.

'What were you doing in Glasgow?' she demanded as soon as they were seated in her car.

Sophie shook her head in exasperation. 'Trying to save Gabriel's life! No one else seems to be doing anything!'

'I told you, Sophie, you're talking nonsense. You've got the wrong end of the—'

'Bullshit!' Sophie interrupted, 'And you know it.'

Eleanor was stunned into silence.

'What I can't figure out,' Sophie went on, 'Is what you have to gain by continuing to lie to me and shut me out? You've got no one on your side — or rather Gabriel seems to have no one on *his* side.'

'Really, Sophie?' Eleanor said levelly. 'That's what you truly think of me? How fucking *dare* you! You know nothing about me, nothing about Gabriel, nothing about how much of my thinking, feeling, *loving* is about that boy. You know nothing!'

'Oh, and that's my fault, is it? You all seemed to think a few nods and winks between you could keep me out of the loop — the *real* loop — not the bullshit loop you all pulled me into. Well, you were wrong. And now I think I probably know more about Gabriel's situation than any one of you does individually.'

'What do you mean? What do you know? *Tell me!*'

'I know the whole story, Eleanor.'

'I don't believe you!' Eleanor fumed, praying Sophie was calling her bluff.

'Try me.'

'No, tell me exactly what you know first,' Eleanor insisted. 'You don't get to hijack me and then expect me to sing like a canary.'

Sophie took a deep breath before replying. 'Okay. It all starts with a block of ice, a mysterious woman, pregnant, and an irresponsible band of scientists who decide to interfere with the past, the present and, quite possibly, the future.'

Eleanor was silent for a long moment. 'Who told you this?' she asked, quietly.

'Carl.'

'Carl? Really?' *Fucking idiot.*

'To be fair to him,' Sophie added, 'I told him Allen had told me everything, so I could help him *manage* you.'

Eleanor's jaw fell open. 'And he believed you?'

'Absolutely.' Sophie sounded more confident than Eleanor had ever heard her. *Had she just discovered this strength, or had she been concealing it?*

'As soon as I told him I knew about the plan to… deal with Gabriel,' Sophie went on, 'His tongue loosened, especially after dinner and wine.'

'Hang on, when was this?'

'The night before I flew back.'

'Ah.' Eleanor remembered Carl's rejection of her dinner offer. Now she understood.

'What exactly did he tell you?'

'He thinks the whole experiment is a disaster and needs to stop ASAP.'

'Hang on, why did you tell him you were in Glasgow?'

'I said I had an interview at Strathclyde University and I thought it would be good to meet up, under the circumstances. I told him I wanted to know more about the real Eleanor, so I could bring my best game to *managing* you.'

'Really? And did he have words of wisdom about me to offer you?' Eleanor spluttered with indignation. 'I bet he *thought* he did.'

'Nothing useful.' Sophie smiled, clearly enjoying the upper hand. 'Anyway, that wasn't the information I was after.'

'What were you after?'

'The data he gathered about the mice he treated.'

'And did he give it to you?'

'Not exactly. I emailed it to myself… while he was sleeping.'

Eleanor's eyes widened. She stared at Sophie.

'Let's just say we both got what we wanted,' Sophie said quietly.

'Can't deny I'm surprised, Sophie. And impressed, I guess. So, you got hold of all the data?'

'Yes, but there's loads of it and it's not well organised. It's going to take some time to unravel it all, but if it gives us even the tiniest ray of hope, then it will all have been worth it.'

Eleanor looked into Sophie's eyes, scanning for any flicker of deceit.

'Eleanor, you can trust me,' Sophie said softly.

'How do I know that? I mean, why are you bothering with all this, stepping freely, of your own free will, into this... terrifying arena?'

'Is it too hard to imagine that I just care?' Sophie looked exasperated. 'Ever since I met Gabriel, I...' She paused as if searching for a way to articulate her thoughts. 'I felt a pull towards him, a strange attachment, like he was someone I was meant to meet, I don't know...' She shook her head. 'It almost doesn't feel to me that I *do* have a choice. All I know is that I cannot simply avert my eyes and let him die.'

'Thanks, Sophie.' Eleanor nodded, suddenly believing in her. 'Actually, it will be such a relief to be able to share this... fucking mess with someone at last. I've been a fool and I know it. But from the moment of his birth, the moment we shared that first... intense... gaze, I fell totally in love with him, and I didn't expect to feel that.' She could feel tears pricking her eyes. 'Every single thing I've done since then, every trail of deceit, has been part of my *campaign* to protect him. But the more complex the web of lies I had to spin, the more entangled in them I became, until now, I feel trapped by my own defences.'

Eleanor paused and stared across at Sophie.

'I'm sorry for shutting you out, Sophie. My secrecy came from fear rather than a desire to exclude. But now…' Eleanor's voice weakened. 'I don't have words… for your sheer persistence… and help…' Eleanor's voice faded as tears cascaded down her flushed cheeks.

Sophie squeezed her hand and said nothing until Eleanor took a deep breath and wiped her hand across her face.

'So, are we trusting each other?' She stared into Eleanor's eyes.

'Absolutely.' Eleanor cupped both hands around Sophie's. 'One hundred percent.'

***

When Eleanor arrived at her desk, she settled immediately to read through Carl's report. There was no meeting formally scheduled, but Carl had emailed a copy of his interpretation of the data that morning to all three of them. They would want to talk.

She knew Carl was an ingenious thinker but not always attentive to detail. She hoped she might notice something he'd missed, something that left a crack of light in what was beginning to seem like a black horizon of hopelessness. She prayed she could hold the fort until she, or Sophie, could come up with a game-changing interpretation of Carl's data.

She hadn't been long at her desk when she heard a knock at the door.

'Eleanor?' Simon walked in. 'Are you free to talk?'

'Sure.' She stood up and followed him to his office where she found Allen, grave-faced and silent.

Simon spoke first. 'We have both received word from Carl…'

'It's all right,' she interrupted, 'There's no need for a tortuous introduction. I know what you're going to say.'

Simon looked her in the eye, searching, she knew, for signs of resistance.

'And I know what you're going to propose.' She had rehearsed this line and the tone of its delivery so often. 'I agree.'

'Good.' Allen took over. 'Simon and I have had a few thoughts on how we might handle this… final phase. At the moment we're favouring the idea of taking Gabriel on a skiing trip at the end of this term. Would you like us to run the details past you?'

Eleanor shook her head. Suddenly, her resolve to remain professional withered and she covered her face with her hands.

'I'm sorry,' she said eventually, trying to pull herself together. 'When all this started, it was just words and ideas, not a baby, a child, a person I have grown to love more than… I can't describe it… there are no words.'

'Take your time,' Simon said gently.

'I had no idea I would feel this way,' she went on, 'That I *could* feel this way, and if I could go back to that meeting, I would make a different choice: I would undo my offer of surrogacy. Now, the thought of losing him, discarding him, is… impossible for me to…' Eleanor looked down at her restless hands, twisting endlessly around each other, and started to cry.

'Oh, Eleanor.' Simon crouched by her side and took her hands. 'This is not all your doing. We all agreed on this; we are all fools together.'

Eleanor could not stop the tears. For the first time since Gabriel's birth, she was speaking the truth to them, saying things she believed and now, having breached her own defences, the floodgates opened.

'Is there really no other way?' She gulped, staring into Simon's eyes.

'Believe me, Eleanor, I have thought this through so many times. We have discussed it endlessly.' He looked to Allen who nodded solemnly. 'But all the signs are that to continue in hope is to play with fire. And from what Carl's research tells us, the consequences would extend way beyond ourselves and almost certainly be a disaster for mankind. We made a terrible mistake, you and I.'

Eleanor nodded.

'And as for Gabriel,' Allen added, 'Can you imagine if even a sniff of this were to get out? There would be no way of protecting him from media interest. Gabriel would become a curiosity, constantly pursued, possibly detained, incarcerated… Quite frankly, it wouldn't be a life worth living. And as for us, we'd be in deep shit, we'd be in no place to support him…'

'I know, I know.' Eleanor pulled herself upright. 'I do understand that.' She shuddered, all the while knowing it was a truth she would choose to ignore. 'And what right have I to put my love for Gabriel above all else? That's just not reasonable. But the problem is, what I am feeling is not based on reason. It's based on emotion and the two are often not on the same side; reason in one corner, emotion in another, pulling in opposite directions.'

Out of the corner of her eye, she thought she saw Allen raise his eyebrows.

'Indeed.' Simon patted her arm.

Eleanor fixed on his hands; those hands she had thought might be too unwieldy to be capable of the intricate task he had undertaken at the start of all this. She remembered the touch of them against her trembling thighs as he gently separated her legs, preparing for implantation, and shuddered.

'Well,' Allen said briskly, 'That's all water under the bridge now. We are where we are and we *must* move on from here, quickly.'

'We thought it would be better if we dealt with things on our own.' Simon's tone was softer. 'But we wanted to give you the option of being included in the planning. We do not want you to feel that things are happening behind your back.'

'And given all the things you've noticed about Gabriel's sensitivity to your emotions, we decided it might be too risky to have you involved in any practical way,' Allen joined in.

'What, you mean, involve *me* in the actual… dear God, no!' said Eleanor. 'I couldn't possibly! No. Never.'

'So,' Allen continued, 'Do we have your permission to take him skiing this winter break?'

Again, she nodded. 'He'll accept that, I think.' Eleanor mused aloud at the invitation she knew she would never deliver. 'He's trusting.'

'When does the term end?' Allen whipped out his phone.

Eleanor consulted the calendar on her phone. 'December 10th.'

'Okay. We'll get something organised.' Allen looked to Simon.

'I really wish we didn't have to do this, Eleanor. Before all of this, I could never have imagined I would even contemplate such an act. But I cannot see any other way. Believe me, I wish I could.' Simon walked to the window and Eleanor saw his shoulders shake as he whipped a tissue from his pocket.

No one spoke until Simon had turned back to face them, his eyes reddened.

'So, what will you do when this sad business is all over? Have you made plans?' Allen asked.

'I'll go back to Glasgow,' Eleanor replied. 'Carl has been making noises about my return anyway. It was meant to be just a temporary absence.'

'Fine,' said Allen.

'Anyway.' Eleanor glanced at her watch after a few moments of heavy silence. 'I should get moving. Got a bit of catching up to do.' She stood up and walked to the door. 'And don't worry about me, I'll be fine. It'll just take a bit of time to adjust.'

'Of course.' Simon nodded.

Eleanor closed the door behind her. She knew they would be waiting for her footsteps to fade before conferring once again. For a moment, she thought about slipping into the ladies' washroom to try to hear what they were saying but decided against it. She couldn't bear to hear them comment on what had just taken place. And what they thought about her didn't matter anymore anyway. There was no going back. She had a plan, she just had to stick to it.

***

It was still dark when Eleanor set off for Cardinal's. She couldn't wait to see Gabriel again and frequently had to hold herself back from speeding, but each thought of him seemed to impel her to press harder on the accelerator. She and Sophie had spent the last few days planning this trip and making all the necessary preparations. Eleanor was both relieved and terrified that the day itself had finally arrived.

The school secretary had hesitated when she'd phoned to say she would be taking Gabriel away for the weekend; they preferred the children to settle for at least ten weeks before visits and outings. But once Eleanor explained there was a family funeral, permission had been granted willingly.

Her spirits lifted each time she thought of Gabriel looking out for her car, only to plummet again when she thought of the meeting with Allen and Simon just days before. It had been an excruciating experience and she flinched each time her memory replayed the words she had heard, and those she herself had uttered. But it had been a means to an end; a way of saving Gabriel, *not* a betrayal of him. And it had left her in no doubt she needed to act immediately; it would only be a matter of time before Carl mentioned his meeting with Sophie and then everything could unravel.

When at last she turned onto the long driveway leading to the school and parked the car, she had to stop herself from running to the entrance. As soon as she reached the door, she heard the heavy steps of someone racing up behind her.

'Mum?' A deep voice startled her.

She turned quickly. There he stood, a handsome young man, now taller than her by a few inches. His hair had darkened to a rich mahogany, his smooth skin roughened around his chin.

'*Gabriel*?' She stared.

He wrapped his arms around her. 'It's wonderful to see you, Mum.'

Eleanor felt tears pool in her eyes but didn't want to cry. She had been expecting to see a change in her son but somehow imagined he would just be a taller version of the child she'd left behind two months before.

'You look really good!' She hugged him again, feeling a new strength in his arms, stretching to encompass the width of his torso. 'I've missed you so much.'

'I've missed you too, Mum.'

As soon as Eleanor had visited the office to sign Gabriel out, they made their way, arm in arm, to the car.

'Homeward bound!' said Gabriel as he clicked on his seatbelt and scrolled through the music menu on his phone.

'Actually, Gabriel, we're not going home,' Eleanor said without looking directly at her son.

'Sounds interesting. Where to then?' He grinned at her but immediately, the broad smile faded. 'What's up? You're sad.'

'I've been up and down, but I feel ten times better already,' she said, reaching across to take her son's hand. 'I do hope you've been happy at Cardinal's, Gabriel.' Eleanor tried to sound strong but she could hear her voice waver as she spoke.

'I think I've had a much better time than you have,' he replied.

Eleanor looked into his eyes. She remembered that first time she had seen them. The helpless infant lying in her arms, his soft skin white in its vernix coat and the tiny fingers that grasped her own shaking hand. He had gazed up at her, and she back at him, sealing a bond like no other she had ever forged.

'Dear God, Gabriel, I'm so sorry. I've made such a mess of things.' Eleanor brought her hands to her face. She felt her body shake; she was finding it hard to breathe. She heard a racking sob and realised it was her own. Her stomach ached with the effort of holding it back, yet also from the pain of its escape.

'Mum!' Gabriel drew closer to her. 'What can possibly be this bad?'

Eleanor knew she had to wait for the tears to stop before she could speak. Her throat felt too tight; no words could possibly be formed. She held Gabriel's hand and felt his tears fall onto the back of her head.

'I'm sorry, Gabriel. Sorry for everything.'

'What is it, Mum?'

Eleanor pulled a tissue from her bag and wiped her eyes.

'Gabriel.' She drew herself up and squeezed his hands in hers. 'There are some things I need to tell you and others that, for the moment, I simply must not. But we can't, or rather, *you* can't… go home. All I can tell you is that it wouldn't be safe for you.'

'Are *you* safe?' he pursued. 'How can it be safe for you but not for me?'

'Gabriel…' She paused. 'I wish, I really do wish I could explain…'

'Is it something about my father?'

'No… no! Whatever gave you that idea?'

'I know I came to you via a test tube. But sometimes fathers *do* try to trace their children. I've read about it.' Gabriel looked away, as if embarrassed by this revelation.

Eleanor reached over to her son and held his hand. 'I'm sorry, Gabriel, I didn't realise.'

'It's fine, Mum, no big deal.' He blushed. 'Just curiosity, I suppose.'

'Of course.' Still, Eleanor felt wounded. *Was she not enough for him?* 'No, it's nothing like that, darling. And the next time we meet, I promise to tell you everything.'

Gabriel looked up at her in confusion. 'The *next* time we meet?'

Eleanor sighed heavily. 'Gabriel, I'm so sorry, but the only way to keep you safe for the moment is to take you away from here and send you to another school. Today.'

'Today?' Gabriel looked over his shoulder at the pathway leading from the car park back to Cardinal's. 'Why? I thought we were going home… and what about my friends? Don't I get to see them again? Ever?'

Eleanor heard hurt in his voice, and possibly anger, emotions she had rarely known Gabriel to express.

She looked away.

Okay,' Gabriel said eventually, his voice now quiet and resigned. 'I'd much rather spend some time with you, but if it has to be this way, then that's okay.'

Eleanor looked over at Gabriel, his jaw was clenched but his lips were trembling. And yet she still had much to say. Fighting her instinct to hug him, to change her mind and run off with him, she pressed on with the plan she and Sophie had devised. It was their best chance. Perhaps their only chance.

'And' she hesitated, 'There's one more thing. You must take another name.'

'Another name?'

Eleanor could see the confusion on his face.

He was quiet for a few moments.

'Do I get to choose?' he asked.

'Sorry, I'm afraid not. You'll be Jude. I'm afraid I had to register you some time ago.'

'Jude.' Gabriel nodded, giving no sign of liking the name or not. 'So, where is this school then?'

'It's just north of Lillooet, about a hundred miles from here. It's out in the wilds, surrounded by nature.' She reached for the brochure on the back seat of the car. 'It'll be a bit of a change from Cardinal's, but I think you'll like it there.'

She handed the glossy booklet to Gabriel. He flicked through the pages.

'I know this will all seem very odd to you, but I must make sure you can't be traced to this school, so I've told them you've just arrived from a remote boarding school in Scotland and that your records are en route.'

'Okay.' He smiled weakly at her. 'Let's go.'

'It won't be forever,' said Eleanor.

'I know, Mum, don't worry. Nothing is.'

***

The further north they travelled, the colder the weather became until, as they approached their destination, snow was beginning to fall. Rocky Falls Academy sat within acres of wooded grounds. As they followed the drive to the entrance, they passed a stable block and a boathouse.

'Hope you managed to get me in on a bursary,' said Gabriel. 'This all looks rather grand.'

Eleanor reached for Gabriel's hand, weak with gratitude and relief that he had accepted the plan.

After the formalities and a brief tour of the facilities, they were introduced to some of the boys in Gabriel's year. Eleanor was glad she had presented him as a sixteen-year-old; he already looked a little older than some of his peers.

After helping her son unpack the bags of new clothes she had brought with her, Gabriel walked with Eleanor back to the car.

'Gabriel.' Eleanor stopped and looked around her. They were some distance from the school buildings now and she saw no signs of life around her. She turned to face her son. 'You must listen carefully to this. *Very* carefully.'

Gabriel gazed into her eyes with such intensity that it silenced her for a moment.

'Everything is going to be fine,' she began, 'But you will hear strange news about upsetting events, things that are supposed to have happened to me and to you. But they won't be true. Do you hear me? *They won't be true.*'

Gabriel's brow furrowed in confusion.

'However, you must act as if they are, but in your heart, know they are not. Do you understand?' She squeezed his arms gently.

'Of course,' he said, with a forced smile.

'One day, I'll explain it all to you and then all this will make some sense.' She threw her arms around him.

'Can I phone you?' he asked.

'Not yet, my darling, not until it's safe. If someone hears us or checks my phone… even with a different name… it's too big a risk. I'm so sorry. But I will write to you.' Eleanor kissed him one more time. 'And you can write to me too. I'll come and see you as soon as I can.' She gripped his hands and brought them to her lips.

'Stay here, please,' she said. 'It will be harder for me to drive away if you come with me to the car.'

Gabriel nodded.

Eleanor walked a few paces, then turned and ran back, pulling him into her arms and hugging him tightly.

'I love you so much, my darling, darling Gabriel,' she whispered.

Then, dragging herself away, she began the agonising walk towards the car, looking back often to catch another glimpse of her child, standing motionless and growing smaller with each step she took until finally, his image melted into a white mist of snow.

Chapter 34

Eleanor's hands trembled as she sped away from Gabriel. It seemed so surreal that she and Sophie had met, just a few evenings before, to discuss the details of exactly how, and where, she would execute the next phase of their plan — and now she was about to do it.

She had hoped to give herself more time to adjust to what lay ahead, but when Sophie told her about the unopened email from Carl she'd spotted on Allen's laptop, ominously headed: *Urgent. We need to talk,* they both knew time was a luxury they could not afford.

The ebony sky shed swirls of snow dust that froze to an opaque crust as soon as they hit the windscreen. The narrow road hugged the side of the rugged hill that stretched back down towards the small town they had passed on their way to Rocky Falls Academy only hours before. The town was the last inhabited area before the school itself, and the approach to it, as Eleanor had discovered during her research, was one of the most infamous accident black spots in the region.

As they'd ascended, Gabriel had been fascinated by the unforgiving landscape. Over each unguarded precipice, the land fell away into a dark and distant canyon, thick with pine and fir and razor- sharp rocks.

But now, there was nothing to be seen beyond the edge, just darkness.

Eleanor checked the temperature gauge on the dashboard. It was thirty degrees Fahrenheit. Perfect. Then she checked the distance travelled from the school gates, noting it was only another fifty yards to the stopping point she had identified on the outward journey. She wondered if Gabriel had noticed her resetting the odometer as they passed.

Ahead of her, she could see the white, swirling cloud of fog that, she knew, would be freezing onto the road below, making a lethal ice rink of it. Taking a deep breath, she drove cautiously into the hazy shroud and edged into the layby she'd spotted earlier.

She began to shake, not with cold, but terror. *Shit! Can I do this? Can I really pull it off? Fuck, fuck, fuck!* She clasped her trembling hands in front of her mouth. *How the hell did it come to this? What kind of a monster have I become?*

A reel of images of her mother played before her eyes, smiling proudly, hugging Gabriel… what would she think if she knew? What kind of a state would she be in when she heard the unthinkable news? She slammed her fist on the steering wheel, accidentally sounding the horn.

Startled, she returned abruptly to the moment and, gritting her teeth, ran through the checklist she and Sophie had rehearsed. Sat nav: on. Radio: on. Child car seat with torn harness in back. Toddler jacket and shoes in footwell. Bag of nappies. Change of clothes. Her coat: on. Gloves and phone in pocket. Handbag: on the back seat of the car. Front window: open. Engine: running.

Bracing herself, she opened the door and stepped out into the fierce chill, gasping as a rush of deafening, icy wind slammed into her. Leaning back into the car, she reached for the handbrake, but pulled back abruptly as soon as she touched it.

No! I can't do this!

She swayed from foot to foot, willing herself to be brave, but she just couldn't make the final move, until suddenly, somewhere way below her, she noticed headlights sweeping the rock face.

Someone was coming.

Horrified, she approached the window once more. It was now or never.

She thrust her hand back into the empty car, released the handbrake, then took up her position ready to push. She heard the roar of the approaching car and paused, her heart pounding in her chest. She could tell the vehicle was travelling at speed and realised it would be safer to wait until it passed. Picking her way across the glistening white road, she squeezed as far as possible into one of the many dark crevices in the rock face. The last thing she wanted was an offer of help.

She held her breath, waiting for the rush of the car passing and bracing herself for the wave of icy shrapnel that would undoubtedly wash over her. It was longer than she expected before the dull yellow of headlights shimmered across the frozen surface, just inches from her feet. She waited, terrified, for it to pass, but when at last the car came into view, she could see its speed had slowed to a crawl.

Fuck! She shrank further back. *Just go a-fucking-way, will you?*

She heard the hum of its engine, its light still making a stage of the road, then the soft thud of the door, the crunch of ice beneath foot.

Fuck off home, hero... She brought her hands to her mouth and tried to hold herself still against the violent shivering that had set in.

Surely he'll look in the car, see nothing and go? She waited. *Maybe report the situation to the police?*

'Eleanor?' a voice barked. 'Where the fuck are you?'

The sound of her own name had Eleanor gasp and immediately a beam of light shot onto her face. Stunned by the glare, she blinked through the shade of her fingers, trying to identify the driver.

'Eleanor.' He grabbed her hands and pulled them from her face. 'We need to talk!'

She recognised the voice. '*Carl?* What the hell are you doing in Canada?'

'Looking for you… and Gabriel!'

'How in God's name did you find me?'

'Pfff. Didn't exactly take the Brain of Britain to work it out from Sophie's search history… *Accident Blackspots in British Columbia,* for example, with this stretch highlighted in an email to you,' he sneered. 'Between that and the dates of the *funeral* you were taking Gabriel to…'

'You hacked into her computer?'

'And thank God I did. I've been tailing you for a few days and you didn't even notice! You're clearly not thinking straight.'

'You what? Why are you here, Carl?'

'To stop *you* doing *this*!'

'Doing what?' Eleanor scrambled to find out what he knew.

'Killing Gabriel, of course. Don't!' Carl shook her arms as he spoke. Eleanor pulled herself free.

Eleanor gasped. 'Why? What have you discovered? Is it safe for him now?' Eleanor clung to Carl's lapels. 'Please…'

'It's amazing, Eleanor! A life changing breakthrough, for all of us!'

'What? Thank God! *Thank you, God!*' Eleanor groaned through her tears.

'You… you won't believe… but it seems Gabriel holds the secret to a longer and healthier life — for everyone! It's almost unbelievable!'

He was breathless with excitement and, even in the darkness, Eleanor could see Carl's eyes sparkle as he spoke.

'His telomeres… they're not like ours. They somehow slow down the unravelling of the chromosomes they are attached to…'

'So…' Eleanor thought furiously. 'You mean they actually delay the process of decay?'

'Exactly. That's why the mice lived longer!'

'Wow… okay, but how can this save Gabriel?'

'Well, it doesn't,' Carl replied, as if it was obvious.

Eleanor took a step backwards. 'Wh-what?'

'We only need his stem cells. I wouldn't need long, Eleanor, just one more week. I'm sure I can find a way to utilise this to…'

'So, Gabriel still has to die? No!' Eleanor sank to the ground and wailed.

Carl crouched down to her level and tried to put his hands on her shoulders but she pushed him away.

'You *bastard*! You let me think…' She lunged at him and battered her fists against his chest.

'I'm pleading with you, Eleanor. Just one week, that's all I need. That boy is worth more than fucking antimatter…'

'Is that all he means to you? Money? Dear God, Carl! You are even more despicable than I could ever have imagined.'

'Oh, come off it. What's your problem? You're the one who's piled a drugged kid into your car and is just about to end his life.'

'Not for money! I'd do anything to save him! And you'd have me go through all this again? All the lies, the tears, the self-hatred at drugging an innocent child… so you can get fucking rich and further your career?' Eleanor pushed him away from her, dizzy with rage.

Carl shot up and marched to the car, pulling out his torch as he approached. Eleanor rushed after him.

'No!' she screamed out. 'Don't wake him!' She snatched the torch and smashed it to the ground then, fuelled by a cocktail of fury and despair, ran to the rear of the car and pressed her hands against the frosted metal.

'No!' Carl levered himself between her and the car, trying to get a grip of her coat to wrench her away.

But Eleanor's anger had brought strength. 'Get out of my way!' she seethed, shoving hard against him, sending him clattering to the ground.

'Fucking bitch!' He scrambled to his feet and snatched his phone from an inside pocket. 'This is filming now, Eleanor. If you don't stop, I'm taking this to the police!'

Eleanor leant into the car with all her strength. She could feel it slowly inch forwards. Carl ran to the front of the car and pushed back at Eleanor. The dark shell of the vehicle was halted in its progress but was still close to the edge. Carl prepared to move it further back.

'Get out of the way, Eleanor!' he shouted.

Then suddenly, Eleanor heard a loud crack as Carl again fell to the ground.

'Jesus Christ.' He rolled quickly onto the road. 'The fucking cliff is crumbling. Are you trying to kill me too?'

Eleanor gave one final push. As the car rolled, she suddenly felt the rear wheels lift. Leaping back, she watched as it lurched forwards, its back rearing up like a wounded animal.

For a moment, she thought she saw Gabriel inside, reaching for her, begging for help. Then all at once, she was surrounded by a terrifying scream, screeching certain death as the car fell, fell, fell, crashing into the ravine far below. The air reverberated to an almighty thud, followed by a shattering explosion as the metal carcass met a bed of rock and the densely wooded ground below. A ball of fire burst upwards and outwards, its pyrotechnic glory a horrifying mockery of the darkness in her heart.

Then, there was silence.

Carl marched towards her and threw her to the ground.

'Fucking mad woman!' he yelled. 'Stupid bitch!' He pushed his face close to hers. 'You'll pay for this… I'm going to make sure of it!'

As he turned to go, Eleanor caught sight of something lying on the ice. Instantly, she grabbed for it and waited until Carl reached his car.

'Carl,' she called to him, trying to mask the triumph she felt.

Carl ignored her and opened the door to his car.

'You dropped this,' she said, waiting for him to turn.

As soon as he saw Eleanor smiling, his phone in her hand, he charged back towards her. Eleanor waited until he was close enough for her to enjoy his expression then tossed the phone into the darkness over the deathly drop.

Carl froze to the spot, his teeth clenched, his eyes fierce. She saw his hand make a fist and waited… then cutting through the charged silence, she heard the faint sound of sirens, vehicles setting out from the town at the bottom of the pass. Help was on its way.

'You will suffer for this!' Carl stabbed his finger towards her eyes then ran back to his car, speeding off before anyone else arrived on the scene.

Eleanor sank to the ground and sobbed, her body shaking uncontrollably as she rocked back and forth. It wasn't long until the fire trucks arrived, their wail screeching louder as they climbed the hill towards her.

It was done.

***

She didn't arrive back at her apartment until late the following evening. Exhausted and distraught, she fell onto her bed and wept. The police had been kind, but still, she had to be questioned. They told her they would check again in the morning for Gabriel, but as far as they could see, there was no chance anyone who had been strapped into the vehicle could have survived either the fall or the inferno.

'No one has yet, I'm afraid,' the chief officer had said. 'And from what we can see, there's nothing left to inspect…' He paused as Eleanor broke down yet again. 'But, of course, we will look, just in case,' he added.

Eleanor lay still, watching night become day, and with the dawn, a new emotion took over. Relief.

She had barely dressed when the phone rang. *Allen*. She'd make him wait. She knew why he was calling and sure enough, turning on the local news, she soon caught the thirty-second snippet.

Meanwhile, further north in the province, yet another life has been claimed on the infamous Lillooet Pass when a car left the road at Devil's Crook. A two-year-old boy was tragically trapped in the vehicle after his mother stepped into the treacherous conditions in a bid to establish the direction of the road ahead. Local officials have promised, yet again, to review safety measures in the area.

Eleanor was taken aback when the old picture of Gabriel as a toddler flashed in front of her. Despite having given it to the police, it was still shocking to see his face staring out at her from the large screen. Hours later, Eleanor returned Allen's call.

'Fucking hell, Eleanor.'

She cried quietly into the phone.

'I'm so sorry… really. You are very brave…'

Eleanor's weeping grew louder.

'Look, I'll call later, just wanted you to know we're thinking about you.'

Eleanor mumbled indistinctly and hung up.

Perfect, she congratulated herself. She would lie low for a few days, as agreed, and would not contact Sophie.

***

It was some days before she returned to work, arriving in the early evening after most of the staff had left.

She saw the horror in Simon's face when he came into her room. She knew she looked awful and was glad he was shocked.

'So sorry, Eleanor. I did not call you, I did not want to… intrude.'

Eleanor tried to reply but no words escaped, resorting instead to a simple nod.

'We are all still in shock, Eleanor. It will take time… Sophie is not coping… She has not been back since she heard…'

Eleanor stared straight ahead, as if hardly listening.

'So… Do you have any plans?' he asked, moving closer to Eleanor.

'I need to go home, to Glasgow,' she said, shoving a few folders into her bag and clearing her desk. 'For good. My mum's in a dreadful state; she needs help.'

'What about you, Eleanor? Do you want to talk about it? It might be good for you. There are not many people you will be able to discuss this with… properly.'

Eleanor could hear the tremor in Simon's voice.

'I'd rather not,' she said without looking up at him. 'What's done is done… and had to *be* done.' She continued to pack her bag. 'I don't want to go there. Believe me, Simon, it won't help.'

'*D'accord.*' He backed off. 'But if you change your mind…'

She nodded her reply.

'He was a wonderful young man, Eleanor, but this just was not his time.'

'I know.' Eleanor focussed intently on organising her desk.

'I will miss you.' He hugged her firmly.

'I'll miss you too.'

***

Eleanor washed down two sleeping tablets with the double gin and tonic she had ordered immediately after take-off. She just had to get through this, she told herself. But nothing in her wanted to leave. She thought of Gabriel, alone and abandoned, wishing he could be with his mum, and her heart ached with longing.

She looked down at the shrinking landscape: their northwards flight path taking them over Lillooet, where, a part of her believed, her toddler lay charred, murdered by his inadequate, stupid fucking mother. She threw back the rest of her drink, closed her eyes and prayed for the tablets and the gin to hasten the oblivion she craved.

***

Miriam had asked Eleanor to stay with her for a while, and despite her longing for privacy, she had agreed, hearing how lost and distraught her mother had sounded on the phone. When she arrived at the front door, there was no cosy glow from the Tiffany lamp shining through the glass and it took several rings before she saw a slow- moving shape make its way towards her.

'Oh, Mum!' Eleanor sobbed as she fell into Miriam's arms, more from shock at her dishevelled appearance than her own grief.

The deathly silence in the house, the candle in front of Gabriel's picture and the smell of rotting food from the overflowing bin were suddenly all too much for her and she fought an urge to turn on her heel and run back to her car. Instead, she called Olivia and asked if she could come over.

'I just can't do this right now,' Eleanor explained. 'I thought I could be here for Mum, but I really need to be on my own.'

Her sister arrived thirty minutes later, just long enough for Eleanor to make them both a cup of tea, and after a brief exchange of hugs and tearful commiserations, Eleanor sped off to her own apartment.

Her beloved Glasgow flat seemed too big now Gabriel wasn't there. His room, once full of toys and books, was back to the shell it had been before his birth: one single bed, one chest of drawers and the plain doors of an empty wardrobe.

The silence was oppressive, but Eleanor knew she needed peace and time to recover from the shock of her own lie. She was finding the stress of living out the deceit utterly exhausting. She wanted to be strong for her mother, but to do that she would need to be apart from her. As an adult, she had never been able to cry in her mother's presence and without that release at the end of each day, she was sure she would crumble.

***

Everyone at the institute had been told of the accident and was primed not to make enquiries. Gradually, within weeks, the aura of tension around her eased and Eleanor began to feel less conspicuous. She had reclaimed her outer shell, her impenetrable emotional defence, but inside the weeping did not stop. She was haunted by visions of tangled metal encasing her child, flames licking around his blistering body, reaching out to her, screaming out her name. *Would this ever stop?* She wanted to scream out the question to the universe and plead for mercy.

Did I do the right thing? Was there really no other way? she asked herself again and again, sometimes fearing she had spoken these thoughts aloud.

Then she would remind herself to give it time. *You will see him again and hug him and all will be well.* But still the aching continued.

Would it really be so wrong to phone him? She stared at the screen in front of her, seeing nothing of it. *Perhaps the sound of his voice would help her remember the truth she had tried to convey to him. None of this is real!* But when she and Sophie had talked it over, Eleanor had reluctantly agreed it would be safer not to.

'Supposing the police are suspicious for some reason and take your phone for investigation?' she had argued.

'I could buy a second phone then, just for Gabriel?' Eleanor had pleaded.

'No, it's an unnecessary risk,' Sophie reasoned, 'And one taken more for your sake than his. The pupils don't have access to any technology. That's the school's policy and that's why we chose it, remember? So, he will know nothing of the car crash. And you've already told him you wouldn't be in touch... I think he would be confused.'

***

When she felt ready, Eleanor took up her mum's offer to join the family for Sunday lunch. It felt strange to be back at the family table, as if nothing had ever happened.

Olivia was there with Kit and the children. She was so lucky, thought Eleanor. She had an ordinary life with regular children she could enjoy openly. Eleanor thought of Gabriel, alone, in a remote corner of Canada, living as Jude. He didn't even have the security of a real identity, never mind the support of a family network. Eleanor felt the warmth of a tear gather, and quickly brushed it away.

As they waited for dinner to be served, there was a heavy silence. Olivia smiled weakly towards her while Bertie and Hannah fixed their eyes downwards on the plates Miriam placed on each raffia mat.

'Blessings on our meal,' she said once seated, her tone flat and sad.

The scrape of cutlery on plates was all that could be heard for a few minutes. Suddenly, Beth paused and stared over at Eleanor.

'Do you miss Gabriel?' she asked in a matter-of-fact voice.

'Beth!' Olivia looked apologetically to Eleanor. 'You shouldn't ask such things.'

'It's all right,' said Eleanor. 'Yes, I *do* miss him. I miss him very much. I think about him all the time. So, in some kind of way that means he's always with me.'

'I miss Daddy like that,' the little girl sympathised. 'He's kind of dead too, isn't he, Mummy?' She looked at her mum.

'No, Beth, it's different.' Olivia put down her cutlery. When she spoke again her voice sounded softer and Eleanor could hear she was picking her words with care. 'But there are lots of ways of missing people… and they're all sad.'

When dinner was finished, Kit looked at Bertie and suggested they take the girls to the park. Miriam went to the front door with them to help with coats and shoes.

'Sorry about that,' Olivia said when they were gone. She reached over and stroked her sister's hand.

Eleanor wanted to say it was fine, that children said those things, out of the mouths of babes… but when she tried to speak, she found no words would come. Instead, she felt a dull heaviness in her chest, her shoulders shuddered and from deep within a whimper gathered force until she heard the wail of her own despair like the howl of the helpless wounded in the wild.

Olivia moved closer and wrapped her arm around her.

'You poor poppet.' She held her tight and buried her head in the hollow of her shoulder. 'He was such a wonderful little boy. I don't know what to say.'

When Miriam returned, she crouched beside her daughter and cupped her hands in her own. They stayed there in stillness for some time, soothing Eleanor as each wave of grief crested then fell away.

'I'm sorry,' she said eventually, sweeping her hair away from her moist cheeks and sniffing.

'There's no need to be sorry, pet.' Miriam drew a tissue from the pocket of her cardigan. 'This is such a hard time, but it will pass. Everything does.'

Eleanor looked up. Her mother looked awful. This grief had aged her and Olivia's kindness was so warm and sincere. What if they knew the truth? What in God's name would they think of her? Gabriel was safe, although his future was not secure, and Eleanor was unsure which emotion was driving her distraught display: a longing for her son? A fear of what might lie ahead for him? Or guilt at the nightmare she was dragging her family through? She really didn't know.

Miriam persuaded Eleanor to stay the night.

'I'd rather you didn't drive in this state, darling,' she had pleaded. Eleanor accepted the offer, more out of guilt than desire. *It's the least I can do,* she thought as she shuffled off to bed in the early evening.

It wasn't long until she heard a soft tap at the door.

'Can I come in?' It was Olivia. Kit had taken the children home.

'Sorry I've been such a handful.' Eleanor looked up from where she was sitting on the edge of her bed.

'What is there to be sorry about?'

'Everything.' Eleanor thought she might cry again.

Olivia sat beside her. 'It's alright to be upset. It's only to be expected. There'd be something wrong if you weren't. And think what I've been like these past few years although my problems were nothing compared to this! I can't even begin to imagine what you are going through, my poor darling… It's every parent's nightmare and you are living it. At least I knew that, hard though it was, all of my problems had, well, solutions — but you…' Olivia hugged her sister and started to cry. 'I am so, so sorry you are going through this.'

Eleanor stroked her sister's hair. 'It's crazy, isn't it?'

'It is.' Olivia sat up and blew her nose. 'And I know it seems impossible right now, but there can be happiness again, believe me. I'm not saying you'll stop thinking about Gabriel or missing him dreadfully. Once a mother…' She held her sister's hand. 'But there will be light at the end of the tunnel, we just don't know how long the tunnel is. I was in pieces, a mess, thought my life was doomed, but...' 'How are things going on that front?' Eleanor sat up and took a deep breath. She was keen to change the subject before she betrayed herself in some way, in the face of her sister's unaccustomed empathy. 'Do the children miss having Charles around the house?'

'Not really,' said Olivia. 'They see him every second weekend and they seem to have accepted Kit. But I suppose that doesn't mean they don't miss their own dad. I'm sure they do, especially Bertie.'

'It does all seem to be going well though. Are you happy?'

'I've never been happier,' said Olivia. 'I feel guilty, things are going so well for me while you are so sad.'

Eleanor shook her head. 'Don't feel guilty. It's not as if there's only so much happiness out there and you've taken it all. I'm pleased for you. It's about time something went your way. I want to hear about it, really. It helps, you know, to hear how good can come from bad, so please... go on.' Eleanor reached for Olivia's hand and squeezed it.

'Okay.' Olivia nodded. 'I... was so angry when Charles left, but really, he did us both a favour. We'd just become so used to our shared misery that we didn't question it. But as each part of my life came into crisis, first my marriage, then my job, then struggling with the children, it was as if filters were lifted. And it was only once I was left with the bare light, the essential me, that I could see each part of my life for what it was, and I could decide which bits I wanted to keep.'

'And you don't miss teaching at all?' Eleanor was struck by her sister's new openness.

'Not at all. It was never the right job for me. I just couldn't think of anything else to do with a degree in modern languages. But in the studio, I feel excited. When I wake up in the morning, I feel enthusiastic about my day. And that's all I've ever wanted, to live a life I believe in.'

**

When Olivia left, Eleanor lay staring at the blank wall opposite her bed, their conversation replaying itself. *To believe in your own life,* that was a good way of putting it. Eleanor knew that for most of her life she had been very lucky on that score. She'd always been absorbed in her job, maybe overly so, given that she'd been oblivious to her sister's distress. And she was still interested in her life despite her current problems and moments of despair. Her happiness might be on hold for the time being, but there could still be a path back to it. She just had to stick to the plan.

Sleep did not come easily that evening. All night she found herself thinking over the email she knew she must write, searching for the phrases she might use. Eventually, she threw the covers back and fetched her laptop. She had the blueprint in her head now and knew she wouldn't rest until she could see the words in black and white.

Dear sir, she started. Her stomach churned at the thought of breathing life into yet another lie. But it had to be done or everything she had endured over the past few weeks would have been for nothing. One letter from Gabriel, one call to her workplace from his school and the truth, the impossible truth, would be exposed.

It is with deep regret that I must inform you of the tragic death of the mother of one of your pupils, Jude Tennyson, who was killed this morning in a car accident. As another party was involved in the incident, I'm afraid I'm not in the position to offer more details at present, except to say she died upon impact and did not endure prolonged pain or distress.

Unfortunately, no family member stays close to the school and given the highly sensitive nature of this news, I would prefer a more sensitive delivery than a phone call could offer. It will, therefore, fall to you to break this distressing news to Jude. As you will know from the registration details, I was named as the next of kin by my sister, Eleanor. I will make arrangements to visit at the first opportunity and will forward details to you of my expected time of arrival.

In the meantime, I would be grateful if you could direct all correspondence to me at the above address as I will henceforth be acting as guardian to my nephew.

Please send my condolences and love to Jude and let him know we are all thinking about him and that his aunt Olivia will visit as soon as possible and bring him home.

Eleanor read the email aloud to herself several times then sat with her finger poised above the keyboard.

Please God, Gabriel, remember what I told you. Please know this is not true.

She paused briefly, then let her finger drop onto the small black button and pressed send.

Chapter 35

It had been just over a month since Eleanor had left Vancouver but returning now, she was struck by how different everything looked. Autumn's glory had faded, and winter's monochrome palette now dominated, like a faded blanket tossed across the landscape. Naked blossom trees reached out to one another above the boulevard, their tips entwined, gnarled hands seeking mutual comfort.

Eleanor hadn't ever discussed her holiday plans with work colleagues, so the only deceit necessary had been with her family who seemed relieved and happy to believe she was going to a luxury spa in Austria for some much-needed recuperation. They asked no questions.

What will he look like now? she wondered. She had noticed his rate of maturity seemed to have accelerated recently and six agonising weeks had passed since she had last seen him. That last image of her son, alone in the snow, waving goodbye, had stayed with her. It woke her in the loneliness of the night, but it also pushed her to keep going each day. Now, she had to get back to him. And he would have known of his mother's *accident* for two weeks. *Surely he had remembered her words and hadn't believed the news…* She pressed harder on the accelerator, desperate for their reunion.

Her stomach churned, its diet of nausea and stress taking its toll as she ran through the plan she and Sophie had devised. She bitterly regretted not confiding in Sophie earlier. She had proven herself to be smart, kind and, most importantly, loyal. Qualities she shared with Gabriel. But fear was the enemy of trust, she realised, and she had been blinded by it.

It was early afternoon by the time she reached the village closest to the school. She turned into the car park of a hotel that dominated a sprinkling of houses and local stores, ordered a coffee but barely touched it, waiting a while before going to the washroom.

There, after several attempts, she managed to twist her hair into a French roll and slipped some heavy earrings into place. Then finally, guided by the memory of her sister's methods, she stroked and brushed on the make-up she'd bought at the airport. A little startled by her appearance, Eleanor turned abruptly from the mirror and walked back to her car.

***

The principal stood in the reception area when she arrived and quickly escorted her to his office on the first floor. If he noticed the similarity in appearance of *Olivia* to her deceased sister, he didn't make any comment but spoke instead in solemn tones of how sorry he was to have heard the dreadful news.

Then he left Eleanor alone in his office to wait for her reunion with Gabriel. She felt grateful that her performance would not be a public one. She paced the wooden floor of the study as the minutes ticked by. *Where was he? Was he reluctant to come? Did he expect to see Olivia?* She pressed her trembling hands to her lips.

Eleanor walked to the window and peered down onto a courtyard. There were no children to be seen, lessons would be in full swing at this time of day, she guessed. A young couple walked arm in arm towards the far end of the quadrangle. They stopped at an arched entrance and Eleanor smiled when she saw the young man kiss the girl affectionately on her forehead as they parted. When he turned back to face her, she realised at once, with a jolt of icy shock, that this young man was her child. It was Gabriel.

'Dear God,' she gasped aloud.

He was taller now and his shoulders broader. His stride was strong and steady as he walked closer to the door beneath her window. Eleanor studied his expression as he came into view. *Who did he expect to see? Would he be confused? Angry?* She had felt sick every moment of every day at the thought of what she'd put him through. He would have every right to be devastated.

But just as he reached the building, he glanced up to the window where she stood. He caught her eye and the broad smile that spread across his face told her all she needed to know.

'Gabriel!' She ran to him and threw her arms around him as soon as he walked in. 'I can't tell you how much I've missed you, how I've worried about you.' She clutched him close to her, breathing in his familiar scent.

'I knew you'd come, Mum,' he whispered. 'I could feel you were alive.'

His quiet, clear words washed over her, and Eleanor felt instantly calm. She believed him.

'Yes,' she said, kissing his cheek, 'Everything is going to be alright.'

Gabriel nodded. 'Of course it is.'

'Let's make the most of every *minute* of this week.' Eleanor stepped back and held her son at arm's length, taking in every detail of him. He smiled down at her. The glint of summer had left his hair a rich, burnished copper that waved in rippled strands towards his eyes, his beautiful blue, blue eyes. He placed his hands on her shoulders and smiled before hugging her again, briefly lifting her from the ground.

Eleanor tried not to laugh. 'Shhh,' she whispered, looking at the door, 'We are supposed to be grieving.'

Gabriel lowered her back to Earth, his gentle hands firm with easy strength, his arms taut beneath his shirt.

'Are you packed and ready to go?'

'Sure am,' he replied. Eleanor smiled at the Canadian lilt to his voice. 'Where are we going?'

'You'll see,' she said. 'I think you'll like it.'

***

The cabin Sophie had booked for them was some distance from Gabriel's school and the drive took several hours. The main highway had been cleared of snow, but as they approached their destination, the roads grew narrower and were often icy. But this was what she had requested, she reminded herself each time the car lost its grip and drifted towards the trees on the side of the road.

Eventually, Eleanor spotted the sign to Riverside Cottage and followed the narrow track. Snow-laden branches stooped and swayed before them, their heavy limbs bowing like actors honouring the star of the show, seizing their moment in the limelight.

Quite suddenly, the leafy curtain parted, and a clearing opened before them. A half-swept path led to a wooden cabin; one single pendant light swinging in its porch.

'What an incredible spot, Mum!' Gabriel jumped from the car as soon as it had come to rest and stood with his hands on his hips, taking in the sights all around him.

The wooden cabin sat close to a lake of liquid turquoise and, at its far end, a stretch of frosted scrubland rose towards a mountain range, the closest ridges rich with pine and fir, while those climbing to the summit wore winter caps of ice.

Eleanor studied her son. He looked fully grown now, an adult. She wondered if the clothes she had brought for him would fit.

Gabriel made his way to the shingle shore, and Eleanor followed. He leapt up onto a small outcrop of rocks that dropped sharply down to the water below. She watched as he closed his eyes and raised his face towards the lukewarm sun. Taking a few deep breaths, he opened his eyes, smiled, and turned back to face her.

'This place…' he said, closing his eyes again and resting a hand on his chest, 'It just feels… right.'

'It does, doesn't it?' said Eleanor. She was glad he loved it. It would be the perfect place to talk, as she'd hoped.

Despite the stillness and isolation, Eleanor felt charged by the atmosphere around her. The calm of the water, the majesty of the mountains and the mere presence of Gabriel all seemed to generate some kind of energy, a power, a tingling.

Eleanor turned to Gabriel. He stared out across the water, and for a moment, she thought she saw him nod, as if in recognition of something. She shivered.

'Hungry?' she asked.

'Always!' Gabriel laughed and turned to face her.

'Good.' She rubbed her hands together. 'Me too.'

The cabin had been described by its owner as *rustic,* which, Eleanor had worried, might mean in poor condition, so she was delighted to discover a freshly painted interior and cheerful soft furnishings and lamps. It would be easy to create a cosy atmosphere, she thought, especially once Gabriel had lit the log fire.

Eleanor selected a frozen meal from the list she had requested.

'Carbonara?' She held the frosted box up for Gabriel to see.

'Ooo, yes, please!' he replied.

Before serving dinner, she lit a small candle that sat within a rough, crystallised rock on the table and watched as Gabriel turned it in his hands.

'Beautiful,' he whispered, before gently replacing it.

'So, what's the food like at Rocky Falls?' Eleanor asked as soon as she had watched her son wolf down his food.

'Oh, it's fine,' he replied. 'Not up to your standards, Mum, but usually tasty enough.'

'And have you made friends?' She was keen to take images of Gabriel's life home with her.

He nodded his reply while chewing.

'And what are classes like? Interesting?'

'Absolutely.' He dabbed each side of his mouth with a napkin. 'But the best thing about the academy is the sport!'

'Really?' Eleanor felt a wave of relief wash over her that he was opening up to her.

'Their facilities are amazing! Anything you want to do, they seem to do it. Basketball, swimming, soccer, even fencing, would you believe.' He placed one hand on his waist and, holding his fork in the other, twirled it like a foil.

Eleanor laughed, realising that was something she hadn't done since Gabriel had left home.

Their eyes met, and there was a moment of silence. Eleanor sensed he was about to ask questions.

'Shall we sit outside?' she suggested.

'Sure.' He nodded.

Eleanor lifted her winter coat from the row of pegs at the door and gathered it around her shoulders. They strolled together towards the lakeside.

'Wow! Look at that!' Gabriel exclaimed.

Moonlight played on the now dark surface, shimmering blacks and whites around the pale lemon orb of its own image.

'Fancy a swim?' He smiled down at his mum.

Eleanor's eyes widened in horror. 'Are you kidding, Gabriel? It's December. It will be freezing!' She dipped her hand in the water and shivered. 'No way!'

'It will be warmer than the air temperature, shouldn't be too bad. Anyway, after a minute or two, you'll get used to it.'

'Dear God, it will kill you!'

Gabriel threw back his head and laughed. Eleanor delighted in his amusement and the way it animated his handsome features.

'Well, I'm up for it.'

Eleanor rose to her feet as Gabriel started to strip to his shorts. 'I'll get you a towel, because I guarantee, you'll soon be pleading for it!'

Gabriel chortled.

By the time she returned, he was in the water.

'How is it?' she asked, placing the towel over her legs for extra warmth.

'Refreshing,' he said, beaming, plunging his head below the surface.

'Jesus,' she called out, 'You must be made of steel!'

'It's fine once you're in, really. Come on; you'll love it!'

Eleanor sipped her hot drink. *How on earth could he cope with this?* She watched as he swam away from the shoreline, the silhouette of his strong arms arching above his back with each stroke, his face held down in the water, rising only rarely on either side.

'Don't forget to breathe!' she called out, hearing a shudder in her voice as she spoke. She ached to join him, to share in the moment, and wondered if she should force herself. Slipping off her shoe, she stretched her foot towards a shallow pool nearby, but instantly she felt her skin burn with the chill and gasped.

'Bloody hell!'

Gabriel laughed.

'You tricked me,' she called to him. 'It's Baltic.'

'Yea-ha!' he hollered, turning and swimming further away from the land.

Eleanor could feel her back, and shoulders sting as a breeze brushed over them. She watched in disbelief as Gabriel's strong, streamlined body glided effortlessly through the water.

She remembered the time she had first taken him swimming. She could still imagine the feeling of his tiny body wriggling as she gently dipped him in and out of the warm water of the little pool at her gym. He had laughed heartily, his eyes sparkling as he blinked away the droplets clinging to his thick lashes.

Dear God, she thought as she cradled the tender image in her mind. *That wasn't even two years ago… only twenty-two months!* She looked again to Gabriel, now effortlessly hauling himself back up onto the rocks. She could see quite clearly that he was nearly a man.

It was time to tell him. Physically, he was mature, and he needed to know the truth. Eleanor shivered. Suddenly, she felt scared, and emotionally way out of her depth.

***

Once he had dried and dressed indoors, Gabriel returned to the water's edge carrying two steaming mugs of fresh hot chocolate. He sat staring across the lake towards the mountains beyond, their crisp white ridges standing stark against the dark. Eleanor, bundled up in extra layers, brought the candle from their dining table, and they sat in its comforting glow, watching insects dart close to its flame, drawn unwittingly to their own demise.

'Gabriel,' she said, still unsure how she would even begin to explain.

'I'm ready,' he replied, looking out across the water.

Eleanor gazed at him and nodded. He had been waiting for this moment.

'Some time ago, you asked about your father, and I explained I didn't know him. Remember?'

'Yes.'

'Well…' She swallowed nervously. 'The truth is… I didn't know your mother either.'

Gabriel stared at her. He opened his mouth as if to speak but said nothing. She saw his lower lip twitch and thought for a moment he might cry. She reached out and held his hand.

'You're… *not* my mother?'

'No. You grew within me, because I so wanted you. All your life, I've loved you, more dearly than I could ever have imagined.' Eleanor could hear her voice crack as she spoke.

'So, who is she then? Who *is* my mother?' His voice sounded higher than normal, as if the words he spoke were those of a younger Gabriel.

'Her identity is a mystery.' Eleanor tried to speak with a stronger voice; she wanted to reassure him and help him believe everything could still be fine. 'Her body, her *frozen* body, was found not far from here, high up on that ridge.' She nodded toward the towering mountains in the distance. 'Mount Meager. How long she had lain there, we're not sure, but almost certainly, she came from a very distant past.'

'She's dead?' Gabriel sounded breathless. He sat open-mouthed. His hand held above his heart.

Eleanor nodded.

'Did you see her body? What did she look like?' Gabriel scanned Eleanor's face as he spoke. She wondered if he was seeing her differently now, as an impostor.

'I have a picture, if you want to—'

'Yes,' he said without hesitation.

Eleanor walked back to the cabin and returned a few moments later with an envelope in her hand.

'You look like her.' She handed it to him without opening it.

Gabriel rose slowly and walked to where the water met the shingle shore. Eleanor knew not to follow him. She watched as he pulled the picture from its package, shining the light of his phone down upon it. She could not see his expression; it was growing dark, and his back was to her. But she saw him still to the image, then ease himself down onto a rock, where he sat, motionless. After a while, he stood up and paced back and forth before halting again to stare down at the picture then across the water to the mountain range.

She listened for the sounds of grief but heard nothing.

It was some time before he returned to her side.

'Should I go on?' She studied his face. For the first time she could remember, his eyes did not sparkle and there was no hint of a smile on his lips.

He nodded slowly.

'When we scanned the body…'

'*We?*'

'There were a few others. You've met them. Allen and Simon?'

Gabriel nodded.

'So, when we scanned her body, we discovered that within her lay the tiniest promise of life and we were captivated; desperate to know what the child of this beautiful woman, this echo from the past, would be like.' She paused but Gabriel said nothing. 'We didn't think it would work, but against all the odds, it did.'

'So, you were the surrogate?'

'Yes. And having you has been the greatest joy of my life. I just pray that I've not been utterly thoughtless of your needs in all of this.' She dropped her head into her hands, unable to bear the search of his gaze any longer. She tried to imagine how it must look through his eyes, how *she* must look. For a moment, she wished herself dead, away from the lies she had nurtured.

'No.' He lifted her hands from her face. 'I've had a wonderful life. And I'm grateful for that. I've always known that I'm… different…'

'What do you mean?' Eleanor suddenly felt nauseous. 'You never said.'

'Neither did you,' he replied, 'But clearly I'm not like my friends in so many ways. I have always just had to accept that I am, well, another kind of person, even if I didn't know why. And I understand why you've tried to hide my differences from people, because I have learnt to do that too. They wouldn't understand. People are unsettled by *differences*.'

Eleanor nodded. 'I had to protect…' she started to say but found her words crumbling into tears.

Gabriel moved closer. 'I can see that,' he said, 'But what I don't understand is having to change my name, my identity.'

Eleanor took a deep breath. 'The others who know about this, about *you*, are scared. They're worried your existence could in some way be a threat, if…' She hesitated. 'If you were to father any children.'

'Why?' Gabriel's normally smooth brow became rucked.

'Your people…' She searched for the words to explain what she did not yet understand herself. 'They seem to have lost their place on this Earth, to have become extinct, because of something that affected their reproduction. We don't know exactly how it worked and we don't know for certain that it could be reintroduced through you, but it does seem to have been devastating. It is possible, Gabriel, that if you were to procreate, we could be opening the door to calamity for the human species, to something we would not be able to control.'

'Wow.' Gabriel shook his head and fell silent. Eventually, he turned back to face her. 'And if I don't reproduce?'

'Then I think there would be no threat,' she said.

'So, what about the others? You say they're scared. Don't they agree with you on that?' he asked.

'There's no firm evidence to support their concerns and they don't know you as I do. They don't know that you would never consciously put others at risk.' Eleanor could see Gabriel was distressed. 'And that's why I'm telling you this.'

'I understand.' He sighed heavily. 'It must have been hard for you, keeping this to yourself, all this time.'

'Much harder for you, I think, Gabriel, to have to face it all now.' Eleanor felt as if her throat had become knotted with barbed wire.

Gabriel went quiet and Eleanor could see he too was fighting back tears. He held his hands over his mouth and closed his eyes.

'But there are solutions, Gabriel…' She moved closer to him. 'There are ways of making sure you can't ever… you know…'

'You mean like a vasectomy?' Gabriel gasped.

Eleanor shook her head. 'No, it would need to be something irreversible, like…'

'Castration?'

Eleanor could hear the terror in his voice.

'No, no… well, not in the physical sense at least… but there are medications that… well…'

Gabriel froze. Eleanor wondered at first if he had understood what she meant, but then saw his jaw tighten and his fists clenched fast.

'I'm so sorry, my darling,' Eleanor whispered. 'I know this must be such a shock to you, especially hearing all this at once. It's not how I wanted it to happen, believe me.'

Gabriel nodded his head but remained silent. He didn't even look Eleanor's way.

'You must have lots more you want to ask,' Eleanor went on.

He stared down at the envelope that held his mother's image.

'Where is she now?' He rocked backwards and forwards as he spoke. 'I want to see her.'

'I don't know.'

'Really?'

'I'm sorry, Gabriel. She was taken from us as soon as the authorities learnt of her, probably transported to a high security research facility. We haven't heard anything since then.'

'Surely someone knows, or can find out, ask questions?'

'We would love to have that information, Gabriel, and more. But it's too dangerous for us to show an interest, in case they suspect something.'

Gabriel buried his head in his hands.

'I'm so, so sorry, my darling.' Eleanor drew her hand down his back. 'Can I get you another hot drink? And we could talk some more?'

Gabriel shook his head. 'No, thanks,' he mumbled. 'Let's talk tomorrow. Tonight, I just want to be by myself.'

'I understand.' She rose to her feet and touched her son on the shoulder. 'I'll be inside, if you need me.'

Chapter 36

Eleanor was aware of Gabriel's restlessness throughout the night. She heard him pacing the floor of the room next to hers. She longed to go to him but knew it was essential to respect his request for solitude. He would come to her if he had questions to ask or if he wanted her company, she knew that.

Sleep evaded her all night and when morning came at last, she got up and went into the kitchen, where she was not surprised to look out of the window and see Gabriel, up and dressed, seated on a rock beside the lake.

Eleanor's stomach was knotted with fear. Was he angry? Just how upset was he? But when she approached with an offering of coffee, he accepted it warmly and made room for her to sit beside him. 'You okay?' she asked.

He gazed out across the water. 'I'm glad you've told me. It's a relief to find out what's been going on. I knew you'd something important to say. There were so many things I didn't understand, and they all have a place now. I feel more complete; aware of who and why I am.' He paused before adding, 'And of where I belong.'

Eleanor nodded, relieved he did not seem angry, or worse still, disappointed in her.

'I've been thinking about her... my mother... up in the mountains. I want to go to the place where she was found.'

Despite herself, Eleanor felt wounded to hear him talk of someone else as his *mother* and felt strangely irritated at the speed of his attachment to Lillooet. He didn't know her — no one did — and she was the one who had mothered him!

Get a grip, she cautioned herself, trying to douse the flames of her gathering jealousy. She couldn't afford to allow this emotion to surface, forcing Gabriel to feel he had to justify his emotions in any way. It was childish of her to seek reassurance from him when what he needed most right now was her unconditional love and support.

'I don't know the *specific* location, Gabriel...' She gazed across at the formidable range and shuddered.

'I do.'

Eleanor felt her heart sink.

'Did a bit of research last night. There was a brief mention of a reported find being taken off Mount Meager two years ago. I think... it might have been her.'

Eleanor nodded.

'I was able to work out the coordinates that will take us to the general area. We need to go to the National Park. There are rangers there who should be able to help. It's not that far.'

Gabriel picked up a guidebook Eleanor hadn't noticed had been lying by his side.

Eleanor sighed heavily. 'It would be risky,' she said quietly.

'I imagine it would,' Gabriel replied, 'But we could at least try, couldn't we?' He spoke softly, but there was an edge of determination in his voice Eleanor had never heard before.

She looked at him and saw his jaw was set and his eyes filled with longing.

'Yes,' she eventually responded, 'I think it's the least I can do.'

***

They drove north through snow-bound vegetation which grew thicker as fields gave way to dense woods and open roads dwindled to winding lanes, hemmed in on either side by oppressive, high trees. The snow lay deep on the ground and no attempts seemed to have been made to clear it.

'Where in God's name is this road taking us?' Eleanor peered as far into the distance as the glare of the snow allowed. 'I think we must have come the wrong way. We should head back before we get lost.'

'Let's keep going a while longer.' Gabriel studied the map on his phone. 'I think this is the right way.'

Eleanor gripped the steering wheel as the car dipped into rucks on the rough track. Gabriel just stared straight ahead, only speaking to read aloud any signs they came across.

After what seemed like hours, they spotted a huddle of wooden buildings set back a little from the track. A helicopter stood in a clearing to one side. To the other lay a yard with a heap of what looked like scrap metal strewn on a patch of undergrowth. Eleanor could see one of the windows in a nearby shed was broken. There were no lights and no signs of life.

'Looks like there's nobody around.' She peered through the windscreen and prayed no one would appear.

'There!' Gabriel pointed to the largest of the buildings.

Eleanor saw a figure emerge from the door then walk round to the back of the shed, out of sight. Her heart sank.

'I'll check it out. You stay here.' Gabriel was out of the car in seconds, running towards where the man had gone.

A few minutes later, he reappeared and beckoned Eleanor to join him.

She followed Gabriel into the office and was surprised, after their unpromising arrival, to find a bright and clean room with two smartly dressed rangers inside.

'So, you're looking for a trip over the Meager?' the older of the two said. He was typing on his laptop as he spoke. On the wall behind him was a map of British Columbia, with swirling concentric lines hooped over vast stretches of the green and brown terrain.

'That's right. We saw the advert for helicopter tours,' Gabriel replied, holding up the guidebook.

The ranger didn't look up. 'Can't do, I'm afraid. Not in this weather.'

'That's a shame.' Eleanor sighed with relief. 'I suppose it's a bit cold for that sort of trip.'

'Oh, it's fine down here,' the younger ranger chipped in, 'But it will be icy up there, and we don't have a "non-icing certificate" for that girl.' He nodded to the helicopter outside.

The older man slapped his laptop shut and stared up at them. 'What you're looking for at this time of year is a private plane scenic tour.'

'So, where could we do that?' Gabriel asked.

The ranger turned to the map behind him and pointed with a pencil. 'There's two airports that offer them... here and... there.'

'How far away are they?' Eleanor leant towards the map.

'A ten-hour drive at least, I'd say, in these conditions.'

'Too far, I'm afraid. Maybe another time?' Eleanor turned to Gabriel, who was staring intently at the man, his jaw fixed.

'And that's all you have?' Gabriel sounded surprised. 'What if someone was hurt up there? How would you reach them?'

'At this time of year? Not by helicopter, that's for sure.'

'So, what *do* you use?'

The ranger rose to his feet. 'A high wing, twin engine, turbo-prop aircraft. Best in the business.'

'So, can't we use that?' Gabriel asked.

'Are you kidding? Have you any idea how much it costs to take that out?'

'We'll pay,' Gabriel insisted, 'Won't we?' He looked at Eleanor.

'Well… how much are we talking about?' she asked.

'Not really allowed to use the plane for leisure,' the younger ranger mumbled.

'Depends what you're looking for,' the other cut across him. 'A quick flyover?'

Eleanor nodded. 'Yes, I think—'

'No,' Gabriel interrupted, 'We need a brief stop, just five minutes.'

'Well, that doubles the price, son. Two take-offs, that's a lot of fuel.'

Gabriel nodded.

The rangers exchanged glances. 'Five thousand dollars,' the older one said.

'*How much?*' Eleanor was aghast.

'That's the best we can do, I'm afraid. And we are bending the rules a bit… if you know what I mean.'

'We'll take it,' Gabriel announced, 'Won't we, Mum?'

When he turned to look at her, Eleanor knew she was going to be unable to refuse him. He rarely asked for anything. It was a small fortune, but it might just be the one thing she could do to help mend things between them.

'Okay,' she eventually agreed, reaching for her purse. 'Let's do it.'

'You'll need these.' The young ranger tossed what looked like two ski jackets and two pairs of salopettes their way. 'Gloves and hats are in the pockets. And boots on the rack behind you. Help yourselves.'

'Better get going. The weather's unpredictable at the moment,' the older ranger said as he took Eleanor's card and processed the sale. 'We can give it a shot now though.'

They followed the young ranger to the furthest building in the complex. A short runway stretched out beyond it.

Eleanor felt sick when the ranger opened the hanger doors to reveal the plane.

'*Dear God!* It's, well, it's a lot smaller than I'd expected,' she stammered.

'Big enough for a rescue team,' he replied.

He unhooked a clipboard from a nail in the wall and walked slowly round the plane, examining it and ticking off items on the list he was consulting.

'And, of course, there's often not much room for manoeuvre. People seem to have the uncanny knack of sustaining injuries in the most awkward locations.' He smiled broadly.

The ranger opened a door to the rear of the craft and pulled down a set of steps. Gabriel climbed aboard eagerly, choosing to sit in the row of single seats to the left. Eleanor sat across from him on the double row. She sat in the aisle seat, preferring not to look out.

She felt a rise of panic as the steps were hauled inside and the door secured.

Shit! She was desperate to call out that she'd changed her mind. They could keep the money, she just wanted out of this claustrophobic capsule but when she looked across to Gabriel, his nose pressed against the glass, right leg bouncing, she knew this meant too much to him for her to allow her fear to shatter his hopes.

'I'm Bill, by the way,' he introduced himself as he checked their seatbelts.

'Eleanor.' She placed a hand on her chest. 'And Gabriel, my son.'

'First time in one of these little beauties?'

Eleanor nodded and tried to smile. Gabriel didn't move from his window vigil.

'Any particular thing you want to see?' Bill placed a hand on the chair backs in front of each of them.

Gabriel shot to attention and pulled a neatly folded sheet from his pocket. 'Yes,' he said, 'We'd like to go there please.'

'Wow! Someone's organised.' Bill unfolded the sheet and examined its contents. 'O-kay,' he went on hesitantly, 'Well, that's a really iffy spot, weather-wise. Can't promise you that we'll be able to land, and if we do, it will be a quick turnaround. Got it?'

Eleanor nodded.

'If you put these on…' Bill handed them each a set of headphones. 'I can point out landmarks.' He turned and climbed through the open archway that led to the cockpit. 'Okay, let's get going.'

He flicked switches that brought the machine to life. It seemed to groan and rattle for quite a while.

Eleanor grasped the armrests. Eventually, she felt the plane roll forwards, accelerate and finally, lift into the air.

The small plane shook and tilted from side to side before steadying itself. Eleanor inhaled sharply, wishing they were coming into land rather than just setting off.

'Nothing to worry about,' their pilot reassured her, 'Believe me. This baby is designed for the remote and extreme. *Anytime, Anywhere, Worldwide*,' he quoted, 'That's the de Havilland motto.'

Gabriel gazed intently out of the window. Eleanor could see he was taking in every detail, his eyes scanning back and forth from the far horizon to near landmarks.

'Quite a view, isn't it?' Eleanor felt unsettled by this new unreachable Gabriel and wanted to pull him back to her.

He continued to stare out of the window as if he hadn't even heard her.

'Gabriel?' She reached over and placed a hand on his arm.

He turned sharply, clearly startled from some reverie.

'Are you alright?' She wished he would sit beside her. But with each minute that passed, he seemed to be slipping from her, as if this was all a dream and only one of them was real and she wasn't sure which one.

From the air, the terrain took on a fresh complexion. Rising above the ancient forests and alpine ridges, the glacial peaks looked all the more staggering. No longer a backdrop, the mountains asserted themselves as the unequivocal lords of the landscape.

'Now, that,' announced the ranger, 'Is a volcano.' He pointed towards a towering mass. 'It's the most unstable in Canada.' He smiled back at Gabriel who seemed unaware of what was being said. 'And over there, you can see the Lillooet River, just south of the ice cap… whoa!' His tone changed suddenly. 'And that looks like some pretty rough weather heading this way!'

Eleanor groaned. 'Didn't you check the forecast before we set out?'

'Of course!' Bill snapped, 'But as I said, this place has its own climate, the weather can turn on a dime and… well, that's one of the reasons why this kind of trip is so dangerous.'

'Brilliant,' Eleanor murmured.

A few minutes later, Bill spoke again. 'Your coordinates seem to bring us here, to this area.'

Eleanor glanced down. Ragged-toothed rocks yawned up from empty planes of snow.

'Jesus!' She felt her stomach lurch. 'How on earth do you land this thing up here?'

'That's exactly what this craft is designed for. The Twin Otter can land on almost any surface — sand, water, snow — and it's perfect for rescue work because of its short runway capabilities. Say, there's not much to see up here. Why this spot?'

Fuck. Eleanor searched for a reasonable explanation.

But Gabriel had one prepared. 'It's geologically quite rare,' he said mildly. 'I want to collect a few rock samples for my research.'

Eleanor wasn't sure how much more of this tension she could take. *Let's just get this over with*, she thought, with gritted teeth.

'Aha, a scholar!' Bill's curiosity seemed to have been satisfied.

Eleanor watched the land expand before her as they started their descent. The wind felt stronger as they approached the ground, so the plane was buffeted about. Eleanor breathed in sharply and clutched the armrests of her seat.

'Nothing to worry about.' Bill sounded calm enough.

Eleanor closed her eyes. Although she was curious to see where Lillooet had been found, she was far more desperate to get this pilgrimage over and done with and start their journey back.

Despite the apparent depth of the snow, it was not a soft landing and the plane slid and bounced violently as it slithered to a halt. Eleanor pressed hard against the seat in front of her, terrified she might crash into it.

'Okay!' Bill turned to face them as soon as he'd completed the manoeuvre, his face stern. 'Five minutes max!'

He strode to the back of the plane to pull open the door. Gabriel was right behind him and jumped down, without waiting for the short flight of steps to be lowered. Eleanor watched as his boots sank into the crisp snow. He stood perfectly still for a second.

'Gabriel?' Eleanor called to him. A blast of iced air instantly filled the cavity of her mouth, freezing it like a spray of liquid nitrogen. She gasped and pulled the muffler she had been issued with tight around her stinging mouth.

He turned sharply.

Wait for me, she gestured.

Gabriel nodded, but his tight lips told her he would rather not.

The ranger looked up at the heavy, white sky and raised an open palm to Eleanor. *Five minutes*. She nodded.

Eleanor walked gingerly down the steps that seemed to be icing over as she looked at them.

Eleanor shivered. There was no warmth in this place and definitely no sign of life. A gallery of rocks towered around them, offering only the occasional glimpse of their steel grey substance, peeping out here and there from behind a seemingly endless curtain of snow. She felt overwhelmed with worry and wanted Gabriel to look around as quickly as possible so they could get back on their way.

She watched as Gabriel walked towards a small outcrop of rocks, his boots sinking deeper with each step. Suddenly, he stopped. He remained still for a while then slowly began to turn, taking in each new vista offered. Eleanor trudged forwards to where he stood, struggling to pull each boot from the dense snow until, at last, she stood by his side and slipped her arm through his. She yearned to reach him, but somehow she could not.

After a few moments, he smiled down at her, patting her hand briefly before freeing himself. With eyes closed, he raised his head, moving it slightly from side to side, as if listening for something, feeling for something, tuning himself into a wavelength beyond her sensitivities. Then, smiling, he paced forwards, his fresh prints forming a path for Eleanor to follow. But she stayed a few paces behind. She could sense he needed this time on his own.

Bill appeared by her side and pointed to his watch. Their time was up.

Eleanor nodded.

'Gabriel!' she called through her scarf. But he didn't move.

'Gabriel!' She pulled down the frozen cloth to give her voice more power. 'It's time to go home.' She ran towards him and touched his arm.

'Yes,' he said, turning to face her, 'It is.' He was smiling but Eleanor could see tears glisten in the corner of his eyes.

'Oh, Gabriel, I am so sorry I've given you this pain,' Eleanor spoke through the agony of the bitter wind.

'You've nothing to be sorry for.' He hugged her. Eleanor felt his body tremble. 'You gave me life and love. What more can any mother give?'

A wave of snow lifted by a fresh gust of wind fell down upon them.

'Guys? We really need to go now!' the ranger called out impatiently.

Eleanor pulled on Gabriel's arm.

'Just one minute,' he said.

'There's no time, Gabriel, please!'

'Really, Mum, you go back. There's one thing I need to do.'

Eleanor realised they were wasting time debating it. *This would be his only chance*, she told herself, *to feel his roots, to be here, at the source of it all…*

'Okay.' She backed off. 'But be as quick as possible… *please?*'

The ranger helped Eleanor climb back into the plane and closed the door behind her. He stood outside stamping his feet and rubbing his gloved hands together. Eleanor stared out through the swirling snow, straining to catch a glimpse of her son. She could see the ranger pacing and looking anxiously up to the sky. Then she watched as he marched off towards the rocks where she'd left Gabriel.

Seconds later, he returned and whipped the door open. 'Where did he go?' he shouted at Eleanor.

'What? I don't know!' Eleanor felt her heart race. 'He said he had something to do, he'd only be a minute!' She pulled her jacket back on and climbed out again. She followed him along the path of churned up snow to the spot where she'd left her son.

'So, where the hell is he?' The man glared at her.

Eleanor spun around, searching for his tracks.

'I left him here,' she stammered, moving to the spot where he'd waved her away.

'Well, he's not here now.' The ranger walked to the edge of the rocky mound and looked behind it. 'O-kay. I see where he's gone,' he called.

Eleanor ran to the spot where he stood gazing upwards. A narrow pathway ascended between jagged rocks. She could see where the deep indentations of Gabriel's boots had left their mark, but eddies of snow now swirled around them, covering the prints and making it hard to see anything above eye level.

'*Gabriel*!' Eleanor screamed up into the sky.

'No!' said the ranger sharply. 'Don't scream! Avalanches.'

She could see the fear in Bill's eyes but felt desperate to call out again. The ranger looked around one more time then began an attempt to climb up the steep ridge, but Eleanor could see it was an impossible task as he gripped the rocks with gloved hands but could not secure a hold.

'Gabriel!' she sobbed, sinking to the ground. 'Don't leave me! I can make everything all right…' Their conversation from the night before came roaring back to her. His sadness when he learnt the truth about it all and his horror at the thought of the *solutions* she had suggested. *Please God, no!*

She rested her head on the only print of his boot still visible. *No, no, no! It doesn't need to be this way!* She traced the groove of his tread with her snow-clogged glove. *It's not too late, my love, you can't be far…*

'Come back, Gabriel, please!' she yelled up the near invisible path he had taken.

The ranger crouched down beside her and placed his arm on her back.

'Shh, shh, shh,' his voice trembled. 'I'm sorry… I'm so very sorry… but we have to go. He's gone. He must have known what he was doing. It's impossible to follow him. I'm sorry but you need to believe me.' He tugged at Eleanor's sleeve. 'You have to come now, right now, or we'll never get off here either.'

'No!' Eleanor hugged the frozen earth. 'No. You go… go!' Eleanor could not move. 'If Gabriel is staying here then so am I. I'd rather die with him than live without him!'

'Please, ma'am.' The ranger was pulling at her arm. 'I want to help you, but this is not the way to do it and I have a family too…'

Eleanor did not reply, instead she willed her body to sink into the chill of the snow.

'If we go now, I can call for a search party, more people, the proper equipment!' he pleaded. 'That's the only chance we have of saving him.'

'Do you think we *have* a chance?' Eleanor roused a little.

'I… well… we'll have to be quick. There's no way any human being can survive up here for long. We've no time to lose.'

Eleanor tried to climb back up to standing, but she felt too heavy to move. The ranger grabbed her arms and tried to drag her up.

'You need to do this if you want any chance of bringing him back.' His breathless voice sounded muffled, far away, and for a moment Eleanor thought she was back by the lake and the voice she heard was Gabriel's, laughing as he swam.

'Gabriel?' She looked up and saw a face she did not recognise, dark eyes beneath frost-crusted brows.

'Please,' she saw him say, although she could hear nothing now above the wail of the wind.

Eleanor crawled to her knees and leant on the stranger's arm. He pulled her up and together they fought their way through the whirls of fresh snow, back to the small craft.

The door had been left open and already a thick covering of snow lay on the cabin floor. Eleanor was only dimly aware of being bundled into the aircraft. The door had iced open and as he fought to release it from its icy lock, Eleanor leapt back to the door.

'Please wait, just a minute or two!' she pleaded. 'Gabriel wouldn't do something like this. He must have fallen — he needs help! He needs me!' She tried to push past the ranger, back onto the snow.

'For fuck's sake!' He pushed her away from the door. 'If I don't get this thing closed within the next few minutes, we're all screwed. So, shut up and sit down!'

Eleanor fell backwards onto Gabriel's seat and spotted his phone on the floor below.

'He'll need this!' She grabbed it.

Bill turned to see what she had found. His face was red and he was panting heavily from his efforts to secure the lock on the door.

'He wanted photos… and he'll want to contact us,' she whimpered, unable to stop the violent shaking that had overwhelmed her.

'No reception up here,' Bill shouted. 'He needs help, Eleanor. Specialist help and that is exactly what we are going to call for now. Fucking idiotic thing to do!'

Bill marched to the cockpit and put out a call on his radio.

Eleanor listened in horror as she heard him, above the whine of the engine, give details to the search and rescue team. He paused and called back to her.

'We need details, name, age, physicals…'

Eleanor came to with a start.

'Eh, Simon,' she stuttered, 'Simon McLean…'

'Not Gabriel?'

'No, that's… a pet name,' she mumbled. 'He's twenty-three years old, six foot two… brown hair, green eyes…' She closed her eyes and listened to her lies being passed as fact.

What had they done? Dear God, what had they done? She sobbed bitterly and clutched her chest as they rose up and away from the ice- sheeted rocks, one hand pressed against the window, Gabriel's window, clawing at the clouding glass.

***

The ranger hadn't wanted Eleanor to return to the cottage that night, but she had insisted. All she had left of Gabriel was there. He drove her back in her car, his colleague behind in another.

Outside the cottage, they stood for a while, Eleanor quizzing them about the search and rescue procedure, aware she was asking the same questions again and again, but unable to stop herself. All she could think of was her son, alone, in the dark, on the treacherous, freezing mountain.

They answered patiently, but Eleanor could tell from the lack of eye contact they held out no hope of finding her son.

When at last they left, she collapsed onto her bed. Her body felt heavy and lifeless. She sat up only twice, each time to vomit onto the floor beside her. Her face lay pressed against the sodden quilt and her hair smelled rancid. She wanted to die. If Gabriel was dead, she wanted to join him.

She wasn't aware of falling asleep, but without knowing how, she found herself in a dream. She was in a railway station with lots of other people. They were young — students, maybe — but she couldn't see their faces. It was snowing and a sign flashed up on the board saying all the trains were cancelled. She turned to leave with the crowd then noticed one carriage on its own in a siding. A dim glow came from it, just enough for her to make out the shape of a person inside. She approached it and as she got closer, she realised an entire family was in there. A woman and some children were crowded around one bent, elderly figure. She was crying, but they couldn't comfort her. Suddenly, the old woman looked up and stared through the window towards her.

'Mum!'

Eleanor was suddenly awake. She sat up and stared around her. It was pitch black and took a while for her to realise where she was. Then she remembered everything.

She eased herself off the bed. She wouldn't allow herself to give up. She couldn't do that. She had caused too much pain already, now she had to try to make things better.

Eleanor wandered through to the kitchen and poured some water into an unwashed glass sitting on the table. As she drank it, she checked her phone to see if search and rescue had tried to reach her but there was nothing but a factual statement of the false description she had given them and a reassurance they would keep her fully informed of developments. He was gone.

As she made her way back to the bedroom, she spotted something on the table. It was a piece of paper pinned down by the candle they'd used two nights before. Eleanor's hand shook as she reached for it. It was a note, written in Gabriel's hand.

'*Dear Mother Eleanor,*' she read, then dropped onto the seat beside her to read the rest.

I love you. I am so sorry, please forgive me. I can't bear to imagine how sad you'll be feeling as you read this. But more than that, I can't justify holding on to a life that could rob others of theirs.

You gave me life, a life borrowed from a less kind fate, and for that I am truly grateful. Your love for me is beyond measure, as is my love for you. But now it is time for me to move on to the place where I should be. I know you'll grieve for me because you must, but don't let it last too long. I'm sure we'll meet again.

Your loving son,

Now and forever,

Gabriel x

'No!' Eleanor wailed as she read the note again before sinking to the floor. 'Gabriel!' she screamed out, then again and again and again, until she had no voice left in her. There was nothing to live for now. She knew she would never feel happy again.

She smoothed the wrinkled paper and held it to her face, kissing his signature before slipping the sheet beneath her head.

***

Eleanor was aware of nothing until she heard the sound of an engine and the crunch of wheels upon the snow outside.

'They've found him!' she cried aloud, shooting to her feet and running outside.

It was midday and the sun sat low on the horizon. A glaring backdrop that made it difficult for her to determine the features of the driver. But she soon saw it was not the ranger.

As she came into view, Eleanor recognised her visitor.

'Sophie?'

The young woman ran towards her, stopping to regard Eleanor in shock.

'What is going on?' Sophie looked ashen. 'You're a mess…'

Eleanor shook her head; she didn't want to give life to the possibility that Gabriel was dead by saying the words aloud.

Instead, she stammered, 'Why are you here, Sophie?'

'Eleanor, I've been trying to contact you, but I guess your phone isn't working out here, so I had to come.'

'Why?'

Sophie clasped both of Eleanor's hands in hers and beamed with excitement. 'The data, Carl's data, he got it wrong! I mean, *badly* wrong! It's possible that Gabriel represents no threat to us, that he is not a risk!' Sophie spoke breathlessly, her eyes gleaming with delight.

'No!' Eleanor screamed, snatching at clumps of her matted hair. 'Why?' she screamed up to the heavens, clenching her fists in the air. 'Eleanor, I thought…' Sophie started, but Eleanor seemed deaf to her and ran into the cabin.

Sophie followed quickly shielding her head as Eleanor made missiles of every object she could lay her hands on.

'Stop!' Sophie yelled, fighting her way towards her. 'Please, Eleanor.' She rushed to her side and held her tightly in her arms. 'Stop,' she whispered, rocking gently. 'Breathe, Eleanor, slow, deep breaths,' she soothed.

As Eleanor relaxed, and a glimmer of awareness returned to her eyes, her tight fist fell open and a crumpled piece of paper dropped onto the floor. Sophie lifted it and smoothed the creases.

'Dear Mother Eleanor,' Sophie started aloud.

Eleanor watched as she fell silent and her sharp eyes flashed down the brief text, her features turning from confusion to horror. The note fell from her hand as she stared at Eleanor.

'Welcome to my hell,' Eleanor groaned, slumping to the floor.

Chapter 37

Eleanor had barely left her apartment in the weeks since her return home to Glasgow. Unable to sleep and reluctant to eat, she hid away from family and colleagues who struggled to understand her wave of deferred grief. Just managing to respond occasionally to her mother's anxious calls, she deleted her voicemails without listening to them and, ignoring the ever-growing heap of letters strewn across the floor of her entrance hall, she no longer cared what anyone thought.

Where was he now? she wondered endlessly, tracing his name on a breath-heavy window. Overwhelmed by exhaustion, she would rouse abruptly from bouts of fitful sleep and stare out to a world she no longer felt a part of.

Sometimes she would imagine he was still a baby, that she could feel his soft skin press against her cheek as he snuggled close to her on a cold winter evening. At other times, she would startle at the sound of his laughter, convinced she could hear him telling her all about his day at school, only to snap back to reality and feel again the weight of that black cloud of despair pressing down upon her.

She must move beyond this, she knew that, but she didn't know how. She had to accept he was gone, that she would never see him again, but she couldn't. There was a part of her that just wouldn't stop believing he was still alive and that he would return. *Mother's intuition*, she told herself. It had served her well so far, why on earth should it fail her now? Then again, she considered, every single person who has lost a loved one probably felt the same. No, she must hold on to reason or she would lose her mind. She would try to silence the maternal whisperings of hope, attending instead to the voice of her rational self, urging acceptance.

She sat in silence by the window, straining to see as far into the distance as possible. The hours passed without her acknowledgment, dark drifting into light then back again. She found the sameness soothing, and having taken refuge in the living room, had begun to sleep on the sofa. This small world, she imagined, she might be able to control.

She watched life unfold on the streets below. It felt like a different planet. Bag-carrying, children-grasping, phone-calling people; wrapped up in the details of their own existence. She pulled away from her vantage point when a courier van drew up, parking clumsily on the double yellow lines and blocking her view. She would put the kettle on, again.

As her hand hovered between the tea and coffee tins, she jumped to a hail of thuds upon her door. But she didn't feel ready yet to see or talk to anyone, so she remained still. Another series of raps left her nervous but even more determined not to be bullied.

She heard mumbling from beyond her door, muffled curses then a shuffling away; they were leaving. *Good*, she thought. She crept back to the window, hoping to catch sight of her would-be intruder, but no one emerged. She turned from the scene, only to be drawn back by the clatter of something heavy falling to the ground and a volley of irate yells.

Two men were arguing, gesticulating mutual blame as they carelessly manhandled a heavy-looking trunk. Eleanor froze. That trunk, it was Gabriel's! Unable to twist the key in the window lock, she banged on the glass, but to no avail. The doors of the van had been thrown open and they were heaving the undelivered goods back into their hold.

'No, no, no!' She ran to the door and hurtled, barefoot, down into the street below, catching up with the men just as they were securing the lock.

Reluctant to repeat their arduous efforts, the men eventually acceded to Eleanor's pleas and once again negotiated the tight corners of the modern stairwell, scraping the aluminium cask across the floor of the communal landing into Eleanor's hallway.

'That's fine, here will be just fine.' She thanked them profusely, remembering only at the last instant to give a tip.

Gabriel's trunk, Jude's trunk. She ran her fingers over the pseudonym, still written clearly on the scratched label, in her own hand.

Fetching the spare key which she kept in her jewellery box, Eleanor caressed the lid before releasing it. *Gabriel's world*, she thought, staring at the array of clothes, books and games equipment.

She picked up a T-shirt that lay at the top of the pile and brushed its soft cotton against her nose, releasing the faintest scent of her child. She hugged it to her as she wandered through to Gabriel's room, pondering how she would organise his belongings within it.

She would not rush this task, she told herself. She would immerse herself in it, make it last, use it to bring Gabriel back into her life.

***

In the days which followed, Eleanor worked her way through the layers of his possessions. She braced herself for torrents of tears but found instead, as she folded away his favourite things and flicked through his school notebooks, that she was strangely comforted by the experience.

She began to eat a little and to sleep in her own bed at night. She remembered to shower and occasionally washed her hair and brushed her teeth. And when she awoke in the morning, she opened the curtains to let the light of the new day fill each room.

It was just as she lifted the final few oddments, that she noticed a bundle of letters, tucked beneath a book. Some were clearly from her, their paper creased. Much read, she hoped. Some seemed to be notes from societies he had joined, meetings, fixtures, lists of names. But one, she saw, had not been opened.

Jude Tennyson, it announced, the looped script giving the name a different appearance. Only his name was on the envelope so the letter must have been delivered by hand, almost certainly from someone at his school. She would not read this letter, she decided. Gabriel had not read it and it looked childishly private. She kissed it and took it with her into the bedroom, feeling Gabriel all around her as she dropped, fully clothed, onto her bed, slipping the letter beneath her pillow.

She fell instantly into a sleep more willing and serene than she had experienced for years. Suddenly lightened, she felt herself gliding once again across a meadow. Alone, but not lonely, she stood beneath a cloudless sky, warmed by its soothing sun. Then, stretching her arms and closing her eyes, she tilted her head towards its warmth and slowly turned.

'Sorry.' She laughed, imagining her sister's childish form beside her, brushing against her as they lost themselves in the dizzying swirl of their favourite game.

'Sorry,' she rejoiced, recalling how they would knock each other off course as they giggled into a giddiness that would eventually bring them crashing to the ground.

Eleanor steadied her gait and listened intently. She could hear it, almost imperceptible but she *could* hear it. Music. She turned to its source and drifted towards the stream.

'*In paradisum,*' it whispered, laying its trail.

'*Deducant te angeli.*'

She quickened her pace.

'*In tuo adventu, suscipiant te martyres.*'

The childish voice grew stronger.

'*Et perducant te.*'

'Gabriel?'

'*In civitatem sanctam.*'

It was. It was Gabriel!

'*Jerusalem, Jerusalem, Jerusalem…*'

It filled her head. The air about her seemed to reverberate to his beautiful voice.

She ran down the slope, through the wildflower-scattered grass, on towards the stream.

'Gabriel!' she called, stepping on the first of a trickle of stout stones that formed a path across the clear, gurgling water. Frantically, she scanned the grass on the opposite side, but there was no trace of him. 'Where are you?' she cried out.

Suddenly, a shape appeared on the mound of the small hill that rose from the opposite bank. Squinting her eyes against the glare of the sun, she saw someone.

'Gabriel?' she called again.

A tall, slender figure stood there but as Eleanor began to discern its features, she realised it was not Gabriel. It was his mother, Lillooet.

'Where is he?' she called to her, stretching to reach the second stone.

Lillooet descended the hill a little, just enough to soften the blinding light. Eleanor could see her clearly now. Lillooet held up her hand, palm first and shook her head.

Immediately understanding the instruction, Eleanor retreated to dry land. Then she noticed that, in her other hand, Lillooet was holding something. A letter. The one she had just found. As soon as Eleanor recognised it, Lillooet nodded.

***

Eleanor awoke abruptly and pulled herself upright, unable for some time to orientate herself back to the moment.

'So real!' she gasped.

She felt different. Not exactly happy, but no longer sad. The black cloud had lifted and she felt strangely hopeful.

She wandered through to the kitchen and switched on the kettle, then froze as she remembered the dream.

The letter. She ran to fetch it. But just as she reached her bedroom door, she was startled by the harsh rasp of her buzzer that seemed to electrify further the space around her.

Who on earth? She crept over to the window.

She heard a scuffling outside of her door and rushed across the living room towards the hall. As soon as she opened the living room door, she leapt in shock as she saw a pair of unblinking eyes staring at her through the metal flap of the letterbox.

'What the fuck?' She retreated, slamming the living room door closed.

'Eleanor, it's me!' A female voice called out to her. She recognised it.

'Sophie?'

'Can I come in?'

Eleanor swept back the bolt and unhooked the chain, her hands trembling so much she struggled to work the lock.

'Thank you.' Sophie embraced her.

Still trembling, Eleanor led her into the living room. When at last she looked at Sophie, she noticed the dark circles under her eyes and reminded herself that this had been traumatic for her too.

'Everyone has been so worried about you…' Sophie started.

'Everyone?'

'Well, Simon mostly.'

Eleanor nodded. 'How is he?'

'He's decided to retire… all too much for him, I think.'

'And Allen?'

'He left too and hasn't been in touch. But I did hear he's taking up a job in Victoria.'

'Good!' Eleanor realised she hadn't thought about them at all. 'What about Carl?'

'No idea.' Sophie shrugged.

'Hang on, why are you here in Glasgow?' Eleanor spoke as if just waking up to the conversation.

'That's one of the reasons I've come to see you. I've been offered the job at Strathclyde University. I think I mentioned it?'

'Yes.' Eleanor nodded. 'Well done.'

'And...' Sophie hesitated and looked down.

'What?' Eleanor glared at her. 'What have you heard? Is it about Gabriel?'

'Not exactly, but... I was wondering if you would like to hear about Carl's research?'

Eleanor slumped forwards. 'What's the point in that now?' she groaned.

Sophie said nothing.

Eleanor eventually pulled herself up again. 'Does any of it matter anymore?'

'Possibly.' Sophie reached over and stroked Eleanor's hand. 'Not in the way we had hoped, but it is still... interesting.'

Despite herself, Eleanor felt a whisper of intrigue. 'In what way?'

'Well...' Sophie paused. 'I don't know if you can remember much of what I said... in the cabin?'

'Not much.'

'Well, once I had time to study the details of it, I could see that the design of the experiment was seriously flawed in so many ways. No clear hypothesis, poor controls, contamination between groups… I could go on but I'm sure you can imagine the rest. His work was at, what I would describe as, a poor undergrad level.'

Eleanor nearly smiled.

'I'm guessing he usually has researchers to organise these things?'

Eleanor nodded.

'Consequently, the data he *analysed* really could not be trusted, especially given his assumptions that a correlation indicates a causal link!'

Eleanor's eyes widened. 'Dear God, it's unbelievable,' she said faintly. 'He is such an idiot! And what a gullible fool *I* was to accept what he told me in Paris…'

'I think you were blinded by fear, Eleanor.'

'True,' she said, sighing heavily, 'And then when Carl eventually sent that document to us, his *report,* I only had time to skim through it, before being pulled into a meeting with Allen and Simon, then everything kicked off…'

'You have nothing to feel bad about, Eleanor. Remember, I couldn't have worked any of this out without studying the details of his raw data on the files I downloaded.'

Eleanor nodded.

'Anyway,' Sophie continued, 'When these errors were factored in, I realised there didn't appear to be *anything* of statistical significance in his data.'

'But what about the excessive birth rate, the maternal deaths and the unusual longevity of the offspring?'

Sophie shook her head. 'Carl clearly knows little about the breeding habits of mice,' she started. 'While one pair of mice may well produce around fifty pups a year, the offspring can also reproduce from six weeks of age, so two mice and their offspring, contained in one space, could become in one year, over *five thousand* mice…'

'But he said he separated them,' Eleanor interrupted.

'He did, but not until eight weeks, by which time the female pups would already be pregnant.'

'Ah, that makes sense. *Idiot!*'

'Moreover, Carl compared the expected lifespan of his mice with those of outdoor mice, but indoor mice generally live two to three times longer, so it was a *false comparison.*'

'You're right. Dear God. Do you think he deliberately misled us?'

'I don't think so,' said Sophie. 'From the grand way he worded his conclusions, I think he believed in his results.'

'And he always likes to be the one to make a *breakthrough*.' Eleanor sighed heavily. 'So, there was never anything to worry about, was there?'

'Not that I could see,' said Sophie, 'But that was just Carl's contribution, remember. There are still lots of unknowns and Gabriel is...' she tailed off, stricken.

'It's okay,' Eleanor said gently.

'Gabriel *was* clearly quite different, and we still don't know what killed his people.'

'True.' Eleanor nodded.

'The only useful piece of information I could glean from the data was behavioural,' Sophie continued. 'Carl's observations of social interaction within the mice colonies did seem to point to a higher degree of cooperation and a lower level of aggression than is normally expected.'

'Okay, that is interesting,' Eleanor said.

'And although I can't be certain of this, from what I could see, only the treated *females* passed on this trait, but obviously that would have required further study under far more rigorous conditions.'

'Of course... and what that might mean is that these traits are encoded within the mitochondrial DNA.' Eleanor pressed her hands to her face.

Sophie nodded.

'So, Gabriel might not have been at risk of passing on these differences!' Eleanor covered her face and gave in to a fresh flood of tears.

'But we don't know any of this for sure, Eleanor,' Sophie said earnestly, 'And none of it might have anything to do with why they became extinct.'

'That's true.' Eleanor grabbed a handful of tissues from the box on the table and blew her nose.

'Can I get you something, Eleanor? Tea? Water?'

'No, I'm okay, thanks. It was good of you to come out of your way to tell me…'

'There is one more thing,' Sophie interrupted.

Eleanor stopped toying with the tissue and looked up. 'What?'

'Okay…' Sophie exhaled sharply. 'I know this might sound ridiculous and the last thing I want to do is trivialise your grief in any way, but… I've been having this recurring dream. About Lillooet.

She's trying to tell me something…'

Eleanor grasped Sophie's hand and squeezed it. 'Dear God, Sophie, spit it out!'

'Eleanor, I'm sorry to sound… mysterious… but she's holding out a…'

'No!' Eleanor shot to her feet and ran to her bedroom. She threw back the bed cover and cast the pillow aside. Snatching up the letter, she ran back and held it out. She watched as the colour drained from Sophie's face.

'How did you know what…'

'A dream. I had it too.' The two stared at one another. It was some time before Eleanor slid her finger beneath the folded crease and eased it across the envelope. She closed her eyes and drew out the neatly folded sheet.

'Dear Jude,' Eleanor read aloud, her eyes flying down the page to the name at the bottom. 'Grace… This must be his girlfriend.'

Her eyes skimmed down the page.

'Dear God,' she whispered, 'She's pregnant.'

Sophie leapt to her feet and ran to Eleanor's side.

'Now I understand,' Eleanor went on, remembering Lillooet's expression as she gazed from across the water. 'Lillooet needs me here, to help Grace and to help the child.'

Eleanor felt suddenly strong and calm. She turned to Sophie. 'And it seems you are part of the plan too, Sophie. Is that okay with you?'

'Of course.' Sophie took the letter from Eleanor and read it several times.

Eleanor drifted to the window and stared again at the people living out their ordinary lives, as she had done so often before. She realised she no longer yearned to be one of them. She gazed beyond the present to a future that now seemed more purposeful. She had been unable to protect her son, but it would be different with his child. This child would survive. But first, they would have to find him.

And deep in her heart, she knew they would.

Printed in Great Britain
by Amazon